HUNTER'S
MOON

HUNTER'S
MOON

CHUCK LOGAN

HarperCollins*Publishers*

HarperCollins books may be purchased for educational, business, or sales promotional use. For information please write: Special Markets Department, HarperCollins Publishers, Inc., 10 East 53rd Street, New York, NY 10022.

FIRST EDITION

Designed by Caitlin Daniels

Library of Congress Cataloging-in-Publication Data
Logan, Chuck, 1942–
  Hunter's moon / Chuck Logan.
    p. cm.
  ISBN 0-06-017643-1
  1. Journalists—Minnesota—Fiction. I. Title.
PS3562.04453H36   1996
813'.54—dc20   95-38432

96 97 98 99 00 ❖/RRD 10 9 8 7 6 5 4 3 2 1

For Sylvia Siegrist Logan

ACKNOWLEDGMENTS

Deborah Howell
Bill Tilton
John Camp
Dr. Kenneth S. Merriman
Jean Pieri

The friends of Harry Griffin never fell off the wagon at a decent hour. The phone rang at 3 A.M. and Bud Maston's 90-proof baritone poured out:

"Harry? You there, man?"

"You're drinking again," Harry answered, half asleep and fumbling the receiver, and Bud's reply was drowned in a clatter of truck traffic. He focused and asked: "Where are you?"

"Where the hell do you think? Up north in a phone booth. On the highway."

"Ten years . . ." Harry said to the dark, very calm now, because he could taste Jack Daniel's ooze in Bud's voice and smell it in the nightcrawlers of sweat that wormed through his own chest.

Bud giggled. "Fuck Minnesota Harry. I wanna talk to Detroit Harry."

"Wonderful, you blew ten years of sobriety," said Harry.

"Don't pull that crap. I love you, man . . ."

Out there, in the drunken night, the phone slammed down and the line went dead. Harry exhaled, hung up the receiver, and rubbed his eyes; then he dropped his feet to the floor and pushed off the bed. He wandered over to the window and stared out into the dark. His high-rise studio faced east from downtown St. Paul and he could see the new moon and a solitary pair of headlights traveling the cold ribbon of Interstate 94. It was a Thursday morning, the first week in November, and he and Bud hadn't spoken in a year.

Since Bud had his breakdown.

And finally Harry was wide awake in the middle of the night with a parched knot in his throat; angry at Bud's reminder that the edge was always right there, just a drink away. So he tried to be reasonable and told himself, Well, shit, there were rules. And even though he hadn't been to a meeting in a long time, the old AA reflexes kicked in; because this was your basic scream for help.

He punched on the bedside light, got his phone directory, and paged to the number that he had never called, which was an area code 218 up in the North Woods on the North Shore with the bears and the moose and the timber wolves—*Goddammit, Bud, it's three in the fucking morning and we're way too old for this shit!*—He stabbed the buttons and waited. A busy signal droned in the Maston family lodge in Stanley, Minnesota. The last he'd heard, Bud lived with a woman up there.

He hung up the phone and thought, Just as well: drunks were like terrorists. You didn't negotiate with them when they were using. You were supposed to let it go . . .

He reached for the pack of cigarettes next to the lamp, debated, put them down, killed the light, and climbed back in bed. But he was pissed now and he tossed in the covers until he curled up on a shallow ledge of sleep.

When the phone rang the next time, he had to pick it up because that was what happened in the dream.

"*Harry, buy a suit,*" said his mother. He couldn't see her in the dream but he could feel her all around him and she sent mixed messages; she'd wanted him to be an artist but she'd sent him to military school and she'd even read *The Iliad* to him while he paddled in her warm amniotic sea. Now, as then, her voice arched with nervous hope, softly protective and fragile as a wishbone.

"*Try on this jacket,*" she said. The jacket was black, double-breasted, and when he slipped it on, it fit him perfectly. A carnation was curled in the lapel, suggesting a wedding or a funeral.

Damn it.

Heart thumping, he swam from the tangle of sweaty sheets and his hand jerked automatically for the cigarettes. He lit an American Spirit and the smoke came at his eyes. Mom had been dead for more than thirty years, so why in the hell did he have to buy a suit?

Gradually, the familiar bite of tobacco laced up his discipline. With a grim smile, he shooed the nightcrawlers from his bed and stubbed out the cigarette and wiped the sweat off his face. Nights like this were the reason he lived alone.

He had stolen an undisturbed hour of sleep when the phone rang again, for real. He reached for it, resigned: shit comes in threes.

"I got married three weeks ago," said Bud in a glum voice.

"Say again?" Harry sat up.

"I need something from you," said Bud.

"What the fuck?"

"I'm having a stand-up ceremony in town next month. The works." His voice was exhausted but steadier now. "I need you to hold the ring. You know, best man—"

"Jesus, Bud . . ."

"The present I want from you is . . . you gotta go hunting with me and my wife's kid this weekend."

"You don't talk to me for a year and you call shitfaced in the middle of the night—"

"You gotta," Bud insisted.

"Bullshit, I don't *gotta* do anything."

Bud mumbled, "Look, I shouldn't have to beg . . ."

So the big debt was being called in. So it was duty. "Christ, I haven't been hunting in—"

"Since before the army, I know," said Bud.

"I have to work. I don't have a rifle," said Harry.

"It's all taken care of. All you need is a deer license for zone one. I already called Randall. He's getting a rifle ready for you . . ."

"You didn't bug Randall at three in the morning?" Randall was as close as Harry came to having a family.

"Look, I called Randall, okay? I already bought you stuff to wear. And I called Tommy over at the paper. You have the time off—"

"Don't go pulling strings, goddammit," Harry muttered. Tommy was Thomas Riker, a distant presence seen on elevators who was the publisher of the paper where Harry worked as an artist. Bud rubbed elbows with Riker at the Athletic Club before he took his belly flop off the top of the social ladder.

"Let's just do it. I'm driving down tonight. I'll pick you up, ten o'clock, Friday morning," said Bud. The phone clicked—and that was that.

Harry lit another cigarette and watched flurries dot an ice-water dawn.

Presumably, Bud's "Detroit Harry" crack was supposed to evoke

Harry's gloriously stupid youth in less tranquil places than St. Paul and provide a dash of northwoods brio to prod him for the hunt.

But that wasn't it. Bud had coined the Detroit Harry line originally to convey a certain audacious style of stepping in.

Harry spread his fingers and drew them in a gentle snare around the moment and weighed it in his palm. The subtle gesture disappeared in lines of force as he made a fist.

He knew a lot of people and as they grew older and paired off and had kids and hunkered deeper into their lives, they didn't invite him to dinner or to their parties.

They only called him when they were in trouble.

2

Harry allowed himself a quiet hour to make coffee and shower before he called Tim Randall. "So Bud Maston's back," Randall observed in a bemused voice.

"He said he called you," said Harry.

"Last night. He's in a manic phase. Married. Full of plans. Plans to open a fishing lodge in the spring. Said he was curious about the current state of your gun phobia. Whether you could handle knocking down a big deer."

"He sounded to me like an experiment where all the mice got out," said Harry.

"You guys," said Dorothy Houston, coming on an extension. "Maybe he fell in love. There's this thing called romance."

"Check it out," said Harry dubiously. "Right in *Webster's*. One definition of *romance* is 'doomed to failure.'"

"We all feel bad about what happened last year, Harry. Maybe he's trying to turn that around," said Dorothy.

Harry pictured them, two lean redheads, sitting in the kitchen of the big house on River Road that overlooked the Mississippi. "We'll see," he said.

"So you're going?" asked Randall.

"Have to. He's calling in his chits," said Harry.

"I have some errands and Tim's got a big old rifle ready for you. We'll drop by," said Dorothy.

Dorothy smiled when Harry opened the door. Randall stood behind her with a cased rifle under his arm.

5

She was four years older than Harry, which put her closer to fifty than to forty. Her prettiness had faded, but not her alert green eyes, or her slender, upright figure, or her long, fiery hair. A wrenching scar ripped the left corner of her smile and puckered up her cheek to her eye.

Colonel Randall remained gaunt and powerful at sixty-three and the spooky shadow of a smile that flickered through chinks in his dignified bearing was the afterburn of a life spent attracting lightning bolts. He wrote history in his retirement from government service.

Harry kissed Dorothy's savaged cheek. He loved these people unconditionally.

"First time he called he was looped. He called again before dawn. That time he was playing whirlwind, organizing the hell out of everything," said Harry.

"Full of plans," said Randall. He leaned the rifle against the wall.

Harry popped his Zippo and lit a cigarette.

Dorothy, a fierce former Pall Mall addict, shook her head. "You stay in shape and still smoke."

"Yeah, yeah," said Harry.

Randall snuck a drag from Harry's cigarette and said, "So Bud took a wife on the sly."

Harry nodded. "Big stagy wedding next month for the cameras. Christ, I'll have to buy a suit."

Dorothy ruffled Harry's longish brown hair. "Good idea, you're the only guy we know who doesn't own a real suit." She cocked her head. "Be happy for him. Don't blow it all out of shape."

Skepticism lined Randall's face. He didn't share Dorothy's enthusiasm. "Are you sure about this?" he asked.

"I couldn't help him when he came apart. Maybe I can do something this time. I owe the guy. The AA thing. He went the extra mile for me back when," said Harry.

"That was years ago. And you quit going to AA," said Randall.

"I'm still sober. Bud isn't." Then Harry laughed. "Gun phobia, huh? He said that?"

The faint smile wetted Randall's lips. "I figured you'd want iron sights."

Harry nodded. "Never liked scopes."

"It's an old, long-barreled Remington ought-six. It shoots dead flat at two hundred yards. You still remember how they work?"

Harry smiled. "Like riding a bike. It'll come back."

They did not undo their coats; just dropping off the rifle. Randall paused. "How are you feeling?" he asked.

Harry shrugged, "Good. Never better."

"You feel strong?"

"Hey, I feel all right, Randall."

"Don't take this wrong, but you and Bud never did fit as close friends."

"He lacks discipline," said Harry, nodding in agreement. "Like his pockets. No bottom. He never learned to set limits."

"One question. If you started drinking again and developed a wild hair to go hunting, do you think anybody'd go with you?"

Harry tried to stare down Randall's ice-blue eyes. He dropped his gaze first. Randall squeezed his shoulder and said, "Watch yourself, son."

3

Harry called it *Das Wortfarben*—the word factory. Ten years ago, the paper had been a real factory with brawny printers and clattering Linotype machines raising an industrial racket below the newsroom. Now it was mainly phony smiles, the plastic patter of computers, and death by memo.

Harry's boss, Arnie Cummings, ran art and photo and was real enough. A fatback Atlanta boy by way of L.A., Arnie looked strangled by his tie as he came across the newsroom and thumped a big knuckle at Harry's sternum. Hug and push was his style. Harry shoved the hand away.

"Must be nice to know people," Arnie drawled. "We're short-staffed as it is."

"Sorry, Arnie, it came up sort of sudden."

Arnie glowered and shoved his thumb toward the ceiling in the direction of publisher country. "You got today and tomorrow off. And Monday. Next time come to me first, Harry." He slapped a pay envelope against Harry's chest. "Walked it through payroll myself. Be here on time Tuesday. Whitetail, huh?" He smiled reluctantly. "Go on, get outta here."

Franky Murphy, a general assignment reporter, fell in step with Harry as he passed the bulletin board.

"Cummings fucking with you?" asked Murphy. He was a wiry, acne-scarred man with a '50s flattop and laser-blue eyes behind wire-rim glasses. Not a friend.

"Nah." Harry kept moving toward the elevators in the lobby.

Murphy followed him. Harry pushed the elevator button.

"So you're going hunting with Bud Maston, huh?" asked Murphy.

Harry squinted at him. "How—"

Murphy shrugged. "He was in town yesterday. Saw him at lunch at McDermit's. He was asking about you."

"Asking you? About me?"

"Yeah, you know, how you're doing. Hey, I didn't know you were in the service with Tim Randall, the writer. That's kinda interesting."

Harry narrowed his eyes. "What the hell was Bud doing in town yesterday?"

"Wouldn't say," Murphy purred, then he cocked an eyebrow, "but he left with Bill Tully. Maybe he's thinking of dipping his toe back in the political sewer. Hear anything, let me know," said Murphy.

"Yeah, sure," said Harry, getting on the elevator. It rankled some, having Bud's style of doing things back in his life so fast. Bud tended to forget that not everybody had his long reach.

Well, shit. Here comes the fucking bride. Harry went directly to Dayton's department store. With a smile, he picked out a black, double-breasted suit.

Later in the day Harry came out of a sporting goods store laden with shopping bags. A cold wind whipped the Minnesota Buck Permit in his hand. He still didn't believe he was going hunting after almost twenty years.

Back home, he looked down from his window at foundries of office lights that burned in the gray afternoon. Arctic air had emptied the streets and turned the sky to stone.

His eyes sought out a particular building, and a specific lighted window on the seventh floor. With an ironic smile he touched the dry fronds of his one houseplant, a spindly areca palm that he always forgot to water; probably because Linda Margoles, the last woman he'd been involved with, had planted it in his bachelor pad like a green expedition flag.

He genuinely enjoyed the company of women and they, in turn, liked him. The problem was making it last.

Linda was on his list. He'd left her for last, after buying warm socks, sturdy wool trousers, the deer license, a Buck knife, and a first-aid kit. He picked up the phone and dialed.

"Law offices," answered a legal secretary.

"Linda Margoles," said Harry.

"Whom shall I say is calling?"

"Harry Griffin."

"Harry," said a wary voice.

"The plant you gave me is dying."

"Like relationships, Harry, they need nurturing to grow. Remember?"

They had been serious until she'd rushed it and laid a baseline for mapping the future and he'd suspected that she'd like to lock him into her briefcase with the other contracts and fine print. Now she resented their breakup. "How's it going?" he asked.

"Let's see. I haven't cut myself and I'm not having my period, so why am I attracting a shark?"

"I need some information."

"Sure." Clipped, precise, like the severe makeup she had started wearing.

"Bring me up to speed on divorce law. Like if someone has a lot of bread and he gets married and suddenly he changes his mind. How much of a bite is he looking at in court?"

"Short-term marriage doesn't generate a lot of marital property. Only the income after the marriage counts."

"Hmmm . . ."

"Does this fatcat have a will?"

"Must."

"Something to think about. He drops over dead intestate and no divorce has been finalized, in the absence of other heirs, the surviving spouse could elect against the whole estate. Somebody we know getting divorced?"

"Bud Maston got married."

"No shit. Keep me posted."

"Thanks, Linda."

Later that evening, after a solitary supper, Harry pulled his cold-weather gear from the back of the closet and stuffed it in his duffel bag. He hefted the rifle case to get a sense of its weight and set it beside the bag.

Then he took a cup of tea to his drawing table where he kept a mirror on the wall as a drawing aid to study expressions. Next to the mirror hung a caricature in which he'd captured himself in fast, nervy line—lean, intense, hooked—plodding with a gorilla on his back who gleefully puffed a cigarette.

Harry lit up, blew smoke at the nagging sketch, and turned his eyes to the framed photograph on the other side of the mirror. As Lyndon Johnson's young dummy, he stood in sweat-bleached tiger stripes and a parachute harness, arm in arm with Randall. Dorothy, then a correspondent, had taken the picture on a funky red dirt landing strip outside of Quang Tri City.

In the photo Detroit Harry bared his crooked front teeth in a fierce grin. Minnesota Harry at forty-two, his muscles still flat as interlocking slats, sent back an orthodontically corrected smile.

He consulted the mirror and wagered with his reflection that he could handle whatever Bud sent his way. His hazel eyes had mellowed—had left tough and were hitchhiking toward wise—but they could still sting with the disciplined snap of sweat hitting a varnished gym floor. His mobile features worked through a repertoire of expressions. Concerned. Quizzical. Stern.

He preferred it quiet but Bud, drinking, would throw slippery grounders.

So he whistled a few bars of "Sukiyaki," some hardball that evoked the beer halls of Fort Benning. Then he turned off the lights and went to bed.

Right after he closed his eyes the first snowflakes began to fall.

4

The radio announcer crooned his signature chestnut about the early onset of "Macho Winter." The weak, he promised, would be quickly sorted out. Then his voice turned serious:

"A winter storm warning is in effect for northern Minnesota. Two feet of snow and winds of seventy miles per hour are expected by ten P.M. tonight north of a line from Fargo to Duluth. On the Canadian prairie, the storm has been upgraded to a blizzard . . ."

Harry glanced at Bud. "Maybe we should pull over."

Bud stared straight ahead and mumbled, "It's a gift for our reunion."

". . . and wind chills of twenty below are reported in the Arrowhead. The Minnesota Highway Patrol has issued a warning to motorists to avoid travel in the storm area. This is a life-threatening weather condition, folks, so shake out those winter driving skills and be careful out there."

Bud Maston turned off the radio and put both hands on the wheel. Mum, elbows locked, he leaned into the storm. The snow started as spitballs and escalated into a Minnesota war whoop; now it looked like a million .50 calibers were blasting fat, white tracers at the windshield.

Bud carried Chrysler's biggest engine in a souped-up Cherokee Sport, a deep diamondback tread on his tires and four-wheel drive, and he'd crammed what looked like the entire inventory of a United Store into the cargo hatch. He had coffee, sandwiches, donuts, and a supply of candy bars that he had been eating methodically since they'd headed north out of St. Paul.

He had everything except an explanation.

When Harry used to talk the AA party line, they called it Twelfth Step work; sticking your nose into a brother drunk's derailed life. With a guy like Bud, who was a success at everything except living, you had to play it very tough and forget the love. Then there was the turnabout personal angle; ten years ago, Bud had been Harry's AA sponsor.

He'd shown up at Harry's apartment with a heavy shopping bag and a heavier hangover. "See if these fit," he'd said with lowered eyes.

Now Harry smelled like a new car. Bud had outfitted him in enough layers of polypro, pile, and Gore-Tex to climb K2. The generosity had erected a barrier. Harry wiggled his toes in his new Gore-Tex boots and resolved to wait until Bud came to him and an awkward silence stretched into hours as they churned north on Interstate 35 East.

Abandoned cars began to litter the snowdrifted highway and emergency vehicles and tow trucks gathered in covens of blue flashing lights. The infrequent low beams of southbound travelers winked bravely as they crept past. By the time they reached the outskirts of Duluth, the road had disappeared as they blindly followed a pair of red taillights across the hilly tundra.

Duluth bustled with siege energy. Busy yellow snowplows worked the downtown cobbled streets and heaped up an igloo village of snow banks. North of town, they pulled into a truck stop to gas up. Semitrailers, waiting out the storm, crowded the apron.

"Where you headed?" asked the station attendant when he stamped Bud's plastic.

"Stanley," said Bud.

"I'd wait," said the guy, staring. "They pulled the plows off North 61. Be dark in another hour."

Bud shook his head. "People expecting us." Their eyes drifted to the TV mounted on a wall bracket over the cash register. On the cable hookup to the weather channel, a loop of sawtooth isobars like the bite radius of a shark slung a cold front down a map of Minnesota and Wisconsin.

Bud went out to the pumps and checked the tires. Harry remembered that he'd forgotten to pack toothpaste and went back in.

"Stanley, huh?" the guy behind the register mused as he rang up the order. "You from there?"

Harry shook his head as the guy handed him his change.

"I went once," said the guy. "Dry socket. Nothing there."

Harry shrugged and opened the door. The guy came around the counter. His chapped face was bitter; his body was caved in by hard labor and a ripple of washboard chest muscle showed beneath layers of quilted underwear at the collar of his grease-stained overalls. Harry knew the breed from his own cousins and uncles back in Michigan.

"That's him, ain't it? Do-good Bud Maston," he said with a razor-thin smile. He pushed past Harry and hawked up a gob of spit and gave it to the wind in Bud's direction. Harry watched the gobber freeze and roll as it hit the snow. Walking away, he heard the muttered: "Fat rich fuck couldn't buy his way into Congress, huh."

The money. Bud had spent his life trying to lose his rich-boy shadow and when the test came, it had eaten him whole. He didn't have the million dollar harelip when Harry met him. Then, he was just another guy back from the war. But the money was waiting. Old Minnesota money plundered from the Iron Range starting back in the fur trade, then timber and mining. The Mastons had exhausted the iron in the Nanabozho Ridge, cursed the wrecked strip of land between Lake and Cook counties with their name, and sought to wash the sweat and blood from their loot through philanthropy. Bud was the last Maston and he had so much money that he gave it away for a living, as director of the Maston Foundation in St. Paul.

Bud might have overheard the station attendant, the way he winced into the churning twilight. Spray some freckles on young Orson Welles playing Citizen Kane, that was Bud a year ago. Now his patrician face had swollen with an alcohol bloat and all that drive had turned to lard.

He wore a blaze-orange vest over an olive-drab commando sweater that bulged tight, like a green innertube around his waist. He'd gained fifty pounds and grown his copper-colored hair shaggy, down to his slab shoulders. A scraggy beard hid his strong chin, his long fingernails were cracked and rimmed with grime, and a button on the fly of his jeans was undone. He was not wearing a wedding ring.

He swung his face toward Harry and his blue eyes could have been painted by van Gogh—contrived to be more brilliant than real life—the way they throbbed, bloodshot with pain. But he didn't say a word.

They got back in the Jeep and drove north and left human scale behind with the lights of Duluth and fell under the power of Lake Superior. Highway 61 squeezed to two lanes and swerved through cuts in the Precambrian hills and pine thrust up and disappeared as the snow came faster, hypnotizing them, and they lost the light and pushed on, all alone, into howling, tunneled darkness.

A slow hour out of Duluth, Bud pulled onto the shoulder and put the Jeep in neutral. Twenty feet ahead in the highbeams, barely legible in the flying snow, a highway sign shuddered in the wind: Entering Maston County.

"You drive," Bud said.

They changed seats. Harry put the Jeep in gear and felt his way in four-wheel drive along the slippery highway that had narrowed to a dogsled trail, winding through the pines. Drifts snaked across the road and Harry accelerated to crash through one that almost breasted the grill.

They careened out of the drift into an open area and the crosswind wrapped them. "Whiteout," Harry muttered and fought the wheel.

"This is the last open spot; we're good," said Bud.

The Jeep lurched and the shoulders of the storm crowded in, predatory, waiting for them to make a fatal mistake. They crossed the open ground into the cover of the trees where granite hills blocked the wind and Harry could see again.

A yellow sign flashed at the side of the road: MOOSE AREA. DRIVE CAREFULLY.

Bud sighed, draped one hand on his belly, munched on a Snickers bar, and finally broke the trance of the storm. "I really appreciate this," he said.

"Does she have a name?" asked Harry.

"Huh?"

"Your wife?"

"Of course. Jesse."

"Where'd you meet her?"

"Local VFW. She was tending bar and—"

"A bartender? *You* married a bartender?"

"What's wrong with that?" Bud countered defensively. "She's not one of those Type-A bitches with an MBA. She's a . . . real woman."

"You going to tell me about it?" asked Harry.

Bud sighed again, fumbled in his pocket, put a filtered cigarette between his lips and forgot to light it. "She's got two kids. Twins. Sixteen years old. Boy and a girl. The girl's all right. The boy, Chris, I'm having trouble with."

Harry reached over, popped his Zippo lighter, and lit Bud's cigarette. Bud took one drag, made a face, rolled down the window, and threw it out. Harry frowned, waiting for more. Bud looked away. He opened his hand and a glob of the Snickers melted across his palm.

Bud went to Harvard and his family had a county named after it. Harry graduated from the auto factories of Detroit and the U.S. infantry and didn't know his father's real name.

They'd both lost parents when they were young and they'd both been busted up in the Big Hit-and-Run-Accident over in the rice paddies. Linda Margoles made a witch's ride across Harry's memory. They both had bad luck with women.

Before Bud got the money, they had been roommates and best friends. Then Bud came into his inheritance and took over the foundation and began to change. The phone was always ringing. He had all these events to attend. His flair for giving spirited banquet speeches did not go unnoticed.

Bud Maston sobered up into the most socially adept person Harry had ever known. He knew innately where everybody was and what they needed and had an uncanny knack for graciously positioning himself with perfect timing to provide it. This personal quality proved to have a downside called politics.

Bill Tully, the Godfather of the Minnesota Democrats, had sized him up. *He has looks, he can talk, he's a war hero. He has the bread. And the guy really fuckin' cares. He could stand for national office.*

Harry had watched the shadow of power come to a point in Bud as an army of freebooting hacks eyed his fortune and told him it could be done; Congress two terms, then a shot at the Senate.

Asked his opinion, Harry flat out told him it was a mistake. Bud had looked right through him the way the first Mastons must have gazed at the virgin North Woods—with a lust that was as scary to the touch as their ax blades. Bud began putting Harry on hold.

A year ago, Bud flashed ahead in the polls going into the Democratic primary for the U.S. Congress seat in St. Paul. He had social magic and polish and that gregarious sweat people love to breathe. And a bottomless campaign chest. The mob picked up the blood scent of doomed charisma and chanted: "Bud, Bud." To Harry it sounded like: "Jump, jump."

His face appeared in *Time* and *Newsweek*, a new Democrat who was compared to Governor Kerry of Nebraska. Accused of being another bleeding-heart liberal, he began to wear his miniature Purple Heart pin in his lapel.

The Congressional Medal of Honor he'd won as a marine lieutenant in Vietnam hovered over the campaign like a halo of stars on a field of blue. Bud never discussed it.

But Harry knew a few things about his old roommate. He knew that behind the elegant public persona, Bud camped precariously at the edge of a black pit inside himself. In most people, the cynical enzyme that filters out human suffering accumulates with age. In Bud, the process was reversed. It was only a matter of time before the political carnival snapped him. He had the best pollsters and consultants that money could buy.

What he needed was a friend.

The insiders whispered and the media hinted at clinical depression when Bud suddenly went into a social coma and quit the race.

He didn't even make a public statement. The campaign sent out a terse news release that he had reconsidered for personal reasons. When the hoopla died down, Harry found him, haunted and disheveled, in his apartment on the top floor of the old Rivers Hotel overlooking the St. Paul riverfront.

Bud just raised his hands, lowered his eyes, and never said a word. Harry had not consciously tried to convey it, but, thinking back, the last expression Bud Maston had seen on his face was "I told you so."

That's where they'd left it, a year ago, when Bud drifted into exile up here.

Harry didn't understand depression. Not really. It was a condition he linked with drinking, with hangovers. With setting yourself up to lose.

"Turn's coming up. Highway 7," said Bud.

Signs winked in a fit of snow—Ace Hardware, Best Western, some churches. To the right, Harry glimpsed shadows of red brick and bare windows. There was supposed to be a big paper mill somewhere. A Holiday gas station levitated in a furor of candlepower, flickered, and then disappeared into the agitated blankness on the edge of Lake Superior.

"Stanley," said Harry.

"Yeah," said Bud. "Tobacco Road North since they closed the mill."

"You had something to do with that, didn't you?"

A little testy, Bud said, "Hell, they were polluting the lake . . ."

The only thing moving, Harry turned left on Highway 7.

"Hope the plows have been out," said Bud.

They climbed slowly up the south slope of Nanabozho Ridge and passed meager tiers of houses with windows illuminated by the soulless waver of TV screens and entered a gauntlet of giant, wind-staggered pines.

The Jeep churned through a foot of snow, deeper drifts. Visibility cut down to five yards. Then three. Harry couldn't see the side of the road. He shifted into low gear and steered inside a set of fading tire tracks. They passed the blur of a general store with a solitary gas pump. "Where's the turnoff?" Harry asked.

"Half a mile. There's a big sign on the right side of the road."

"Where the fuck is the side of the road?"

"Maybe we should put on the tire chains."

"We got wheels. We need eyes."

"According to the speedometer we still have four-tenths of a mile. I clocked it from when we turned off the main highway," said Bud.

"If we get stuck, no heroics, we stay with the car," said Harry, mindful that it had been a long time since he'd been out in this kind of weather. The last ten years he'd mostly watched it gnash its fangs against city windows.

The Jeep labored at the tight end of a funnel and the tires started to wallow and sideslip. The tracks in the road were blotting out.

"Shit." The right wheels churned sideways and they were off the road; the shoulder was snow pudding. The wheels spun, dug a trench, forward motion ceased, and the Jeep stalled.

Bud pursed his lips. "It's only a tenth of a mile. We could try to walk in."

"No way. We dig it out."

Outside took on a whole new meaning: instant disorientation. Harry's breath went small in his chest as the wind wrapped his fancy mountain parka around his spine. They were buried in a snow bank almost up to the passenger door window. Harry dug furiously with his hands to free the exhaust pipe. The cold put needle teeth in the snow. Chastised, he yanked on his gloves. The red flash of the hazard lights revealed how swiftly the snow was filling in their tracks. Take ten steps in any direction and you'd lose sight of the car. Bud carried two shovels. One was a big snow scoop, the other was a surplus army entrenching tool. Harry took the bigger shovel and began dragging snow away from the packed wheels. Bud worked next to him with the smaller one. In minutes, Bud was gasping for breath.

Bud got behind the wheel. Harry tried pushing. The Jeep threw gravel but did not move except to settle deeper.

"Shit," yelled Bud. "We almost made it. I'll bet you we could walk it. We got the gear. We could put on the snowmobile suits. The snowshoes. Jesse'll say we're weather wimps."

"Uh-uh. Keep digging. Put something under the wheels."

"Warm up first," said Bud. Back inside, they turned on the heater and smoked a cigarette in silence. Harry switched the lights on.

"Wait," said Bud. "Turn 'em off again."

Harry turned them off. A flicker of light up ahead. A pattern. Harry flashed the lights three times. The flicker came back. Three times.

"The cavalry to the rescue," said Bud, more animated the closer he got to home.

The blue monster truck that trundled from the wall of snow had jacked-up suspension, monolith tires, roll bars, decks of running lights, a broad snow blade, and a winch for tusks. Two people sat up high in the brightly lit interior.

The truck stopped ten feet away and the two people got out. The driver resembled a ponytailed Abe Lincoln come back as a middle-aged Hell's Angel.

"That's Jay Cox," said Bud. "He's not as rough as he looks."

Harry took in the leather-patched denim and the jut of the scar-lumped face and wasn't so sure. Cox hailed from the white backwoods tribe that burned leaded gasoline and carried their young full term in a grease pit and delivered them by chain-hoist and suckled them on a sharp stick.

The girl danced into the headlight like a wild spark from the storm, agile and lanky, and mocking the cold in tight jeans, tennis shoes, and an old army field jacket that wasn't zipped. Her high youthful breasts swelled against the flimsy protection of a T-shirt and, defiantly hatless, her long black hair whipped around her face like a cap of tarantulas.

Harry cranked down his window. Cox gave a lupine grin and

shouted, "You're crazy to be driving in this, Mr. Maston. But Jes said you'd make a try, so I ran some tracks down to the main highway a couple of times to give you something to go on." His eyes were silver-gray and as fixed and shiny as two over-tightened bolts.

"Thanks, Jay," said Bud. "Meet Harry Griffin. Jay Cox."

Harry hadn't met a Jay Cox in a while. Guys like him didn't work at newspapers. The patch on his long-billed black cap was of Snoopy in his aviator hat, hand upraised, middle finger flipping the bird under the stitched caption: FUCK JANE FONDA.

"Howdy," said Cox, squinting, unable to make out Harry's features buried in the parka hood. Harry shook a leather hand that was tempered in gasoline and callus and there was definition in the finger muscles. "This is Becky," said Cox. She poked her head in the window.

"Hi," she said. Her eyes were dark beneath an inquisitive frown.

Cox yelled over the wind, "I'll turn my rig around and hook up a tow strap. I got the road into the lodge plowed out." He tipped his hand to his cap and jogged back to his truck. The girl leaped into the truck bed. Cox manhandled the giant truck in a turn, following the girl's hand signals. He popped out of the truck, took the thick strap from the girl, disappeared under the grill for a second, fiddled for a moment at his rear hitch, then was back at the window.

"You want me to gun it a little to bust free?" yelled Harry.

"Nah. Just put in the clutch and enjoy the ride."

After a wild lurch, they careened through the snow drifts. Harry steered off the road, passed a big hand-lettered plywood sign—SITE OF SNOWSHOE LODGE—and was on a freshly plowed roadbed.

"That the daughter?" asked Harry.

"That's the daughter."

"How old is she?"

"Sweet sixteen."

"She doesn't look sixteen. She looks like a fucking Indian."

"Got some Metis in her. Jesse's dad was French and Cree. And maybe a little Gypsy. Mom was Serbian."

"Who's the guy?" asked Harry.

"Jack of all trades. Good carpenter. He's building this new stuff."

Thick spruce cut the wind and they passed under a poled archway with a pair of snowshoes for a crest. A peaked roof thrust up among the trees, slabbed with cedar shakes, and rugged as a fort. An addition and garage appeared quaint, diluted with gabled gingerbread, next to the massive original timbers. Blond ribcages of new lumber winked in the snow. Cabins under construction. A satellite dish sat in a clearing like a stranded space traveler. Beyond the buildings, Harry sensed the lake.

They ran up the steps into shelter. Cox retrieved his tow strap and joined them and Bud handed him a folded bill. He pocketed it quickly with a shrug. A surreptitious smirk zigzagged between Becky and Cox as the money changed hands.

"Stay for coffee," said Bud.

They were on a large, snug mud porch, peeling off gloves, opening their coats, and stamping snow off their boots. Harry shook off the parka hood and Cox got a good look at his face. The tight eyes unscrewed, the hard grin clotted, and the blood drained from Cox's pitted cheeks.

Jay Cox looked like someone who had lost his place.

5

"C'mon," said Bud, grinning for the first time, "cup a coffee will warm us up."

Cox's prominent Adam's apple bobbed as he tried to bring up spit. "Naw. Gotta plow out other folks," he rasped and closed his hands to hide the chewed patches of red meat that rimmed his cuticles. Becky edged over and touched his arm. Cox nervously moved her aside.

"Don't be bothering Jay, Becky."

The husky voice brought Harry around: Jesse was a chance you take by firelight or the dark of the moon. With her beauty barely in control, she walked up to him and she was innately man-wary and man-daring and she had a bold lower lip and raven eyes and black hair twisted up in a tangle of braids. She wore skintight Levi's and a crisp blue-and-white-checked blouse that crackled under a loose wool cardigan.

He bisected her face, covering up one half, then the other. *Beware,* warned her cool, untouchable right eye. *Come a little bit closer*, suggested the left.

The rangy boy stood behind her and, like his mother and his sister, he was a little too good looking, the way Cox was a little too much of a fright.

Chris had raccoon circles under his tense brown eyes and had harlequined his appearance with long hair, tailed in back and shaved to his scalp over the ears. A death's head emblem decorated his black T-shirt; under the grinning skull, the crooked lightning insignia of the Waffen SS pimped some heavy metal band.

He favored his left leg with a slight limp.

Bud put his arm around Jesse. "Harry, meet Jesse," he said with a

22

goofy grin. She held out a cool left hand. A barbaric diamond glittered on the third finger.

"Hi."

Their hands met. Left-handed shake. She smelled as dangerously fresh as ozone coming after lightning and their eyes and their fingers lingered together a fraction of a second too long as the ghost of Harry's sex drive sat up and took a ragged breath.

Everybody grinned. Cox's gray eyes wobbled and he looked like he'd chugalugged a gallon of flu virus. Harry grinned, too. They weren't grinning with Bud. They were grinning at him and to each other.

"Chris," said Bud. "C'mon over here and meet my friend Harry." Chris's eyes flashed.

"No way to be," Cox quietly admonished. Dutifully Chris came forward and shook Harry's hand. "Pleased to meet you," he said.

Chris's lean hand crawled in Harry's grip.

"So you're the guy who knows where the big deer are," said Harry, making a stab at conversation.

Chris avoided Harry's eyes.

"We'll get that deer, tomorrow morning," said Bud, putting his hand on Chris's shoulder.

"We'll see what we get," said Chris. He shook off Bud's hand and went into the lodge.

Bud turned to Harry with a hurt expression. Standing behind Bud, Jesse wrung her hands together and her knuckles bleached white. She fired one probing glance at Cox. Cox just stared, spooked.

"Let's go inside," Jesse said. "It's cold out here."

Bud, myopic with hangover, missed the eyes working all around him. And Harry knew that, this time, Bud wasn't mired in the neurotic, indulgent morass of city slicker love. Bud had really stepped into it out here in the sticks.

Jesse and Cox carefully did not look at each other as Cox made his farewell, went out, and got back in his big truck. He sat for a moment, gripping the steering wheel with his hands. Then he started the truck and drove away.

Harry shook out his senses and cast them in a wide net. He'd been around these kind of folks before.

They were outlaws.

6

Six apartments the size of Harry's would fit in the lodge's main room and a man could sleep in the fieldstone fireplace. The woodwork was hand hewn and inlaid with Ojibway design.

An antique bowsprit, carved in the shape of a bare-breasted Indian maiden with streamlined hair, jutted out from the apex of beams over the fireplace. "Looks like a goddamn meadhall. What was your grand-dad's real name? Beowulf?" Harry's eyes wandered up to the cathedral ceiling and wagon wheel chandeliers.

"Grendel," said Bud, winking.

"His name was Stanley, like the town," said Jesse. Becky darted past them in a youthful flap of arms, legs, and bouncing breasts and disappeared down a hallway at the other end of the building.

In contrast to the Mission Oak furniture and Navajo rugs on the oak plank floor, the walls were decorated with grim, framed prints from Goya's Disasters of War. The prints were interspersed with tribal masks: Indian, African, South Sea Islander; collections of spears, bows and arrows, and war clubs clustered around the masks.

Harry inspected a large bearskin, complete with head and claws, stretched on the wall. The plaque under it had been carved by a child: GLACIER LAKE ROGUE BLACK BEAR. SHOT BY SHERIFF LAWRENCE EMERY.

Bud explained, "The stuff on the walls is left over from when public TV was up here."

"You know," Jesse dead-panned, "all these treehuggers from the Cities came up here to play Indian. Beat on drums. Get naked and," with elegant barroom vulgarity, she looked Harry in the eye, "pretend it don't matter who's got the biggest pee pee in the teepee."

24

Harry felt like he'd known her all his life. Strength and mystery were at her fingertips, but she kept part of her brains squeezed down in her pants and she liked to see men fight.

"Tad Clark's men's group, that show they did?" said Bud with a pained smile.

Harry nodded vaguely. Then his eyes fastened on a sheet of stationery that lay on the writing desk next to the fireplace. A fancy printing job, the paper had a beige birchbark ripple. He scanned the business letterhead:

Snowshoe Lodge, Stanley, Minnesota
In friendly Maston County
Jesse Deucette, Manager

When he looked up, she was watching him. He pointed to the letterhead. "So you didn't change your name?" he asked.

"Neither did Bud," she parried. He continued his inspection. No wedding pictures. No cat. No dog. No houseplants. With all these windows, if this was a home, something should be growing.

Bud stooped and fiddled with the fire. Jesse showed Harry around. "You caught us kind of in between, we plan to get this place up and running for the fishing opener in the spring," she said, pointing up a broad stairway. Thick plastic sheeting walled off the balcony and second story. Harry smelled paint and plaster spackling compound; several paint cans and a 10-gallon bucket of spackle sat next to French doors that opened to a long porch where new wood shone in the shadows. A long carpenter's level was propped up against a wall of bare Sheetrock.

The level had a coat of dust and looked like it hadn't been touched in weeks. Just sitting there.

"Jay's redoing the porch so we can turn it into a dining room," explained Jesse. They stepped onto the unlit, chilly porch, which gave off a cold wood scent. More dust crunched under Harry's boots. The ceiling beams were pegged in tongue-and-groove joinery and gabled with a flourish that went beyond mere craft.

"Jay does nice work," said Harry.

"He's good with his hands." She pointed out the roughed-in addition next to the porch where opaque sheets of plastic were stapled over the framing and masked several large packing crates. Plumbing equipment was strewn around. "Whirlpool and sauna go in there," she explained.

She glided to the windows and Harry followed, drawn by the train of her energy, which was stronger in the dark. "Can't see much now, but there's a hell of a lake out there," she said.

Their wrists grazed and he felt the tension in the taut, twisted braids and imagined setting it free.

"Two hundred feet deep. Muskie, Northerns, and Lake Trout," said Bud, coming up behind them. "We even have some Indian caves at the other end with pictographs." Again that goofy grin. "The good life in Minnesota," he said.

Harry watched her face as Bud spoke. She regarded her new husband with the poise of a high-wire artist glancing down on a clown.

Bud clapped his hands together. "We'll need the snowshoes tomorrow. I'll unload the Jeep."

"I'll help." said Harry.

"Nah, you get comfortable," said Bud, going out the door.

Harry followed Jesse off the porch, across plywood decking, through Sheetrocked partitions, to a restaurant-sized kitchen under construction. Wires dangled and bare fixtures jutted from holes in the drywall. A blueprint gathered dust on a piece of plywood supported by sawhorses. More dust shrouded a Skilsaw tilted on the blueprint and the circular blade was chalky orange with rust.

They ducked through a double thickness of plastic sheeting and entered the remains of the old kitchen. Maple cabinets, a butcher block island, and more scuffed maple on the floor. A stained, cast-iron Wagner kettle bubbled on the tarred burner of an old gas stove. He smelled venison stew, coffee from a tall stoneware pot. The temporary kitchen opened onto a den.

"This'll all change," said Jesse.

The den had the unlived-in feel of a furniture showroom. There was a rich red Persian carpet and tall oak bookcases lined with books; the couch and chairs of deep, crushed coffee bean leather on Scandinavian oak frames looked like they'd never known human contact. The desk, an IBM PC, and a printer were brand new and the TV, stereo, CD player, and VCR were stacked in an oak console and exuded an electric whiff of welded circuits. A hallway opened past the kitchen and led, Harry supposed, to bedrooms.

Chris hunched over in a chair toying with a long, black hunting knife at a long trestle table that occupied the area between the old kitchen and the den.

"Chris, put that away," said Jesse.

Chris smiled and tipped the knife mumblypeg fashion off his index finger. It flipped end over end, pierced the rug, and stuck in the floor with a loud thunk.

"Oops," said Chris. "Sorry."

"Put that away, right now," she repeated. Chris pulled the knife from the floor. He did not put it away and Harry got the distinct impression the boy was pushing new limits. Jesse didn't strike him as a woman who put up with defiance.

"Why don't you help Bud bring the stuff in?" Harry said in a friendly voice.

"He said he'd do it," said Chris, his dark eyes were quietly hostile.

Jesse interceded. "C'mon, let's get some coffee. You look like you could use some after being on the road."

"Yeah. I'm bushed," said Harry as he inhaled the vinegary steam of venison and peppercorns mingled with fresh perked coffee. On the island, two stainless steel bowls were covered with damp, swollen dish-towels and the heavy scent of baking apples and brown sugar wafted from the oven. A radio played country western down low.

Jesse relaxed her erect posture and leaned back on the island between the bowls of rising dough. The stove-moist air was tactile and crowded with fumbling, yeasty fingers. Standing three feet apart, it felt like they were touching all over.

Physically, she implied tremendous leverage. A straight line and a few simple, perfect curves. Harry was moved.

Her hands were vigorous and efficient, the fingernails trimmed, unpainted, used to work. He found himself wanting to see the firm clean flesh of her upper arms.

"Becky, get the man some coffee," said Jesse. Harry turned. The girl had reappeared and had changed into short, cut-off Levi's and a T-shirt that had the neck, sleeves, and bottom scissored out. She wasn't wearing a bra. The muscled dent of her navel showed an inch above the shorts and her thighs rippled smooth along the ragged denim fringe. A serious runner or a swimmer.

Becky poured coffee and handed the cup to Harry. Bud came into the kitchen, picked up the telephone, dialed a number, and began to talk to somebody about plowing the roads. Jesse's posture took on an erect propriety.

"You want something in that to warm you up?" asked Jesse. She reached for a pint of Jack Daniel's that sat next to a spice rack on the counter. Harry hadn't been this close to a pint bottle in years.

"I don't drink," said Harry.

"Up here everybody drinks. Unemployment and long winters don't go together real good," she said.

"Mom's a bartender. People who don't drink are bad for business," said Chris.

"I just helped out at the local VFW, part time. More straightening out their books," said Jesse curtly, raising her chin and giving her son an indignant glance.

Harry nodded politely. She was a regular sensual crowbar. Maybe just what Bud needed to rebuild his life. Or demolish it. Chris looked like a crippled Mowgli, the wolf boy. Becky, the forthright Amazon, seemed to have inherited all the mother's strength.

His eyes drifted to the table where Chris turned the knife in his fingers, staring along the gray honed edge.

"You ever see one of these?" Chris asked, boldly engaging Harry's gaze.

Harry walked over and took the knife away with a firm snap of his hand. It was a K-Bar. A marine fighting knife. As he thrust it into the scabbard that lay on the table he noticed the initials BM carved in the frayed leather. "Yeah," said Harry, returning to the kitchen. He opened a drawer and dropped the big knife out of sight.

"You know what it's for?" Chris asked, all of a sudden smiling sweetly. Harry tried to stare him down. The dark eyes didn't waver.

"It's for cutting the Gibionici," Chris grinned. "You know what Gibionici is?"

"Nope," said Harry.

"It's what's in the oven," said Chris.

Becky laughed, a sweet girlish sound at odds with her mature body. "You ain't from around here, are you, boy?"

"Like an apple turnover. My Serbian mother," explained Jesse, meeting his eyes. They both had high wide-set cheekbones and a trace of tannic spit to their skin that shed age. Her Serbian mother flirted with his Slavic father about the Mongol ponies that had raided in their blood.

Chris got up, walked to the drawer, took out his knife, and went back to the table.

"Plow's on the way," said Bud, hanging up the phone. Automatically, he plucked the pint bottle off the counter, unscrewed the top, took a quick nip, and then tucked the bottle into the inside pocket of his vest. No one seemed to notice except Harry.

"Bud's got pull," said Becky, letting her tongue drift lazily along her lower teeth. She had put on a kind of white waxy lipstick that Harry hated and too much purple eye shadow bruised her face. "Push and pull. He gets things done. Don'tcha Bud?"

"Mind your manners, smarty pants," said Bud.

Pulling away, Becky sideswiped Bud with a hip.

Bud sat down across from Chris. "Put that away," he said. Chris put the knife down on the table and spun it. The point stopped ambiguously, aiming out toward the lake.

The knife and the way Becky threw herself around put Harry on edge. Too hot in the kitchen, too many sharp things, too much of the girl's flesh exposed. He took his coffee to a chair in the den and sat with his back to the wall.

Jesse punched the bread dough down and formed it to fit in loaf pans. Bud talked to Chris about tomorrow morning. Becky set the table and tossed an iceberg salad.

Jesse didn't strike him as a disorganized person, so it surprised Harry the way everything proceeded backwards. Jesse took the pastry from the oven and Chris cut it into steaming strips with his big knife. Dessert came before supper. Then Jesse ladled out bowls of venison stew. They ate it with the salad and cornbread that had been in the oven with the pastry.

The electricity wavered and the radio signal cut out. In the sudden darkness, the wind leaned an icy shoulder to the lodge: a roof timber creaked.

"Candles . . ." said Bud.

Then the lights came back on. For a brief second, all the faces around the table were unmasked in tableau. Jesse and her children tensed in their chairs, staring at Harry. The muscle in Harry's left cheek twitched.

Silverware grated on plates and reminded Harry of the spooked expression on Cox's face.

Jesse moved quickly into the vacuum. "Bud says this is your first time hunting?"

"First time in Minnesota," said Harry.

"You'll never get that deer unless you go out in the dark," said Becky. "You can't see him in the daylight. And he only shows himself to certain people."

"You are so full of shit," said Chris.

"*I* showed you where he is. *You* get lost in the woods even with a compass."

Chris snorted. "Only good thing about the woods is the road leading south to the Cities."

"You drop out of school, the only thing you'll find in the Cities is a job taking orders at McDonald's."

Brother and sister exchanged tight smiles.

"I know why you go hunting," Becky announced.

"Why's that?" asked Bud. Smiling. Oblivious.

"To get away from women," said Becky.

Jesse's lips turned down in a savvy expression. "Men don't have to go anywhere to get away. They're gone sitting right next to you. Most of them."

"But I know why," said Becky, her agitated fingers jerked in conflict with her bright smile. Awkwardly, she took one of her mother's cigarettes, popped a lighter, and held it experimentally between her thumb and index finger. She stared pointedly at Harry until she had his full attention. "Are you circumcised?" she asked blankly.

"Gross," muttered Chris through a suppressed giggle.

Harry's face flushed under her bold scrutiny.

"It's common for men to be circumcised today," said Bud quickly. "For hygiene reasons." Like a man performing a repetitive task, Bud had the pint out, splashed a shot into his coffee, and whisked it back out of sight.

"That's what they tell you," said Becky. "But the real reason is it's a thing from way long ago, this kind of memory from when men sacrificed their genitals. Cut them right off. Even today, there's these primitive tribes in some parts of the world where the men have their penises cut up so they look like vulvas and they squat to pee."

Becky spoke self-importantly with her chin tilted up. The brightest kid in the class.

"Vulvas?" ejected Chris in feigned ignorance.

"That's pussy to you, dummy," said Becky, flicking cigarette ashes on her plate.

Jesse watched her daughter carefully. "Where'd you hear that? On 'Donahue'?" she asked.

Becky explained. "I read it in a book that Bud gave me. The mutilation of genitals is a holdover from an earlier time when women used to run the world. When men tried to make themselves look like women."

"Look like women?" laughed Chris.

"It was their religion, and everyone ate vegetables. The men rebelled and went off hunting," said Becky.

"Our pussy who art in heaven," Chris quipped.

Harry watched Bud wolf down stew and cornbread, all aglow with Jack Daniel's paterfamilias, presiding over native intelligence emerging from the trash of the popular culture.

"Well, that clears that up," said Jesse. "Now you guys do the dishes," she ordered her kids. She turned to Harry. "C'mon, I'll show you where you sleep."

Harry picked up his duffel bag and followed Jesse down the hall past the kitchen that ended in twin bedrooms. Midway, another bedroom faced the bathroom. They went in. "You're in here. Chris'll sleep out on the couch," she explained and tossed her head toward the kitchen. "Sorry about Becky. They skipped her a grade in school and she's enjoying being precocious. She's worse since Bud's been around. He encourages them both to talk. Becky more than Chris. You know Bud. He means well." She punctuated her last sentence with a searching glance.

Harry stood flat-footed. A huge print was framed on the wall over the bed. Another Goya. But this one was a particular horror. A mad-eyed titan held a limp decapitated naked body to its ravenous mouth. It was called "Saturn Devouring His Son." Harry turned to her.

"I drew the line on that one being out where people could see it," she said. "So Chris brought it in here. Kinda fits in with David Bowie and the Sex Pistols, don't you think?" Her eyes scanned the room. A cheap boombox sat on a desk next to dusty schoolbooks. Another IBM PC rested on a side table in a litter of floppy disks. The walls were papered with posters from contemporary rock groups. An iron cross hung from the light cord.

"Yeah," said Harry noncommittally. He threw his duffel bag on the rumpled bed.

She lingered at the door. "You're a surprise," she said very directly. "Funny, when Bud said he was bringing a friend up, last minute and all, I didn't figure someone like you. You're real different from him."

Harry shrugged, aware that neither of them knew what to do with their hands. She put hers on her hips. Seemed like a good idea. He put his the same way.

"Bud showed me some of the things you used to draw," she said.

Harry nodded politely. It was conversation. "It's more computers now," he said.

"It resembles you, the way you draw." She cocked her head. "Kinda quiet and nice to look at but there's an edge . . ."

Her eyes softened and it would have been a sweet moment if she wasn't the new bride of his once best friend. Something ran deep and artesian in her and Harry couldn't tell if it was loneliness or cunning.

Her eyes pried him open. "I know stuff about you. Bud told me, about Minnesota Harry and Detroit Harry. How he found you in the gutter drifting toward an open manhole and dried you out."

"Well, you know Bud. He gave me a hand," said Harry.

"Riiight, now maybe you're thinking about returning the favor, huh?" Her sporting laugh had a bitter trickle and Harry went with the loneliness. She'd never see thirty-five again and she had yet to be discovered.

But her smile was pure heroin. Once you had it, you wanted more and nothing else mattered. "Yeah," she mused, "I know Bud all right. I only got an idea about you."

She left a shiver of physical intrigue in the room and if there was an open manhole she was it but he couldn't stop himself from going to the doorway to watch her walk away down the hall.

Damn.

7

Jesse plus one hour and counting: the raw dirty copper taste started in Harry's mouth that signaled that his nerves were acting up, so he took a shower to soak out the chill of the road, then he resorted to an old nervous habit. Dripping dry in front of the bathroom mirror, he worried at his teeth with a toothbrush.

He meditated on the tabloid disorder that was Bud; with his body out of control and his life out of control and all that bread like helium gas that allowed him to drift above the law of gravity.

Well, that was the booze for you. Met her in a bar. Hadda be shit-faced drunk when he married into this bunch. Harry tasted blood. Too long, too heavy with the brush. He took it out and grimaced at the red-tipped bristles.

He ran his finger along the line of his lips. Then he grinned, revealing the straight, even teeth. His face relaxed into a modestly handsome grin. Cost five grand at the orthodontist to straighten out Detroit Harry's crooked teeth. Cost Bud. A gift to commemorate Harry's first year sober.

And Bud *had* dragged him off the street. And into AA. And sponsored him in every sense of the word; had arranged his late-start break in the straight world with the job at the paper.

So he owed Bud. The way he saw it, he owed Bud honesty.

The bathroom door swung open and Chris stood in the doorway. "Oops, sorry," he said, as his eyes traveled boldly over Harry's body and stopped at hip level with intense scrutiny.

Harry slammed the door shut. That did it.

He dressed quickly and went down the hall. Bud sat at the dining room table, staring at a sheet of paper. Chris had joined his mother and sister and they stood, heads close over the sink, whispering, watching Bud.

"C'mon, we're going out. I need to buy some smokes," said Harry.

Bud squinted at him, then out the windows. "You kidding?"

"That place we passed down the road should be open. Get your coat on."

Jesse, Becky, and Chris eyed Harry suspiciously.

For emphasis, Harry gripped Bud's elbow. Tight. Bud winced. Harry insisted. "Let's go. We gotta talk."

It was still snowing, but the wind had backed off. Harry had Bud's keys in his parka so he drove. At the end of the driveway they watched a road grader with a V blade smash a swath down Highway 7. Harry steered in behind it.

Bud hunched in the passenger seat. He knew what was coming. Harry turned on the radio and caught some Northland news: the worst of the storm had passed to the southwest, warmer air was moving in.

The store looked deserted but the lights were on. There was a large maple tree next to a swayback garage with a ladder placed against the thick trunk. Ropes dangled from the branches.

Going in, Harry jerked his head at the tree and quipped, "They going to have a lynching?" His serious voice did not carry the joke.

Bud winced. "For deer."

Inside were big round oak tables and mismatched chairs, dry goods, and cooler to the side, kitchen in the back. A sturdy woman in jeans and a blaze-orange shirt was counting receipts at the cash register. "Not a good night to be out, Mr. Maston. The heat off at home?" she crooned with a sly smile.

Bud crumpled into a chair. Harry went to the counter and selected a pack of Camel straights from a slotted shelf and ordered two cups of coffee. He brought the coffee back, sat down, and slit the cellophane on the cigarettes with his thumbnail.

"Time to go to the Camels, Bud."

"Fuuck." Bud drew it out. Going to the Camels was an AA ritual they used to have that preceded straight talk.

Harry placed his Zippo on the table with a firm click. Bud reached out reluctantly, fumbled with the pack, and raised the lighter. His hands shook.

"You quit going to meetings, didn't you?" Bud asked.

"I think I figured it out. Don't put it in your mouth," said Harry.

"That's Detroit Harry talking, doing it on guts," said Bud. His smile turned down at the corners and he looked away.

An elaborate silence separated them. Harry was more visceral and direct. Prone to act, to use his hands rather than words. Bud was always the more verbal, traveling circles in his head. Reluctant to offend.

Bud had dubbed him Detroit Harry after Harry had taken what is known in AA as a Fifth Step: Admitted to God, to himself, and to another human being the exact nature of his wrongs.

Under the seal of AA, Harry had confided to Bud why he'd left Detroit in a hurry. That was ten years ago, in a glibber time, when Minnesota was the first M in the MMPI. In the reborn zeal of sobriety, Harry had signed on for the whole extended-warranty Minnesota therapy jive package; treatment, AA, stress groups through the VA.

Now Bud owed him that kind of honesty in return.

"What the fuck is going on up here? How long you been drinking?" Harry asked.

"Shit, ever since I . . . left town."

"Dammit. Why'd you isolate yourself and wait a year to call?"

"You knew where I was, you could have called," Bud shot back.

Harry unburdened himself of a long-standing resentment. "Right, when you were playing bigshot you started treating me like the hired help."

Bud's voice dropped to a whisper. "You think this is easy. Letting people who knew me see me like this. I finally just panicked, I guess."

"You just got married. People get nervous, but panic?"

Bud drew in a sharp breath and gritted his teeth; his eyes glistened and his distended body arched in his chair.

Harry said it for him. "You were drunk when you got married, am I right or wrong?" Bud dropped his eyes. "Now you're thinking of getting out but she's a wolverine and you don't know how to drop the bomb."

A tear crept down the rust of freckles on Bud's cheek. He shook his head from side to side and his eyes drifted, became dreamy, the way they used to get when he looked out from behind a podium and microphone, into the lights across an auditorium. He shook his head. "I came up here thinking Buddha was right, man. You don't solve human suffering through direct action. Politics was an ego trip . . ." Bud grimaced and his voice was a whisper. "But I miss the action. I miss it real bad."

"Cut the bullshit. What's coming at you right now?" Harry was a little shaken by Bud's tears. Maybe this was beyond his competence. Maybe it really was depression. Harry didn't want to believe that, because if he did, he had to worry about covering all the bases and he hated the sound of the word *suicide*.

Bud's face quivered. *Christ.* Like looking at Orson Welles with triple chins in a wine commercial. Harry suppressed an urge to knock the needy expression off Bud's face. God—what happened to the guy? The day they'd met at an antiwar rally at the University of Minnesota, they'd sniffed each other out like two skinny dogs who had lived out in the rain. Bud had stood straight on his crutch, his freckles were scorched pennies, and he'd worn this amazed Huck Finn grin from a year gone fishing in Hell—just back from Nam and Woodstock in the same week.

For a few heartbeats, the predator in Harry was off the leash and padding in step with his conscience. Bud, the consummate player, had emerged from the crisis of his life as a mark. The perception bothered Harry, who believed you were innately one or the other.

"You want out of this scene up here." Harry stated it as fact, not a question. Bud pursed his dry lips and stared at the plastic tablecloth.

Harry exhaled. "Okay. Bud. Look, you just need a little help getting off the meat hook . . ."

Crying muscles bunched around Bud's eyes and his mouth. "Easy for you to say."

"Bud. Buddy. It's the good no-fault life in Minnesota. No one has to be right or wrong. You just have to have irreconcilable differences." Harry tried for some levity. "Hell, when I got divorced back in Michigan I was guilty of acts of extreme cruelty."

Bud didn't laugh. He growled and swung his head around, at bay. He clamped his arms to his chest to stop a spasm of shaking. "Fuck this." He mumbled and reached inside his vest pocket, pulled out the pint of Jack Daniel's, unscrewed the top, and poured two inches into his coffee.

Their eyes met. "Okay?" Bud asked defiantly. Harry shrugged.

Bud took a long sip and the whiskey toned his face and tightened his eyes. His freckles seemed to pop out like brass rivets. He sighed and made a ceremony of lighting another Camel with a snappy barroom display of reflexes, twirling the cigarette in his blotchy fingers. His eyes slouched across the table. "Are you ever tempted, Harry?"

Drifting hooks of alcohol came trailing and Harry sat absolutely still, not giving them anything to snag on.

"Listen. You can do whatever you want. But you take another drink of that shit and I'm not going anywhere near the woods and loaded rifles with you."

Bud grimaced and screwed the top back on the bottle and stuck it back in his vest. "You can be a real drag. Does it ever go to your head? Being the designated hero everybody can count on?" Resentful words. Well, tough shit. Harry's plan was simple. Get Bud out of the situation. Then get the booze out of Bud. Until that happened, talk would just be a devious game.

"Another thing," said Harry. "From what I've seen of Chris, I don't think he should be around a rifle."

Bud tipped his cup, stared into the contents, and moved it aside. He dragged on his smoke so hard that strings of tobacco stuck to his lip. A tiny bead of blood welled up around a dot of white cigarette paper that tore his dry lower lip.

"Bud, it's all wrong up here. I've watched you and women for years. From astrologers to community organizers. They all wind up going to law school. I figured you married some backwoods feminist, Our Lady of the Whole Food Coop or something. Jesse might have the hottest ass in Maston County but she's not Minnesota congressman's wife material."

"What the fuck is that supposed to mean?"

"What do I have to do? Draw you a fucking picture?"

Bud glowered at him. Harry reached in his pocket for a felt-tip pen. He quickly sketched on the tablecloth. A Scrooge McDuck moneybag with a serpentine dollar sign on the side. Then he drew a grasping feminine hand descending from above.

"Subtle," said Bud dryly.

"She's a hustler. And Cox? I smell institution all over that dude."

"They're hard-knocks folks. Takes a while for them to warm up to people who are better off. I just wanted to get lost up here. Be this ordinary guy . . . She took care of me. She had all these great ideas about fixing up the lodge—" Bud was gearing up to give a speech.

Harry cut him off. "Don't con the con, man. You running a fishing lodge in the sticks? C'mon. I can't believe you let her get her hooks into you this deep. She's turning your house into a hotel, for Chrissake. And now she's got spousal rights. That's half of something."

Bud's expression belonged in a textbook over the caption: delusion. "She's really got her heart set on opening the place next May—"

"Bullshit, the tools in that place haven't been used in weeks, there's dust all over them. And when you leave her it'll break her heart and she'll cry great big tears for about twelve minutes until she finds a lawyer who can put a dollar figure on it." Harry took a breath. "Enough of this shit. Do you want to be married to this woman?"

"Jesus," Bud groaned and avoided the eyes of the lady at the cash register who was pretending to read a magazine but who was really straining her ears to eavesdrop.

Harry kept coming. "Look me in the eye and tell me you love her," he said.

Bud drew himself up in an attempt to meet Harry's eyes. He burst into helpless laughter and muttered, "I *can* look you in the eye and tell you it's like sticking your crank in a sack of wildcats."

He drew his meaty hand across his eyes. "Aw goddamn. What the fuck do I do? She thinks we're going to have this social wedding in the St. Paul Cathedral. She's asking me for an invitation list of everybody I know. She's looking at dresses for Chrissake."

"I'll talk to her, man. I'll explain—"

"Explain what? That I fell apart? A year ago I was so close I could taste it." Bud's fingers fondled a shapely vision of success. Then they balled into fists and he began to tremble.

Harry reached over and put his hand on Bud's arm. "You trust me on this?" he asked.

"Yeah," Bud sighed. "I can't get out on my own. That's why I called you."

Harry nodded. "We go back, get our stuff, and split. Let me do the talking—"

Bud banged both fists down on the table and overturned the coffee cups. "No! We go through with the hunting part. I can't write it all off to drinking. I made a promise to that kid. I'm not running out on that. I have to start turning it around somewhere."

Harry shook his head.

*   *   *

They drove back in silence. Harry pulled into the driveway, braked, and put the Jeep in neutral. He leaned forward and draped both elbows on the steering wheel and watched snowflakes tumble in the headlights. He'd never known such a feeling of physical inevitability about a woman. Like gravity pulling him down.

Bud spoke in a rush. "Chris's been getting in trouble. He gets thrown out of school. He's been in some jams with the law. The sheriff up here is a good guy, he's been trying to work with him, but I figured it was more my job if he's living under my roof."

"What kind of jams?" Harry tried to fight it.

"He got caught with some pot, some uppers. No way he's going to listen to me about that. You're more like the guys up here, a little scary. I thought maybe you could get through to him."

"Too many things going on," said Harry. "Forget playing daddy."

"Harry, when I was a kid up here in the summers I was . . . not real strong. I had asthma, hay fever. The town kids always put me down for a weakass. I cop out on this hunting, they'll laugh at me." Bud's voice turned poignant. "My father always wanted to take me hunting . . ." His mother and father, brother and sister had gone down in a freak sailboat mishap on Superior when he was twelve.

Harry felt it turning, beyond his control, almost like it was meant to happen. "You should get your ass into detox, not the goddamn woods."

"Look. Let's make a deal. We hunt opening day, then you can make your pitch. I'll go back with you, go into treatment maybe—whatever. I'd rather confront Jesse about all this in a counselor's office, not in my kitchen. C'mon, man, we drove all the way here through the fucking blizzard. We got the guns and the clothes . . . one day."

"Shit."

Bud grinned. "It was Chris's idea to go hunting." Bud held up the piece of paper he had been studying at the dining room table. "Treasure map to the big deer. Chris knows where he is. These ridges over a swamp. We built deer stands and I put him through a gun safety class with the sheriff. That tree with the ropes on it back there? Every year they hang the biggest deer and the winner gets a steak at the VFW cooked by . . ." Bud sighed. "Jesse."

"Jesus," Harry groaned.

"Like a contest, we all put in ten bucks, the money goes to the food shelf. I already put in for you. So what do you think? We stick Chris on one of these ridges. Then you and me sit on another . . ." Bud bit his lip.

Harry glanced around. Not like he could hop a bus. "Okay, okay," he said. Giving in was a guilty thrill, like the first time he stole something. "So we set up on these ridges—"

"Thing is, shooting was never my strong suit," Bud said. "I had to go back to the range three times in boot camp to qualify at the bottom of my company. You never had that problem . . ." He stared at Harry expectantly.

"Where's Cox going to be?"

Bud smiled. "He's the hired help, not a hunting buddy."

"Okay. We hunt tomorrow. But you have to lay it on the line with her."

Bud gripped Harry's elbow. "Just get me through tomorrow. Go in there and try to talk to the kid, you know, about hunting. What do you say?"

Harry reached inside Bud's vest, seized the pint, rolled down the window, and threw it out. "No more booze."

8

Back inside the lodge, Bud put on the clown face he wore around his wife and Jesse challenged Harry. "You get all the mantalk straightened out?"

"I'm going to take a shower," said Bud nervously, stepping between them to stop the staring contest. He rolled his eyes toward the main room where Chris slouched in a chair. Harry didn't move.

"Harry?" Bud insisted, then, embarrassed, he dropped his gaze and walked to the bathroom.

"Your master's voice," Jesse said under her breath, going past him down the hall.

Harry went to his room, grabbed his rifle case and a cleaning kit, and came back out to the main room. Bud's expensive Sako .30-06 rifle with a Leupold scope lay on the sofa. A cheaper new Marlin, bolt action .30-30 with a Redfield scope sat next to it. A lighter load for the kid.

"That your rifle?" Harry asked as he sat down on the floor in front of the hearth.

"Bud bought it for me," Chris said. He pulled his hair out of his eyes and his expression quieted into a puzzle of adolescent curiosity.

"Looks all cleaned up and ready to go," said Harry. Man and boy warmed to each other as the old American flint and steel threw out a spark. Guns.

"Larry showed me how to clean it."

"Larry?"

"Sheriff Emery. I had to take a gun safety class, because, like, I'm just sixteen." His eyes flitted in the firelight.

"He shot the bear?" asked Harry. He pointed to the hide on the wall.

"Yeah. We used to live with Larry. We thought mom was going to marry him."

Harry absorbed this large piece of information without blinking. "What about Jay? Your mom ever think of marrying him?" he joked.

Chris laughed. "Mom says Jay is just this walking hard-on." Chris leaned forward. "You see those scars on his cheeks? He shot himself once on a dare, right through. Missed his teeth."

"Dumb," said Harry.

"Yeah," said Chris. "But he works like hell building all that new stuff out there. He's going to retire and be a guide when they open this place."

"That guide stuff isn't for you, huh?"

"Fuck that," Chris said. "If I never see another walleye it'll be too soon."

Harry took Randall's rifle out of the case and pressed the catch under the trigger housing and the bolt slid out with a soft, oiled click. He set it aside and threaded a cleaning rod together.

"That's an old gun. How long you had it?" said Chris. The boy's fascinated expression reminded Harry of the faces of uniformed children in Civil War photographs.

"Not mine. I borrowed it."

"Guns are beautiful," said Chris. "They're . . . perfect." The turbulent drummer-boy eyes queried Harry for a response.

Harry shrugged. He'd never particularly liked guns. Just a tool that brought to mind a certain kind of work.

"How come you don't have a scope on it?" asked Chris.

"I learned to shoot without a scope."

"They teach you to shoot in the marines?"

"I was in the army, not the marines. Uncle back in Michigan taught me."

"You and Bud were in the war together, weren't you?"

Harry shook his head. "We were around some of the same places."

Chris gave him a taunting look of disbelief. "Bud says you shot a lot of people in the war?"

Harry answered the inappropriate question with busy silence. He looked up and saw that Chris was watching him. Demanding an answer. Harry said, "Lot of people did."

"He said you did creepy stuff. Like at night."

"Bud tends to exaggerate."

Chris, riveted to Harry's every move, accepted this answer without comment. Harry screwed a bore brush into the rod and dipped it in a bottle of cleaning solvent. His fingers warmed to the smell and feel of solvent on machined steel as he ran the brush down the barrel. Then he tipped the rifle up and squinted down the muzzle, inspecting the rifling against the firelight.

"Listen, Mr. Griffin, I'm sorry about walking in on you in the bathroom," said Chris.

"Harry."

Chris nodded and slowly extended his hand and touched Harry on the forearm above his left wrist. "Harry, could I see that tattoo you have on your arm?"

Harry tensed at the gentleness of Chris's touch. He started to reach over with his right hand to roll up his sleeve.

"I'll do it," said Chris. He turned the sleeve away and for a brief second held Harry's left forearm in his hands. The tattoo was losing its edge, blending into the pigment; a winged Griffin below a word like a fading shout: AIRBORNE.

Chris pulled his hands back and folded them in his lap. "You ever have any other tattoos?" he asked.

Harry shook his head. When enough time had passed, he asked Chris, "How'd that happen? Your leg?"

Chris grinned. "Becky's got nice legs, don't she? She's got nice everything. That's because she took my leg before we were born. When we were tangled up in Mom's belly like two little red skinned rabbits."

"So you were born with it?"

"Uh-huh. Bud says he's gonna take me to a specialist to get an operation. Some kind of muscle graft deal. We just haven't got around to it yet . . ."

"You like Bud?" Harry asked offhand as he replaced the brush with a slotted tip and ran a patch down the rifle barrel. The patch came out pure. Randall had cleaned the gun before giving it to him. Harry was just going through the ritual. Getting acquainted.

"Mom likes him right now." Chris said. "She married Bachelor Number Three. They should all go on the fucking 'Dating Game.'" A drip of poison.

Harry felt eyes on his back and glanced up. Bud stood in the kitchen wearing a baggy brown terrycloth robe. He smiled, seeing Harry and the boy sitting in front of the fire. Becky came down the hall. Harry heard Becky open the refrigerator. Close it.

"So what are you going to do if you see a deer tomorrow?" Harry asked.

Chris fidgeted. "Shoot the sucker."

"Where you going to shoot him?"

Chris's eyes glittered at the fire. "Larry says an animal's life is between its shoulders. So aim there."

Harry squinted at Chris. He wasn't used to being around kids. Maybe he was reading it wrong. "First time hunting, huh?" he asked in a fraternal voice.

Chris bit his lip. "Yeah," he smiled sheepishly.

"Tell you what you do: you count to three," said Harry. "One, make sure it has horns. Two, while you're aiming, make sure you have the safety off. Then put the sight right on the front edge of his chest and move smooth with the shot. Make sure the crosshairs stay in the same spot. That way you're moving with the target. Three, squeeze. Don't jerk it."

"What if it's standing still?"

"Then it's easier. But you'll be real excited if you see a deer. That's why you should count, to control yourself."

Chris chewed on his lip and glanced around. "One—two—three."

"Good," said Harry. He slid the bolt into the rifle, pointed it at the fireplace, and pulled the trigger with a hollow click.

Abruptly Chris got up, went into the den, and turned on the television. A stereo came on in Becky's room at the end of the hall. The quiet interval had ended.

Jesse, barefoot in a purple silk robe, came out of the hall and glided down the steps and firelight licked her carved ankles and calves and the glowing moisturizing cream on her face. With a languid, utterly female gesture she raised her arm and placed her hand behind her head. Harry caught every rustle of the silk sleeve and saw and smelled the dusky roundness under her arm as she slowly pulled a binder from her hair. The braids loosened and breathed. "We're hitting the sack," she said. "You know where everything is?"

"I'm fine."

44

"It'll be crazy in the morning. Bud wants to get up at four." She paused, almost shy. *Jesus.* She had more forward gears than a Mack truck. "Well, goodnight," she said. Just being polite, seeing to a guest.

Alone in front of the fire, Harry snapped the Remington 271 to his shoulder and sighted down the barrel, getting its feel. He set the rifle aside, lit a cigarette, and savored Jesse Deucette, the manager. For a married woman, she sure had a bold way of showing her ass. The kind of female who trips a man up in his balls. Same principle that had the red-eyed bucks rampaging out there in the dark, lips curled back, noses tilted to the estrus in the wind as they thrashed their horns against the trees in the grip of the rut and were led around by their dicks right under the hunters' guns.

Too much woman. Like . . . he shut his eyes . . . being inside Grace Slick's voice with the volume turned all the way up.

Eyes again. Chris stood in front of the TV, looking down into the main room, watching him. A hulking brown shape moved past the kitchen. Bud in his bathrobe, going down the hall.

Harry flipped his smoke into the fireplace.

"Guess I'll turn in," Harry said as he walked into the den. He stopped in front of the racket of some rock group video on the TV and tapped down the volume key. "That'd wake the dead," he said.

"That's the idea," Chris shrugged.

"'Night," said Harry, moving toward the hall.

"Hey," said Chris. Harry turned. Chris pointed his finger and cocked his thumb. "One, two, three." The boy's grin was too bright. His eyes too hot. He was high.

"I'm not afraid of you," Chris said in an even voice.

Harry smiled grimly and turned his back on Chris. The minute he closed the bedroom door behind him, the TV jolted back up to high volume. He heard Bud go down the hall and have a long convoluted conversation with Chris, trying to convince him to turn it down. Bud's voice was a reasonable drone. Harry debated walking in there and shaking the kid. Turn it down. Do it. He flopped down on the bed. It was a house without rules.

Bud entered the room and Harry smelled marijuana.

"That kid smoking dope out there?" Harry asked.

"Jesse. She smokes a little grass before she goes to bed."

Harry lit a cigarette with jerky motions and blew smoke to blot out the cannabis perfume. "You talk to her?"

"Jesus Christ, man, I took a year to get into this . . . give me a few days."

Harry scowled.

"What's going on with you? You're getting all pointy." Bud said.

"I don't like people smoking dope where I sleep," said Harry.

"Take it easy. There's other people in the world besides you."

Harry thought about it. One of his basic rules was, if you get uncomfortable, leave. Before something happened. Now here he was waiting for Jesse to happen.

And now Bud's ruddy face looked pleasantly bedraggled. The ends of his beard were damp and stuck to his meaty chest and his robe fell open at the waist and showed the hairy sag of his belly. A chunk of his left calf muscle the size of a fist was missing, the skin twisted over the concave whorl of scar tissue. The wound gave his leg, below the knee, the slick appearance of a scalded drumstick.

"I'd feel more comfortable tonight in one of those log cabins," said Harry.

"The roofs aren't on those cabins. Hey, hey," Bud said in a soothing voice as he put his hands gently on Harry's shoulders. "It's been a long day. We're both burned from the drive. And we've talked down some heavy shit. Maybe you're just a little nervous about . . . tomorrow."

"Nervous?"

Bud cuffed him warmly on the neck, his fingers lingered, kneading the taut muscle. "I don't know. Guns. Moving targets."

Endless bullshit, thought Harry. And the woman, right next door, smoking dope in a silk robe.

Bud paused at the door and glanced self-consciously down the darkened hallway. "This won't be easy. She really turns me on," he said in a hoarse voice.

Harry looked away and tried to put sternness in his voice. "That kid, Chris, needs a kick in the pants."

"He'll be all right once we get in the woods—"

"Shit," Harry laughed, pointing to the Goya over the bed. "Lookit this room. There's probably an altar around here someplace with the bones of little children on it."

Bud shrugged. "You're not used to being around kids, Harry. I've been learning. You have to be flexible."

But not too flexible, thought Harry. Too hot, the absurdly loud music beyond the door. The marijuana seeping—permissive, unraveling—in the air.

"Well, she's in there, waiting," said Bud in an amazed voice. "More than I can handle."

"When you met her, she approach you?" Harry asked.

"Actually I *met* her a couple of years ago. She came down to St. Paul. Put the bite on me for a political campaign she was managing."

"Whose campaign?"

"County sheriff. And after that, it was the new hospital—"

"You check her out? Her background?"

Bud shrugged. "She's from here. Moved to Duluth, went to UMD. Got knocked up her freshman year. The guy split. Kids were born out of wedlock. She married another guy. He died, then she moved back here."

"Was there ever anything between Jesse and Cox?" Harry asked abruptly.

"Cox? Be serious. She's got more class than that," Bud grimaced.

"What about this Larry? The sheriff?"

"They used to go out—"

"Chris said they used to live together."

Bud swallowed. "She does stuff that . . ."

Harry exhaled. Bail out, man. Beyond this point it gets real fucked up! *Problem is, buddy, your wife turns me on. And it ain't all in my overheated imagination.* "This is dumb, me being here, Bud."

"I need you, Harry. To . . . talk to . . ."

"Jesus Christ," Harry muttered. "Get outta here." He pushed Bud through the door.

"Right. We got a big day tomorrow," Bud forced a grin and closed the door. His departure caused a sudden quiet to fill the lodge. The TV, the stereo. Off. Absolute silence. The cold wrestled with the roof and the furnace came on.

Listening. The whole hot lodge turned into an acoustic device.

Harry shut off the light, stripped down, crawled into bed, and lay on his back, smoking. Faintly, he could hear Bud and Jesse on the other side of the wall. A low domestic conversation. Several times he thought he heard his name.

They were discreet at first. The individual sounds were subdued. Harry stubbed out his smoke, rolled over, and lay facedown.

A thump? A giggle? Right against the wall next to his bed. Christ, the headboard of their bed was banging on the wall. *Jesse* tapping out Morse code with her hips right through the partition.

Harry's imagination amplified the muffled sounds as the springs squeaked. There was a throaty yelp of pain or pleasure. Slow then fast then slow again. Harry shut his eyes. Bud in there. His sticky flab slapping her like a tub of hamburger.

Harry took a deep breath and tried his tricks. Part of sobering up had been learning transcendental meditation. Now he tried to find the ladder to climb to a calmer depth. All Harry is divided into three parts. He tried to separate his mind from his heartbeat from his breathing. Let it all float.

Bang. Ram. Groan.

No good. There were other relaxation techniques. Older, surer ones.

Because One-Eyed Lazarus, the dead twig he peed through, was up and jolly red. Christ. An erection. Thought he'd used them all up and would spend the rest of his life paying interest on a wanton deficit. To break the tension, he masturbated slowly, outdistancing the faint sounds next door. Tried to hang there, defying gravity, on the very top arc of sensation. The universal problem. How do you make anything last?

There.

But just as quickly gone. A spilled memory. Practical now. Hide the evidence. Bent over, he tiptoed to the door. Opened it. Quiet. Except for the kid snoring in the living room. He ducked across the hall into the bathroom, cupping his groin.

Clearing up outside. Moonlight hit the snow cover and bounced through the bathroom window. He reached for the toilet paper.

"Oops, sorry," drawled the amused husky voice behind him. Besides her smile, Jesse wore nothing except a soft sparkle of sweat, shadows and scallops of moonshine. She watched him flush the soiled tissue.

Boldly, she entered the room and he inhaled Bud's raw booze-marbled sweat and her clean salt and the damp business of her thighs—Bud's jiz and her barn-musk—rioted among the porcelain and tile. Harry's bare butt backed into the chilly sink and her hand glided out and touched him on the left hip.

"You missed some," she said, with one eye cocked. Her profile, in a cascade of mussed hair, looked as cool as Liberty on a dime.

"Get out of the way," Harry said tersely.

She moved left, a feint because as he stepped around her, she shifted back and her erect nipples grazed his chest and her sweaty hair teased along his bare shoulder.

He pushed her away and crossed the hall to his room. Her voice chased him. "Bud fell asleep on me. But you don't look like you're going to sleep at all."

9

Harry woke up with a bad case of nerves hammering dirty copper nails into the roof of his mouth and somebody was shaking him and shouting, "Daylight in the swamp." He batted a hand away.

Bud. With sidelight from the hall molding the grin on his fat cuckold's face. As he turned and lumbered from the room, his grape-colored polypro long undies rode down his chubby hips and showed the hairy crack of his ass. On his way out, he yanked the light cord and the dangling Iron Cross swung back and forth.

The glare of the naked bulb punched up the debris of Chris's discarded cigarette packs, ashes, socks, and underpants. A Kmart boombox sat on the desk in a clutter of tapes and its overbuilt plastic case was redundant with ledges that were designed to collect dust. An executed schoolbook lay facedown on the floor.

Jesse's chanteuse voice lilted down the hall, singing in the kitchen. She was good, with a throaty Linda Ronstadt edge, but this morning it sounded like mockery.

You missed some. A wave of folly stood Harry up. He had to go out there and see the look on her face.

Towel wrapped around his waist, shaving kit in hand, Harry went into the hall ready to see how Jesse would put the day in play. Instead he saw a drowsy Chris, leaning his long mop of hair against the wall next to the bathroom with his raccoon eyes grainy and red, glued half shut. He wore a T-shirt and droopy Jockey shorts and tried to hide his withered left leg behind his good one. Harry got in line for the bathroom and avoided looking at the leg.

"Shake it up, you guys, if you want to eat before it gets light!" yelled

50

Jesse as utensils tinkled over cast iron and the sound of frying bacon, eggs, sausage, hash browns, and onions crackled behind her voice.

Becky came out of the bathroom wearing a shapeless nightie, with her hair all askew around a face pink and puffy as chewed bubble gum. She plodded by Harry with downcast eyes. Chris went in.

"Set the table," ordered Jesse in the kitchen.

"Leave me *alone*!" The half whine, half snarl of the teenaged oppressed.

"Hurry it up. Hubba hubba." Bud. Making a busy clatter in the main room, moving around rifles and snowshoes. "Fucking beautiful out, no wind, thirty degrees . . ." Dropped cartridges clinked on the oak planks.

Harry's turn in the bathroom. Where Jesse had stood last night like a pillar of fire was just chilly tile under his bare feet. Fast shower. Quick shave. A mouthful of Listerine to chase the corrupt taste. He returned to his room and pulled on long underwear under the mad gaze of Goya's cannibal giant.

He tossed aside the fancy Gore-Tex trousers—Bud's gift—and put on his own heavy wool trousers. Resentment welled in his throat. "Get me up here in this."

Jesse waited in the kitchen with her Gypsy braids in black ranks, twisted tight to her skull. Proper as starch in an ironed blouse, she placed a cup of coffee in his hand. "You don't look so high and mighty this morning, Harry," she said with lowered eyes.

They both looked up at the same time and saw Bud, entering the den, caught in midstride, staring at them. "Eat. Eat," ordered Bud, averting his eyes, flapping out his arms as a sleepy Becky loaded plates of food on the table.

Harry needed a minute to get organized so he opened the French doors and took his coffee out on the frigid porch. Turning, he caught Jesse's quick glance as she pushed off the kitchen counter with a restive thrust of her hips. He thought of a dirty book, the well-thumbed pages opening right to the good parts.

He turned to the windows. The wind and snow had left behind a vast Tiaga stillness and a horned moon that wedged in a canyon of clouds and scattered silver dollars on Glacier Lake.

Jesse moved beside him and their shoulders touched. "You have anything this pretty down in your Cities?" she asked.

"What is it with you?" he said and their voices were clandestine, thick in their throats.

"People can't help when they meet," said Jesse, matter-of-factly.

"He's my friend, Jesse."

"Your friend is the greatest show on earth," she said and before he could respond, she walked back into the lodge.

He stared into the darkness. Below a cape of clouds, the glittering points of Orion the Hunter hung low in the east and he picked out the icy diamond of Rigel and above it, the three studs in the constellation's belt. A crack appeared above the crooked hump of Nanabozho Ridge and a sliver of purple and vermilion stretched solemn as a church window clear to Canada.

At the table, Harry fed his bunched nerves sparingly with toast and a little scrambled eggs while Bud went over the plan of the hunt on the worn sheet of lodge stationery and Chris sat unusually attentive at his side and Jesse stood in the kitchen and puffed nervously on a cigarette.

Their eyes were loud and sticky and stumbled toward each other.

Becky, face washed and wide awake now, came down the hall in a gray wind suit and cross-country ski boots. She pulled her hair back and knotted it into a practical ponytail.

"What are you doing?" asked Bud.

"I'm going to ski."

"You can't ski today. The woods are full of hunters. There's two feet of snow on the trail around the lake," said Bud.

"Some snowmobiles went through last night. The trail's fine. It's the first snow of the season," said Becky, sitting down and tightening the laces on her boots.

"She shouldn't go out there," Bud said to Jesse.

Jesse nodded. "Maybe you should wait."

"Mom," said Becky, drawing out the sound.

"Hush," said Jesse.

Then Bud stuck his elbow into a puddle of syrup from the blueberry pancakes and Jesse scolded him lightly as she came to his aid with a damp dishcloth. As she tended to Bud's spill, her eyes ambushed Harry through Bud's thick cowlick.

"We go along this ridge that skirts the shore," Bud was saying. "Then we follow it east away from the lake till we come to where it peters out into these three fingers that go down to the swamp."

"Once the first shot goes off, all the deer head for the swamp, that's what Larry says. The deer we want has thirteen points and the long tine on his left antler is way bigger than the other side. You can't miss him," said Chris in a touching attempt at mimicking a man's deeper voice. He looked focused, purposeful, his hair combed straight back; a different person from the punk of last night.

Bud nodded. "We'll set up on the ridges. Harry on the first one, then me, then Chris." Bud marked *x*'s on each of the three crooked fingers he'd drawn.

Becky piped up. "Give up. Larry always shoots the biggest deer. Five years in a row."

"Not this year," said Bud.

It was time to bundle up in blaze orange. Chris went to the bathroom. Bud fiddled with the snowshoes out on the porch.

Harry carried his plate to the kitchen counter. Jesse stood a bare inch away and said in a low voice, "You don't have to go out there. They'd probably have more fun, just the two of them."

For a moment there was only the sound of their breathing.

"Look, I know why you're here," she said with tired candor. "He doesn't have the guts to bail on his own." The left side of her smile jerked. "When I met him he was too good to be true, we were going to put this town back on the map. He can get you to believe almost anything."

"So what happened?"

The other side of her smile twitched. "What he was running from in the Cities caught up with him and he started changing on me, drank himself into that tub of guts out there. I gave up *a lot* for him. And not just to be his sport fuck. So yeah, I got him to make it legal. And when he splits I have no qualms about taking his money. Answer your question?"

Becky approached with her leggy runner's stride and thrust her body between them. "Oops, sorry," she said, in a mocking imitation of her mother's voice. She dropped a pile of dirty plates into the sink with a crash and gave them both a look of pure disgust as she moved away.

"And last night?" asked Harry.

"Life goes on, Harry. It's going on right here. Isn't it?"

Harry exhaled carefully. *Ten years of discipline slipping, every day a sober penny rubbed shiny with his sweat. Bud with his idle fucking millions.*

"You could tell them you forgot something. And come back for a cup of coffee and I'll tell you a thing or two about Bud Maston," she said simply.

Revenge Fuck was beautifully written all over her face. She read his mind and gave him a man-weary expression. Her eyes tightened. "Bud's not the only one in need of help," she said under her breath.

"Kid's stuff," Harry muttered but his eyes were manacled to hers and he knew he was going to throw his life at her like a pair of dice and it was an exhilaration he hadn't known in ten years sober.

She reached over and plucked a red cord that draped from his parka pocket. Slowly she drew out his compass. She slid it on the counter behind the toaster.

"You could say you forgot your compass," she said in a steady voice.

Sleepwalking, out of breath, Harry retreated to the mud porch. He put on a blaze-orange coverlet and tried to look busy, checking the contents of his backpack. Through the doorway, he saw Becky grab Chris by the arm and pull him back into the lodge. A muffled disagreement tugged between them, fast, their heads close. Chris's eyes caught Harry's glance and burned with a look of such intensity that Harry guiltily broke eye contact.

They know. Becky must have overheard the scene in the bathroom last night.

Chris stared straight ahead, holding a piece of pancake in his hand, munching, as Becky continued to whisper in his ear. He shook his head. Becky lowered her eyes. Chris's face had transformed since he'd left the table and gone to the bathroom. He looked like he'd just stepped out of a wind tunnel.

Outside, on the steps, they struggled into the snowshoes. Bud handed out ammunition and made sure Chris was loaded and on safe. By the porch light, Harry loaded the Remington—four bullets, copper-yellow streaks, with fat, soft lead noses. With Jesse's plea careening in his head, he pushed the bolt forward, slid a round into the chamber, locked down the bolt, and set the safety.

Jesse and Becky stood in the doorway, watching them hunker back and forth, testing the snowshoe straps. Bud bent to help Chris with the buckles. Chris took a step back. Rods of tension transfixed all the people standing in the cold. Could be just me, thought Harry.

Then Bud came next to Harry and said in a low voice. "I'll lead, then Chris. Keep your eye on the kid, he's not used to handling guns." Then he swung his hand and grinned. "Follow me."

"I'll keep the coffee hot," said Jesse. She stood hunched, hugging herself. Becky raised her hand once to Chris, then turned and dashed inside. When Bud and Chris had their backs turned, Jesse inclined her head at Harry and winked with her hot whore's eye.

They set off across the powder, fine as flour, that had sifted off the trees onto the plowed drive, passed between two of the roughed-in log cabins, and followed a clear-cut trail.

It was sharp out, but not that cold. Mist pooled in low places.

Just like Becky had said, a snowmobile trail was carved into the drifts. They followed it for a few minutes, then Bud turned off at another clear-cut and they began to climb.

Over the scrunch of the snowshoes, Bud's labored breath wheezed white gusts in the menthol air and a broth of sweat pasted Harry's underwear against his ribs. Not used to this snowshoe routine in the dark, he settled into a web-footed lumbering gait.

Bud, who wore the biggest snowshoes, took care to beat a track for Chris, who dragged his left foot. Slow going in the black pines and then, fifty yards away, something big started and bounded away with muffled urgency. They poised alert, handling their guns, peering into the dissolving darkness. A minute later, Bud pointed to fresh tracks. Harry nodded. Deer.

More serious now, they plodded up the trail.

There was enough light now to pick out the faint contour of the ridge rising through the pines. They continued to climb, soundless except for the squeak of the laminated catgut on their wickered feet.

Harry brought up the rear. Reliable Harry. Everybody agreed, when the chips were down, depend on Harry to do the right thing.

Words: *Temper. Temperance. Tempt. Tempest.* Most of life was just so much goddamn talk.

"Wait," Harry called out.

"What?" Bud turned.

"I don't have my compass. Left it back in the lodge."

"Can't get lost in this snow. Just stay on the tracks," said Bud.

"Should have a compass," said Harry. His eyes were fixed in the gloom an inch to the left of Bud's frosted beard. "You guys go ahead. I'll catch up to you on the ridge."

"I'll go with you," Bud said nervously, "but we have to hurry. We should set in before light."

"I'll make better time on my own." Harry started to unsling his rifle and pack. Bud seized the leather sling in a gloved hand, holding it to Harry's shoulder.

"Hang on to your rifle," said Bud.

"Okay, but you might as well wait here . . ."

"I'll go part way with you, so you don't get lost," said Bud lamely.

"Can't get lost in this snow," said Harry foolishly and was embarrassed by the absurdity of their words. *He knows too. And I'm going to do it anyway.*

Chris listened passively to their silly conversation and they left him standing silently in the middle of the trail. Bud kept up for a hundred yards, then bent over, wheezing, he waved Harry on. Harry looked once over his shoulder and saw Bud slip off the trail into the cover of the trees.

Harry's snowshoes flew over the moon-dappled snow.

10

The clean slice of skis cut through the trample of snowshoe tracks on the snowmobile trail. So Becky had gone skiing after all.

So he'd be alone with her.

For years, he'd treaded cautiously between anger and fear and his blood had thinned running in strict sober lines. Now it was up, hammering in his throat.

Be straight Harry or be crooked—either way, be real.

He stacked his rifle and pack next to the trail, kicked off the snowshoes, and broke into a run.

And he saw the pale lunar figure in faded denim come up from a dip in the trail and stride out of the low hanging mist with the plaid lining of her jean jacket rosy against her bare neck.

She held the compass at arm's length on its cord, and then she cast her hand and threw the compass away and, not missing a step, she removed her wedding ring and stuck it in her pocket and raised both arms and put her hands back and tossed her head—another step, another toss—step and toss and the long black hair swung free.

She moved to the left, off the trail, into a grove of long-needled pine and Harry paced her, step for step. Sideways at first, they stole silently through smaller pines that were bowed with snow, prostrated in the wake of the north wind and then the thick branches closed in and dissembled the moonlight.

They approached each other by feel, by smell, in the still green maze of pine needles that vibrated in the misty air, erect as slender tuning forks.

Soundlessly they closed the distance until he threw his hands wide and pushed the pine boughs aside and uncovered her trembling on tip-toe with her eyes shut and her lips parted. Moonlight etched her teeth and hung a tinsel of silver and shadow on her upturned face and the bristling pine folded around them.

They crushed together and buttons, zippers, and belt buckles made welts in their flesh and their hips grated and her hair hummed through his fingers, inky as a sweaty June night.

Their hands explored and it was impossible this way, hobbled in clothes and boots, so she turned around and they fumbled in the moon-splashed dark and a button popped off his wool pants in his haste as she kicked one tennis shoe free of her wadded jeans.

She flung out her arms, grasped two branches in her fists, and bent from the waist and her smooth thighs shuddered as she stamped one shoe in the snow and then the other and took the stance and thrust her back in a powerful arch.

Harry would remember the antler curve of the moon, the pines shivering, the snow tumbling down.

Their breath joined in one great cloud, then tapered off into plumes and on fire in a foot of snow, they dropped to their knees and, face to face, began to laugh. Quickly they covered each other's mouths with their hands and hugged and looked warily after their echoing laughter. Starved to touch, their fingers silently gobbled each other's faces and only their eyes sparkled with laughter: *isn't this the way it's supposed to be—wild. Magic.*

The moment ended and they put their clothing back in place and she tugged his wrists, inclining her body back toward the lodge—toward hot coffee, clean sheets. Words to span the wreckage of impulse.

No. He wanted this moment pure. He shook his head and she tightened her grip. They began to struggle because she was very strong and deliberate thought replaced the passion in her incendiary eyes. Stay.

Harry resorted to a fighting technique to break her grip. She rebounded quickly and threw her arms around him. He held her off and pushed through the pines. A crimson thread drew him to the side of the trail where he retrieved his compass. She followed him as he retraced his steps and, as he buckled on his snowshoes and shouldered his rifle and pack, she stood with her arms upraised, beckoning. Finally, the cold gripped her face like censure; she hugged herself, turned and walked away.

Not a word had passed between them.

He was caught in a riddle of time. Somewhere just up ahead he had stepped through a door in the forest and now he had to find his way back into his life. Irony twirled around him but his muscles moved smoothly with dreamy power and his eyes had never been so clean. He could feel the blood shoot the rapids of his heart.

Cursed or blessed, he wanted to shout.

Floating, he seized the rifle with both hands in a burst of exhilaration: *I'll shoot a deer while it's still running down her leg.*

Then the first twinge eclipsed the euphoria. Have to tell Bud. Be honest. Just happened. Like a car accident. Still hard to think right now, all tactile, pulsing . . .

Every surface of the forest stood out with a shadowy gleam. Pristine, never cut in here. Towers of white and red pine reached up 80, 90 feet before they branched. Thickets of snow-tiered fir and spruce. A tremble of aspen stirred heady resins of sap and tangy bark and pine cones nestled like tiny hand grenades.

His heart thumped in his throat when he picked out Bud hiding behind a tree next to the trail, stooped over, chin on his chest. He stepped back into his life and everything looked different. Bud looked weak, pathetic.

For the first time, Harry consciously resented Bud Maston his messy, monied life. Walking those last few paces, his mind swirled with numbers; his age, salary, the years until retirement. Not that many good years left.

Could he afford a woman like Jesse? Crazy damn thoughts.

"You all set?" Bud whispered.

Harry nodded and held up the compass and looked around. "Where's the kid?"

"Up ahead. He started down already. Something was moving this way. I think he saw that deer."

"You think? Not a good idea to split up in the dark."

Bud watched his breath drift in the chill air. "Wind's this way," he motioned to the left. "If we jump a deer, he'll run into the wind, that way."

"Yeah?" Harry's senses were still reeling. Wind? And Bud, his voice goofy for that big deer, went on talking.

"So, you take the trail, I'll drag along about thirty yards into the trees to the right. Maybe you'll push him out my way." Bud gripped his rifle and his eyes glowed in the faint light, Harry wondered if he could sniff the sweet babyshit of sex lingering in the crisp air.

"Let's do it. I'm going to hang that deer from that fucking tree and show these morons," said Bud. "I'll meet you where the ridges split off over the swamp. Keep an eye out for Chris, he's to the left."

Harry didn't like it, split up and all, but he didn't want to be around Bud right now, so he stalked the trail while Bud moved silently on snowshoes through the trees. He just walked, not even unslinging his rifle from his shoulder until he came to the end of the trail where the ridge broke into three meandering fingers and sloped gradually. Below, flanked by tamarack and aspen and fringed by a thick hedge of tall reddish brush, the gray grass and clumped cattails were bent with frost and driven helter-skelter by a stampede of wind.

Bud's voice came from the cover of the trees to Harry's rear. "You're in here. I'll find Chris and set him in and be right back."

A few yards away, astride the ridgeline, a platform of new lumber peeked stark as bone among the rotting branches of a fallen white pine. A deer would see it a mile away.

Bud disappeared into the trees down the second finger. Harry unbuckled the snowshoes and quietly hoisted himself into the platform and scooped away snow. He had the highest position, overlooking the other two fingers.

He got his bearings and quickly figured his field of fire: 200 yards of open swamp and slope in front and 100 yards of tangled forest to either side.

A red squirrel raced chattering through the underbrush in a miniature frenzy and set the forest echoing and the first hush of dawn smeared honey through the trees and dripped pastel shadows on the snow.

The heavy rifle swung balsa-light in his hot hands as he traversed an arc, sighting along the gray marsh grass. Slowly, his body began to cool and a sheet of sweat turned icy across his chest and a curl of steam rose from his bare throat and he inhaled the happy scent of crushed berries. He whispered: "Jesse."

Then the rabbit-assed squirrel bolted again, marking Bud's progress through the thicket across the ravine.

Friend's wife. Technically. Bargaining now. Bud didn't really love her anyway.

He strained his eyes to see through the filmy light. Everything was flat. The shadows without edge. Hard to see.

He shifted the rifle and blew into the peep sight to make sure it was free of snow. Then he flexed his fingers in the soft deerskin glove shells, switched off the safety, tested the trigger pull, flipped back to safe. With the stock snug to his shoulder, he rested his cheek along the smooth walnut. Last time he'd fired a rifle it was dirty black plastic itching his cheek, stinking of sweat and mosquito repellent and it'd been 100 degrees in the shade

Now what? That was Chris—but why was he down at the bottom of the ravine, stepping out of the thick stuff by the swamp. Too far down. C'mon guys, get some cover. Almost light.

Times like this it was hard to believe Bud had been a marine on another ridge years ago. A spiky, laterite, red dirt ridge that had been fertilized with napalm and twisted down from the Annamite Cordillera below the DMZ in Vietnam. Harry had read the citation. Bud had stayed behind with the machine gun to cover the retreat of his platoon so they could get to better ground. Held off a North Vietnamese flanking attack for crucial minutes, like Chamberlain on Little Round Top. Saved his whole company.

The first trickle of true remorse seeped over him. Friends were the people you lied for, who you didn't steal from.

A panorama of memory nailed down the slow stain of guilt. Spring 1971. The big Vietnam Veterans Against the War demonstration in Washington, D.C.:

Harry and Bud, holding hands, stepped forward when their time came in the long line of veterans who were tossing back their medals and moved up to the pig wire Nixon had strung across the Capitol steps to keep them away from their government and flung their Purple Hearts and a jackal pack of reporters and photographers scrambled across the steps to drool at the twinkling stars and hearts that showered down on the cold marble and Bud and Harry charged the fence and started to scale it, shaking with a holy rage.

Almost sun up. Noble memories didn't help. He was alone in all of God's nature with a dirty movie in his head. Only sin there was: letting a buddy down.

Bud was moving down the ravine and Chris was starting to climb to meet him. Now what the fuck were they doing, maneuvering? Maybe they spotted something. Harry stood up on tiptoe, but the ground was tricky where Bud and Chris approached each other and the edge of the ridge and brush blocked his line of sight.

A puff of snow fell from a pine bough and slapped his face. His ears rang. Too long in the city. The sheer quiet made him nervous and he glanced from side to side in an effort to locate its source.

Muffled voices, but angry. An argument. What the hell now? Harry tensed up on the balls of his feet.

"Why you ungrateful little shit!" Bud's bellow shook the trees as a blur of orange jackets collided in the thicket. Christ, they were fighting.

The two spaced rifle shots blew a hole in the pastel dawn and the day gushed out at red combat speed and Harry vaulted from the stand and was in midair when Bud screamed and his senses—razor sensitive from Jesse—flicked toward the sound of mortal terror like a school of sharks.

He thumbed off the safety as he hit the snow in a dead run for the edge of the ridge with his rifle held at high port.

11

There was time.

Harry on the ridge, synapses popping like firecrackers.

Real close. But time. Ninety yards down the slope, Chris's hand shook frantically, struggling with his rifle bolt. Trying to clear a jam.

Bud flopped, tangled in his long snowshoes with blood running Day-Glo bright and wet on his orange jacket, his hands, and spattered in the snow. His red hand strained toward where his rifle was buried, only the stock showing. Out of reach.

Harry saw it etched with eyes rinsed from the sprint through the adrenaline shower; prisoner to action, his reflexes decided between two runaway heartbeats.

A high nasal squeal came from Bud's throat as he tried to claw his way into a tangle of jackpine, away from Chris and the echo of the shots that still thrashed the air like a barbed cordite whip.

And then Chris's manic fingers stopped fumbling. His hand shot forward on the bolt and locked it down.

"*One!*" screamed Chris as he raised the rifle and curled his finger around the trigger.

And the high-resolution shit roared a million miles a second and the sting that turned his blood to burning needles had already shaved a hair off the split second . . .

"*Two!*" A flash from the white of Chris's right eye. Saw Harry—a chance. No. The rifle never moved off Bud. Eye back to scope, aiming. Only 30 feet to his crawling, flopping target. Couldn't miss.

Bud was a blur outside the indifferent steel ring of the peep sight.

Maybe he looked up. Couldn't tell. Downhill, don't overshoot . . . It was happening.

"Three!" Chris's scream blended into the crack of a rifle shot and bark snapped from a tree trunk a foot from Bud's head where Chris's shot went wild when Harry took him low in his right armpit and he twirled like a string-cut marionette and time still spread out, jeweled and as perversely beautiful as a peacock fan.

Yes!

Harry watched over his sights as Chris's hat and rifle flew away and his long hair swirled and his arms flapped out and his hands and fingers reached.

As he spun, Harry could see the expression on his face—not the eyes, too far—but Chris's mouth gaped in a stricken circle and his cheeks contorted in a mask of surprise. He was dead as he made the last quarter-turn of a clumsy snowshoe pirouette and pitched, arms outstretched, into the thorny branches of prickly gooseberry bramble bush.

Harry watched a clump of snow collapse from the shivering brambles as he came down the slope, swiftly working the bolt, mashing another round into the chamber. Chris's body trembled and Harry's rifle came up. Wary. Ready. Just the bush shaking. But Harry came forward cautiously, covering the prone form.

"Oh my God!" Bud's scream let time out of its cage.

No movement from the bush. He dropped the rifle. Running now through the deep snow. Down. Down. Stumbling in the muskeg at the bottom of the ravine. Pine crowns whirled overhead.

Out of time. And now Harry desperately wanted time. Time to talk. Time to reason. Time to make it better. Fear and shock closed in and a ragged crimson tunnel squeezed his vision. The sun poked through the clouds and the snow glittered brilliant and was blinding except for the red stain that led to Bud.

Bud's face was cold in the hot snow, the texture of gray congealed grease going into shock.

"There's pieces of him . . ." gasped Bud, hyperventilating, staring, wide-eyed. "Pieces of him . . ." His bluish lips were stringy, dribbling blood, bitten through and pulled tight across the chattering red-stained Chiclets of his teeth.

"Don't look," panted Harry as he dropped beside Bud. Soft-nosed hunting bullets didn't make clean holes coming out. Harry's hands tore at Bud's jacket. The damn zipper stuck. Harry pulled out his knife and hacked.

"His eyes . . ." gasped Bud.

"Calm down, dammit." Fear was very detailed in Harry's hoarse voice.

"His eyes . . . close his eyes," whispered Bud.

"What?" Harry turned. Chris's face had come to rest on its side. The dark eyes were wide open, staring at them. One eyelid hooked on a thorn.

Trembling, Harry hacked harder at Bud's coat—destroyed the zipper, ignored Bud's cries—yanked it off and threw it at the thorn bush. The bloody coat covered the eyes.

"I . . . I was trying to . . . get his gun away and—" panted Bud.

"He fucking tried to kill you, man!" snarled Harry. He was thinking with his hands and his anger masked a terror that he was about to reach into blasted intestines and the half-digested slop of Jesse's breakfast and stomach acid. God, if he's gut shot, what do I do?

Bud's sticky red hands seized at Harry's collar. "Did you have to . . . have to—?"

Roughly, Harry rolled Bud on his side, slashed through two hundred dollars worth of Gore-Tex trousers and exposed the quivering flab of his flank.

"Ow," moaned Bud as Harry squeegeed blood away with his palm. A small entrance wound puckered in Bud's left-side love handle, rouged with powder burn. In back, a bigger ragged wound bubbled where the bullet came out in curls of yellow fat that peeled back around the ripped skin. Lucky. Nothing like the hole in the kid.

"Blubber saved your ass," said Harry, relieved, jerking off his pack, thankful that he'd brought the first-aid kit. Efficiently he took out sterile pads, gauze, tape.

"Is . . . is he . . . is he?" Bud reared, gasped.

Harry slapped him hard across the face. "Shut your mouth. Breath through your nose. Do it! All that bullet did was blow a thousand calories outta your spare tire, but shock could kill you, so calm the fuck down!"

"But you . . . *killed him*," groaned Bud.

"I fucking know that!" Harry shouted. He dropped the dressing and pounded his thighs with his fists. Seeing Bud's eyes go even wider into shock at his tantrum, he controlled himself and willed his hands to stop shaking as he washed the blood away with snow. Still a lot of blood. Lot of capillaries to feed all that fat. Bud screamed when Harry splashed some iodine on his wound.

Quickly Harry taped on a compress, then he unlaced Bud's boots and removed his own parka and covered Bud with it. He stood up and lit a cigarette to calm himself and took a quick inventory. Clear the airway. Stop the bleeding. Treat for shock.

Steam came off him in waves. He was still on fire with adrenaline. His eyes stopped on his rifle, half buried in the snow.

"Don't touch anything," he told Bud.

"What? *What?*" Bud shook, his eyes welled up.

"There'll be cops. Don't touch anything," said Harry.

"If only I coulda talked to him! I was trying to talk to him," Bud stammered.

"Get your head outta your ass," Harry shouted, annoyed. "What happened, Bud? What happened?"

"He said if I ratted him out he'd kill me, I tried to get to him but the little shit shot me." Bud blinked several times and shuddered.

Harry knelt, took off his wool cap, pulled it over Bud's wild hair. He stroked Bud's face and said, "You're all right. Just . . . calm down."

"I'm not all right," Bud heaved and began to cry. "It's all fucked up."

Harry gritted his teeth and held him in his arms as sobs wracked Bud's thick body. "It's all right, give it all to me," he mumbled. What I do. How I keep going when the air is made of tears. Grow gills. Do my fucking job.

Suddenly, fiercely, Bud flung his arms around Harry's neck and clung in a spasm of fear. As Harry struggled to quiet him, he felt Bud's torn lips streak his own, tasting of hot, wet, dirty pennies.

Bud's mouth worked, pronouncing some silent word as pain and tenderness and relief made a bloody sponge of his face. Harry noticed the salt-and-pepper bruise along Bud's forehead. Another powder burn that turned the freckles black. He leaned forward to hear and Bud's sour, harsh breath bussed his ear and tears carved crooked salty channels down Bud's dirty Kabuki face as he gathered himself and gasped, "You saved my life."

"No shit," said Harry. He was numb. Times like this you had to keep it real simple. No wasted motion. He eased Bud back down and rummaged in his pack, pulled out a space blanket, unfolded it from its cellophane wrap and tucked it around Bud.

A sharp volley of gunshots echoed through the trees, off the ridges and from the corner of his eye he caught movement—gray—a shadow darting up the ridge where it wasn't supposed to be. Could be a deer. Or . . . Harry crouched alert. His rifle was back by the body. His eyes scanned the treeline. "There could be more of them," he muttered.

"What do you mean?" said Bud, wide-eyed.

"That guy Cox . . ." Harry's voice trailed off. He stared at his rifle buried yards away. A cliché from detective movies about disturbing evidence. Better leave it for the cops. He reached for Bud's rifle. "I heard two shots and saw him fire once. Either of those first two yours?"

"Never got it off my shoulder. Dropped it when—"

"You sure?"

"Fuck yes, I'm sure. He fired three times and missed twice. Christ, if he hadn't jammed up after the second one—"

"You'd be one dead-stupid-fucking-drunk millionaire, getting me up here in all this. Serve you right, dammit." Fingers trembling, Harry broke open Bud's rifle and sniffed the chamber. The cold steel bolt smelled greasy of solvent and oil. Not fired. He unloaded the rifle and quickly assembled a cleaning rod from his pack and rammed the plug of snow from the barrel, flung the rod aside and reloaded the rifle, shoved a round in the chamber and checked the surrounding woods.

"Don't do that," wailed Bud. "You're scaring me."

Harry set the safety and laid the rifle across Bud's chest.

Bud clutched it. "What are you doing?"

"I can't carry you out of here. I gotta go get help," said Harry. "Until I get back, that weapon is the only friend you've got."

Bud's eyes bulged at the woods. "Harry, don't leave me!"

"Fuck you, you been shot before. Worse than this. Why'd you call me in the middle of the night, dammit?"

"I was scared. I dunno. Just a feeling. I just wanted you along."

"You sonofabitch, you gotta talk to me. What was that argument about?"

Bud shut his eyes. "I don't know. It's nuts . . . I caught him with some stuff he stole. I told him he had to go to the police and turn it in. It was all settled, we were going to the sheriff, but he wanted to go hunting first. He said the sheriff'd never let him hunt after he turned the stuff in."

"What did he steal?"

Bud gulped for air. "Guns."

"Jesus, we went *hunting* with a drugged-up kid who steals guns? Where is your fucking brain?"

"He went wild. Said to get off his back or I'd never live through deer season. He threatened me, the little asshole, threatened me with a gun. So I tried to take it away from him." Bud panted, caught his breath and continued. "Shot right at my head, can you believe that? I grabbed at the gun but got tangled in the snowshoes and he stuck it right against me and shot again."

Harry shook his head. "Man, you don't know how close you came to checking out."

Bud swallowed. "I don't believe how quick it happened."

But Harry wasn't thinking about making the shot. He was thinking about the charms of Jesse Deucette.

"I wasn't supposed to be here," Harry thought out loud.

"What?" asked Bud, gray-faced, eyes huge with confusion and pain.

Harry shook his head. Not now. His head wasn't working real good beyond the immediate situation. The immediate situation called for a medic and the cops.

Harry turned and walked up the slope to the sagging brambles where Chris lay. He lifted the torn coat and stared into the lifeless face. Looked diminished. The dead always did. Like leftovers. Just a kid. Jesus.

Don't think about it. Do your job. Get help.

"What are you going to tell her?" Bud moaned in agony as he hugged the rifle to his chest.

"The truth," said Harry, as he took a last, unflinching look at the boy's corpse. Gently, he let the coat drape over the face. Then he gathered himself and began to run through the deep snow.

12

Panic played its clumsy slow-motion joke and tripped him in the under-brush and the knee-deep snow. Snowshoes? No time. Keep going. Brambles whipped his face and he lost his footing again and this time he went ass over end downhill. Getting up, he saw Becky bent over her skis on the snowmobile trail. Her breath came in tortured clouds and she was sticky with snow to her waist. "*Becky,*" he yelled.

She turned with a waxen expression when she saw him coming full tilt down the ridge. Her face was all wrong, but then he realized that he was smeared with blood. In a frenzied movement she fastened the bind-ings and grabbed her ski poles.

"Go," he yelled. "Get to a phone. Get an ambulance! Bud's shot!"

The muscles of her back and buttocks bunched against the clingy metal-gray fabric of her wind suit and rippled as she sprinted down the trail in long strides and her voice filled the woods with an eerie, high-pitched cry. "*Mom! Moooommmmmm!*"

And he was spent and he couldn't keep up and he staggered and tripped again and got up and tried to run on wobbling legs. Finally he came between the log cabins and fell to all fours in front of the porch steps. "Ambulance." He gasped and coughed as he wiped spittle from his chin.

Becky stalked back and forth on the porch with her face twitching and her fingers pulling at her hair. Jesse ran down the steps. "I called the hospital . . ." Her face was bright with slow horror and her jeans were still wet from their romp in the snow. "You're bleeding," she said.

Thinking with his hands, he seized her shoulders and shook her.

"Bud's shot," he said in an icy voice. "And if I'd of spent another ten minutes doing it like dogs, he'd be dead."

"Oh God," Jesse's eyes went vacant.

"Not that bad. He'll be all right," he panted.

"I'll get something," said Jesse, but she couldn't move.

"No. No. Wait for the ambulance," said Harry. "We need some cops."

"Cops," said Jesse, paralyzed.

"Mom, we gotta get out of here," wailed Becky as she paced in a caged circle and opened and closed her fingers and plucked at the air.

"Where's Chris?" asked Jesse starkly.

He pushed her away. "He tried to kill Bud. I had to stop him. There wasn't any time . . ."

"Where's Chris," she whispered fiercely. "Where's my boy?"

Harry looked straight into Jesse's clouding eyes. "He's dead, Jesse. Chris shot Bud and I shot Chris and he's dead."

Then it was faces by Diane Arbus in a wraparound funhouse mirror. Becky's features elongated into horse eyes swollen in fury and terror and Jesse's teeth and gums enlarged as her lips contracted and pores cratered her skin.

Becky came off the porch and grabbed at Jesse and yanked her away from Harry, *"Mom, don't you see? He's going to kill us all!"* and her hysteria erupted from inside her but the shock was hitting Jesse from the outside in waves that glittered like rain on a marble statue and it was as bad a moment as he had ever known.

But he got on them and shook them by the arms: "Calm down. We need a medic."

"Don't you touch her," Becky screamed and jumped in front of her mother and she charged in a blur of gray and they went down in the snow and her fingers raked his face, tearing the skin, barely missing his eyes. *"Killer,"* she screamed over and over. *"Killer! Killer! Killer!"*

"Stop this," Jesse ordered, trying to get her arms around Becky.

Harry had blood in his eyes as Becky squirmed beneath him in a manic flurry of fists, elbows, and knees. Finally he pinned her arms and Jesse started to bolt toward the woods. "I've got to go out there," she panted.

"No, not till the cops get here." And he tackled her, and Becky came at him again. The siren was faint, between the shouts and grunts of struggle. Then louder.

Jesse's hair was still down, with a wild shine from their lovemaking and warm in his hands when he yanked her head back. "You bitch, you tried to kill Bud," he whispered fiercely.

Terror softened her lips and swelled them and tears brimmed in her eyes. But she met his glare straight on. "And any doctor who examined me right now would diagnose rape the way I'm wracked up," she whispered right back. Their lips were an inch apart and they breathed the supercharged air from each other's lungs. Becky lunged away from them and rolled over and came to her knees and pressed both hands to her ears and screamed: *"Why are you whispering?"*

A whirling blue strobe from a police flasher slapped Jesse's face and the Maston County deputy's Chevy Blazer practically ran the three of them down as it slid to a sideways stop in the drive. The first thing the deputy saw when he bolted from the car was the blood all over Harry's face. The first thing he heard was Becky's high quavering scream:

"Killlerrr!"

13

Eight A.M. in Maston County. The low clouds sagged with arsenic amber, black, and gray and Harry hugged himself and shivered at the top of the ridge. Nauseous, he wanted to brush his teeth real bad.

The deputies strung piss-yellow tape through the trees to cordon off Chris's body, the spot where Bud had fallen, and the slope leading up to Harry's deer stand in the down pine. The tape billowed slack, then reared and snapped in a gust of wind. Shots popped several ridges away where someone was shooting at deer, not people. Harry started at the reports and the Maston County Sheriff's deputy who was the first to answer the call placed a steady hand on his arm. In his Prussian blue winter uniform, the cop made a trim cutout against the poison sky.

Four Highway Patrol deputies, another local deputy, the sheriff, and the medics from the ambulance were down below with Bud. More cops were back at the lodge seeing to Jesse and Becky.

The sheriff, a tall man in a red Hudson's Bay mackinaw, stood near the orange blob of Chris's body, keeping everyone away from the tracks in the snow that choreographed the fatal seconds in the ravine.

And Harry could see Bud's face—Brillo beard stuck in dirty Ivory soap—between the backs and shoulders of the medics.

His deputy escort was young and competent, very correct in his bearing with tragic excitement animating his athletic Scandinavian face. Maybe they didn't get this kind of call much up here. He had asked questions and methodically taken notes in his spiral notepad and had photographed the scene with a Polaroid as the medics went in to get to Bud. He had directed their initial approach with care so as not to disturb evidence. Procedure had set in, setting boundaries for shock.

Harry gagged and tried to spit the taste from his mouth.

"How you doing?" asked the deputy.

"I'm good," said Harry, wiping spittle from his lips. Probably the wrong thing to say. He gingerly dabbed his face with a bloody wad of gauze and loose meat wobbled like thawing steak. Four deep lacerations started on his left cheek under the eye, raked across the bridge of his nose, and clawed down his right cheek.

"Where's your coat?" asked the deputy.

Harry nodded down the slope. "Used it to cover him."

The deputy yelled down the incline. "Somebody bring Mr. Griffin his coat."

Harry grimaced. The hemorrhaging adrenaline that had carried him this far had flamed out and now his guts were charred hollow and dirty as a chimney fire. The deputy watched him closely for signs of shock.

"We got this under control here, Mr. Griffin. We can get you back to town. Get you somebody to talk to."

"Talk to?" Harry shook his head. "A lawyer?"

"No, uh, they got people trained in crisis counseling—"

"Christ," muttered Harry. Minnesota cops. They probably all had counseling degrees. "You got a cigarette?" he asked the deputy.

"Don't smoke."

Harry hugged himself. "Cold," he said.

"Hurry up with that coat," the deputy yelled. Down below someone held up the coat. They were putting Bud on a gurney.

"I'd like to ride with him to the hospital," Harry said.

"You just wait here, sir," said the deputy. "Here comes your coat."

Another county deputy jogged up the slope, staying outside the yellow tape perimeter. He carried Harry's jacket, a blanket, and a Thermos. Harry put on his parka, pulled the hood over the cake of sweat frozen in his hair, and grabbed for a high-energy bar in his pocket. He tore at the plastic wrapper and his numb, blood-stained fingers spasmed. He dropped it. The deputy picked it up and opened it. Harry gobbled it down. The other deputy draped the blanket over his shoulders and held out the Thermos.

"Sheriff thought you might need this," he said, screwing off the cup and pouring it full and steaming.

Harry took it and drank greedily and the warmth flooded his veins and enlarged his throat and suddenly there was all this new room inside him. An involuntary parched "Ah," came from his lips and he forced the cup away with both hands. He spat out the residue in his mouth as a smoky wind, one part coffee, nine parts whiskey, raced through him. He spat again on the snow and handed back the cup. "Booze in it," he said, unable to stop the grin spreading across his torn face. "Not the day I want to lose ten years of sobriety."

The cops exchanged glances and the one who brought the Thermos spoke apologetically. "It's Sheriff Emery's. He ain't on duty today. Was going hunting."

Harry nodded, found his cigarettes in his pocket, and lit up. Tendrils of fire spun hot and lacy inside his fingertips and the whiskey washed the decomposed taste from his mouth. Huddled in the coat and blanket he felt stronger. He nodded down the slope. "How is he?"

"Shock. Lost some blood, but you patched him up pretty good," said the second deputy. "That's what the Smokeys say, anyway. What happened to his face, Jerry?" he asked.

"Jesse and Becky went apeshit when Mr. Griffin told them what happened. Becky took a swipe at his face."

The second deputy spit thoughtfully. Dark brown stain on the snow. Chewing tobacco. "Maston says he saved his life. That Chris was trying to kill him, which don't exactly surprise me. I'd a never let that kid go near a gun myself."

Harry started to ask a question, but something about the way the deputies were talking warned him to shut up.

"Larry shoulda done something about that Chris . . . the shit's going to hit the fan now—"

"Sweet on Jesse and the kids," said the one named Jerry. "Be sweet on her after Maston's gone."

Bud's hasty marriage didn't appear to be engraved in stone in Maston County.

"Yeah, but will he still be sheriff after this?" said the tobacco chewer.

Jerry toed the snow with his boot, the other cop spit his tobacco. Any minute now one of them would start whittling, thought Harry. The hayseed schmooze routine didn't fit with their otherwise highly trained style. Consequences, he thought, on guard. If Jesse made good on her rape threat, how would his story look to these canny backwoods cops?

The second deputy inspected Harry's face. "You should get back to town, have a doc look at that kisser. Need a tetanus shot for sure. Lots of dirty stuff under a person's fingernails."

"It can wait," said Harry. He had given his driver's license to another cop who'd stayed back at the lodge. By now they'd made a radio call and he wondered what kind of picture the criminal justice system kept on Detroit Harry in its national computer.

The second deputy said, "I'll be getting back down there, help them bring the stretcher up."

"I'll go with you," said Harry.

"You best wait up here, sir," said the second deputy. "Anybody in this county's going to get first-class treatment, it's Maston. He had the new hospital built. You just sit tight. Sheriff'll want to talk to you." He took off down the hill.

"Am I under arrest?" Harry asked.

"No sir, you're under no legal constraints other'n we'd like you to stick around to help clear up some questions the county medical examiner might have. You weren't planning on leaving, were you?"

Harry shook his head. It was interrogation. Keep the parties involved separate for questioning. Routine. Sensible. Different though, if you were in the middle.

"And if the medical examiner has . . . questions?" asked Harry.

"Well, then the county prosecutor gets involved and there'll be an investigation. Gets to where two and two don't add up . . . well, then we're required to advise you that you might want to talk to an attorney . . ."

Harry started to ask another question. The deputy cut in polite but firm. "Just rest up, Mr. Griffin. Save it for the sheriff."

They were bringing Bud up the slope. Six cops man-hauling the gurney with a medic jogging alongside steadying an IV rig. More medics with bags and gear followed. Bud grimaced with every jerk of the stretcher and Harry pushed through to him and squeezed his arm through the blankets. "Hang in there," he said.

Bud grinned wanly and fell back exhausted and the cop-powered dogsled huffed and puffed down the trail and disappeared in the pines. A voice bellowed commands down by the swamp:

"Awright, we got the hurt guy outta here, so square away this clusterfuck, and *be careful, people*! Nobody go near that body till the medical examiner gets here. And the BCA are coming from Duluth. You know how finicky those guys are. Film it, but don't be mucking up them tracks. An' don't fuck with them rifles. Or the packs. Leave 'em lay. BCA's bringing their lab, so we gotta keep this place clean. I don't want no dumb-ass hunters walking through."

Out-of-place voice in the North Woods, with a lilt of Southern cadence.

Sheriff Emery plodded up the slope and Harry had an impression of butternut and leather and thought: he'd own a horse. The kind of man Jesse might have married before she met Bud.

No badge. No gun. His person was his authority. He moved with shambling grace; a powerful man with a deceptive softness to his loosely chiseled features; hatless, his long dark hair ruffled almost to his shoulders, softly curly, in the breeze.

Emery drew close and his watchful tobacco eyes were mournful and bloodshot and teared with the cold. He stopped a few feet away and seemed to loose his balance.

Deputy Jerry immediately went to him. Profound sympathy softened the vigorous lines of the young cop's face as he took the sheriff by the arm and steadied him. "How you doing with this, Larry?" he asked.

The sheriff took a deep, shuddering breath and released it. "I'm okay," he said but the scary way his eyes flashed told Harry to get ready to meet the most pissed-off and most dangerous man in Maston County.

Emery let Harry have another second of the glare, then he folded it back into his eyes like a jackknife blade and said, "Jerry, you go down an' help Morris with the video camera so's we got more than just treetops on that tape. And don't have him spitting tobacco juice on any evidence. Do it right. And don't piss off the God almighty State fucking Patrol."

"Morris knows what to do," said Jerry and didn't move. They had a quick conference, heads close. Emery perused Jerry's notebook, then returned to Harry. Jerry hovered a few feet away.

"I'm Larry Emery. Sheriff here." He said, icy with control.

"How is he?" Harry asked.

Emery squinted at him. "You want a lawyer? Go back into town, get a lawyer. Or talk to somebody 'bout being upset? We got this preacher works for us you can talk to now when your heart starts going pitter-pat."

"Is he all right?" Harry repeated.

"Seems to be. Looks like you've bandaged a gunshot wound before."

"Nothing went into his guts or anything?"

"Flesh wound. Through and though." Emery slowly scanned Harry's face. "He's more worried about you."

Harry nodded and winced as the ooze from the claw marks cracked in the cold.

"Girl really did a job on you," said Emery. "Need that looked at."

"Your deputy said you had some questions?"

"Bud says you saved his life. What d'you say?" Emery asked. He took a small wooden cylinder from his pocket, twisted off the top, and withdrew a toothpick that he held between his fingers and put it to his lips like a smoker. His fingers shook.

"It was real fast," said Harry.

"Um-hum," nodded Emery. He was looking down the slope. At the kid's body, hugging the bush. "So you was up here, in this dead pine," he walked the yellow tape to the platform 20 feet away. The angle of the land and the brush below just blocked the line-of-sight view from the stand to where Chris had stood. Emery's eyes took this in. "And you hear this shot—"

"Yelling. They were yelling at each other."

"What'd they say?"

"An argument. Bud called Chris an 'ungrateful little shit,' I heard that."

"Then what?"

"Two shots and Bud screamed. I jumped out of the tree and ran to the edge of the ridge where I could see. Bud was down, the kid—"

"Name was Chris," said Emery. "Christopher Warren Deucette."

"Chris was reloading, tearing at the bolt like it was jammed, then he aimed it at Bud—"

"How long you know him—Chris, I mean?"

"Met him last night. We just drove up from the Cities. Bud married his mother . . ."

"Lives with her. Keeps her." said Emery with distaste. He threw the toothpick away. "You got another cigarette?"

Harry handed him his pack. Emery tore off the filter and took a light from Harry's Zippo. He dragged for a moment and exhaled. "You talk much to Chris?"

"A little, about hunting—"

"Anything between Chris and Maston come up? Anything explain why he'd put a deer gun on Maston?"

"Right after it happened Bud said something about stolen goods. Not real clear on that part."

"You get that in your notes?" Emery queried Jerry, who nodded. Then Emery studied Harry carefully. After an interval, he went on. "An' you see Chris shoot at Bud. Was they standing close?"

Harry shook his head. "Bud was down, crawling away, bleeding. The ki . . . Chris, he was working the bolt—"

"So you didn't see him shoot?"

"Not the first two. Third one hit a tree next to Bud's head. Same time I fired."

Emery peered down the slope, at angles and distances. "So his shot went wild when he was hit? Or he missed?"

"Too close to tell." Harry remembered Bud's agonized statement—that he was trying to talk to Chris. Did he react too fast? His memory was starting to function again and it served up the image of the gray movement he'd seen in the trees right after the shooting and matched it with the image of Becky in her ski suit racing down the trail, coming off the porch at him. "Maybe I should talk to a lawyer," he said.

"I don't think we're to that yet, Mr. Griffin. Don't think this is headed that way. But that's your right. Take you back and you make your phone call. You get your legal advice, then we'll get your statement. Like the law says."

There was something heavy and remorseful in Sheriff Emery's manner when he pronounced the phrase, "the law."

Harry and Emery walked in silence back along the ridge and down to the trail with Deputy Jerry just behind them. The herd of cops and medics had made a wallow of the snow, obliterating any snowshoe tracks. As they approached the grove of pines, Harry stiffened as he watched Emery's alert tracker's eyes inspect the two sets of footprints that left the trail and went into the trees.

Harry stopped flat-footed. The tracks ended abruptly in recently feathered snow. Sprinkled pine needles and curls of rusty bark traced the path of someone who had swept the entire area with a pine-bough broom.

Harry held his breath and heard the leather creak on Jerry's gunbelt as the deputy shifted his weight. Trying to look calm, he followed Emery into the grove. All swept over. No trace of the stamped snow where he'd been with Jesse less than two hours ago.

Without comment, Emery walked a circle through the grove. Harry and Jerry followed. Harry's fingers were exploring the nubbin of thick thread on his trousers where a button was missing when he saw what Emery had paused to study. The sweep-job led to ski tracks, distinct as two rails that fanned a turn around on a slight rise at the edge of the thicker timber above the grove. The tracks did not lead off toward the snowmobile trail. Instead they cut overland through the cover of the trees parallel to the ridge. Hard going for anyone unless they had something very deliberate in mind.

Becky. Had to be. Snooping. And cleaning up after her mother? Harry was no expert on police work but he could follow fresh tracks in clean snow close to the site of a shooting and pose the obvious question. *Were there any other witnesses or an accomplice?*

Harry's face closed tight to hide a flush of shame and anger. Bud could be the one lying dead out there if . . .

And Emery, who looked like he could follow a butterfly through a tornado, just knelt over the tracks and slowly rotated his eyes with his weather-cured face showing no expression.

No one was connecting the dots strewn all around the countryside and things were getting tricky in Maston County. Harry resolved to keep his mouth shut until he got a big-city lawyer like Dorothy Houston's dad to back him up.

Emery motioned Harry and Jerry back to the trail and they continued on to the lodge without speaking.

14

Laconic after-the-fact police traffic droned on car radios. County Blazers and Highway Patrol cruisers jammed the horseshoe drive in front of the lodge. They'd taken Jesse and Becky away.

Cops. Watching him out of the corner of their eyes. A van showed up with CRIME LAB stenciled on the side. The guys in the van had the scene explained to them, then they watched Harry from the corners of their eyes as they talked to Emery. Jerry, ever-present and competent, helped load travel cases of forensic gear on a gurney rigged behind a snowmobile.

When somebody looked at him, Harry looked back with a hard glance that said, Fuck you, I didn't do anything wrong. He had a metal whir in his chest and his eyes were a camera.

Deeper down, Sheriff Emery's whiskey crept in him, silently, opening doors, and the walls of his memory started to move.

A snowbridge of the shock crumpled beneath his feet, his knees misfired and his hands went out for balance. Emery caught it from the corner of his eye.

His thoughts spiraled: Chris spun and fell. The smooth muscles at the base of Jesse's spine trembled.

He could feel the electric charge of Chris's life go from his body. Weigh the corpse. He knew it would be lighter. Put the whole fucking world on a scale. Lighter. Minus one.

The snapshots of desire and death had a specific slippery, corrosive taste. *Gotta brush my teeth. Now.*

"I want to make a phone call," he told Emery. The sheriff was talking to the state guys; he nodded and pointed to the lodge. A deputy lounged in the kitchen near the coffee pot. Harry asked to use the phone.

The deputy checked with Emery, who dismissed him with a wave of his hand and turned back to the BCA.

Two cops were going through the room where he'd slept and the contents of Harry's duffel were neatly spread out on the bed, exactly where he'd left them. He asked if he could have his shaving kit. They handed it to him. In the bathroom, he scrubbed at his teeth, swigged mouthfuls of Listerine, gargled, and swallowed some in his haste. It only managed to coat the taste. He grimaced in the mirror at the gummy stripes that were riven into his face.

The deputies came out of Chris's room and emptied the contents of a shoebox on the table in the den and began to bag and tag three hand-guns and an assortment of pills.

Looked like a snub-nosed .38, an automatic, and a bigger revolver with a long barrel. Guessing. Didn't know much about handguns. No idea what the pills where. He was a couple generations removed from street pharmacology.

"What are you doing?" Harry challenged them.

"Maston gave us permission to search the place," said one of the deputies politely.

The clock over the stove said 8:35. Over two hours since it went down. Still worrying his teeth with the toothbrush, Harry dialed Randall's number in St. Paul.

"I'm in the shit," Harry said simply when Dorothy answered. "Lemme talk to Randall."

Randall skipped the drama and went right to the relevant facts. Had they given him his rights? Had he been charged with anything? No. But he was on his way to the local cop shop with the sheriff. Harry mentioned the medical examiner, who might have questions. He finished by saying, "I need Dorothy's father."

Randall and Dorothy held a quick conference, then Dorothy came on the line.

"They're giving you what's called a 'soft Miranda.' If the local prosecutor rules justifiable homicide, you're in good shape. If they decide something kinky went down, then it could get tricky. Either way, they might give it to a grand jury. It's up to the prosecutor. What Bud says is real important."

"Bud told them I saved his life."

"They'll pull up your police files. They may want to take a closer look at you. I'll call my dad and see if he knows somebody who can talk to the local prosecutor. Is there an airstrip up there?"

"Must be. Bud flies in and out all the time." Some comfort. Dorothy's dad was a senior partner in an old St. Paul firm, also a bigshot in Democratic politics.

"We'll grab a charter and be right up. And another thing. Look out for the press," said Dorothy. "This kid you shot just tried to kill a light heavyweight prominent Minnesotan. That's a big story on a slow news day."

"Christ, I never thought of that," said Harry.

"Button up, Harry, till we get there."

"Will do," said Harry.

Randall came back on the line. "Hang tough," he said. "Don't let it fuck with your head. Help's on the way."

"Thanks," said Harry.

Emery drove. Harry sat in the passenger seat of the sheriff's Blazer with his duffel between his knees. Jerry took up his silent post in the back.

They turned onto the highway, went around a curve, and the land fell away. Superior stretched flat and endless looking like God's level beneath brooding clouds. Way too much sky for Harry to handle right now. He lowered his eyes. The town of Stanley hid below them in the trees.

He ran his toothbrush over his teeth. Emery glanced at him. Harry slipped the toothbrush into the chest pocket of his shirt.

Emery sipped from his Thermos cup and slouched behind the wheel. Sorrow stacked up ledge on ledge in the sheriff's face and his somber eyes mirrored the distant thunderheads.

They slowed down. Decaying white clapboard houses lurked in the undergrowth and straddled the road on the heights above Stanley. The old mining ghost town was just two rings of company housing surrounding the skeleton of a company store. A sturdy WPA brick schoolhouse had its windows boarded up and scrabbly jackpine grew to the second story. Harry recalled there'd been a bloody labor dispute here back in the '30s.

People still lived among the ruins in swayback houses bailed together in Jackpine Savage squalor, in yards fenced with barbed wire and landscaped with rusting cars. A solitary Holstein cow walked a muddy path along a fence line. A new snowplow idled in a cloud of exhaust in front of a large pole barn.

Emery turned off at a crossroads. Several pickups were parked in front of the general store. Hunters in orange pulled a deer carcass from one of the trucks. A single eight-point buck dangled from the birch tree. Emery stopped, got out, and inspected the deer. The hunters did not greet him. They stepped back solemnly, giving him a wide deferential berth. Emery got back in the Blazer.

Across from the store, a cinder-block building was painted bulkhead gray-green. A cold neon sign over the door announced: VFW. The marquee sign in the parking lot had remnants of a bingo announcement that had been cannibalized to spell out DEER HUNTERS WELCOME.

The hospital was right off Highway 7, set into the hillside among the houses sprinkled above Minnesota 61. The new brick- and-glass facade was gracefully landscaped with pines and junipers. In back, 55-gallon drums stuffed with hunks of drywall and electrical conduit littered the raw slope. A granite slab near the entrance bore the chiseled dedication: Stanley Maston Memorial Medical Center.

A dozen pickups were parked in front of the emergency room door. Two had stiffening deer carcasses protruding from their beds. Orange men milled around.

Emery grumbled. "Everybody's come to see the show. Shit . . ."

The snow made a loud Styrofoam squeak under Harry's boots and captions of freezing breath hung over the crowd of hunters.

A haggard-faced Jay Cox exploded from the crowd and came straight at Harry and pushed him.

"Why isn't he under arrest?" Cox growled at Emery. His eyes sparked as if powerful machines were stripping their gears in there.

"You're outta line, Jay," Emery said softly, easing between them. Then, out of nowhere, Emery had springs in his feet. Graceful as a puma he moved on Cox and acquired Cox's face in his hand, fingers spread, like he was palming a basketball. He heaved him off balance and sent him sprawling into the snow. Jerry interposed his body, watching Emery, not the furious Cox.

"Get him outta here before . . ." said Emery in a calm voice, leaving the threat hanging in the air. Some of the men surrounded Cox, took him aside to walk it off. Harry took a mental note. Sheriff Emery: question mark. Second line: doesn't like Cox.

Emery guided Harry, in front of him, through the hospital door.

"Need you to look at his face," Emery said to a nurse at the desk, walking into the emergency room.

"How are you, Larry," asked the nurse. "You need anything?"

"Where you got Jessica and Becky?" asked Emery.

"In the lobby. They're calmed down. You got any more shot-up city people out there, or is this it?" asked the nurse, turning Harry's face in her cool fingers as if she were inspecting a hat she might buy.

The interior of the ER revolved in a clean spin of antiseptic tile, bright lights, and gleaming stainless steel. Harry yielded to trembling fatigue and his knees collapsed. Emery caught him.

"Delayed shock," Emery said to the nurse.

The nurse led Harry to a chair, popped a thermometer into his mouth, told him to strip off his coat and roll up his sleeve so she could strap a blood pressure cuff on his arm. A young doctor, his green surgical suit spotted with blood, walked over, drying his hands on a towel. "Larry, I think you should sit down," he said.

Emery shook him off. "Can Maston talk?"

"The man's been shot," protested the doctor.

"Ain't shot that bad. Wait'll you see the boy."

"Two minutes," said the doctor.

"Normal," said the nurse, raising an eyebrow, taking out the thermometer and unstrapping the cuff.

They had Bud across the ER, screened off. Emery went behind the curtains. Harry walked over and heard Bud's voice, foggy with pain.

"Oh God, Larry, I'm sorry . . ."

Harry stepped in. Bud was pale and naked except for a blue hospital sheet thrown across his gut. He was hooked up to some machine by electrodes taped to his chest. The wound in his side was painted mercurochrome orange; the actual holes were a ragged black.

Bud muttered weakly, his face ash-white. "Forgot how much it hurts to get shot."

Emery escorted Harry back outside the curtain. "Just as soon you two didn't talk till we get us a preliminary report from the forensic bunch outta Duluth. He can't talk much anyway, they got him wacked out on Dilaudid."

Harry froze. Jesse Deucette, her face as bloodless as chilled ivory, had found time to braid her hair. She stood in the center of the room with the ostentatious diamond sparkling on her left hand. Their eyes played fast paddycake. If they blinked, their infidelity would crash to the floor and writhe like snakes.

Emery broke the spell. His usual watchfulness gone, he missed the eye play. He only saw Jesse. He moved surprisingly fast, silently. Her presence turned his face buttermilk smooth and soft. "Now Jessica, this ain't the time . . ."

The mask of grief on her face crumpled into tears as Emery held out his arms to her. Wracked with sobs, she shook her head, but Emery persisted patiently and she was drawn into his embrace. She shuddered against his shoulder and couldn't get words out.

"Best to cry, just . . . cry now," said Emery, stony and patient, gently patting her shoulder.

The people in the ER seemed to shrink back, like the hunters had done when Emery inspected the deer at the general store. Harry followed Emery's eyes, which looked past Jesse.

Becky stood poised uncertainly on the balls of her feet in the corridor. Emery raised one hand toward her. The girl's face spooked and she broke into a run, past the tableau of people who were watching Jesse cry in Emery's arms. No one moved to stop her.

Harry watched her dart out the door. A green Jeep Wrangler shivered on its suspension with a keyed-up nervous clutch in a cloud of exhaust just outside the plate-glass entrance. The driver threw the door open for her. Harry caught a glimpse of the driver's tow-headed hair and the gray flash of Becky's wind suit and the Jeep fishtailed away.

Jesse had stopped crying. Sniffling, she scrubbed her palm down her cheek to wipe away the tears and said, "I have to see Bud."

"They got him doped up," said Emery.

"You'd better wait a little," said the doctor gently. "We're monitoring for shock. Then you can talk."

Jesse looked at the floor in front of Harry. Her eyes came up slowly. The despair in her face was drained of tears and had become precise, faceted fire and ice, a larger version of the rock on her finger.

Emery floated warily on the toes of his boots between them.

"Why isn't he under arrest?" she said and Harry's heart stopped.

"Don't tell me how to do my job, Jessica," Emery said patiently. "Not sure what we got here. Fact is, Griffin'd be within his rights to file an assault complaint on Becky. That's some permanent damage on his face."

Harry's fingers crept gingerly up to his face and felt a dangling flap of his cheek. Emery nodded to a nurse who took Jesse by the arm and walked her away.

Another nurse led Harry back to his chair. Emery followed. His shadow, Jerry, was just a step behind. "Take down your trousers," ordered the nurse, squinting along a hypodermic.

"Tetanus," said Emery. The nurse stuck Harry in the rump and then sat him down next to a table. Small curved needles lay on a towel. A stainless steel tray smelled of alcohol.

The young doctor returned and adjusted a light on Harry's face. He dabbed with alcohol-soaked gauze. Harry trembled. The doc was moving pieces of his face. He yanked off a flap of skin.

"Two of these need stitches," said the doctor. "Are you allergic to novocaine?"

"I don't want novocaine in my face." Harry wanted to stay alert.

"You sure?"

"Sew," said Harry. He stared at Emery as the doctor sewed. Emery's eyes didn't waver, but a commotion at the door allowed them to break eye contact.

A tall, red-faced, beefy man wearing hunting boots and a blaze-orange parka stomped into the ER. In contrast to his ruddy complexion, his hair, eyebrows, and mustache were fleecy platinum. He swiveled pale falcon eyes.

"Larry? Jesus Christ, I just heard," he yelled. Six other men followed in his wake. All but one was dressed for hunting in blaze orange and had the same hawkish features and white-blond hair. Emery ambled over to them.

The doctor grimaced as he forced the needle through Harry's cheek. Surprisingly tough stuff, skin. Harry used the pain to sharpen his attention.

The big guy put his hands on Emery's shoulders. For a moment Harry thought he might embrace Emery. But he shook him, getting his full attention. They talked, their heads close, then the big guy turned and pummeled the tile wall with his fist. "You don't fucking get it, do you?" he yelled at Emery. Emery put his hands on his hips, stared at his boots. Emery talked. Harry couldn't make out the words.

The big guy blew up again. "I told you to do something back then, goddammit! God, we could get sued for negligence." Then the big guy stepped back, warned by Emery's eyes. "I'm sorry but goddammit . . ."

They went back to talking low. They all turned and looked at Harry. The nonhunter walked over. His scrubbed face was fringed with a closely barbered mustache and his dry blue eyes were set in contemplative wrinkles behind horn-rim glasses. His sandy hair was styled past his ears and was shot with gray.

"How you doing, son?" he asked.

"I'm not your son. I'm probably older than you."

"You need anything?"

"You got a cigarette?"

"You can't smoke in here," said the doctor, yanking the knot on the last stitch a little harder than was necessary. Then he dropped the needle in a pan of antiseptic and walked away. The tense discussion Emery was having with the hunting party was making the ER jumpy. The new guy sat down in the doctor's place. He held out his hand. "Don Karson. Local minister. Lutheran. You Catholic? We have a priest in town."

"Is he out hunting, too?" asked Harry, sizing Karson up. A soft Christ. Not a carpenter.

"You know, I think he is," said Karson.

Harry's palm was smeared with dried blood. Karson wiped his hand on his pants.

Jesse reappeared and joined in Emery's conversation with the big guy. Harry breathed through his nose, deep diaphragmatic breathing to slow his racing heartbeat.

The men formed a respectful circle around her. Then she walked toward Bud's curtained bed. Emery moved to stop her. The big guy physically yanked Emery back.

Now it was Emery's turn to get mad. "Am I running a criminal investigation or what!"

"You ain't running shit. We better start thinking about damage control," said the big guy. Harry noticed that everyone in hearing distance of this shouting—the nurses, the doctor—ducked their heads down into their shoulders.

"Who's the big one?" Harry asked the minister.

"Mike Hakala, county prosecutor."

"And the others?"

"The county board," Karson said. "Terry Hakala, owns the lumber yard. Used to be mayor till we cut the position. And there's Greg Hakala, the banker, and the little one is Morris Hakala, he used to run public works, now he operates the garbage business. Couple of cousins. They used to manage the paper mill cooperative. When it went under, they scrambled onto the only thing left afloat, the local government."

Harry appraised the Hakalas, who tended toward piratical mustaches and longish hair. All they needed was horned helmets to be a gathering of Minnesota Vikings logos.

Jesse's voice rose in argument behind the curtain. Harry was up. Everybody raced to Bud's bed. Jesse was crying again and pointed her finger at Bud whose dilated eyes yawned in alarm. Physically, he cringed from her.

"I told you to listen to Mike, goddamn you. This wouldn't have happened if you had the guts to stand up to Larry. But you had to try to be one of the boys! . . ." She saw Harry and drew herself up. "Instead you had to bring *him* . . ."

Harry braced himself for her accusations.

She yanked the ring from her finger and threw it at Harry. The diamond bounced off his chest and rolled under the bed. Then she slapped Harry in the face. Right in the stitches. He didn't even feel it. He was completely absorbed in the deft intelligence working behind the grief in her eyes.

Emery grabbed her. Bud tried to sit up and tipped over the IV stand. It clattered on the tile, a sound as stark and hollow as Jesse's voice. "How much is Chris's life worth, Bud? That's how much your fucking divorce is going to cost!"

Movement suspended. Everyone pretended to be invisible and Harry and Jesse stared at each other across a roomful of statues. A nurse swooped down and pulled the curtains tight around the bed.

"He killed my son. Isn't anybody going to do anything?" Jesse sobbed. Numb stares. Karson moved to intercede. Emery seized the smaller man by the arm and pushed him away. "You stay away from her," he hissed. No one looked at Harry except Karson and Harry sensed that the minister was another outsider here.

Jesse the magician, who was going to turn her son's corpse into gold, bowed her head and walked from the silent room. When she was gone, Harry asked an orderly where the bathroom was.

On unsteady feet he walked to the bathroom that was at the opposite end of the hall from where Emery and Hakala were trying to calm Jesse. He washed the blood off his hands, stared into the mirror over the sink, and tried to get used to the four claw marks that crossed his face.

The blood was persistent, etched into the creases of his hands. He wanted to feel sorrow, but all that came was a flush of the triumphant adrenal fury he had felt on the ridge.

The rust-tinged water swirled down the drain and took with it the last ten years of his life. He'd paid all his bills on time and drove the speed limit and went soberly to the nice little office everyday where the people said "excuse me" instead of "outta the way, motherfucker" and he was a kind of artist like his mother had wanted and he went to groups to learn how to control his anger because it was the anger that had always got him in trouble. And the anger was worst when somebody tried to use him. And damn if Jesse hadn't used him in the baddest way because he was willing to break all the rules for her.

Harry stared at the bloody drain and finally the revulsion came. A sixteen-year-old kid lay dead by his hand and not twenty minutes before he'd pulled the trigger he'd been knocking around right next to the womb that bore him. And the locals were playing blindman's buff.

The vertigo and nausea wobbled up his throat and he barely made it to a stall to vomit. That's how Jerry found him, hugging the toilet bowl, coming down from the dry heaves, still gagging, with hot salty tears streaking his torn cheeks.

15

Maston County was governed from a one-story building of yellow masonry with a flat asphalt roof and opaque glass brick plugs for windows. The structure took up one of the four city blocks that was downtown Stanley. The county occupied the half of the building that faced the waterfront. The other half was the municipal liquor store.

Emery went into the building. Jerry waited as Harry took a look around. Older people mainly, carefully walking through heaps of snow the plows had thrown up on the sidewalks. Several groups of orange-clad hunters hurried by. He did not see a single mother with a child.

A seagull stood sentinel on a lamppost overlooking a breakwater made of granite boulders. At the south end of town, the silent smokestacks of the paper mill were stapled against the sky, as incongruous among the granite, waves, and pine as a cement space platform that had toppled out of orbit. The gull cried. The gray, unhurried white-capped rollers of Superior sloshed ice cubes against the boulders. It could have been a dying town on the coast of Maine.

Across the street from the county offices, dusty windows in four brick storefronts caught the morning light. Military recruiters had set up in one of them. The Minnesota Department of Human Services had a sign in another. The third had been the *County Gazette* and was now a food shelf. The faded sign on the fourth advertised the Maston County Economic Development Coop and was empty.

The next block was doing a little better. It had the bank, the hardware store, the drugstore, a diner, and some antique stores. Newer stuff, a tourist restaurant, the IGA grocery, a motel, and the Holiday station were up on the main highway.

Jerry nodded across the street. "Military's the only ones doing any hiring these days." His pale blue eyes traveled up the mass of Nanabozho Ridge. "Wolves are coming back though."

Three Indian winos hobbled around the corner from the liquor store and engaged Harry with bleary curiosity. Must be the big event in town. Watching the cops take a man with a busted-up face and blood on his clothes from a police car to the station.

Jerry ushered him through a door with peeling stenciled letters: COUNTY SHERIFF. They crossed a lobby with a radio dispatch desk and went down a dim corridor of buckled green linoleum and walls of cheap imitation paneling. Mike Hakala popped out of an office and motioned them down the hall.

They took Harry into the lunchroom and sat on folding metal chairs at a Formica cafeteria table. There were crumbs on the table and a half-eaten ham sandwich curled on a crumpled paper bag next to a pint of milk and the last house fly in Minnesota buzzed in a drunken circle above their heads.

Harry declined to make a statement until his lawyer called. Hakala temporized, told him that no criminal charges would be filed. That it looked like self-defense under very tragic circumstances. A domestic, he called it. There might be a grand jury to review the incident and Harry could be called to testify.

Hakala asked him if he was considering charging Becky for clawing his face. Harry shook his head. He cruised right through. No hint that Jesse had said anything to complicate his story.

Hakala told him to sit out by the desk and wait for his call.

Harry waited on a cheap couch and stared at the frayed copy of *Guns & Ammo* that lay on the chipped plastic coffee table. A deputy brought him a cup of coffee as a succession of serious-looking people trooped in, tracking snow. He assumed they were the forensic techies from the crime lab. They conferred with Hakala and Emery in an office behind a glass partition that faced the radio dispatch desk.

Harry kept feeling his pockets. He must have lost his cigarettes at the hospital, probably in the bathroom. He looked up. The minister, Karson, stood in the doorway, watching him pat his pockets. Karson tossed him a pack of cigarettes.

"I just talked to Bud and decided I should look in on you," said Karson.

"They let you talk to him?"

"What I do," said Karson, sitting down on the couch. "I marry them and bury them. The rest of the time I talk to them. Mostly I listen."

"You marry Bud and Jesse?"

Karson sighed. "No. The Honorable Judge Toyvo Hakala did that in his offices three weeks ago."

"You going to bury Chris Deucette?"

"Yes, I suspect I will do that."

Jerry walked past them and nodded to Karson with a civil smile. His body language was dismissive: *Tits on a boar*. Karson nodded back with the superior, inhibited air of a vegetarian at a buffalo roast.

Harry and Karson smoked together for a few awkward minutes. Then Harry motioned toward the office where Emery and Hakala were hunched over a desk. "What do you think *they're* talking about?"

"Politics."

"Why politics?"

"It's called cover your ass and protect your political supply lines," said Karson.

"Explain," said Harry.

Karson cleared his throat. "Well, Bud Maston was going to be the golden goose for this town and now he's up the hill with a gunshot wound. Maston bankrolled Larry Emery's run for office. That makes Larry Maston's man on the Hakala pirate ship. It would behoove Larry to look after Maston's general well-being to ensure his own."

The fine web of wrinkles tightened around Karson's blue eyes. "Except Larry has been falling down on the job. Last month, Chris Deucette, whose body is now in a little room in the hospital being dissected like a laboratory frog, walked into high school, late for class, and outrageously stoned. When his homeroom teacher took him aside, Chris pulled out a very large handgun and threatened the teacher's life."

Harry sat up and narrowed his eyes. "Where'd he get the gun?"

"Broke into Emery's house, where he used to live, and stole it."

Karson puffed on his cigarette and continued. "Well, everybody got called in, me included. We've never had a gun incident in our school. Mike hit the roof. He wanted Chris to do some kind of time for it. At least a stint in a drug-dependency program, with family counseling tacked on. Larry got Bud to convince Mike to let Chris off, put him in their joint parental custody. So now Mike's nervous that that decision might come back on him."

Karson flicked the ash from his cigarette. His voice flicked too. "Larry Emery is a very advanced thinker. A troubled kid pulls a gun, so you take him out and teach him how to shoot a bigger, more powerful gun so he can go slaughter deer . . ." Karson shrugged his shoulders. "Maybe that spirit won the West, but it sure fucked up in this case."

"You and Sheriff Emery aren't real close, huh?"

"He hates my guts."

"Guy looks pretty spaced out for a lawman from what I've seen today."

Karson chuckled ironically and his forehead furrowed with wrinkles. "Now we come to the interesting part that everyone, including Bud, seems to have neglected to tell you in all the confusion."

"What?"

Karson's lips jerked in a faint smile. "You killed Larry Emery's bastard this morning. That's why Hakala has him on such a tight leash."

The walls of the police station started marching in and Harry felt a suffocation and a fear that didn't pass with a few rapid breaths.

"Yes indeed," said Karson, in a tone that conveyed sympathy with Harry's goose bumps. "I have a feeling that if you didn't work for a newspaper in the big city and weren't Bud's pal, Emery might have you down in the basement right now. He's an expert with resisting arrest."

"I'm not under arrest," Harry said quickly.

Karson put his hand on Harry's shoulder. "That's true and you won't be." Karson lowered his voice. "Nobody wants to dig into this. Look, Chris Deucette was a member of my congregation. All the danger signs were there. I tried, with both him *and* his mother, but Emery blocked me."

Harry stared at the hand on his shoulder. Karson withdrew it and puffed on his cigarette. "They're not charging you. Legally you didn't do anything wrong . . . unless you want to talk about breaking the Tenth Commandment . . . and, from what Bud told me, it isn't the first time you did that."

The Tenth Commandment was about not coveting your neighbor's wife. Harry assumed he was talking about number six. Thou shalt not kill. Karson had his commandments mixed up. Or did he?

"Subtle guy like you wouldn't be a local, would he?" asked Harry.

"Nope," said Karson.

A third man joined Hakala and Emery behind the glass. Chubby fellow who rocked from foot to foot.

"Tony Camp. Our medical examiner. He's the town undertaker, not a licensed pathologist," said Karson as he stood up and ground out his smoke in the ashtray. He shook Harry's hand. Then he produced a card. Reverend Donald Karson with a K. Trinity Lutheran Church. Phone numbers. "If I get down to St. Paul maybe we could talk again." His voice became a little too casual. "I assume you know some good reporters."

"Karson. You here on your own?"

"Not exactly. The county retains me to counsel people in crisis."

"Who do *you* talk to?" asked Harry.

"Well, people who—"

"No, I mean when you're in crisis," said Harry.

Karson looked Harry directly in the eye. "You maybe . . ."

Hakala waited in the hall and watched Karson leave. Then he gave Harry a firm, concerned public-servant smile. "Don get you all straightened out?" he asked.

"Seems like a good enough guy," said Harry, putting on his own broad phony smile, a mask that he had learned from the Vietnamese. The more nervous they got the bigger the grin.

"For a bleeding heart treehugger . . ." Hakala plopped down on the couch and put his beefy arm around Harry's shoulders. He came on solid, part corner grocer, part big-league linebacker. His pale eyes managed to be deep, shrewd, and warm at the same time. "Let me tell you what's happening. First of all, Bud's fine, they'll keep him for a couple of days to make sure there isn't an infection. But he's going to be all right."

The deputy behind the desk yelled, "Mike," and held up a phone. Hakala excused himself. He spoke for a minute and then called Harry over. "Your lawyer," said Hakala.

Harry picked up the phone. "Harry," said a calm voice. "Gene Houston."

"Hello, Mr. Houston."

"Sounds like you've had a hell of a morning, son. But Hakala says that your version of things matches the facts so you can calm down. I made a call to make sure this doesn't pick up the wrong spin."

"Anybody I know?"

The calm voice shrugged. "Bill Tully, he talked to someone up the street and they had a prayer meeting with Hakala."

Harry took a deep breath and let it out. Tully was the chairman of the Democratic Central Committee.

Gene Houston went on in his calm voice. "You're not under arrest and you're not going to be charged. Hakala does have one question: they found a cleaning rod threaded together out where it happened. If there's a plausible explanation, tell Hakala. If there's some reason you don't want to discuss it, well, I'm prepared to hop a plane and fly up there."

"He's, like, standing right here," said Harry.

"Your call, Harry," said the attorney. "Hakala's the DFL county chair. He's not gaming you."

"Okay . . ." said Harry. "It was a reflex, I guess. Bud was freaked out. He didn't want to be left alone. I wanted to give him something to hang on to till I got back with help. I didn't know what else to do. His rifle was plugged with snow. So I cleared it, rammed it out real quick, and reloaded it."

"Uh-huh," said the attorney. "Let me talk to Hakala." Harry handed over the phone.

Hakala spoke to Houston and nodded his head. "Yup. That's pretty much what Bud said. BCA'll run paraffin tests on Bud's rifle but the chamber's finger-clean. Looks like it hadn't been fired. Sure, Gene, no, I don't foresee anything other than him having to take some time off work if there's a grand jury. Yeah. Justifiable. All the conditions are there."

Hakala handed the phone back to Harry.

"Go ahead and give them your statement," said Houston. "But if anything comes up that makes you uncomfortable, stop the interview and call me immediately. Dorothy and Tim are flying up to bring you home. So sit tight." He gave Harry a phone number. Harry used a pen from the desk to jot it down on a piece of blotter paper.

"Thank you, Mr. Houston," said Harry.

"On the contrary, Harry. *I* thank *you*, for Dorothy."

Harry smiled and hung up. Hakala blew on his fingers and shook them. "Gene Houston. That's some heavy legal artillery."

They went back to the lunch room. Jerry ran the tape recorder.

Emery sat with his large arms folded, chewing a toothpick. His eyes were very quiet and still and meeting them, Harry experienced a pang from childhood. Fear of the dark.

Harry gave a succinct statement about the morning's events. He did not seek out Emery's eyes, but he didn't avoid them either.

Hakala asked the questions. Did Chris exhibit any odd behavior prior to the shooting? Specifically, did the boy look like he was using drugs?

Harry mentioned Bud's notion that Harry might talk to Chris about drug use. And, yes, Chris looked tense the night before. But it was hard to tell with hindsight fractured by the shooting, meeting new people, driving up through the storm. Harry let them guide the questions. Jesse's name did not come up. And no one mentioned his police record in Detroit. Harry had been grilled by law enforcement types before. This was a walk in the sun and it was the first time he'd been in a roomful of cops with the powerful intuition that everybody present, not just him, had something to hide.

At the conclusion of the statement, Jerry, who now clearly had the role of watching Emery, shepherded his charge from the room. Harry stood alone in the hall with Hakala.

"That's it for now, Harry. You're free to go. The coroner and I agree. Open-and-shut justifiable homicide," said Hakala with an appropriate touch of officious remorse in his voice.

"So I just walk?" asked Harry, pushing it a little.

"You're a pretty stable citizen. Sound work record. Good people vouching for you—Ah, look. Some reporters from Duluth TV showed up. We could go to my office. Maybe they'll go away."

Harry smiled. He was still scared being in the same building with Emery, but he was curious now about the links between Jesse and Emery and their crazy kid.

"Actually, there's a favor I'd like to ask . . . privately," Hakala said blandly.

"Sure," said Harry. Hakala led him in back of the sheriff's office and down another corridor.

"You know Houston's son-in-law, Tim Randall, the writer?" kibbutzed Hakala.

"We go back a ways," said Harry.

"Always meant to read his Pulitzer book." Hakala nodded and

stopped in front of a doorway with his name and title on a thin plastic strip. "He knew Kennedy, didn't he?"

"He met Kennedy. He knew Matt Ridgway."

"Who?" Hakala smiled politely.

"Forget it."

Harry entered a corner office. Meager light filtered through glass brick. Hakala turned on the overhead lights. A new computer looked out of place among the antique furnishings. The desk was an enormous oak table. Everything was big, including the twelve-point buck mounted over the desk.

Harry inspected a broad, framed photo on the wall, set between Hakala's academic degrees and a picture of the governor. Another antique. John L. Lewis, the bushy-browed president of the United Mine Workers, addressing a Depression-era crowd at the dedication of the monument to the Stanley Massacre.

Hakala sat in the swivel oak chair behind the desk and motioned Harry to take a seat. Then the beefy prosecutor turned and took a glass pot from the Mr. Coffee machine behind his desk. He poured two cups and placed one on front of Harry. "How's the face?" he asked.

Harry smiled gamely and sipped his coffee. "Tell me, do you usually let someone involved in a shooting go so quick?"

Hakala assumed a dignified posture behind his enormous desk and gave Harry the official word. "Specific conditions must occur to excuse or justify the use of deadly force, Harry. The killing must have been done in the belief that it was necessary to avert death or grievous bodily harm. In this case, your judgment that Bud was exposed to grave peril has to be reasonable under the circumstances. And your decision to kill must have been such as a reasonable man would have made in light of the danger apprehended. This incident matches the statute almost verbatim. A second-year law student would make me look like a fool if I were to charge you. Especially with Bud as a witness . . . and Chris's history."

Harry tried to see the morning in terms of a cut-and-dried legal diagram. His left hand moved to his right bicep and massaged the tender spot where the rifle had kicked into the muscle.

Hakala steepled his thick fingers. "Bud tells me you're his best friend. And you're a reformed alcoholic. He discussed Chris Deucette's drug use with you. What about his own drinking?"

"We're just talking? Right? Nobody has given me my rights."

"Relax. Look, I'll give it to you straight. Bud's in a sticky situation. When Don Karson refused to marry Bud and Jesse Deucette, I took Bud aside and told him not to do it. Hell, I tried to talk him out of shacking up with her in the first place." Hakala sighed. "Trying to talk to the drunken millionaire who owns the county is like trying to talk to a gorilla. He does what he wants."

"His drinking was that obvious?" Harry asked.

"Started to stink in the summer when he put on all that weight. People would coffee up in the bait shops and talk of little else between welfare checks." Hakala shook his head. "We knew Jesse would blow up in his face. But not . . . this way."

Harry kept his voice cautious. Let him do the leading. Don't offer anything. "I took one look at him and decided he belonged in a treatment center."

Hakala came forward in his chair. He rubbed his thick palms together and lowered his voice. "I'd go discuss it with him. In fact, let me lend you a little leverage." Hakala leaned back, resteepled his fingers. "Let's say I've received a little incentive to work this out."

"Yeah?" said Harry.

Hakala rotated the swivel chair to the wall and studied the autographed portrait of the governor—a fellow Iron Ranger. Then he swung back to face Harry. "If Bud agrees to go inpatient and complete a treatment program, I'd be less inclined to a grand jury. I mean, if the guy sobered up . . ." Hakala's smile was an effortless blend of concern and self-interest. "And put all this behind him in the right way—you know, humble, wiser for the pain—he could get that House seat. Maybe even make a Minnesota senator someday."

Harry smiled. "As long as he observes a decent interval. And remembers who his friends are, huh, Hakala?" He stretched in the chair and connected the dots. Gene Houston to Bill Tully to someone in the governor's office who made the call to Hakala. Bud and his prodigal millions were being brought back into the fold.

Harry had committed adultery, justifiable homicide, and now he was brokering a political deal. All before lunch. It was tranquil in the office. Sitting in the eye of Hurricane Jesse.

Hakala held up his finger. "If he *won't* take a quiet vacation in a place like Hazelden, remind him that this wasn't the first time Chris was mixed up in stolen guns and drugs. And the other time I erred on the side of leniency because Bud wanted to try straightening out the kid. That comes out, the press could blow this way up, start digging around. It could get messy for all of *us*." Hakala stressed the "us," inclined his head back, and looked at Harry down his nose. "Oh yeah, we looked you up in the computer. You, ah, did a little time."

"County jail stuff, nothing serious, years ago," Harry minimized.

"Couple of pretty serious assault charges . . ."

Harry casually opened his palm, a gesture of affirming the obvious. "Just as soon let all that lay."

"Fine." Hakala smiled. "Then I see no reason to exacerbate the tragedy of an open-and-shut case by putting everyone through a grand jury." His big hand waffled deftly. "You get Bud to agree and I'll handle the vulture control with the media. Bud can take the cure and get on with his life."

"So you think you have a motive?"

Hakala smiled briskly. "Do we understand each other, Harry?"

"Perfectly."

"Off the record?"

"Sure."

Hakala rocked back in his chair. "We have Bud's sworn statement. Chris said he'd never let Bud turn him in and then he shot him. Bud's damn lucky to be alive. He's got a serious powder burn on his temple where Chris missed him point-blank the first time. And we have evidence. A small drugstore and an armory turned up in Chris's room. The guns match the serial numbers of three handguns heisted from the Ace Hardware three weeks ago."

Hakala shrugged. "Bud told me how he found that stuff and threatened to turn Chris in for violating the agreement we worked out the last time Chris got busted. But he was willing to give it one more try, bring you up here and do some kind of intervention. In his condition, he underestimated the kid's capacity for violence with predictable results. This is what happens when civilians try to do the work the system is set up for."

"Uh-huh," said Harry, unable to hide the skeptical edge in his voice.

"Well," Hakala knit his brows conscientiously, "we can't read minds. But it looks to me like Chris figured that hunting season's a good time to kill somebody . . . Kinda like a war. Lots of men with lots of guns. Accidents happen."

Damn straight, Harry thought. Jesse, the instant bride and instant widow, might have been in line to inherit the farm; especially with a blind sheriff on the case.

Hakala sighed and ran his fingers through his fine hair. "Well, we'll know some more pretty soon. BCA has a gizmo that does blood analysis. We'll see if Chris was jacked up on something—"

"Another crazy kid hopped up on drugs, huh?" asked Harry. "Probably not a good idea to take a kid like that deer hunting?"

"Up here, everybody goes hunting. Hard to sort out the crazy from the sane once they're all dressed up in orange. Last season we had an engineer from 3M shoot three cows. Hell. We practically close the high school. Now that the mill's shut down we got forty percent unemployed. These people live on venison most of the year."

Harry stood up. "I've got the picture. Now I'd like to go talk to Bud."

"Good. I'll have Jerry run you up. Take you out through the garage. Avoid the vampires with the TV cameras out there."

16

Bud wasn't fine.

The IV was back in his arm and his green hospital smock was pulled to the side. A glass tube stuck from his wound to drain bullion gruel into a kidney-shaped pan and his stitched lower lip looked like a gob of purple sausage with flies on it.

But Harry wasn't real long on sympathy at the moment. "You sorry drunk bastard," he swore softly. "I had to hear from Karson who I just shot. The fucking sheriff's kid."

"Illegitimate," Bud mumbled. "Jesse wouldn't marry him."

"I should have known better to come up here with you when you were drinking. Randall tried to tell me." Harry swung his head from side to side. Then he saw the stupid grin on Bud's face. "What's so damn funny."

Bud ducked his head into his shoulders and said in a tiny apologetic voice, "It's the Dilaudid. I'm stoned."

"Great. Okay, look. They're not charging me. I talked to Hakala."

Bud nodded with dreamy eyes. "I really messed up . . . So much for playing Dad. Being married. It all came apart."

Harry leaned down and whispered in Bud's ear. "Not quite. The fix is in. Hakala's been on the horn to Bill Tully down south and now he's playing God. Here's the deal. You agree to go to treatment. No grand jury poking around in your life. That giant sucking sound you hear? That's everybody lining up to drain you dry. You owe Hakala and Tully for the rest of your life."

For the first time Bud noticed Harry's face. His hand drifted up, nearly touched. "Christ, what happened?"

"Becky clawed me up when I told them."

"You'll be scarred," said Bud. "Christ, I'm sorry I got you mixed up in this. I thought . . ." Bud's voice cracked and his eyes brimmed with tears.

Harry pursed his lips and looked away. That's right, go on. Lose it on me.

Bud sobbed and an enormous tear rolled down his cheek and trickled along the stitches on his lip. "I thought bringing you along would be good for everybody. You too. You know, if it worked out next year we could have done it again, the four of us . . ."

"Four of us?"

"You know, your boy back in Michigan—"

"Jesus, Bud. Get a fucking grip!"

Ashamed of his tears, Bud hid his face in his hands for a moment. The shudder passed. He dropped his hands and controlled his voice. "We'll get through. I owe you big time. I'll take care of you."

"Take care of yourself," Harry said sharply. "Did you hear anything I said?"

"Don't yell at me. You always yell at me."

He was ducking down that open elevator shaft, into the thing Harry didn't understand. In a softer voice, Harry said, "Take Hakala's offer. Dry out. Get divorced. Lay low in the weeds for a while. Start over."

Bud avoided Harry's hard gaze.

Harry tapped him on the shoulder. "This morning your new bride was one bullet away from probate court."

Bud's peeked out nervously from a window in his fluffy Dilaudid cloud. "The thought crossed my mind."

"Hakala seems to have overlooked that angle—"

"No love lost between me and the Hakalas. Family thing goes way back—"

"Get her out of your place. Get a lawyer . . ."

Bud pointed at the diamond ring that lay burning a hole in the bedside table. "She threw it away."

Harry wanted to grab him and shake him till his teeth rattled. "Goddammit! We're going to put you on a plane. Fly you down to Ramsey in St. Paul. Get you in a decent hospital, out of this fucking county."

"Okay. I can see that. When you get back, call Linda Margoles. She'll know what to do." He smiled again and sailed away.

"Jesus, Bud. There's a million lawyers out there—"

"Call her—"

"Bullshit. You call her." Harry picked up the phone on the bedside table and handed it to Bud. Bud shook his head and looked away. Harry placed the phone back on the cradle.

Bud said, "It really happened, didn't it?"

"Yeah, it really did."

Bud squeezed Harry's hand and his eyes widened into blue saucers. "Harry, don't let this morning mess with your head. Maybe you should just accept it, don't dwell on it, huh?"

"Right. The Serenity Prayer. Accept the things we cannot change. Gotcha, except you gotta revise the rules a little when somebody brings live ammo to the therapy group," said Harry.

Bud dropped his bearded chin to his chest and stared straight ahead. Harry said, "Randall and Dorothy are flying up. I'm going back with them."

Bud nodded, raised a hand, and let it drop. "Talk to Hakala for me. Tell him it's fine what he said. And thank him." He tried to smile but all that came was a loose, watery stare.

"Hey, Bud, who drives a green Jeep Wrangler in town?"

"Huh?"

"Green Jeep Wrangler."

"Ah, Mitch. Mike Hakala's boy. He goes out with Becky." The words came out softly. So many blown bubbles. Then: "Harry, you think there's a Hell?"

"You're stoned, man. Just crash and we'll get you out of here." Harry squeezed Bud's arm.

He stepped through the curtains into the antiseptic tile emergency room but the chill on his heart told him he was standing in the shadow of sudden violent death. Maybe not Hell, Bud . . . but something. Love and hate were strong enough to leap across the grave. They canceled each other out. The last one standing walked your soul into the darkness.

17

Jerry, apparently under orders not to discuss anything with Harry, didn't say a word round-trip. Turning onto the waterfront, they saw the mobile TV van double-parked in front of the county offices. And two print photographers with Nikons around their necks hunched at the door. They talked to an auburn-haired woman in a belted trench coat who had good legs and one of those quick faces.

Seeing her, Jerry broke his silence and whistled. "Sherry Rawlins from Duluth. Duck your head."

Harry stayed low until they were in the garage and the door closed behind them. The decibel level in the sheriff's office had picked up. The TV crew was clawing for information in the lobby. Phones rang. Harried deputies scurried from room to room.

Emery slouched against a pop machine in a pool of melted snow from his hunting boots and watched Harry and Hakala approach from different directions. Hakala, with shaving lather dotting his left ear, wore polished wingtips, a T-shirt, and his suit trousers trailed suspenders. He nodded at the men's room.

Emery spit his frayed toothpick on the floor and walked away.

In the john, Harry stood over the sink and methodically cleaned the residue of crusted blood from between his knuckles and from under his fingernails. As he dried his hands, Hakala stooped to check that no one was in the toilet stalls.

"Get an air ambulance to fly him down to Ramsey in St. Paul," said Harry.

"Right away," said Hakala.

"He said to thank you."

Hakala cleared his throat. "I'm preparing an appropriate statement to read to the press."

Randall and Dorothy marched into Hakala's office as primed and cocked as a matched set of dueling pistols.

Dorothy hugged Harry quickly and then appraised his face with her long, cool fingers. "You talk to my dad?" she asked. Harry nodded.

"There's a TV crew from Duluth camped in the lobby," said Randall. He reached over, pried the toothbrush from Harry's fingers, and put it out of sight.

"It's on the wire," said Dorothy. "I heard a report before we took off."

"Where's your stuff?" Randall asked. Harry kicked his duffel bag.

A cloud of Old Spice preceded Hakala in a suit coat and tie, hair slicked back. Harry introduced them. Hakala stooped over in manly genuflection and reconstructed his conversation with Dorothy's father. Harry stood back while they shot the legal breeze. Emery filled the doorway.

The sheriff's face was puffy and loose, his caged eyes mainly inspected the floor, and his breath was a potpourri of mints and alcohol.

Harry drilled Emery with a cold look. "He get off all right? No accidents?"

"He's en route to St. Paul Ramsey," said Emery tightly.

"Will you be taking this to a grand jury?" Dorothy asked.

Emery drew himself up, about to say something.

"Don't think so," said Hakala, warning Emery with a quick glance.

"So that's it," said Randall briskly.

Harry turned to Emery. "Consider Bud and Jesse separated. Get her and her kid out of that lodge."

Emery lowered his eyes, his face reddened, and the veins of his neck bulged. "If that's what Mr. Maston wants."

"It's what he wants," said Harry.

Dorothy, a former member of the working press, planned their exit. "Is there a side door?"

Hakala walked them past the garage to a service door. Dorothy checked out the approach and strode off. A few minutes later a Jeep Wrangler wheeled up to the door. Dorothy sat in the passenger seat.

"Who's the driver?" Harry asked Randall as they went out.

"Hakala's son. Met us at the landing strip. He's being very helpful," said Randall.

"You're outta here, Griffin. Sorry about all . . . this," said Hakala. He extended his hand. "You've been real cooperative."

Harry took the hearty handshake, expecting Hakala's hand to be oily. It was hard and dry. Hakala stepped back and Emery did one of his puma-footed moves and was right in Harry's face.

"We'll meet again, motherfucker," said Emery.

Harry met the fierce, suffering eyes without flinching, but he had to pucker up to keep his spine from turning to ice and dropping through his sphincter.

Jerry was there, summoned by the threat in Emery's voice. Randall was right behind him. Jerry walked Emery back into the building.

"What's that about?" asked Randall. Harry shook his head. "Time to go," said Randall as he opened the door of the Wrangler. Thirty yards away, a TV crew rounded the corner.

Harry caught a flash of trim calves above slipper snow boots as the chesty lady in the trench coat stepped from behind the service door.

"Sherry Rawlins, Duluth paper," she said quickly. "How many shots? How many times was the kid hit?"

Randall elbowed the reporter aside and pushed Harry into the backseat.

Hakala's kid was Iron Range gut-tough in his varsity hockey jacket and scarred platinum eyebrows. He drove tight-lipped, never taking his steely eyes from his route, which avoided the front of the police station. No one spoke. Five minutes later they drove out onto a recently ploughed tarmac where a Cessna was warmed up and ready to go.

As Harry was getting out, he put his hand on the driver's shoulder. "Hey, where's Becky . . ." he started to say. Mitch Hakala shook off the hand, averted his face, and stared into the ramparts of snow that lined the runway. Randall tugged Harry from the car.

The plane taxied into the wind, took off, and gained altitude and the dollhouses of Stanley, Minnesota, and the secrets they held, pinwheeled away and Harry looked down on a rash of blaze-orange measles sprinkled through the blank tundra.

"Wow," said Dorothy. "What the hell did Bud get himself into?"

"It's seriously weird up there," said Harry, shaking his head. "His wife could bump Kathleen Turner out of *Body Heat*. This clan of Finns runs the town. There's this character named Cox who acts like he knows me."

"That sheriff looks like he wants to secure your heartbeat," said Randall.

"No shit. That's his bastard kid I shot."

"Jesus," said Dorothy.

"Slow down. Let it settle," said Randall, quieter than Dorothy. "Don't let the déjà vu fuck with your head."

Harry nodded. He had carefully not allowed himself to think about *that*. "It was just like that all over again. Quick, you know?"

"We know," Dorothy's voice caught in her throat.

Harry turned away and looked out the window at the snowy hills unreeling below them.

Other hills. Layered in mist. Emerald, jade, turquoise, shamrock, moss-green till hell wouldn't have it and ferrous red Martian dirt that stored the day's heat like a furnace. Sweat and fear and no sleep.

Crazy damn operation. Randall's brainchild. Trying to rescue a renegade Viet Cong leader from the North Vietnamese. Complicated by Dorothy tagging along, hot to interview the renegade. All screwed up into a confused, running fight down a jungle mountainside. Got separated. Randall and Dorothy captured. Had them digging their own graves when Harry broke from the tree line at the run with his M16 walloping his shoulder.

Defining moment of his life. He was twenty-one years old and touched with dead-on magic and he'd sprinted through a hole in the day and even now, he smiled remembering it. *Every move perfect.* The bullets meant for Randall and Dorothy had sizzled around his head. Couldn't remember exactly. A scream. A prayer. *Fuck you! You can't have these people that I love!* The three North Vietnamese executioners went down.

"You might want to get away from the paper for a while," said Dorothy.

"What?" Harry blinked.

Dorothy cocked her head with a wry expression. "A newspaper's a funny place. All these people sit around and wait for something bad to happen to somebody else out in the world. They have their filters to deal with reality. To keep it manageable. You just got turned into a story. Reporters like to write stories in newsrooms and put their byline on them like a seal of approval. They don't like the stories walking around, talking over their shoulder. It'll be weird."

"I'm more worried about Bud—" Harry started to say.

"The more you help Bud, the deeper in shit you get. Leave it alone," said Randall.

"I think you should stay at our place tonight," said Dorothy.

Harry nodded, leaned on his duffel bag, and studied the faded Air America baggage tags looped to the grip. Same bag he'd packed in a rush when he split Detroit. Now he and his bag were on their way to Randall and Dorothy's place again. Maybe nothing ever changed.

18

Flurries blew across Holman Field in St. Paul. The storm had merely swished its petticoats through town as it passed to the northeast. On the way to the parking lot, Randall asked, "How are you feeling?"

"Adrenaline bends," said Harry. The corrupt taste festered in his gums and only a drink could wash it out when it got this bad.

"You need some sleep," said Randall.

The city whirled past with the cramped aspect of a childhood home revisited as an adult. Randall took the freeway, exited on Cretin Avenue, and went south, past the College of St. Thomas. Apple-cheeked Tommies toted bookbags. Girls in plaid skirts.

They turned onto the River Road. The homes were bigger. Larger lots. Ice winked on the crumbling grin of a Halloween jack-o'-lantern.

Randall and Dorothy lived in a solid, three-story, wood-frame home set back from a screen of oak and maple. They entered the side door and went through a dining room hung with tourist plunder from three continents. They couldn't have kids, so they had trips.

In the kitchen, Dorothy heated water for coffee. She turned and stared at Harry. "Not to put too fine a point on it, Harry, but those clothes have blood all over them."

Harry showered and changed to a pair of clean jeans, turtleneck, and a heavy wool cardigan. Dorothy handed him a cup of coffee and said, "He's in the den."

Randall's den overlooked the backyard. The tiers of limestone retaining walls jutting from the snow were a memory in Harry's hands.

He and Randall had landscaped the yard ten years ago, working in July heat. Harry had watched Randall's raw-boned strength start to slip away that summer by inches as they struggled with the rock. The project had been a changing of the guard. Harry, tireless, panther-muscled, the PFC, had finally put out his hand, and told Randall, the colonel, to slow down.

Let me do it.

To know Randall was to be lost in the long shadow of three wars and eleven Purple Hearts and the autographed portraits that peered from the wall: Eisenhower, Kennedy, the great airborne chieftains Ridgway and Gavin.

Randall reached over and took Harry's cigarette, dragged, then handed it back. His pale eyes scoured Harry's face.

"What really happened up there?" he asked.

"I wasn't supposed to be there. I was a last-minute change," said Harry.

Randall's gaze took on the stony focus of a sphinx.

Harry laughed nervously. "Bud's wife." He bit his lip. "We . . ."

Randall cocked his head.

"The minute I saw her I just knew I was going to fuck up. She figured out that Bud brought me up there to pry him out of a bad marriage. I tried to get him to leave last night. He belongs in detox."

"Did you fuck the woman?" asked Randall.

Harry threw up his hands. "Yes. I went back after we started out to hunt. She met me on the trail. We went into this grove—"

"Really? Outside, in the woods, in the snow?" Randall appeared impressed.

Harry exhaled. "She tried to drag me back to the lodge with her. Get it?"

"You think Bud was supposed to die in a hunting accident. And the grieving widow was supposed to pocket the Maston fortune. And she could manipulate her son to do that—" Randall pondered.

"Not just the boy. Jesse's daughter was out there, the sheriff's other bastard kid. And this guy Cox who works around Bud's place—he's wrong from the git go." Harry shook his head. "It was too easy. The sheriff and the DA were a little too eager to look the other way. I'm out by noon. Hakala parleys a deal, if Bud agrees to go to treatment, no grand jury. That's not for Bud's benefit. They're hiding something. It's a dying town and Bud washed up on Main Street like a ton of drunken blubber. Everybody had their knives out."

Randall chose his words carefully. "Harry, you can watch my back anytime. You have excellent instincts in a tight pinch. But when the smoke clears, your thinking has a way of becoming fucked up."

"What's she like? Bud's wife?" asked Dorothy. She had been listening in the doorway.

"Jesse?" He watched Dorothy's eyes pierce him and then soften as he pronounced the name. "The hell of it is—I can't shake this feeling she was asking me for help somehow. I gotta know—"

"Randall," said Dorothy, "you better talk to him. I do believe he's thinking of going back for her."

Harry clicked his teeth. "She's—"

"The blackjack dealer," Randall inserted in a wry voice as he shook his head. "Harry. You were playing it safe, getting your life together. You had nineteen on the table and you planned to stay with that. Then you went on your mission of mercy, the woman appears and tempts you to stand up and take a hit."

"Poor Harry," sighed Dorothy. "I thought we were through with all that."

"Apparently not," mused Randall. "Look at him. He's found a drama and he's spilled some blood and screwed this Jesse and now he thinks his testicles are tetherballs again."

"Hey, Bud coulda been dead, and the people who set him up are still walking around up there," Harry protested.

"Really," said Randall. "Most folks have a day like this, they'd reach for the Valium. You, you dummy, are thinking about going back for more. And not out of concern about Bud."

"They used me, Randall, like I was some dumb recruit," said Harry flatly.

Randall's knees creaked when he rose to his feet. "Here's my advice. Right or wrong, you're free of it. No charges. No blame. Walk away. No more temptation. No more trying to relive," he cleared his throat, "something that's gone." He went into the kitchen.

"What's eating him?" asked Harry.

"Sympathy. He was forty-two once thinking he was still twenty-five." Dorothy narrowed her green eyes and the scar from the wound she'd suffered on the day Harry had saved her life accented her smile.

"Say it," said Harry.

"Just thinking," she pondered in a bittersweet voice. "What a terrible way to fall in love."

The bruise on Harry's upper arm from the rifle kick spread blue on sickly yellow, the size of a grapefruit. The bruise in his mind was much larger and talk was no good and thinking was suspect and memory failed. Chris's death and Bud's life were in his belly.

Dreading the dream that might wait, Harry lay down on the couch in the living room and slept. When he opened his eyes the windows were dark. He'd slept for six hours.

Dorothy and Randall sat in the kitchen at the long trestle table under a squadron of hanging copper pots with their heads close together. Dorothy was talking on the phone. When Harry walked in, she said, "Sorry, Lucy," and hung up. "Three kinds of bullshit," she said brightly.

"Who is it?"

She mentioned a local TV anchorwoman. "Word's out that Flattop Franky Murphy at the paper has weaseled out a juicy angle on the Maston shooting. To wit: not the first time Harry Griffin has saved a friend's life with some snickersnack rifle work. Prepare for a trip down memory lane."

"Nam?" asked Harry.

"My God," said Randall. "It's going to be a circus."

"Shit," said Harry. "How'd Murphy get onto that. It's ancient history."

Dorothy shrugged. "Well they dug it up somewhere. Slow news day, Harry. People must of glommed on. Just a few paragraphs to brighten up the story. Personalize it a little. Hip hip hooray for the new flash journalism," said Dorothy with a sour smile. She taught the old-style journalism part time at the U of M.

"Fucking scribblers," muttered Randall. "Tecumseh Sherman was right. Shoot the bastards."

"So now what?" asked Harry.

"I called Bud over at Ramsey," said Dorothy. "If none of us play into it, they don't have a sexy sidebar. Just the basic story. So we'll just tough it out. Lucky you. You get your fifteen minutes in the footlights," said Dorothy.

"Bud." Harry remembered. "He was in town talking to Murphy . . ."

The phone rang. Randall answered. "Fuck you." He paused. "No comment." He listened for a moment, looked at Harry. "Not here." Another pause. "No idea." Randall hung up.

"Who?" Harry asked.

"Murphy."

"I'm gonna set the fucker straight," Harry said.

19

Harry insisted that Randall drive him home.

Chris Deucette's death, but not his name, made headlines in St. Paul. PHILANTHROPIST MASTON SHOT—stripped in six column Bodoni Bold type across the top of the early outstate edition. Harry slapped quarters in the street sales box next to the elevators in his building and took out a paper.

If he'd been shot, the headline would say, HUNTER SHOT. NOBODY SHOT. A photo of a slimmer Bud Maston accompanied the story. Back when he was a prince, before he turned into a frog.

Going up in the elevator, he saw the sidebar below the fold. DÉJÀ VU HAUNTS HUNTING TRAGEDY. His face made page one. An old library file photo. His hair was longer, teeth crooked. A picture of Tim Randall from one of his book promotions ran alongside.

> It wasn't the first time Harry Griffin saved a friend's life with a fast rifle shot, a reliable source told this newspaper. In January 1968, Harold S. Griffin, then a PFC in the U.S. Army serving in Vietnam, rescued another friend in a dramatic, almost identical situation. "Harry [Griffin] hasn't touched a gun since the war," added the source.

Which was not true. "Bud, you dumb shit," he muttered. He skipped the war story part and continued to read:

> The other recipient of Griffin's shooting acumen is St. Paul author and former army man Timothy Randall. Randall, who was Griffin's commanding officer, retired from the army under a cloud in 1968. His Pulitzer Prize–winning book on the Vietnam War, *The Bitter Coming of Age,* was published in 1972.

The story quoted an old review of Randall's book, written by some creep from the Nixon administration.

Jack Kennedy once described Randall as "a killer who wrote books." Randall had a reputation for being a lone wolf warrior-scholar with a flair for "black operations." Black operations is a term from the Vietnam era used to describe covert activities that included kidnapping and assassination.

The main story was off the wire from the Duluth paper and bore Sherry Rawlins's byline. It tersely described the incident, quoting from an "exclusive" interview with Mike Hakala—"tragic result of drugs making an inroad in rural Minnesota . . . a patent case of justifiable homicide . . . friend coming to the aid of a friend"—and Bud's recent "quiet" marriage and doomed political campaign. Jesse was not mentioned by name, her picture did not appear, and she wasn't quoted. Hakala had kept the lid down tight.

Chris was sketched fast as a troubled kid who possessed drugs and stole guns. A blurry high school picture. No mention of the teacher Chris had allegedly threatened at gunpoint.

Harry crumpled the paper and threw it across the room. The phone rang. It was Linda Margoles.

"Jesus, Harry. Bud called me from Ramsey. He wants to file for divorce. Then I saw you on the six o'clock news and talked to Dorothy Houston, she said you were back home. You need a lawyer?"

"Not me. Bud sure does."

"He said you think his wife . . . tried to kill him?"

"I was him I wouldn't stick around to find out."

"Christ, he just got married."

"Linda, just get the papers ready." He imagined the intricate gears of her mind shifting through his rushed words.

"Okay, okay, calm down," she said in a steady voice. She was humoring him. Everybody was being nice. Floating with the shock waves. In a more intimate voice she said, "How are you doing with this?"

"Not so hot," said Harry.

"Dorothy said you haven't eaten. I could pick up some Chinese. Come over."

Harry exhaled. "Linda, we've been through all this."

"You shouldn't be alone tonight."

Harry thought about it. "Yes, I should."

"At least have something to eat." Her voice hovered.

"Okay. Jesus. Give me an hour." He hung up. Dialed Randall's. "You see the paper?" he asked when Dorothy answered.

"It's on the ten o'clock news, too. I told you it could get weird," said Dorothy.

Randall came on. "Is this Murphy a friend of yours?" he asked.

"Just a guy I work with. A hotshot," said Harry.

"Well, he's good, I'll give him that. I just got a call from D.C. Remember Hollywood from special ops?"

"Yeah," said Harry. Hollywood. A blond gorilla with dry ice for eyes. Navy SEAL he'd worked for after Randall split the war.

"Well, Hollywood is a United States Attorney now working for the Justice Department. He said the phones are buzzing among the old gang. Murphy looked through all my old book reviews and called the hostile ones."

"Shit, Tim, I'm sorry you got dragged into this."

"Hey, I'm used to being notorious. It's you we're worried about. If you read between the lines, they're setting you up as the psycho vet from central casting. Dorothy thinks you should take a leave of absence. Bug out for a while."

"I'll deal with it. I'll get 'em to kill the story, the part about you."

"Don't kid yourself. You don't deal with something like this. You just turned into a story."

"Fucking Bud. He musta said something to Murphy. Put the blood in the water."

"It doesn't make any difference where it started. Technically, it's all accurate information. The clever juxtaposition gives it lurid texture. It's what you get for living an interesting life in a world of newspaper subscribers and voyeur reporters who grub along in quiet desperation."

"You're a lot of help."

"Screw 'em," Randall chuckled. "What are they going to do? Send us to Vietnam? Let's invite Murphy over. I'll get out the twenty-two and we'll sit around and shoot squirrels in the backyard while he interviews us about back when we were 'assassins' together."

"They've no right, man," said Harry.

"Hunker down. Let it blow over," said Randall. "Why don't you come back here tonight?"

Randall's concern was practical, not emotional like Linda's. Randall knew he could sweat some sheets.

"I'll think about it."

The minute he put the phone down, it rang. A reporter from Channel 7. Harry pulled the phone connection out of the wall.

His heart started to race. Steady down. Do the tricks.

In sobriety he had evolved disciplined routines; first he put the water on for coffee, then twenty minutes of meditation till the water boiled.

He sat on the carpet, folded his legs into a half lotus, shut his eyes, and let his thoughts scatter into the darkness behind his eyelids. He imagined them swirling in a slow-motion, underwater storm. The heavy ones sank. The lighter ones trickled up like ribbons of bubbles.

The tension was supposed to start seeping through a pressure ridge along his brow and slowly bleed away.

Jesse's face didn't sink, it didn't ascend. It said, "People can't help when they meet." Over and over, until the kettle whistled.

She was still whispering through the caffeine star clusters as he groomed the strong Colombian with boiling water.

Christ. He scrubbed his knuckles in his sweaty hair and broke into absurd laughter. This was the year he was going to quit smoking. Loosen up. Trade in the boxing gym for cross-country skis. He had even looked in a pet shop. Birds and cats. Linda Margoles had suggested one or the other. Chided that both were not a real good idea.

He'd even considered getting some new furniture to splash a little color around.

The studio was a woodcut of where a man should live, dreamed up by a boy raised in pretelevision America that Harry kept quiet with antiques, bookshelves, old nautical maps on the wall, a globe, and the smell of tobacco.

A ship captain's room, Linda Margoles had remarked on making her final exit. The narrow single bed was a bunk that could accommodate sex by the night.

Not wide enough for love.

Harry paced and touched his belongings. A gritty blowup from Bill Mauldin's World War II classic *Up Front* hung near the drawing table. Joe and Willie. Two cartoon uncles who had taught him to draw as he copied them on the long nights of his youth as a military cadet in Georgia. He'd ridden the holiday trains between Georgia and Michigan and his cartoon characters had come to life for him in the faces of GIs in transit to and from Korea.

He smiled ironically at his reflection in a black window. "I got my teeth fixed, Ma." He laughed, adding, "I got a good job. I'm not punching a clock at Chrysler anymore . . ."

Almost pulled it off. For a few years he'd drawn dark laughter for the editorial page. But times changed. He changed. He'd found himself getting comfortable. He detoured around the mean streets that he'd once walked. The computers came. He traded in his steel pen for a plastic Macintosh mouse.

A safe life. Too safe. Like the artwork he created that was two steps removed from his fingertips behind a wafer of plastic and a video monitor.

A stamped, addressed envelope lay on the drawing table. His child support payment to the Wayne County Friend of the Court in Detroit. Forgot to mail it in his haste after Bud called.

The kid was in high school now. Harry hadn't seen him since he was in diapers. But this year, with ten years sober in the bank, he thought maybe . . .

Touching all the bases didn't help. Minnesota Harry's comfy life was trickling away. The sharp edges that he had learned to fold discreetly inside had flashed out. In the grove, on the ridge—that was him. Not this. Not books and pieces of paper. Not predictable habits.

Detroit Harry grinned at him from the picture hanging over the drawing table and he saw how he would sandbag Murphy and kill the story.

He had his pride and a certain reputation and Murphy could dig up pieces of his past that didn't square with his image. It was fine to be a reformed drunk in Minnesota. But not some other things.

He called the newsroom and asked for Murphy.

"Frank Murphy." The voice was tense, self-absorbed.

"Murphy, you sonofabitch—"

"Griffin! Where are you?"

"What the hell're you doing with this story?"

"My job. We have to be thorough on this one, Harry. You work here. We have to bend over backward to dot all the *i*'s; we could be accused of favoritism. Besides, it's a hell of a story."

"Your ass. Look, I'll talk to you, off the record, but I want you to leave Randall and his wife out of it."

"His wife? Dorothy Houston. She teaches journalism at the U. She used to work here—"

"She was there that day, they were together. That scar on her face—"

"No shit, this is great stuff."

"I'll talk about what happened this morning. But not the rest. You know where I live?"

"I'll get it from the city desk. We'd like to bring a photographer."

"You bring nothing."

"Be right there," said Murphy.

Tactical on Murphy. Scrappy competitive guy. Short. Napoleon complex. Hungry for front-page ink. He measured his column inches every week and let his peers know whose was bigger.

Harry broke the cellophane on a fresh toothbrush and scrubbed his teeth as he paced. But would Murphy play fast and loose when his blood was up for the hunt?

Harry moved one of his easy chairs against his drawing table, directly under the picture of him and Randall all strapped up in warrior garb.

Then he dug an old scrapbook out of the closet and found four prints of the framed picture. He put the scrapbook on the lamp table next to the chair, the loose pictures strewn, peeking from under magazines.

Harry was hoping that the fastest Franky Murphy had ever had to think on his feet was playing golf.

The intercom sounded. Harry buzzed him in. A few minutes later the knock came. Harry grabbed the front section of the paper in his fist, opened the door, and brandished it in Franky Murphy's face.

"What the fuck are you doing to me, Franky? Making me look like some kind of nut?"

Franky shrugged. "It's news."

Harry looked into the hall. He'd come alone. He glared at Franky. "What happened up north is news. This other stuff is bullshit."

Franky walked in, unbuttoned his overcoat, and regarded Harry with a look of pitying condescension; that someone who worked for a newspaper would commit the cardinal sin of being written about in its pages.

"I had a copper run you through NCIC. Didn't know you had a police record in Detroit," said Murphy for openers.

"So what."

"A year in the Detroit House of Correction. Two separate counts of ag assault. Some beef with a guy in a bar." Franky paused. "And, uh, apparently you roughed up your wife. Didn't know you were married."

Harry responded with a nervous tick, popping the toothbrush in his mouth. Franky went on. "There's a more serious prior charge, an armed assault conviction in Detroit in July sixty-seven. But you got a suspended sentence on that one."

"I wipe my ass with my right hand. You wanna write about that too?"

"Harry." Franky spread his hands and pursed his lips. "What I'd like to do is a big feature follow. Three separate lives joined by a violent incident. The rich dropout, the veteran, and the punk rocker kid. But you'd have to agree to being interviewed to make that fly. I mean, it'd look better if you'd comment on it, put it in perspective." Franky paused. "You, uh, willing to go on the record about any of this?"

"Where'd you get the thing about me and Randall?"

"It's in the public record. You got a medal. I can get a copy of the citation from military records in St. Louis but that'll take a couple of days. You wouldn't have one handy?"

"Bullshit St. Louis. Who, Franky?"

"Sorry, Harry. That's a source."

"A source, huh? What do I think? I think you got creative with your sources. I think you were shooting the breeze with Bud Maston—who's a bit of a mess right now—and he said something about hunting. That I hadn't been around guns since the army. Then this happens . . . and you sail that quote in there out of context . . . I thought you guys had ethics."

"But it's accurate, isn't it?" said Murphy. "That quote."

"Jesus, this really sucks. The kid isn't even all the way cold yet."

"Why do you think the kid did it?"

"Fuck if I know. Kids used to get drunk and drive cars fast, now I guess they shoot people when they're pissed off."

"What's it like to kill someone?"

Harry pulled the toothbrush from his mouth and Murphy's eager eyes blinked nervously.

"Ah God, Harry. That's blood—"

"Fuck you, Murphy."

Franky grimaced and his eyes flitted around Harry, probing. Finally they settled on the picture hanging over Harry's head. He leaned forward.

"That's you and Randall . . ."

Harry stood up. "Screw it. I don't care what you write." Harry made a face at the bloody toothbrush. "I'm going to the bathroom. When I come out, I don't want to see you."

Harry walked down the hall to the bathroom. He left the door ajar. He heard Murphy scurry by. Heard the apartment door close.

One of the smaller pictures was missing.

Now give it about half an hour. Time for Murphy to get back, run the picture through photo. Call Arnie Cummings at home just about the time the picture editor takes the picture to the news desk.

If it didn't work, Harry could only hope that a bigger story would come along. Something juicier for the nearsighted papier-mâché shark to chew on. Like a big local plane crash. An earthquake. Some nut to take a shot at the president. He needed something bad to happen to somebody else.

Harry paced and brushed his teeth and spit a wad of bloody saliva into the kitchen sink. Then he called Arnie.

"Harry?" Arnie's voice was concerned and awkward, distancing. "I saw you on the tube. You all right?"

"Hell no, I'm not all right." Harry laid it on him. How Murphy had sticky fingers and lifted a picture behind his back. Then he let Arnie be Arnie. Arnie was predictably furious. A picture was involved; Murphy was messing in his turf. If there was an ethics dispute about swiping a picture, people would see the picture and associate it with the photo staff. He'd seen the early edition and sounded genuinely pissed that they'd dig into Harry's background to jazz up a story.

Harry agreed. Said he'd prefer to let it slide if the personal stuff stayed out. He wondered aloud why they didn't just stick to the basic story. Another thing. It might be awkward, coming back to work after everything that had happened. What if he took two weeks' vacation until it blew over?

Arnie said he'd get back to him. He was smoking to stop that picture getting in the paper.

"Damn shame what happened, but they cleared you," said Arnie.

"Fucking Yankee yuppies don't know shit about guns, or hunting . . . or these kinds of matters."

"You're absolutely right," said Harry.

He hung up and paced in a caged circle, picking up velocity. Old feeling. Embattled. Not a bad one.

The intercom rang. Shit! Linda. Food. He buzzed her in.

20

Mistake, all the lawyers in town, Bud calling her. And he knew it was a mistake letting her come over the minute she tossed off her Marmot and he saw her in a snug beige skirt and sweater and when he saw the melting bridal veil of snowflakes scattered in her short chestnut hair and in her long eyelashes.

She grimaced at his gouged face. She did a lot of pro bono for a women's shelter. He must look like a doorpost marked by a woman. *Beware, violent man inside.*

"I look like hell, huh?" She looked great. And sensible and safe.

She had a narrow face and oval brown eyes and a slightly crooked nose that, with her long, clean neck, gave her a touch of Europe—Modigliani would have spotted her a mile away and painted her and called the portrait Loneliness.

She held up a bag. Harry smelled Chinese.

"You should eat," she said. No kiss. First things first. If you didn't watch her close, she'd take you right over. And if he was smart, right now, he'd let her.

With quick efficient moves, she was past him and put the bag on the kitchenette counter and her alert eyes spied the toothbrush where he'd stuck it behind the toaster. She held it up and noted the bristles with concern. "God, this again?" She dropped it in the sink.

They split an order of Princess Chicken at his small kitchen table and tried to make conversation.

"You want to talk about it?" she asked finally.

"No." He chewed and swallowed. "You talk to Bud?"

"Uh-huh. He said prepare the papers but he wants to hold off on serving them. He thinks he should go to the funeral first."

"Idiot, the only place he's going is a treatment center. He's going to sit the rest of this one out."

"The rest?" Her voice sped up.

"What else did you talk about?"

"Standard stuff. Told him to change his life insurance. He said his new wife specifically had asked not be named on the policy. Names the foundation as beneficiary. But the will . . . that's a different story. The foundation again, but if that bullet would have been six inches over, the surviving spouse could pop it open."

"Is he aware of that?"

"Actually . . ." She folded her brisk demeanor and filed it away. "We spent most of the time talking about you."

Mistake. He just knew it. She had that basic look back in her eyes: *I slept with you, now you take the Boy Scout oath.* Dammit. His own eyes darted. "Bud's been drinking a lot lately. You can't take him literally."

"He sounded sincere about his worry for you. That you're enjoying all this."

Harry cleared the plates and returned with cups of coffee. Linda sat back, crossed her lean legs, and cupped her chin in her palm. A purple vein curved on the olive skin of her wrist. He remembered that the exact vein also curled over her ankle. Ankle and wrist were the same size.

"Are you? Enjoying this?" she asked.

Harry stood up abruptly and began to pace. "God no. That's nuts." He snapped his lighter and lit a cigarette in a fast reflex. Linda wrinkled her nose in disapproval.

"He's worried *you* might start drinking again." She probed. She looked softer without the precision-attired bitch makeup she wore to the law office. But she'd taken the time to put on a subtle touch of green eye shadow. "Bud thinks you have two gears, neutral and full tilt. He says you can't handle the excitement sober."

Harry continued to pace and had to laugh. Sonofabitch, funny wasn't it, how trauma was a jack-in-the-box. She was trying to express concern, but the lid flies open and you get all these tangled longings and resentments. Like Jesse, you reach for the love of your fucked-up life and death pops up wearing a clown face.

He stabbed a finger at the bed across the room. "Don't give me that about excitement. You're the one whose pulse never gets much over ninety."

Another thing about Linda. She had the stamina to run horizontal marathons in bed. You had to qualify because she didn't come until after she hit the wall.

Her eyes tracked him as he paced. In a very deliberate voice, she said, "Dorothy thinks you're going to have a rough night. I'll stay if you'd like."

"Mercy fuck?"

She braced at his language. "Company," she said.

He plucked up the newspaper. "You see this? Nutty vet picks up gun first time in years and finds an excuse to shoot somebody."

Her voice was reasonable, at first. "They're just trying to sell newspapers. You're not crazy, Harry." Then it took on a weary edge. "Jesus, God, if there's one word that'll never die from overuse with men, it's *bullshit*! Look, the only connection you have to Vietnam is repeating a pattern of ignorance. What's the cliché? We weren't in Vietnam ten years, we were there one year, ten times. That's like you and being sober. You've been sober one year and repeated it ten times . . ."

She raised her chin. "That adds up to one woman a year. By the time you got to me you had the routine pretty refined."

Her sangfroid took a hike. He liked the street fighter in her, except when her eyes hexed him with the glint of broken beer bottles. "Uh-uh, we been over this before," he protested.

"It's sad. You can get it up to kill somebody. No problem. But committing to a relationship . . ." For emphasis, she arched her index finger and let it fall flaccid.

"I don't need this right now, Linda."

"No, you've been through a lot. That's always your excuse, isn't it?"

He used to like the way she looked you straight in the eye. But now he turned his back on her and retreated to his bookcases where he rummaged in his box of tapes, found one, and slapped it into his tape player and pushed some buttons.

Motown, shivery as an old Detroit street kata, filled the apartment. He tried to evoke the feel of the factories, the freeways, the bitter wind off the river. But it was gone, that jump where the muscle hits the steel.

Linda smiled sadly and put on her coat. He crossed to her, holding out his hands in an invitation to dance. She raised her voice to carry over the music. "Get a life, Harry. They use that music on TV now. To sell fruit."

As he watched her walk out he compared her to Jesse Deucette. Linda was the opposite of danger; she was forever, a keeper, the good serious girl who went with the decent job and his straight new smile. He'd almost got it right with her.

Harry danced alone with the same old problem. Life presented choices. There was this princess and this dragon. Before he met Linda he'd always chosen to kill the princess and fuck the dragon.

But . . .

She lived in a house on Lake Como. In the summer she trained for marathons on the park trails, in the winter she skied cross country. Kept the stuff in her cupboards lined up. A woman who made lists.

He'd read the list in her mind when she looked at him a certain way and decided it was full of children's names.

The old panic had set in. The first cold fumble that untied the blood knot of sexual performance. He ran from the scourge of impotence and masked his retreat in pyschobabble about sobriety.

The phone rang. Arnie, his voice tired and irritable. Murphy would be reprimanded. They'd kill the background stuff. Harry could have his two weeks off. The editor wanted a sit-down discussion of ethical guidelines in situations where staffers get involved inadvertently in stories.

Harry said he'd drop in the office Monday morning.

"What's that noise?" asked Arnie.

"Music," said Harry.

"Sounds like that raisin commercial," said Arnie.

He sat in bed chain-smoking to blunt the lousy taste in his mouth as he watched traffic crawl along the interstate. Lights going east and west. The moon swung a sickle at the curve of the 35 interchange where the road curled north to dragon country.

Go back. Yes. For the woman *and* the truth.

The night waited like a stretch of tricky open ground he had to cross and his body knew and he clamped his elbows tight to his sides, crossed his forearms rigidly across his chest, and drew up his knees.

Sleep swung open beneath him like bomb bay doors.

21

The jack-in-the-box had slanted eyes and onion breath and carried Karl Marx in his pack and the bastard popped out of the inky rain on springs of fire and steel. And they were all scared, all the young lives that clawed at the melting ladder of a last breath in the muscle-scented night and Harry wet his pants, but it was blood.

And all the ones he'd killed were there and people he'd seen die and every goddamned corpse he'd ever touched.

And the explosion embraced him in white line as strict as a winter bush and two South Vietnamese militiamen took the full force of the booby trap that sprung the ambush and he was clubbed into the slime of a paddy dike with their tangled corpses.

Death was a happy whore on a busy night who put the French kiss to him. He bit off the steaming tongue and spit it back and gagged on a mouthful of digested rice as a dead Vietnamese farm boy's supper leaked out from the uncoiling yarn of his guts and a slick fishbone sensation tingled along the blood-drenched canvas ankle of his jungle boot and that was vertebrae at the bottom of a chest cavity.

With the oblong eye of perfect fear he saw the implacable shadows swarm up from the paddies and he saw the thigh muscles bang like slats beneath their muddy shorts and he saw the magazines of the Kalishnakovs in their determined hands curve wickedly and drip with the rain and the VC ghosts wore flesh tonight when they came to finish the job.

Don't move, play dead, and hide in the guts and eat the rice. Wash it down with hot sticky blood and the primal ooze of paddy water and stay alive.

He'd always thought that the angel who drifted across the pond of death and quieted his terror was his mother because she was there, mixed in with the rest. The water where he lay glowed from the still-burning lamps of a '51 Packard that lurched nose down between the smashed rice stalks with the doors popped open and the dome light still on and a hole in the windshield, passenger side, where he'd catapulted free. And the dome light flickered in the gory ruffled halo of cracked glass that she wore around her face.

And now he saw in the sputtering magnesium light of a parachute flare that it was not his mother who came with outstretched arms.

The North Vietnamese soldiers who tried to shoot Randall and Dorothy were there talking to Chris, comparing their wounds. And one of them leaned against the fender of the Packard and Chris put his finger in the hole in the Vietnamese's chest with fascination on his face at how tidy it was compared to the wreckage of his heart and lungs and the Vietnamese turned to display his dangling scapula.

Not an angel who lifted him from the killing ground and carried him into the grove of pines. Who pulled him down beside her and threw aside her shining robes. Jesse Deucette had the ram's head configuration of her ovaries and uterus drawn on her belly with blood.

Harry lay motionless and patiently let the brew of dread and mosquito repellent dry in his sweat. He stared at the quiet winter moon that hung over I-94 and massaged the starfish-shaped scars that quilted the muscle of his left shoulder.

And the dream was just another scar that reared up and screamed and bled and thrashed and stank when he was a little too tense. And through the years he'd come to appreciate its symmetry and scored it to the keening cries of grieving Vietnamese peasant women as they prepared their dead for burial; as they placed bananas on the corpses' chests to confuse the ravenous Celestial Dog and as they filled the gaping mouths with rice.

After he'd quit drinking, the jack-in-the-box joke was that the nightmare liked to hide in the sweet itch weeds where sex tangled up with love.

So for ten years he'd played hide-and-seek with women. Then he'd met Linda and, with ten years sober as a hedge, he'd wanted to believe he was past it and he'd pleased her with the joy of being free. But the joke was just being patient for the right moment to shove down the visceral plunger and he could feel her insides swell all around him and he was dreaming wide awake that he was back in the gut pile and he'd just told her that he loved her and he'd meant it and the joke convulsed with slippery hungry glee: *What do you suppose she had for supper?* The hydraulics of sex dried up on the spot.

She'd suggested therapy and she'd wanted to work it out, but he knew she'd never get the joke because outside the womb the only time most men got inside another human being was making love.

So Harry lit a cigarette to chase the loathing in his mouth and laughed because Linda the feminist thought women should be in combat. And a voice in the back of his mind that sounded like Randall cautioned him. *You're too old, too soft, to play out a hand of blackjack with Jesse Deucette.*

The phone rang just before dawn and the Reverend Donald Karson of Stanley, Minnesota, sounded like he'd been up all night.

"Bud gave me your number," said Karson. "He feels a duty to come to . . . Chris's funeral. That's *not* a good idea, Harry."

"When's the service?" Harry asked calmly as a vision of Jesse floated across the burial plots and stood next to an open grave.

"Tuesday, eleven A.M."

"It'll be all right," said Harry. "Bud will be checked safe and sound into a chemical-dependency ward. I will attend the funeral."

"You can't be serious," said Karson.

22

So how serious are you, man—St. Paul serious or Detroit serious? At dawn, Harry in his sweat suit put his Nikes to the Sunday quiet streets of St. Paul.

The snow crunched and the fresh air seared his breath and he remembered how he'd come north to St. Paul, where it was clean, to put the first half of his life to sleep. Almost a Canadian town. Hell, back then, he'd cross the river to Windsor, Canada, and sit in a well-tended park where things were tidy and under control and dream of a better life.

He headed up Wabasha Street toward the Capitol and came to the Maston Building and slowed to a walk and read the bronze plaque next to the doorway: Maston Foundation. Richard Stanley Maston, Director.

Two rampant griffins stood vigil over the entrance. Griffins are guardians. Bud said that. The first day they met.

Well, he'd be one fucked Griffin if he laid down for this one.

He let it percolate at the edge of his thoughts—Jesse, Emery, Becky hiding in the woods—as he ran up the hill and crossed over the empty moat of the freeway and the Capitol loomed, iced with frost, with a team of gold horses prancing over the door.

He stopped at a marble bench and a granite pedestal where the statue of Stanley Houghton Walker Maston posed in weathered bronze with birdshit for epaulets. The old robber baron extended one green hand, flicking a spitball in perpetuity at the back of his blood enemy, another statue across the way. Floyd B. Olson, Minnesota's Red governor during the Depression.

Well, Richard, you have your karma to work out and I have mine.

He ran eight-minute miles down Summit Avenue to the river and pushed it on the way back until the nicotine stitches burst in his lungs and the old screws that thrived on pain started turning and he had to keep going to shake the flat out of his ass from all the years stuck at a desk. In front of his apartment, he coughed up a decade's worth of caution and hawked it into the snow, then he went upstairs and showered.

Time to call Bud in the hospital. He worked through the switchboard, found the ward and was told that Bud was being carted around for tests.

With energy shooting from his fingers, Harry cleaned his apartment, laid out clothing, studied a map of Minnesota, and traced the road north. He checked the balance in his savings account.

Ravenous, he got in his car and drove east down the Interstate, crossed the St. Croix River, and pulled off in Hudson, Wisconsin, into an empty landscape of cement and brand names. Perkins. Country Kitchen. Amoco. Anywhere USA. He went into the Perkins and ordered eggs, sausage, pancakes. Poured on the syrup. A man in the next booth was reading the St. Paul paper. Harry glanced at the front page and grinned.

A grainy AP photo showed corpses in the Third World mud and the headline story in the final Sunday edition was the murder of three American clergymen in El Salvador. The shooting in northern Minnesota was stripped in a small headline at the bottom of the page. Most of the story had been kicked inside.

For diversion, he wandered down the shopping mall and went to a movie and took a tub of popcorn into the dark to watch a blockbuster thriller about a cop taking on a gang of terrorists. Someone was killed in the first three minutes and people kept dying in orgies of automatic gunfire and lots of explosions served up supernovas of flying glass and bodies were dropping, coming apart, impaled, burned, flying into the air.

Harry had to laugh at the audience, at how they cheered the special effects, oohing and aahing when the ketchup packets splattered in long, drawn-out slow-motion arabesques, heehawing at the heroes' quick one-liners as he reloaded.

Chris Deucette would have liked to watch the movie with hog tranq boiling in his brain.

The last pane of glass shattered. The last plume of gasoline burned away, the last car crashed, and the last of a million gunshots echoed over the carnage. The good guy won in the end.

He walked out of the theater grinning and people in the lobby averted their eyes from his torn face. He passed down an arcade of coming attractions and in every poster movie stars held out guns in the new American handshake.

Outside, Detroit Harry sniffed the melancholy afternoon. It smelled drunk out. The whole glass world was tipped on its side.

Get Bud in the hospital first . . .

23

Six pillows propped Bud up in the hospital bed and his hairy gut hung out and his face was the same color as the thick gauze that swathed his wounded side. He spooned soft ice cream over his distended lower lip and watched the Vikings tumble on Astroturf like steroidal Easter eggs. Harry switched off the TV set.

"Going to that funeral is the dumbest thing I ever heard," said Harry firmly. "You had a deal with Hakala, remember? You're going into treatment. Tomorrow."

Bud put down his spoon and looked at Harry thoughtfully. "I've . . . had time to think. I have an obligation to attend that service."

"Bullshit. When can you get out of here?"

"Tomorrow. You talk to Linda?"

"She was over, doing her Angel of Mercy number. More like a Cuisinart with nipples." Harry scowled. "I don't need people practicing amateur shrink with my life right now . . ."

Bud dropped his eyes. "Déjà vu. They really got into that. Murphy tried to talk to me. I didn't say a word."

"It's already blowing over. Some American church people got killed in El Salvador. That bumped us to the bottom of the front page. Tomorrow it'll be inside. TV will drop it if nobody talks to them."

"A Duluth station had a camera crew out there. I saw it on the news last night. Those yellow ribbons . . ." said Bud. "I talked to Hakala this morning. They did an autopsy. He was flying on angel dust. Who names drugs these days?"

"Pick a hospital, with a good inpatient program."

"I've always thought highly of St. Helen's. It's right in town. And I built their new children's wing—"

"Call them. Reserve a bed."

"I'll call Louise in the morning. She can make the arrangements." Louise was Bud's personal secretary at the foundation.

"No, you call, now."

"What if they don't have a bed open?"

"Pick up the phone."

Bud picked up the bedside phone, balked, and appealed, "You think I really need to go, like, in the hospital?"

"Dial," said Harry.

It took half an hour to get the bed reserved. Bud had to call the director of the hospital at home during dinner. When it was done, Bud grimaced and held up a tiny paper cup and peered inside. "They took me off Dilaudid. Fucking Tylenol."

"Noon tomorrow," said Harry.

"St. Helen's, Christ they run their CD ward like boot camp."

"Good," said Harry. "When did Linda say she could have the divorce summons ready?"

"Huh? Oh. Tomorrow. Why?"

"Somebody has to put them in her hand."

Bud pulled his sheets around his shoulders and snuggled deeper in his pillows and his eyes drifted out the window and watched St. Paul light its lamps against the desolate twilight.

The El Salvador killings and Washington reaction dominated the six o'clock news. Video footage of a muddy field filled the screen with adobe-colored earth and heavy, moist saffron air. The Latin cops wore white shirts, tight gray pants, and sunglasses. Their slim physiques, long black hair, and large pistols were reminiscent of the Vietnamese Special Police.

Harry understood the scene on the TV. The friction of living in a match factory with open vats of gasoline led to a certain fatalism and sensitivity to the spark of violence.

But that violence was tied to social and political forces. The scene up north was Perry Mason shit. Stuff he didn't understand.

He'd have a clearer picture when he talked to Reverend Karson.

Randall called and said he had a care package from Dorothy. Harry told him to come on over. Thirty minutes later, Randall showed up with a casserole. Harry put it in the fridge.

"They killed the story," Harry said.

Randall's eyes wandered the apartment, paused on the travel gear laid out on the bed, and returned to Harry's face. He raised an eyebrow. "How was last night?"

"Wet," said Harry.

For a long time they watched each other; a conversation with their eyes that went back over the years. The older man sought a patience in the younger man, an acceptance. Harry felt a flush of envy. Every line in Randall's face bore the name of a battle or a great man. He'd done it all.

Randall slowly shook his head. "Look. Bud's a devious fuckup. His life is a wreck, so he's trying to avoid it by worrying about you. He called. He's concerned you're not working the AA program. Quote, that your life is starting to get unmanageable, unquote. He says I should tell you to go to a meeting."

Harry laughed. "I'm checking *him* into a treatment program at noon tomorrow. You telling *me* to go to a meeting?"

"I'm telling you to pay more attention to your blind side."

"This is for real. People up there want to see Bud dead."

"And you owe him so much. Why is that? Because he helped you sober up, get a job? You would have done that on your own. He cultivated your friendship. It wouldn't have happened normally. There's something off in the chemistry."

Harry shook his head. "Bud had shrapnel pulled out of his ass in Third Med at Dong Ha just like you and me. He left the best part of himself on that ridge in Nam when he got the Congressional . . .

"That's romantic bullshit. The Purple Heart's the only medal you can't fake."

"What are you saying?"

Randall shrugged. "I pushed paratroops for twenty-five years. Bud isn't like you. He's a taker, not a giver."

"Bud's all about giving. It's what he does for a living."

"He gives advice and money, neither of which cost him squat."

The air turned brittle. Harry shook his head. "I gotta do this. This is my fight."

Randall pointed a finger in an uncharacteristically rude gesture.

"Your blind side is your loyalty. It's exaggerated. It saved Dorothy and me, and it's still exaggerated."

"I stepped into the middle of something. I'm going to walk out the tracks."

Randall stood up and put on his coat. "What about the woman?"

"She's part of it," said Harry ambiguously.

"You've been sitting at a desk for ten years. We're not who we were, thank God. You could tangle with some real rough-cut people up there. Loyalty isn't just a blind side. It's a predictable pattern. Remember patterns?"

"Riddles don't help me right now, Randall."

"You've got it fucked around in your head to where your buddy is up to his ass in shit and you can't let him down. You can't run away. This has nothing to do with Bud, this is a bad old tape about your father." The finger stabbed again, lecturing.

Harry was starting to get pissed off and the flash of anger raised the shadow that dwelled deep in his muscles. The story in his family was that his dad's physical gifts were terrifying in a man, but just about right for a wild animal.

His voice snapped. "You taking up amateur psychology in your old age, Randall?" It came out flat and nasty, a particularly brutal resentment between a younger man and an older man. Between a father and a son.

Harry had never seen Randall show anger. He parried Harry's hot eyes with the bland, accommodating smile he'd learned to wear all those years hanging out with the Vietnamese. "I just hope you remember what I taught you. I have a feeling you're going to need it," he said.

Harry closed the door after him and muttered, "Goddamn you, Randall, if I could have picked my own father I would have chosen you." You're wrong, old man. I *can* handle it. I have to. Because it scares me.

He took the shoebox that contained ten numbered one-year AA medallions and his medals out of the closet. He cast them, ribboned stars and brass circles, in a random pattern on the table. He selected the ten-year AA pin and set it aside.

Carefully he unrolled a musty Buddhist wall hanging. Mildew had eaten parts away and the once brightly colored threads were faded now and his fingers came away from the frayed cloth dusted with a fine talcum of red dirt.

Some Buddhist tough love. Go to your worst fear, embrace it, and see it as a product of your mind.

The Tibetan tanka portrayed a Buddha sitting in the lotus position. A blood-red naked woman sat in his lap in a sexual posture with her legs wrapped around his waist. Her violent hair streamed up into flames and her upstretched arms turned into claws. The Buddha's teeth projected as fangs. Skulls were woven into the woman's fiery hair.

She is here, the Vietnamese used to say. In groves of bamboo, not pine . . .

Go see what was in the card she had facedown on the table.

Bet it all.

24

"Circle the wagons, the bitch is on a rampage!" Bud shouted on the phone.

Harry had overslept. Awake now.

Bud's voice was outraged. "I've been on the phone all morning to Stanley. I called the locksmith at the hardware store and sent him to the lodge to change the locks. He gets there and finds Jesse and that shit-bird Cox *with a fucking chainsaw* hacking the figurehead out of the woodwork over the fireplace. They got Cox's truck and they're loading it up with everything that isn't nailed down . . ."

He took a breath, "So I call Emery and get him over there and he at least gets them to put down the chainsaw, but he says she's got a right to half the stuff we bought after we got married . . . Jesus. The locksmith calls me and says he's isn't going near the place till things settle down. Then he tells me he was having coffee with one of the Hakalas, Greg, who owns the bank, and hears the latest gossip. Jesse drained the business account we set up for the lodge. There was 125,000 bucks in that account. Every cent I had that isn't tied up in investments. I've been shot and now I've been fucking robbed!" Bud paused, "What?"

"Welcome back, Bud," Harry laughed.

"Very fucking funny. Thing is, according to Emery and Margoles, it isn't robbery because, technically, the business account—since Jesse and I set it up jointly after the goddamn wedding—can be considered marital property. Sonofabitch! And while this is going on I'm in a hospital doped up. I gotta get outta here, man, and get up there before she carries off the whole damn lake bucket by bucket!"

"Calm down," said Harry.

"*Calm down?*"

"It's a game. Get it? She's negotiating. First she softens you up with a Mau Mau routine, then she lets you off if you give her a truck full of money."

"Easy for you to say. She's got my plastic, man, my Visa, American Express—"

"Sit tight. Get on the horn and call Visa or whatever and tell them to freeze the accounts."

"Stop by Linda's office and pick up the summons and petition. I want that snake served. A chainsaw, Harry. They were cutting my house apart with a *chainsaw!*"

"Look. You clear Ramsey. I'll pick up the divorce papers and tuck you into St. Helen's—"

"No shit," said Bud. "I need a court order. An injunction, something to freeze assets. Emery won't keep an eye on the place. He's still carrying a torch for her. Jesus, what a mess."

"Hey, Bud. Trust me. You sit this one out. Get your head straight. Now listen. I'm going to ask you for a favor."

"Sure. Hell, Harry, anything."

"I want the keys to the lodge. I'm going up there and take care of your things for a while. Until this settles down."

"No way. That's definitely out. I don't want you anywhere near that place. Not after—"

"You can't do it. You made a deal with Hakala. I'm the logical one."

"God, Harry."

"Think about it. I'll be at Ramsey at noon. Meet me in the lobby." Harry hung up. Bud would fight it, but he'd cave in.

The introspection of last night was gone. He enjoyed the slant of bronze sunlight against his skin and the texture of the carpet under his bare feet. The day felt brand new and a little bit dangerous.

The phone rang again. It was the department store. His suit was ready. He pulled on his sweats and went through the skyways to Dayton's, picked up the suit, and charged a pair of dress shoes, two silk ties, a belt, and two shirts.

He hung the suit on his closet door, black and authoritative. Flipped on his FM tuner and searched for the station that didn't have a lot of commercials, that played vintage '60s. He called Linda Margoles at her office. Linda was way ahead of him. The papers were being typed up as they spoke.

He turned the radio up and took a shower. Shaving was tricky, with the scabs, but he grinned and sang along with Bob Dylan's "Positively Fourth Street."

With a scissors, he trimmed the stitch ends down closer to the knot under his left eye. Then he dug out his shoeshine kit and slapped a spit-shine on the new shoes until the leather gleamed and twisted the reflection of his face into a crooked smile.

Dressed. Threw the Italian silk tie in a half-Windsor, smoothed his hands once down his lapels.

On his way out he slipped the AA medallion in his pocket. He took the elevator to the parking garage and tossed his duffel into his car. Then he hit the skyways with a roll to his walk, cutting smooth angles, a ripple of hipster muscle in a hot-shit black double-breasted suit.

He went to his bank and withdrew $2,000 from savings. The twenty $100 bills were crisp and new. He had never seen an old $100 bill.

Harry walked into the first hair salon he came upon. A blond receptionist stared up from her morning coffee.

"Fit me in. I got a heavy day," he said, handing her a twenty.

She would have been pretty, the genuine Scandinavian article, if her skin hadn't been artificially tanned to the texture of a Zulu shield. She grinned at his face. "Rough night, huh?"

"And I'm going back for more," Harry smiled.

Down on the street the air nipped the fresh tonic on his ears. He hailed a cab. "Selby and Dale," he told the driver.

Selby and Dale was an intersection in the Hill District behind the cathedral where turn-of-the-century mansions gave way to vacant lots and run-down storefronts.

"Stop over there," Harry pointed. "Keep the engine running, I'll be back in five minutes," Harry got out.

The bar's name was a mystery of broken gray neon and two slit windows gave it a besieged inner-city squint. The door was sprayed with the tangled prophecy of gang symbols imported from Chicago.

The interior smelled of stale beer and smoke and the felt on the pool table was patched with duct tape. Beer cases stacked on the peeling linoleum. Cheap Formica tables. Goodwill aluminum tube chairs.

Two sets of eyes clicked on him through the gloom; the bartender and an old dusty fucker in a shapeless overcoat whose knotty fingers grew out of the bar and twisted around a glass.

Harry bowed his eyes to the shrine of bottles.

"You lost?" asked the bartender, who was bald, with the wide, calm face of a world-weary African Buddha. His ropey forearms shone with scars.

Harry inhaled, shot his cuffs, and swung onto a barstool.

"Yeah," said Harry. "I'm lost. Find me a drink."

"So whaddya want?"

"Jack Daniel's. Double, straight up."

The bartender shrugged, wiped his hands on his apron, and poured two shots into a glass. With the deliberation of ceremony, Harry placed the ten-year AA medallion next to the glass. The bartender chewed the inside of his lip and looked directly into Harry's eyes.

"Know what this is?" Harry asked.

"Uh-huh. But it don't buy no whiskey," said the bartender.

"Like a medal," Harry said, picking up the medallion and weighing it on his index finger. "Got me another medal. *That* one they give me for saving somebody else's life. So I'm gonna keep that one. But this one"—he studied the medallion—"they give me for saving my own life. Now what do you call a guy who gives himself a medal for saving his own ass?"

The bartender studied him. "Man, what the fuck is your story?"

"I missed a payment on my clean, safe life and they took it back."

Harry tipped the drink to his lips and drank half of it. The gasoline tingle evaporated through the roof of his mouth and he felt a boost of fuel-injected sweat. He left the glass half full to prove he was in control.

"Keep the change," said Harry. He tossed down a twenty and left the AA coin on the bar.

He had the cabby drop him at the cathedral. Down the hill, the windows of St. Paul shimmered like purple seashells in a cold cloak of steam.

He wasn't wearing an overcoat, and it was freezing, but he walked unhurried toward the downtown loop. Halfway there, he stopped in a cafe and had a cup of black coffee.

Then he walked again, using the cold to work an edge. He walked until his nose and his hands were red and his ears stung. The alcohol traveled through his body and affected his balance. Like walking in a pair of ten-year-old shoes.

He'd read somewhere that it takes an hour for your system to process an ounce of alcohol.

He headed for the word factory.

Perfectly creased and coiffed but skewed by the cold, he stepped off the elevator. A female reporter stood waiting for the door to open. Suzanne was married now with two kids and had filled out in an appealing way, but she still had those great fucked-out eyes . . .

"Ye God," she raised her hand to her mouth, seeing his face.

"Trick or treat," said Harry.

"Nice suit," she said as he went by. People saw him and froze. Ha, he thought. The Story Walks Among You.

He stopped at the bulletin board and looked around. Franky Murphy moved across the newsroom, a mobile zit in a tableau of statues.

Someone came up behind and took him by the arm. Arnie Cummings.

"Harry, there you are . . ." Arnie paused, sniffed. "Christ, you smell like a gin mill. This is a hell of a time to fall off the wagon."

Murphy danced into Harry's vision. "You set me up, you sonofabitch."

"Two things I hate, Franky. A liar and a thief."

Franky pointed a narrow finger. "I'll get you, fucker, just wait."

So much for the ounce-an-hour theory. Squirt one shot into the swamp, add a dash of hassle, and the shadowy figure bubbles up from its enchanted sleep. "Why wait?" Harry grinned, poised on the balls of his feet, ready for something.

The pressure of Arnie's hand turned rough, pulling him away from Murphy.

Harry bristled. "Don't mess with me, Arnie."

"You'll blow this if you talk to the boss smelling like booze."

"Hands off!"

People standing, at desks, in midstride, all eyes glued to the tugging match at the bulletin board.

Arnie pulled him toward the lobby. "C'mon. Let's take a walk. There's time. Get you something . . ."

Harry broke Arnie's grip with a sharp, combat-speed arc of his forearm. Arnie tottered back, off balance. Recovering, he stepped forward, angry now, struggling to keep his voice down.

"I'm trying to help you, you dumb shit." For emphasis, Arnie thumped Harry on the chest.

"Don't touch me," Harry warned.

"Listen, you!" Arnie said, determined, his knuckle rapping over Harry's sternum.

"Get back!" He meant to push Arnie away, just get him out of his face. But Arnie's hands came up defensively like he might throw a punch.

The shadow sprinted in Harry's blood, showy and nasty.

Somebody screamed. Harry got control of the punch at the last second and the viscous left hook arced an inch from Arnie's shocked face. Harry's knuckles furrowed into the bulletin board, crushing a plastic stick pin. Harry recoiled into a fighting stance with blood on his knuckles. Dots of it on Arnie's cheeks.

"What is this? The parking lot in high school?" Arnie's voice shook.

Harry dropped his hands.

"Outside," ordered Arnie. Harry pushed past him into the lobby and down the stairwell exit. They left the building and went out on the street.

"What the fuck was that all about?" yelled Arnie.

Harry sucked his bleeding knuckle. "You pushed me."

Arnie shook his head. Diplomatically, he said, "I'll take care of it. We can talk to the boss when you get back." There was a resigned plea in his voice. Just get out of here. Take the mess out of sight.

Harry gave Arnie a vacant grin. The idea of coming back had not occurred to him.

"Watch yourself, man. You got a lot of people freaked," muttered Arnie, not making eye contact.

"You bet." Harry walked off toward his parking garage.

25

Harry left his Honda Civic parked illegally in front of the First National Bank building and dashed for the elevator. Linda's office was on the seventh floor.

She saw him when he entered the reception area. At work, she drew herself down tight as a health-spa panther in a blue power suit. She padded toward him.

"Harry, your hand is bleeding," she said crisply. "I suppose it's apt that the first time I see you in a suit you look like you came from a brawl."

Harry sucked on the bloody knuckle. "I love you, too. Where's the divorce papers?"

"What do you mean? Bud picked them up a half hour ago."

Harry firmly took her by the elbow. "Say again?" he asked.

"You're getting blood on my jacket," she enunciated. Harry released his grip. "He came by and asked for the papers. Said he was going to serve them. I told him to have someone else do it. He's not supposed to actually hand them over himself."

"Christ. He's out—" Harry started for the elevators. Linda kept pace.

"He didn't look well, even considering that he'd been shot. And he was dressed . . . weird. He asked to borrow some cash," said Linda.

"Why didn't you keep him here?" Harry spun on her.

"He's my client. Not my swim-check partner at summer camp. I assumed he was on his way to see you."

"He's bottoming out of a year-long drunk and he's devious as a snake. I'm supposed to haul his ass into treatment at noon today so he ran from Ramsey. If he comes back this way, hold on to him. I'll call." The elevator door closed before she could reply.

It would be funny if it wasn't so damned serious. The million-dollar kid, on foot and penniless in his hometown. Christ. He could still have credit cards. What if he chartered a plane? Hopped a Greyhound? Was in a Hertz rent-a-car right now cruising north on 35?

Next stop, the Maston Foundation. This time he double-parked in front, leaving his flashers on. He bounded up the stairs into a marble-pillared, oak-paneled atrium. Louise Lennon, Bud's elegantly appointed mastiff, sat behind her desk. Her color looked a little steamed.

"Bud," said Harry.

"Mr. Griffin, in my opinion they should have not let Mr. Maston out of the hospital in a gymnasium suit and tennis shoes."

"How long ago was he here, Louise?"

"Fifteen minutes. He asked . . ." Her cheeks reddened slightly, "for a loan and for the use of my automobile. That alarmed me, after everything that has happened."

Harry drew in his breath. "Did you give him your car?"

"No, he withdrew the request when he saw this on my desk." She held up a poster that portrayed an American Indian drum. An *Assembly of Men—Tad Clark.* Sponsored by the Maston Foundation. Today. At the old Rivers Hotel on Kellogg Boulevard. Louise cleared her throat. "He called Steve Cotter and asked to borrow money."

Shit. Cotter was the manager of the Rivers Hotel. He'd give Bud the shirt off his back.

"Tell him to wear a hat," Louise sang out after Harry. "There's a storm . . ."

The Rivers. Shoulda figured. Bud still kept a suite of rooms. The wounded animal always returns to its den.

Bud had lived there for years. The Rivers was a crumbling brick relic that had been slated for demolition for three decades. George Armstrong Custer had reputedly received his last haircut in the hotel barber shop. Bud had a soft spot for the old wreck and had managed to get it on the Historical Register. The hotel bar had been their old drinking haunt.

He ran six blocks and a red light in fourth gear and left the Honda idling, flashers on, in front of the hotel, and went into the lobby. Bennett, the reception clerk, had a startled twitch to his handlebar mustache as if he just seen an elephant graze through the ferns in the lobby.

"Where is he?" Harry demanded.

Bennett rolled his eyes toward the bar, which had swinging doors that Harry knocked wide apart going in. A small early luncheon crowd looked up from their small sandwiches and large tumblers. An aroma of sawdust, whiskey, and tobacco smoke cured the air. The long horseshoe bar had a rail. Tall stools. Circa 1860 spittoons. No Bud. He walked to his old stool and drummed his fingers over the scarred teak bar. He kept his left hand out of sight.

Snowflakes as big as half dollars cartwheeled against the windows.

Tony, the bartender, wore a vest and a look of discreet curiosity held close to it. As he wiped the bar and put down a fresh ashtray, he purred, "Harry, haven't seen you in a while. Read about you though. What's up?"

"You seen Bud?"

"He's in the back with Steve." Tony glanced at the windows and made bluff conversation. "This one's coming from the West. Lifted the roof off the Rockies and is going to drop it smack on us. You want some coffee?"

Steve kept a safe in the back. Harry stared at the office door at the rear of the room. So play it safe with nineteen showing or push it a little. "Hit me," said Harry.

"Come again?"

"Jack Daniel's. Double. Straight up," said Harry, putting a five down on the bar. Felt right. No. Necessary. No way he could pull off tomorrow morning straight. *Damn.* He needed those divorce papers.

The drink arrived. He raised it and peered through the distorted prism of the thick tumbler at the mural of Custer's Last Stand that stretched across the back wall next to the office door.

Custer stood in the center of the painting, his sword raised as the redskins closed in. At first Harry didn't recognize Bud when he came out of the office with a wad of folding cash clutched in one hand and a drink in the other. No beard. He'd cut his hair, shorn it, penitent-fashion, down to the scalp. A baggy maroon U of M sweatshirt hung from his shoulders.

Bud stared at him and the stalk of celery protruding from the sturdy Bloody Mary in his hand began to shake. Bud gulped the drink, dropped the glass, scuttled around the bar, went between a screen of tall potted palms, and out the side door.

Harry gave chase down the hotel corridor. "Hold it right there," he yelled.

"You're drinking. All bets are off," Bud yelled back as he hobbled, favoring his left side. He turned a corner and went down a corridor of banquet rooms. The hall stopped in a dead end. Bud looked left and right and choose the door to the left, the one with a drum poster stuck to it.

An Assembly of Men.

Christ. Harry paused at the door and took a deep breath. Like two more symptoms of desperation, the men's movement and the state lottery had surfaced at about the same time in Minnesota. Same bunch that staged the production for public TV up at Bud's lodge. He opened the door and entered the large hotel suite.

The furniture was shoved in a big circle and an elusive Plains Indian flute played low on a stereo. Stuff on the walls. Masks. Spears. Pine scent trickled from sticks of burning incense.

Thirty guys who didn't need to be at work on Monday morning stood around. They tended toward carefully groomed beards, sensitive eyes, and affluent bodies starved from exercise.

Bud's disheveled entrance and now Harry's bloody left hand created a nervous murmur. Bud talked urgently to a portly dude in a fringed buckskin shirt with a leonine mane of black Grecian Formula hair crawling down his neck.

Bud's electric blue eyes danced around the room. Gregarious Bud, trying to work the crowd, groping for his social magic.

But this gang had read the papers. They regarded him as if he'd staggered down off a sand dune on Mars; sloppy, wild-eyed, badly dressed, stitches in his lower lip, and a round, messy stain leaking from his bandaged left side, soaking through his sweatshirt.

Bud stepped behind the endomorph in buckskin. "Leave me alone, I mean it," he challenged as Harry went straight for him.

"Hold on, there," rumbled the big man. Tad Clark had had a reputation in the Cities as a "cause person," now he'd trimmed his political sails. Now everybody was his own cause. Harry moved Clark aside and seized Bud's wrist. The Assembly of Men began to assemble.

"Look out, he's been drinking," Bud warned in a loud voice.

Coldly, Harry said, "Make a hole. I'm taking Mr. Maston back to the hospital where he belongs."

Bud tried to pull free. Harry snapped his wrist into a gooseneck come-along. Bud resisted and Harry discovered there was still considerable physical strength in his large body. Harry wrenched the arm violently, locking the elbow and wrist, stiffening it into a fulcrum. "Ow!" Bud cried out in pain.

Clark stepped forward and put a loose hand on Harry's shoulder. "No rough stuff. Don't you know Bud's been . . . hurt?"

"Watch it, Tad. He's dangerous," said Bud.

With his free hand, Harry pulled Tad Clark close and his face, with the scabs streaked across his nose and cheeks, could have modeled one of the Algonquin warrior masks Clark had hung on the wall.

He whispered in Clark's ear. "I'm his best friend. See. He's under a great deal of strain because his life just blew up in his face and he's been drinking. I'm taking him where he can get proper attention. And I'm about out of patience. Call off the tribe or I swear to God I'll pop out your left eyeball and skull-fuck you to death."

Tad's large eyes turned to Bud. Bud sagged and his swollen lower lip trembled. "I can't let you go up there, Harry. It's my responsibility."

Tad Clark stepped back. "Where are you taking him?" he whispered.

"St. Helen's. There's a bed reserved on the CD ward. That's not for broadcasting, you understand?"

"You're the one who saved his life. You shot the boy," said Tad Clark. "Your picture was in the paper."

"Okay, it's all over, folks. Out of the way," said Harry.

Bud went docilely. Harry collared his arm around Bud's shoulder and walked him to the lobby where he pried Cotter's money and his car keys from Bud's hand and left them with Bennett at the desk.

"Take it easy, asshole," muttered Harry as they walked out into a blast of snow.

Bud began to shake. "Harry, one of us has to stay straight. When I'm fucked up I might marry the wrong person. You . . ." A violent spasm of shaking ended his sentence. His teeth chattered. "No shit. I think I might have a touch of the DTs."

At the curb, Harry reached in the backseat, pulled out his parka, and threw it over Bud's shoulders. Then he helped Bud into the cramped front seat and got behind the wheel.

"Jesus," breathed Harry. He wiped his palm across his forehead.

"Almost made it," said Bud. "Would have if I hadn't ordered a drink—"

"The papers," ordered Harry.

Bud reached under his sweatshirt and pulled out the legal document. An unhealthy glaze of spoiled meat slicked his face as he rolled his eyes and said, "I've never seen you in a suit before. You look good."

26

The storm dumped on St. Paul and it was twilight at noon. The street-lights switched on and the edges of buildings turned grainy at 100 yards and the street became a skating rink. Cars skidded. The drivers, descendants of Scandinavian berserks, looked up and grinned.

They were a block from the hospital when Bud quipped, "Heads up, gook in the open."

Harry hit the brakes and just missed hitting a short brown man who tried to cross against the light on one leg and a crutch. The Hmong tipped over in a light jacket and one dilapidated tennis shoe and a safety pin fastened his empty flapping pantleg and long black hair streamed around his square, lined face as he plopped on his ass in the snow. He cocked his head and fixed Harry with onyx eyes and raised a wrinkled hand in a disturbing gesture. Harry averted his face from the black shaman gaze as a crowd of pedestrians rushed into the slippery street.

"No shit. That's Billy Tully," said Bud, suddenly energized as he recognized a pin-striped rhino with a shock of white hair who lumbered from under a restaurant awning to the cripple's aid. Harry groaned. The one-legged Hmong had to fall down in front of McDermit's, where the Democratic party faithful ate their long lunches. It was a small town.

"This'll just take a second," said Bud briskly. Manic, he surged out the door. Harry immediately was out after him, poised for another escape attempt. Bud and Billy Tully outdid each other, helping the guy to his foot, handing him his crutch.

"It's Harry, right, we've met. Party at Tim and Dorothy's," Tully said smoothly under his breath as he deftly shook Harry's hand in the commotion. His Scotch-gored eyes took in Harry's battered face and the spectacle of a shorn Bud Maston appearing out of the snow in a baggy sweat suit. Unfazed, he inquired, "So how is our boy doing?"

"Shit," muttered Harry. "I'm trying to get his ass to St. Helen's to take the cure. It's turning into an all-day job."

"You did good up there. We won't forget it, son," said Tully. He patted Harry and the Hmong on the shoulder simultaneously. "Now let's get Bud off this street full of voters, shall we?" Harry was for that. He clamped a hand on Bud's elbow as cars honked their horns and people gathered.

Tully turned to Bud and a sirloin grin parted the webbed capillaries of his face. "Christ, Bud, you look like you been shot at and hit." He winked and wheezed as he handed the stoic Hmong a business card.

"Well I have been, Billy, I have been," said Bud, gushing sweat that steamed in the blowing snow, oblivious that a watery nosebleed crept down his upper lip and reddened the horror-show stitches in his purple, swollen lower lip.

Caught in the conjunction of a gathering crowd and Bill Tully, the ultimate fixer, the grotesque stump of Bud Maston's amputated ambition waved out of the delirium tremens and the snow came down like the confetti of the victory parade he never had and he threw his free arm around the Hmong's shoulder and hugged him like they were old asshole buddies.

"No, Bud," hissed Harry but Bud had already launched into his best Bud-Maston-Cares baritone: "This man fought for America and we bugged out and hung him out to dry. I'll bet he swam the Mekong River to get out of Laos. With one leg. And now he can't even get benefits from a veterans hospital." He paused for breath and shot a quick aside to Harry in a low voice. "You have any money, so he can take a cab?"

"Fuck me dead." Harry dug out the roll of bills. Bud pulled one off the top and handed it over.

"What a minute! That's a hundred!" Harry protested. But the Hmong had already pocketed the bill and was making like Long John Silver toward the nearest building lobby.

Bud steepled his hands in a Buddhist devotion and called after him. "Najoong." He turned to Harry. "Is that the right word?"

"Time-out, Bud," said Tully. He pinned one of Bud's arms, Harry had the other and they dragged him to the Honda.

Bud wagged a finger in Tully's face. "Guy should at least have an artificial leg. All our fucking fault, Billy, all that crap we did, the dope and the marches and the fucking McGovern campaign. We were partying and left the Neanderthals to mind the store." The crowd had drifted away. Bud was babbling to the snow.

Tully glanced at the ghostly lights of St. Paul and laughed. "And empty office buildings and beggars on the street. Wipe your nose, Bud."

Bud wiped his nose but tatters of old speeches still fell out of his mouth: "Thirteen-year-olds joining gangs, carrying guns. Reagan's children—they grew right out of the goddamn concrete."

Tully's pouchy eyes glowered. "Put the cork in it, Bud. Let Harry here take you to the hospital and here's the word: you do this right and maybe you can pull off a come back."

Bud gave Tully his full attention. "Well, I don't know, Billy, after that thing up north," he said dubiously. "And now the CD ward."

"Nothing wrong with that in Minnesota. It's an acceptable rite of passage. Like losing your virginity. As far as up north goes, figure out how to put that kid into a nice rap about drugs." Tully smiled. "You know, turn it into a fucking speech. In there." Tully pointed at the brick bastille of the hospital down the street. "And make that marriage go away. Then call me after a decent interval, we'll talk," said Tully tartly. Bud's five minutes were up. They shook hands.

"Get in the car," said Harry. He shoved and Tully's hand guided Bud's head so he wouldn't bump it on the door.

Bud wheezed, fitted himself back in the front seat, and dusted snow from his scalp. He waved bye-bye to Tully, who gave him thumbs up.

"Hmong die in their sleep, you know that," said Bud with a perplexed grin. "For no apparent medical reason. They get yanked out of their jungle and get dumped in a city on the other side of the world and they fucking die. Weird, huh?"

"Look, showboat, I need the keys to the lodge," said Harry doggedly as he skidded to a stop in front of the hospital.

"What?" Bud shook his head. His teeth chattered. "Man. I don't feel so hot."

"You'll be fine. They'll take care of you. Give me the keys."

Bud winced as he reached in his pocket and pulled out a thick key ring. Each key had a neatly printed legend on a strip of adhesive. "This one is to my grandfather's gun cabinet. Make sure they didn't take any-thing. This one's the Jeep. Garage-door opener is under the front seat."

Harry took the keys. "You all set?"

"Wait—what are you going to do?"

"Make sure the rabble don't sack Castle Frankenstein. And serve the divorce papers."

"You don't know your way around up there, Harry—"

"I know where she'll be at eleven o'clock tomorrow morning."

"Christ, you're serious." Bud had a lucid episode, aghast through his pallor.

"C'mon. Let's get you inside."

They were expecting Bud at the desk. "I think he may be in alcohol shock," Harry told a nurse.

"We'll get a wheelchair," the nurse replied. But nobody moved.

Bud grinned weakly. "No tickee, no washee," he said as he pulled his wallet from his pocket and dropped a Blue Cross card on the counter.

They stamped the plastic, resumed their efficient attentiveness, and called for a wheelchair.

"Get some rest, Bud. I'll be in touch." Harry squeezed Bud's arm.

Bud reacted with a loud tantrum of resentment. "You're the one who belongs in here, not me!" Heads turned in the reception area.

Bud Maston slouched over, feeble and bitter in his baggy sweat suit, with his cueball haircut and a ring of flab hanging around his neck, he looked like a lost recruit on the first day of basic training being shunted off to the fatboys' platoon.

27

With Bud under wraps, he was free.

Free also from Randall with his Geritol advice and Linda. Didn't need their nagging or Bud's raving. Never did believe that stuff about alcoholism being a disease. Doctors and hospitals and weepy therapy groups. Nobody's fault. Let's all be victims together. Through being sick. Be weak or be strong. The Honda idled at the curb. He was traveling in his head.

He pawed through his tapes, found the one to blow him out of town, slapped it in the deck, and cranked the volume way up.

He sucked the blood from his skinned knuckle, glanced at his scarred face in the rearview mirror, and popped the clutch to a thunder of guitar chords and the bawl of Waylon Jennings. The Honda fishtailed onto the streets of St. Paul.

Now that would be an AA group he'd love to sit in on. Waylon, Kris, Willie, and Johnny Cash singing through raw holes in their livers, wallowing in Confederate self-pity . . .

Harry leaned on his horn. Goddamn Minnesota drivers. Car in front too slow coming off a light. Stop-go-red-green-walk-don't walk. A block later, he ran an amber, and forced a car onto the shoulder on his way to the freeway ramp.

He had blowing snow and the open four-lane ahead of him. And a full tank of gas and a roll of new $100 bills in his pocket. Johnny Cash waved him on singing about gunplay in Reno.

Driving the wrong car. The Honda had a lot of heart—no, his old Plymouth Valiant had heart. A Jap car wouldn't have heart; it would have what they called *ki* in Shotokan karate.

He drove out of the storm at Forest Lake and Interstate 35 ran straight to the horizon fouled with billboards. Visualizing the gray, rolling Gobi of Superior, he made good time on plowed, salted roads.

Kris Kristofferson warbled in his whiskey-cured, bedroom voice about ribbons and hair falling down and again, he felt her, fire and ice in the moonlight, double-crossing her legs over an intersection of deceit and maybe murder. Harry stepped on the gas.

By late afternoon he was past Duluth. On North 61, orange men left their pickups and plodded up logging trails with rifles. Twilight netted the black pines with creeping shadows and a diamond-shaped yellow sign danced in his headlights with the imprint of a leaping white-tailed buck. He crossed into Maston County and a tingle of fear enhanced the dark. Sheriff Larry Emery owned this night.

But crossing that line clarified his unruly exit from St. Paul. He knew for the first time in a long time—maybe ever—exactly what he was doing. He had killed a sixteen-year-old boy, and while the official version of events might satisfy the local politicians, it didn't square with his conscience. He wasn't leaving Maston County until he knew why Chris pointed that gun. Period.

He passed a clapboard church with a nativity scene arranged in the snow. Six-foot plastic camels were planted under strings of gaudy Christmas lights with three wise men, and baby Jesus was some kid's doll in a bale of hay. Those dudes are lost, he thought—Mediterranean desert nomads making their wish against the black Ojibway forest. Wasn't even Thanksgiving yet.

A stand of shadowy red oaks hitchhiked among the pines and Harry grinned. He'd been raised by Germans, his mother's people. Druids, under the Protestant shellac. Had learned superstitions from his grandmother. The Christmas tree was put up the night before Christmas. Bad luck to start the symbolism too early.

If only the trees out there that morning could talk. You could try and try and you'd never understand all the detail in a tree, all the gnarls and turns and subtlety of foliage.

The insides of people were like trees. You could never see it all.

Harry drove toward the lights of Stanley, turned off the highway, and made a run down Main Street. Like bad omens, a festive crepe of red and green Christmas decorations draped the street and the lights burned in the Camp Funeral Home.

He rolled down the window and let the pure oxygen suck the city from his lungs. Not even the murmur of Superior broke the vast snow quiet, and soft woodsmoke chains drifted up and moored the little town to the icy northern stars. And somebody in this peaceful illusion had a reason, and enough influence, to get Chris Deucette to pull that trigger? Emery, out of jealousy? Jesse certainly, for the money. But Jay Cox was the wild card. Where did he fit?

He pulled in back of City Hall and parked in front of the liquor store. A trio of Indian winos stamped their feet next to the door. Going in, Harry threw them a snappy fraternal salute.

He bought a fifth of Jack Daniel's, then went to the pay phone next to the entrance, dug in his wallet, found Reverend Karson's card, and called the residence number.

A woman answered. "Uh, he's meeting with some people," she said.

"This is Harry Griffin. Tell him it's urgent."

Subdued conversation carried over the connection. "Harry," said Karson, "this is bad timing. I'm preparing a funeral service. Where are you?"

"I'll be staying out at Maston's lodge for a while."

"I see—"

"I need a favor, padre."

"Uh, let me take this in the basement on another line," said Karson. A minute later, Karson's voice came back on. "Martha, would you hang up the upstairs phone, please."

"Martha your wife?" asked Harry.

"We are used to dealing in confidences in this house. My wife is part of my ministry in that respect." He paused. "Where's Bud?"

"Tucked away in a CD ward in the city."

"You shouldn't be up here."

"Why? You said I didn't do anything wrong."

Karson exhaled. "What do you want, Harry?"

"I want to know about Jay Cox. I need his birthday and Social Security number—"

"Is this for a story? The newspaper?" Karson's apprehensive voice turned curious.

"No, no. Just me. I'm on vacation, making sure nobody rips off Maston's house."

"Vacation? My God. Uh, I know Cox. Not well—"

"He's a real sweetheart, isn't he?"

"Look, I don't think I should say anything directly about Cox."

"Hey, padre. I thought you were the local good guy."

Silence on the line.

Harry tried again. "I wouldn't want you to say anything directly. Indirectly would be fine."

More silence. "After the funeral, Harry," said Karson. He hung up the phone.

The preacher was scared.

28

Harry wheeled into the lodge drive and Jay Cox froze in the headlights, stooped under the weight of an outboard motor he was lifting into the back of his truck. Harry left the brights on and got out.

"Put it down and clear off the property!"

Cox's face was a fistful of witch doctor bones in the harsh glare. *Watch yourself. They line up right and you're dead, brother.*

"Who're you? Maston's idea of a joke?" Cox grimaced as he heaved the motor into the bed of the truck and bent down for a can of gas. "She talked to a lawyer. She's got a right to half of everything new in that pole barn."

"Get her lawyer to convince a judge. Till then, everything stays."

They started to circle and Harry tried to keep the lights at his back, in Cox's face. Basic math. Cox went around six-one and two hundred pounds. An inch and twenty pounds on Harry. A real hard twenty pounds.

Box him, wear him out. Who was he kidding? He hadn't been in a real fight for twenty years. Cox was a brawler who'd close and break him in his powerful hands. Old street wisdom. Crazy covers tough. Harry looked around for an equalizer as their breath came in taut, white jets.

Cox bared his teeth. "Maston thinks he's pretty smart, bringing you up here. You threw me for a minute but you're just a game," he was talking himself into a rage, "just a soft-handed city guy. Go back down there and do whatever you do in some office. I'm only going to warn you once. This ain't your affair," he growled.

Harry wore a crazy grin as he stepped into the jerky pins-and-needles of a fight and felt his way toward the first punch. He reached over, seized the stem of the outboard motor and, with a shift of his weight, toppled the motor off the tailgate. Cox backed out of the way.

"You're asking for it. I ain't opposed to beating up on crazy people," Cox warned. He slid sideways toward a big chainsaw sitting on a stump.

Cox's eyes darted and he started for the chainsaw. Harry, faster, cut him off, scooped the big red Jonsrud up by the handle, hoped it had gas in it, and flicked the switch.

He balanced on the balls of his feet, the saw casually in front of him, one hand on the handle, one hand gripping the ripcord. *Careful. Don't get gas on your new suit.*

"I always wondered," he shouted to keep his voice from shaking. "Put one of these to a big new radial tire. Would it go hiss or would it go bang?" he yanked the cord and the saw whirred alive. He let the blade fall in a lazy arc that stopped an inch from a rear truck tire.

"Watch it there, goddammit," Cox yelled, genuinely alarmed for his truck. "Those things are tricky."

The rage in Cox's eyes raced in a loop, as trapped as the necklace of steel teeth whipping around the chain bar. Might have to fight this man, but not tonight. He stepped back to give Cox room to walk to his truck.

Up close, in the brilliant headlights, Cox looked spooky as hell, but no longer scary. He looked . . . old. Tired. Breathing heavily with the strain of this confrontation.

For a moment they panted, measuring each other. Harry percolated with fear, but he knew it would vanish at the first blow. Cox's hooded eyes showed confusion. Dry-mouthed vacant pain.

Harry cut off the saw and put it to the ground. He lowered his eyes and stepped back to let Cox leave.

Cox hauled himself up, one hand on a big mirror bracket, and opened the door of his truck. When the door opened, the interior light came on and Harry saw the butt of a deer rifle half out of the case suspended in the gun rack over the seat.

I need a gun.

Cox snarled, "You don't scare me, you fucking faggot!"

Harry folded his arms across his chest.

Cox backed out of the driveway, one eye on his rearview mirror, the other on Harry. When the sound of the truck faded down the highway, Harry took out Bud's key ring and went to the lodge.

*   *   *

He expected more of a mess. A tall stepladder was tipped over in front of the fireplace in a pile of sawdust and, like Bud said, the bowsprit carving had been removed from the beams above the fireplace. The new furniture in the den was gone, but the sound system, TV, computer, and trestle table remained. The bookshelves were undisturbed. The kitchen was tidy, the silverware still lined up in the drawers.

The head and one paw of Sheriff Emery's bearskin dangled off the wall. Above it, someone had written in garish green spray paint: BUD IS A FUCKER!

He changed into jeans and boots and approached the sturdy oak gun cabinet next to the fireplace and found the heavy lock untampered with. Opening it, he saw a double-barreled shotgun, a 12-gauge pump, and an old lever-action .45-70 rifle. Ammunition was stacked in the drawer at the bottom of the rack. And something wrapped in a chamois cloth. A military Colt .45.

He pulled out the beautifully restored old Remington 12 gauge, searched in the drawer, opened a box of double-ought buck shells, and loaded it.

Back outside, he looked around. Nothing but the wind in the pines. Keeping the shotgun close at hand, he opened the pole barn, moved the pile of tools that Cox had assembled back inside, closed the sliding door, and locked it. Then he walked a slow circuit of the lodge grounds and paused to listen at the road. Convinced that Cox was gone, he switched on a flashlight and started cautiously down the trail between the log cabins toward the snowmobile trail.

He came to the frozen remnants of Becky's ski tracks where they'd left the trail and gone overland. Slowly he paced them until he came to the place where Emery had stooped in thought. The crusted snow was pocked and wind-spoiled and the trail disappeared in the drifts.

Something moved. He shined the light into the thicket of pines and a sharp nasal snort—not human—brought him to tingling alertness. Something big in there. Harry backed away and retreated down the trail.

He started Bud's Jeep in the garage under the addition. Almost full of gas and the tires looked all right. Then he took a look at the furnace and the fuse box and located three fire extinguishers.

Sleeping in one of the bedrooms was out. Too closed in. Averting his eyes from Chris's room, he went into the master bedroom where Bud had slept with Jesse. A musky morning scent, faintly perfumed, lingered in the stale air. The king-size mattress was bare, the dresser drawers pulled out and empty. Harry knelt to the floor in back of the bed and found spilled candle wax, some curls of incense, and several tiny, yellowed butts of marijuana cigarettes.

He dragged the mattress and box spring down the hall and positioned them in front of the fireplace. Then he heated water, searched the cupboards, and found some Lipton tea. With a hot mug of tea, he went to the desk in the den and methodically searched the drawers. Jesse said she kept books, seemed proud of it. Maybe there was something written down he could use to ID Cox.

Randall knew a lot of people. He had access to national databanks. Government computers. Dorothy knew some cops in Minneapolis and St. Paul from her days as a reporter.

The desk drawers were empty except for envelopes and the Snowshoe Lodge letterhead and some floppy disks.

He switched on the IBM computer. Simple office software. He went through the floppies, opening files. Text for brochures. Correspondence. Projected rates for lodging and fishing parties. He turned off the computer and flipped on the FM tuner and spent an hour cleaning up the main room: put the stepladder out on the front porch, swept up the pile of sawdust, retacked the bearskin, and brought in some kindling from the pile on the porch.

Cleaning out the fireplace, he found a fried can of charcoal starter among the ashes. A thick plume of soot disfigured the mantle from where they'd burned the Goyas and the wall artifacts on the hearth. Tilted on the endirons, a ferocious eye and gaping jaws leered from an unburned portion of the print that had hung in Chris's room. Harry built a fire and watched the flames consume the mad cannibal stare.

After a shower, he heated a can of Hormel chili from the cupboard and ate it with saltines.

He laid out his suit, flicked some lint from the jacket, and touched the divorce papers in the pocket. The new dress shirt was slightly wrinkled, his shoes a little scuffed, but they'd do.

He poked at the fire and tried to figure Cox. The guy had a rope-toughness you don't see on a white man unless he's done serious jail time or seen a lot of combat, but Cox had acted with restraint. He had been prepared to see Cox as Jesse's blunt instrument. Now he seemed more the damaged tool.

Not afraid of you? Same line Chris had used the night before it happened. Lot of people shook up in the wake of the shooting. Becky. Karson. Cox. Harry turned off the lamps and stared at the fire. What would Randall do in this situation?

Hell, Randall wouldn't get into this scene in the first place.

White pencils of light flashed through the darkened lodge, threaded the woods. Snowmobiles, on the trail around the lake.

He jumped when the phone jangled.

Karson's voice sounded like he'd been holding his breath since Harry hung up in the liquor store. "Ginny Hakala works at the Timber Cruiser Cafe. She used to go out with Cox." He hung up.

Harry made a note of the name and cautioned himself. Take it one step at a time. He glanced at the whiskey bottle that sat on the dining room table.

Better make that one drink at a time.

Didn't need it now. Would in the morning though. A couple shots to light the fuse.

He built up the fire, brought sheets, quilts and pillows, and made the bed. He checked the shotgun safety and placed it next to him on the mattress. The last cigarette of the day made an arc of sparks into the fireplace and Harry closed his eyes and exhaled, *If I should die before I wake . . .*

He drew up his knees and crossed his arms rigidly across his chest in the hopeful foxhole posture that attempted to cover his vital parts.

29

On Tuesday morning fog lay thick on Maston County. The kind of day Randall used to call Hitler weather.

Harry meditated in reverse. Not to relax. To twist himself tight. One by one, he detached the wires to faith, hope, and charity.

His plan was direct. Stir up the funeral with the divorce papers and watch the faces. The one with Freon in his veins, the one who had controlled Chris, might show himself—or herself. Look for the one who cracked first and go after him and get him to talk.

Get under the lie a few layers, then go back to Hakala and remind him that he had skipped impaneling a grand jury for self-serving reasons. Getting Bud in the hospital was the only deal Harry'd made. So fuck a bunch of politicians.

Hell, man, you just want to see her.

He pushed the unsettling thought aside. It all came down to Jesse and whose bed she was rising from on this gloomy morning. She was the only one with the strength of will to plan cold-blooded murder for money . . . and behind her loomed the shadow of Larry Emery. They'd be together today to bury their trigger-happy son.

He padded to the bathroom, undressed, and twirled the nozzle on the shower faucet. When the water turned icy he braced both palms against the shower tile and counted to a hundred.

So screw their funeral.

Stark fluorescent light bounced off the tile and painted the scabs on his face livid purple in the mirror. As he shaved, he mentally downshifted. Have to operate in one forward gear. No second thoughts.

They started it. They weren't the only ones who could play rough.

He sagged, splashed cold water on his face to clean off the lather, and inspected himself. Once he could have done it without remorse. But then he was young and didn't feel things.

Whole town might be there. Jesse, Emery, Cox, and Hakala for sure. Karson. Becky. Be walking across their graves. Their history.

He dressed, remembering Emery's cold parting promise. *"We'll meet again, motherfucker."* His fingers shook as he tried to knot his tie and he stared at his shivering hands.

For the first time in his life, he didn't kid himself about why he needed a drink. Minnesota Harry couldn't do it. Detroit Harry could. The bottle and the empty glass waited on the dining room table.

You don't see this through you'll be carrying that dead kid on your back as a question mark your whole goddamn life. He poured the glass full and let it run down his throat and into his caged places.

Steady now, with a Jack Daniel's snap, crackle, and pop in his fingertips, the tie flew into place. He transferred the divorce papers into the inside pocket of his jacket. Drive Bud's Jeep. It was black, like his suit.

The digital clock in the Jeep dashboard read 10:30. Plenty of time to stop for breakfast at the Timber Cruiser Cafe and check out this Ginny. Slowly he drove down Nanabozho Ridge.

Twelve deer carcasses dangled by their antlers from the big maple beside the General Store. Beads of frozen blood clung to the matted hair along the gutted bellies and twinkled in his low beams. Harry drove on, prowled into Stanley, and went looking for the Lutheran church.

Trinity Lutheran was an obstinate, red brick fist, its steeple hidden in the fog. He found it just past the Hakala Lumberyard, north of the business district, on a cape of compacted liver-colored shingle that formed the north shoulder of Stanley's harbor. He rolled down his window.

An organ played "Nearer My God to Thee" and the sound turned with the waves that broke against the granite boulders to either side.

Trucks, snowmobiles, and four-by-fours crowded the parking lot. Jay Cox's big rig—scrubbed clean—sat in front of the hearse. A county sheriff's Blazer was parked in front of the truck.

He continued down the road that led out to the end of the jetty and a sign materialized in his lights: MASTON COUNTY HISTORICAL SOCIETY. Harry squinted to make out the nebulous mass of a two-story, pillared building. A figure appeared in the mist and he slowed. The woman wore a pleated black skirt and a black sweater. She had prominent cheekbones and graying raven hair pulled tight along her skull and the erect carriage of an elderly ballerina. She was attaching an American flag to a pole and raised her hand to her forehead and peered into his lights. Then she hoisted the flag and walked to the church.

Harry made a U-turn and drove back toward the glow of town. The brightest lights came from the plate-glass windows of the Timber Cruiser Cafe. After he parked, he paused at the door. He'd be able to see the cortege headlights when they left the church parking lot.

The cafe's rough-hewn beams and crannies leaked an aroma of cigar smoke, meat and gravy, of jokes told. A Fisher wood stove in the center of the room pumped out heat. Double-bladed axes, two-handed logging saws, and mounted bucks thronged the walls.

There were sepia pictures like the ones in Hakala's office. Lumber-jacks. Miners marching under a CIO banner. Deer hunting expeditions. A 1920s shack with a crudely lettered Hakala Lumber sign next to a proud proprietor. A brass Wurlitzer squatted next to the door.

The red-leather stools along the counter, the booths by the windows, and the tables in the back were empty this morning except for a lanky blonde waitress with milk-white skin who lounged on a stool next to the cash register. Olympic Nordic legs spilled from her miniskirt and tapered down to bobby socks and sneakers. The two top buttons of her blouse were unbuttoned to ease the strain of her breasts.

She looked up from the book she was reading and her bee-stung lips smiled self-consciously. Longish teeth broke the spell. With lidded eyes and two moles—one on her left cheek, the other at the corner of her left eye—she straddled an intriguing, willowy line right between horsey and gorgeous; an inch either way and she'd be someone else.

She set a bookmark in her place, put her book aside, and sauntered down the counter.

"Coffee, black," said Harry, opening a menu. "Oatmeal. Grape-fruit—"

"Only got the canned slices," said a breathy voice as her gray-green eyes took in his ripped face and she sniffed the whiskey on his breath.

"Naw, give me a big orange juice." Booze loosened his tongue and his smile as he watched her sing the order over the counter into the kitchen. The cook had a blaze-orange knit cap perched on his head and balanced a two-inch ash on the cigarette in his lips.

Harry turned over the book she had been reading. *Functions of the Unconscious*, lectures in psychological astrology.

He got up and went to the jukebox. The antique selections matched the decor. Harry dropped in a coin and punched "Unchained Melody" by Al Hibbler.

She set his coffee down and blew a strand of hair out of her eyes. Electric with Jack Daniel's, Harry found her scent sensual and exhilarating on this morning. A scoop of rich vanilla ice cream after sex.

A pickup with a three-wheeled all-terrain scooter in the back pulled up. Three ruddy youths climbed out, swaddled in orange hunting duds. Their loud young voices drowned out the jukebox as they tumbled into a booth. High school boys.

"Hey, Ginny," one of them yelled, "Mountain Dews."

Ginny swung her stuff as she rounded the counter with three green cans and glasses on a tray. She stood with one hip slanted at an angle as she took their orders. Her tight skirt molded the panty line against her buttocks.

Harry turned on his stool, waited for a lull in the conversation, and asked. "Have any luck?"

"Ah," said one of the boys, "you can't see nothing out there."

"You guys go to high school here?"

They studied his torn face. Their apparent spokesman appraised Harry. "Yeah, so?"

"They let you off school to go hunting?"

"Just the first few days," another piped up.

A third boy put his hand across the table, palm down, in a warning gesture. "That's the guy," he said. "Becky did that to his face. And that's Bud Maston's Jeep out there. Remember, Saturday, at the hospital . . ."

Conversation dried up.

"Any of you know Chris Deucette?" Harry asked.

One of them giggled. "Nope, we all got girlfriends." The boy next to him elbowed him sharply. "Funeral's today, you dweeb."

"So I guess you're not going to the funeral, huh?" asked Harry.

"Guess not," said the spokesman. They all hunched their shoulders and looked at their glasses. Harry spun around on his stool. One of the boys griped, "Christ, Ginny, when you gonna get some decent music on that damn ole jukebox?"

* * *

"Nice kids," said Harry, spooning brown sugar on his oatmeal. "Real friendly."

Ginny wrote out his ticket and placed it on the counter with a shrug. "You heard 'em. You're the guy."

Harry blew on a spoon of oatmeal to cool it, then took a taste. He made a face, put down the spoon, and eased the bowl aside. The oats and orange juice couldn't occupy the same space with sour mash. Ginny watched him concentrate on his black coffee.

Then she reached under the counter, pulled up a folded front section of Sunday's outstate edition of the St. Paul paper, and held it casually against her hip. She tapped his picture. "It's a small town, mister."

Harry pointed to the book she'd been reading. "You believe in that stuff?"

"Must be something to it. It's been around for a long time," she said.

"You do charts on people?"

"Sometimes . . ." She drew her fingers down an errant strand of hair.

An indolent heat swung in his belly. Maston County was a magic place where he had rediscovered women. "How do you do that? I mean, what do you need to start?"

"Exact time of birth and where." She crinkled her eyes. "You interested in astrology?"

"Could be."

The orders for the kids at the booth came up and Ginny carried them to their table. When she returned, she sat one stool away, near the cash register, and turned back to her book. Halfway through his coffee, their eyes met. She lowered hers and a slight flush crept above her collar. Her hand floated up and lightly touched her hair.

Harry finished his coffee, stood up, and went to the cash register and handed her a twenty. As she made change, she asked, "You come up for the funeral?"

"Why?"

"The suit." She dropped her eyes. "Did Becky Deucette do that to your face?"

Harry nodded. Their fingers touched when she handed him his change. He dropped a five next to the register. "You know Jesse Deucette?" he asked.

Her mobile lips turned down. "'Course. She's better'n the soaps on TV."

"She been around lately?"

"Hard to tell, the way she switches her ass from bed to bed so fast."

"I have something for her."

"She figures every man does."

Harry eased the divorce petition out of his pocket, unfolded it, and held it in front of Ginny long enough for her to read the names. She glanced toward the church, then back at Harry. She relished a smile. "I'd like to see that."

"Check you later," said Harry.

She came around the counter and put herself in plain view for his appraisal. "You staying in town?"

"Out at Maston's."

She held out her hand. "Ginny Hakala."

"Like in big Mike, the prosecutor?"

"He's my uncle."

"Harry Griffin," he shook her hand.

"I know," she said. "It's in the paper."

Harry drove back down the jetty and waited for the service to end. Finally, the church doors opened and the pallbearers slowly descended the steps and loaded the casket in the back of the hearse. Snowmobiles started the cortege, outriders, their lights piercing the gloom. The sheriff's Blazer led the procession, its blue flasher turning slowly, silently. Harry waited until they passed, then made a U-turn and paced them out of town.

The cemetery was up Highway 7, back toward the lodge, off a road past the old mining company housing. It took several minutes for the caravan to reach its destination, creeping along the winding gravel path. The vehicles parked in an L-shape and left their lights on. Fog seeped in beams that crossed over a fresh grave.

Harry parked back on the road and walked in. The front of the cemetery was set aside for a miniature Stonehenge, sixteen stones in a circle around a tall granite boulder. The Stanley Massacre. This was one local attraction the Maston family didn't bankroll. The United Mine Workers put in the rock. Mike Hakala had the picture of the dedication on his office wall.

The date, 1933, was chiseled in the stone. Pinkertons with machine guns faced unarmed striking miners. Names: Slovak, Croat, Swedish, Finnish, Italian. His eyes focused. Three Hakalas. Two Emerys. One Deucette.

He walked slowly among the burial plots toward the gathering. Tall arbor vitae lined the path and Harry stepped behind one of them 20 yards from the grave. Black figures arranged themselves. Six of them assembled behind the hearse.

His breath caught in his throat. Jesse Deucette stood next to the grave, fastened in spokes of light. A mud-spattered backhoe crouched over a pile of earth behind her with the digging arm frozen in apex above her head.

She wore a gray raincoat over a black dress. Harry couldn't make out her expression, only the pale oval of her face under a black scarf tied babushka-fashion around her hair. She held white roses.

Now we'll see who's who. Do it.

Harry on parade. Shoulders squared, chin up, his muscles oiled with 90-proof resolve, he marched down the arcade of light, straight at Jesse. Her color turned as pallid as the roses in her hands as she watched him approach. Don Karson detached from the crowd of mourners, a scurry of black robes, quick toward the grave.

The only sound was the creak of the hearse suspension as the pallbearers wrestled the coffin.

Cox and Sheriff Emery stood sergeant-straight, first in line on either side. Cox's hair was severely ponytailed, his cheeks blue as sandpaper from a clean shave. The narrow lapels on his shiny suit were twenty years old.

Emery projected massive dignity in a tie and black cloth. Mike Hakala hulked behind Emery. Three other guys manned the back. One of them could have been Jerry the deputy.

They all saw him at once and everybody froze. Something wrong with the waxworks? He glanced around. Where was Becky? Then he saw her, standing back next to the green Jeep Wrangler. She wore a red high school jacket with athletic awards pinned to the front. Her face was pinched and white and dark purple lipstick bruised her lips. Her hair was unkempt and she looked like she'd slept in her soiled gray wind suit and Nikes. Mitch Hakala, also wearing a high school letter jacket, stood protectively at her side.

Hanging way back there. Why not up with her mother?

Harry stepped up to Jesse.

She came forward ever so slightly, rising on her toes, as if he were going to ask her to dance, and Harry felt the strange premonition that their breath was linked.

Face to face with her, his voice shook. "I want to express my deepest sympathy for your great loss." He extended his right hand. Jesse, captive to ceremony, adjusted the flowers and cautiously reached to take the handshake.

He was not prepared for the moist rush of hope that crowded the wary realism and grief in her eyes. He almost balked. Then she smelled the whiskey on his breath and her outstretched hand arched, fingers pulled back, tendons prominent. Swiftly, Harry brought his left hand from his pocket and placed the papers in her hand.

She read them in a glance and a bitter smile yanked the strings of her face—the joke's on me—and her eyes were struck with so much sadness that Harry felt a surge of emotion to hit her or hold her.

What have I done?

Jesse regained her poise in a rush of tears. She struck him across the face with the papers. "You!" she sobbed, swinging again. She hurled the flowers at him. They sailed past his shoulder. Harry looked back. The bouquet hit Emery in the face.

"Larry! Jay! Mike!" she demanded. "*Do* something!"

Cox let go of the coffin and leaped at Harry. Emery, tiger quick, threw an arm to restrain him. He stopped Cox. He also lost his hold on the coffin handle.

"Shit," yelled Hakala as the weight of the coffin twisted in his grip. The other three men bringing up the rear swayed as the long box tipped. A woman screamed and the coffin dropped with a dull thunk on the cold ground. A gasp issued from the crowd of mourners and became a muffled growl when the latch popped and Chris Deucette's cadaver flopped stiffly into the muddy snow and rolled over.

Karson darted forward, grabbed Harry by the arm, and walked him swiftly away. Harry was aware of Emery manhandling Cox. Hissed words. The other pallbearers struggled with their unbalanced load, the body out on the ground, the clothing ripping in their hands as they tried to shove it back in.

Jesse shouted, berated, "Somebody make him pay. Aren't there any men around here?"

No one moved. Emery held them in place, hands raised. Harry examined the fear in Karson's expression, felt the minister's hand tremble on his arm. "Who you scared of Karson?" he asked. "Which one?"

Jesse surged forward. Karson let go to ward her off. He comforted her in his arms. "Jesse, Jesse," he soothed.

"Jesus Christ!" she sobbed. "Somebody pick him up and put him back in the damn box!" Emery knelt and gently did her bidding.

Harry walked swiftly back toward the road. Becky darted in front of him with her head cocked and a crooked smile. The Hakala boy hovered, hands out defensively, eyes warily watching the crowd. Not Harry.

"You're the only one with the guts to stand up to them," said Becky. She turned suddenly and sprinted with the boy for the Wrangler. They jumped in and sped away.

Before Harry could figure out Becky's odd behavior, Emery overtook him. Sober this morning, he moved with relentless grace. Absolute calm.

This is where I get arrested.

But Emery just looked at him. Harry, his heart pounding, stared back at the visage of beaten bronze, into the man's deadly, patient, hunter's eyes.

"You," said Harry. Not Cox, not Jesse, but *you.*

"Get the hell outta here," ordered Emery with the authority of Old Testament wrath.

30

They'd come after him now. Good. Get it out in the open.

He felt hollow. Famished.

He drove back into town, wheeled into the IGA parking lot, and went in among bright aisles and waxed floors and grabbed on impulse and dropped $200 on a grocery-shopping binge. He laughed at the headlines at the checkout: GHOST OF ELVIS FATHERED MY TWO-HEADED SON.

Standing in the parking lot, he saw the dirge of headlights wind down the ridge and a clean thrill of fear squeegeed his stomach.

Let 'em come.

Turning up Highway 7, he passed the end of the cortege. Eyes straight ahead, he stepped on the gas.

When the bottom falls out: cook. The kitchen was the strong cradle of his childhood. He was, in fact, a better cook than Linda Margoles. He hauled the food inside. Started a fire. First you had to clean up. He scoured the stainless steel sink and washed down the butcher-block counter and bleached it with white vinegar. Grandma had used vinegar for everything. Bowls throughout the house to capture odors.

Apple cider vinegar in the summer, mixed in ice water, dippers of it sweating on a hay wagon. Swizzle, they called it.

He turned on the radio and scanned the dial past polkas and country until he found some bluesy, '60s ballads. The station drifted in and out.

He found a sharpening steel and honed a long kitchen knife and slapped down a slab of lean sirloin on the clean countertop. Casting aside the butcher paper, he saw his fingerprints smeared in red whorls against the white crackle. He mashed the paper in a ball and hurled it into the trash.

He cut the steak in narrow strips, marinated it in vinegar, Worcestershire, red cooking wine, and Tabasco. Doused it with pepper and paprika, then set it aside in the fridge. Exhaled, lit a cigarette. Laid out vegetables.

Jesse. Real suffering on her face.

But Emery was cool. So cool.

They all feared Emery.

Me too.

He drove the heel of his hand down and splintered a head of garlic. Then he mashed each individual clove and peeled away the husk. The sticky power of the herb smudged his fingers.

Maybe he was a fuckup, but so were they. They were hiding something. Something about Chris. About themselves. Becky, hanging on the edge of the ceremony. Find her. Talk to her.

You're the only one with the guts to stand up to them.

Papercuts of fear. Cox had a screw loose. He wasn't cool, could be out there, working up to it. He'd make a move.

Harry's wet hand hovered over the whiskey bottle on the dining room table. Square away. Arm yourself. Even back when he was fucked up, he'd never mixed booze and guns. The one time that he did . . .

He dumped Jack D down the kitchen sink, started the coffee water, and went into the main room. He came back from the oak cabinet with his arms filled with guns.

He laid the two shotguns, the .45 Colt automatic, and the rifle on the dining room table. Went back for boxes of shells.

The pile of weapons stared at him as he rinsed the vegetables. Sliced the onions, mushrooms, green peppers, enjoying their shape and color and their innocent scent. And as the knife went snick-chop against the maple grain the thought of Jesse ran like a thief under his skin. She stole all four directions, up and down, right and wrong . . .

"FUCK!!!" he shouted. As if the word, the sound, presented with enough force, could make her materialize in the kitchen right before his eyes.

For Unlawful Carnal Knowledge. Knowledge, knowledge who's got the knowledge.

Karson. Becky maybe.

He wiped out a deep Wagner cast-iron frying pan. Shook in some olive oil and turned on the gas. Threw in the garlic and the sliced steak.

Watched the strips of beef singe and curl in the spattering oil. Then he tossed in a double handful of loosely sliced onions. While the meat browned he opened cans of tomatoes, tomato sauce, and paste. Deep breaths to inhale the steam of onion, meat, and garlic.

Chris. Doll face in the muddy snow with a massaged-in mortuary smile, rouge, and makeup. Somebody had grabbed at him, tried to catch him, maybe Cox, spooky old Cox, had pulled his suit coat up over his shoulders so his skinny white chest . . .

Harry threw in the rest of the vegetables and stirred them with a long wooden spoon, added olive oil, oregano, a bay leaf, and a pinch of sugar. He lay two miniatures trees of parsley and cilantro on the block. Minced them. Dumped them in.

Lost track of time. Emptied the ashtray twice. Brewed another pot of coffee. He added the rest of the ingredients to his spaghetti sauce, stirred, tasted, added spices, and all the rest of the red cooking wine just ahead of an impulse to drink it. Set the burner to simmer.

Steam brought sweat to his brow and coated the kitchen windows. He rubbed a porthole with his fist. The afternoon was one deepening blue shadow.

Be dark soon.

Well Bud, here I am, out of the office. In the woods, getting back to nature. He jammed shotgun shells with double *O*'s on them into the 12 gauge. Wracked the pump action. The steel clashed with the fatality of a gate closing.

Locked and loaded.

"*Fuck*," he shouted again. While the pasta water boiled, he began to clean the counters. His finger traced the letters in the spattered spices, salt and pepper.

F-U-C-K. The opposite of death.

He'd lost his appetite. He turned his back on the kitchen, took a cup of strong black coffee to the table in the den, lit a cigarette, and methodically loaded the double-barreled shotgun with birdshot.

Harry exhaled, set the shotgun aside, and pressed stumpy slugs into the pistol magazine. Never liked the .45. Always struck him as an over-built American way to end an argument. No finesse, too many catches along the slide. Cock it and the hammer stuck out, caught on stuff. He hefted the pistol in his hand. The other weapons in the cabinet were for hunting. Not this baby.

He slammed the magazine into the handle, yanked the slide, and thumbed the safe. *What the hell, man; you never planned on living this long anyway . . .*

They came for him at sundown. Harry had turned out all the lights and waited on the porch steps, sipping coffee, smoking a cigarette in his cupped hand. The 12-gauge pump rested across his knees. The double-barrel leaned against the porch rail. The .45 was in his waistband and a spare magazine jutted from his back pocket. Probably should have put the Honda in the garage.

He heard them and then he saw them.

A dozen riders on snowmobiles, their lights streaking like vigilante torches as they came wild weasel through the black trees.

Harry's guts tightened. His heart raced. A qualm of sweat popped on his palms. Then the adrenaline boost.

Ohhh shit!

The growl of engines came fast between the cabins and swirled in the driveway. A ragged volley of beer cans and rocks clattered off the porch, windows shattered. Escalation. One of the riders stood up in his seat and threw a long-neck bottle. A smoky sparking arc. The corner of the porch burst into oily flame.

Cox in his biker denim. Playing for keeps. Okay, motherfucker . . .

Harry backed off the outside porch, into the doorway of the mud porch, and fired the double-barrel one-handed. Two loads of birdshot skinned off snowmobile suits and metal. Muffled cries.

One of the snowmobiles crashed into his Honda. The rider ran. Harry dropped the double-barrel and took deliberate aim with the pump. Buckshot slammed into the riderless machine. The gas tank exploded and a shock wave billowed. The mist snapped back full of fire and the Honda's gas tank blew in a sunburst not unlike a Japanese flag.

Down on one knee in the doorway with fire licking the side of his face. All flame and smoke and scurrying shadows, but he held his fire. Even in the chaos there were rules. No one was directly threatening his life. He couldn't bring himself to fire the killing buckshot directly at the milling figures.

The siren and flasher exploded out of the flickering dark with a whoop-whoop scream as the Blazer, Deputy Jerry at the wheel, did its patented four-wheel skid down the driveway and the snowmobiles scattered like cockroaches in a Raid commercial. The dismounted rider leaped onto another sled, hugged the driver. In a snarl of motors, the pack lunged back into the woods.

Jerry was out of his truck, yelling on his radio handset. Harry dived for a big coal-scoop snow shovel that leaned against the doorway and hurled shovelfuls of snow at the burning porch. No way. The roof was already kindling.

Jerry screamed. *"Axes! Fire extinguisher!"*

Harry came from the kitchen with an extinguisher and emptied it into the flames. Jerry found a chopping maul and an ax. His boot on Harry's shoulder, he scrambled up to the porch roof, reached down, and pulled Harry up with him. Back to back, they danced in the flames, swinging at the cedar shakes. Wood chips flew as they hacked the joists that held the porch to the lodge. Somewhere in the frenzy, two firetrucks manned by stout Viking types arrived. They attacked the porch with crowbars, axes, and bigger fire extinguishers. Tore the sucker free, nails shrieking in the cold, threw a chain around the whole shebang, hooked it to the back of an engine, and dragged it clear of the main building. The porch joined the bonfire that consumed the Honda and the snowmobile. A circle of firefighters doused the pyre in a chemical cloud.

Deputy Jerry, black-faced with smoke, probed among the smoldering wreckage. "What happened?" he demanded.

"Assholes came through and tried to burn it down."

"You ID anybody?"

"You kidding?"

The alert young cop kicked at a spent shotgun shell. He evaluated the buckshot stipple in the smoking black hull of the dead Arctic Cat. Bent down, gingerly rubbed away soot, shined his flashlight, and wrote in his spiral notebook.

"You, ah, shoot anybody else tonight, Mr. Griffin?"

"Gave them a couple barrels of number eight birdshot. Doubt it even went through their snowmobile suits."

Jerry scribbled more notes in his notepad. "We'll check the hospital emergency room. And I got the serial numbers off this sled."

One of the firemen muttered loud enough for Harry to hear. "Lucky they didn't stuff a walleye up his ass and set *him* on fire after this morning!"

Jerry grimaced and pushed his Russian-style fur cap back on his sooty head. "Hope you and Maston got your insurance paid up. You ain't gonna get a lot of sympathy around here today." Then he waved his pen and notebook at the stuttering embers. "But this is arson. That's serious."

"What's your last name, Jerry?" asked Harry.

Jerry explored the inside of his cheek with his tongue. "Hakala."

"Which part of the tribe you from?"

"My dad owns the bank." He coughed and tried to look official. "So you gonna come in, press charges?"

Harry laughed. "What good would it do in this county?"

"We'll investigate."

Harry turned on his heel, clambered up to the mud porch, and went inside. He sat down at the dining room table and methodically cleaned the shotguns while firefighters sprayed the porch one last time. Then they climbed back on their rigs. On the way out, one of the trucks demolished the landscaping in the middle of the horseshoe drive, grinding a five-foot Japanese yew into powder.

Fucking hayseeds.

Not Deputy Jerry. He was no country joke. He stood awhile, warming his hands over the collapsed embers. When Harry looked out the window again, he was still there. A few minutes later, calmed down enough to recognize that Jerry's timely entrance saved his ass, he realized that the young cop was doing his job, guarding him against further harm.

Harry took him a cup of coffee.

Jerry sipped, toed a smoking hunk of porch, cast his blue eyes around at the tires still fitfully burning on the greasy chassis of Harry's car, and said, with deep sincerity, "Mr. Griffin, why don't you go home?"

Harry grinned and went back inside. Jerry left the cup on the mud porch and repositioned his Blazer across the entrance to the driveway.

The chemical tang of fire retardant leaked into the lodge's main room through the shattered windows. In the garage, next to Bud's Jeep, Harry found packing boxes from the new stereo. As he tore the corners out of the cardboard, flattening it, a sheet of stiff paper fell out. A photograph, blurred emulsion, enlarged, printed on 8½ by 11. Someone had cut the face out of it. Neck and naked shoulders remained.

Weird? He shrugged and went after the broken windows, piecing cardboard plugs and securing them with duct tape. Then he swept up the glass and aired the place out.

With a flashlight and the 12 gauge, Harry went back outside. Coals hissed in the quiet. Jerry kept watch down the driveway.

Harry stalked up the trail in the direction the retreating snowmobiles had taken and found fresh tracks that led all the way up the ridge. He followed them to the fallen pine and put the light on the bare wood of the tree stand. The tracks went down the slope into the dark near the swamp.

Harry stopped ten yards from the gooseberry bramble bush where Chris had died. The night visitor had collected the yellow police tape, tied it into a large, many-ribboned bow, and fixed it to the bush. Walking closer, he saw a dozen white roses beneath the bow, stiff with freezer burn. Becky. Hadda be. Messing with his mind. First claws his face. Then the strange routine at the funeral.

Harry played the flashlight beam over the snow beneath the flowers and saw deep slashes in the frozen pink rime. Blotches of coffee-colored urine. An enormous deer track was setting up in the red slush.

He turned off the light and squatted when something moved in the brush. Pincushion alert, Harry peered into the dark. Really big. Thrashing. It stamped and made a blowing noise, like a kid blowing into the neck of a Coke bottle.

Deer. Maybe Chris's deer.

He waited for the sounds to come closer. Finally, unable to be still, he switched on the light. Just a wall of brush, tamarack, and brambles. The sounds moved off, deeper into the darkness.

He walked back up the ridge, stopping every few feet to listen to the silent tickle of the mist. He imagined Becky, out there tiptoeing in the woods, watching him.

A wild grind of engines slipped through an eddy of breeze. Faint yells. Snowmobiles threw spindles of light at the far end of the lake. Jackpine savages drinking beer in the cold at Chris's Iron Range wake.

Back inside, he had the operator connect him with the St. Helen's CD ward. A nurse informed him that patients could only receive calls between noon and one P.M. He left Bud a cryptic message. Had the nurse read it back.

"Papers served. The serfs are restless. Things are heating up."

They could come back with scoped deer guns. More serious the second time. He pushed fat bullets into the lever-action rifle. No more birdshot.

As he brewed a pot of coffee, the FM tuner jumped loud and clear and a ghost signal danced in on the ions from Reserve, Wisconsin. The fireplace shadows shook with a spooky treble of high keening voices and the tachycardia of Ojibway drums.

Harry built up the fire, selected a thick Civil War history from the bookshelf, and lined up his arsenal by his chair. With the tom-toms for company, he settled in to wait.

31

The next morning it was like a basement out. Tree trunks jutted, holding up a cotton ceiling of fog. The damp air reeked of chemicals and charcoal ruin and a black sugar of soot lay on the snow. Harry was in the driveway, sighting in the heavy .45-70 rifle when Don Karson drove up in a Kermit-green Subaru station wagon.

So they sent the preacher. Soft approach. Harry arched his back to ease the crook in his neck from sleeping in the chair.

Karson, the serious intercessor doing God's work on this shitty overcast day, picked his way through the Battle of the Snowmobiles in a tweed sports coat with leather elbow patches and a tightly knotted red wool tie.

Harry adjusted the rear notched rifle sight with the blade of his Buck knife. "Shoots little to the left," he said by way of greeting.

"Last thing you should be doing today is playing with guns," said Karson in a level voice.

"Who's playing?" Harry snapped the heavy rifle to his shoulder and fired offhand at the target he'd tacked to the side of a stump 80 yards away. He worked the lever, snapped it up, fired again, and repeated the process. The echo of the shots elongated and slapped back against the ridge. Then he yanked the lever, threw the bolt open, and slung the rifle over his shoulder.

"What?" he asked blankly to Karson's face.

"I thought we could talk."

Harry pointed to the ebony junk that had been his car. "The Friends of Jesse visited me last night. Anybody in your congregation like to throw Molotov cocktails from speeding snowmobiles?"

"You pissed off some people yesterday. Probably the VFW crowd had a little too much to drink."

"Probably Jay Cox," said Harry.

"You call Emery?"

"Jerry Hakala was out with the fire department." Harry turned and walked down to the stump. Karson followed. Harry knelt and inspected his last three shots. Two of them were low, an inch off the two-inch bull's-eye he'd drawn in black Magic Marker. The third was dead center.

"Trouble with me," said Harry, "is I'm real good, but erratic. Always envied people who were steady. You strike me as a steady sort of man, padre."

"Someone should teach you respect for the dead, Griffin." Karson drew himself up and Lutheran steel glinted in his blue eyes.

"Lot of shoulds. Let's just say I don't confuse the living with the dead."

"That was sacrilegious, what you did yesterday."

"I guess that depends on your religion."

Karson studied him. "And what kind of religion raised you?"

"Born again buddhism, small *b*," said Harry.

"I take it you don't believe Jesus Christ died for your sins."

"A lot of Vietnamese died for my sins, padre, yours too."

"You desecrated that boy."

"Whoa . . . I respect the process of dying," said Harry, "when it happens, but I don't confuse that with burying the gum wrapper in a hole in the ground. I think the Tibetans are more honest and practical. After they have their ceremony they take the body to the edge of town and toss it out for the animals to eat. Sometimes the young monks cut off the choice portions of meat for the critters prowling around." Harry looked Karson directly in the eye. "They sit among the bodies and meditate on the impermanence of life."

Karson made a face. "I keep seeing that woman, losing her son, getting divorce papers slapped in her hand at his funeral, and then having the body roll out of the coffin . . . the suit slipped around when they put him back in and there were these big staples holding his chest . . ."

"Get off it, Karson. She didn't lose her son like you lose a pair of socks. He tried to kill somebody." Harry tapped Karson on the chest right in the middle of his red tie. "And Jesse Deucette would steal a hot stove."

He motioned for Karson to follow him into the lodge. They walked across shards of glass, through soggy embers, and up the jury-rigged steps Harry had hammered together to get up onto the mud porch.

Harry brought two cups of coffee to the table in the den and shoved the shotgun, the .45, and a cleaning kit aside to make room.

"You expecting a war?" asked Karson.

"I'm not going to be run off, you can tell them that."

"Don't you think there's been enough macho bullshit?" Karson sat down and loosened his tie. He reached in his coat pocket and took out a pack of Winstons. They lit up.

Harry sighed and looked around. "Bud must have had some wedding. Chris with a needle stuck in his arm, Becky with her tits popping out."

"The kids didn't attend."

"Anybody interview them before the fact? You know, discuss the seriousness of the marriage vows with them? Didn't it register that Bud has been falling-down drunk?"

"Hard to tell with Bud. He has . . . excellent social skills. Everybody up here drinks to some extent." The minister paused. "You were drinking yesterday. I could smell it on your breath."

Karson's remark landed on target. Gravity replaced the banter in Harry's voice. "So where do you come down on the question of Jesse? Does she have carry-on baggage or steamer trunks full of skeletons?"

Karson measured him. "I tried to tell Bud that Jesse and Larry Emery have a peculiar way of fighting with each other. That she might marry him to spite Larry."

Harry raised his eyebrows.

Karson continued. "Bud said he'd take his chances."

"No shit."

"They were quite a team when they first started going out. They opened the development Coop downtown and came up with this ambitious plan to convert the paper mill to a hydrogen peroxide closed cycle system. No more pumping dioxin into the lake." Karson smiled. "Those were exciting times. Jesse can be very convincing. She used to sing in the choir. She has a beautiful voice."

"What she's got is a beautiful ass. And the will to use it."

Karson cleared his throat. "She has a promiscuous edge. But that's just part of her."

Harry scrutinized Karson for thirty seconds. Karson sighed and cast his eyes back, remembering. "Then last summer it all started falling apart. The Coop, the plans—"

"Coffee and cookies is over, Karson. Did Chris act alone?"

"Things can get murky. Mistakes were made," said Karson.

"Things don't get murky. Things happen. The way we think about them might get murky, like when we don't want to look at them straight on, when we deny, or lie or forget."

Karson bit his lip. "Bud's in the hospital and you served the divorce papers. Maybe you should go home. I could come down to St. Paul."

"C'mon, *Don,* everybody's covering for everybody. Is that in your job description? Lying, cheating, stealing . . . arson? How about manipulating a kid to commit premeditated murder?"

Karson's eyes leveled with sincerity. "Watch out for Larry Emery. He's a very dangerous man. Especially when he's been drinking—"

"Yeah?"

"And when he's jealous." Karson's upper lip was a tidy pink stripe that accented his neatly barbered mustache. His small red tongue flicked at it. "Everybody saw the way you and Jesse were looking at each other. Right at the grave."

Harry raised his eyebrows.

"It was pretty steamy. The two of you there," said Karson. "Emery didn't miss it."

Briskly, Harry asked, "Emery's not from around here, is he?"

"He was born here, lived with his father in Memphis when his parents split. Moved back to live with his mother. After the service, he was a cop in Duluth. The previous sheriff had to retire. Health problems. Mike Hakala hired Emery to fill out his term. Then he got elected."

"So back when, he followed Jesse to Duluth and knocked her up?"

"That's the local legend."

"And Jesse wouldn't marry him."

"She's obviously always had her sights set a little higher on the socioeconomic ladder."

"In the cop shop you said you'd talked to Jesse and Chris. And that caused Emery to hate you."

"Those were private conversations."

Harry saw what Karson was angling toward. "You guys have an ethical thing about confidentiality, don't you, like priests in a confessional?"

Karson pursed his lips. "Something like that."

"So you have this office in back of your church with a comfy chair where people come and confide in you. Under the seal, as it were. And Jesse's been in that chair, and Chris. What about Jay Cox?"

"I don't know about Cox."

"Sorry, I forgot, you gave me Ginny Hakala for that purpose."

Karson reacted stiffly. "A lot of people had a hand in pointing Chris Deucette in the wrong direction. Some of them had good intentions—"

"Like you?" Karson didn't respond. Harry's voice softened without losing any of its edge. "Hard, isn't it? Trying to figure out what to keep inside, what to let out into the world. You have all their stories in your head. And maybe you talk to God about these people. How's that work when you talk to God? Is it mystic, like a spirit? Or is it the old anthropomorphic version—God the father by Michelangelo, with eyes and hands and ears? Becky might give you an argument on that. She gave this little speech when I met her. I don't think she has much faith in a deity that doesn't have a uterus. You had a chance to talk to her lately?"

Karson shook his head.

"She left the funeral service in a hurry. Wearing running shoes," said Harry.

Karson exhaled. "Since the shooting she's been . . . hiding, I guess is the way to say it."

"What's she hiding from?"

Karson shrugged. "Her brother was killed. She's been through a traumatic time."

"Haven't we all. I just wonder, if I hadn't been out on that ridge that day and Chris would have accidentally shot Bud Maston to death— how traumatic would that have been for this quaint little community?"

"There's a lot of anger in you, Harry. I can get angry, too," said Karson softly. "But my job isn't to judge."

Harry shook his head. "You didn't bury Chris Deucette. You flushed a toilet. Get angry, padre. It does wonders to light up a moral vacuum, which is what you got up here."

Karson coolly met Harry's eyes. "How far are you willing to go with this?"

"All the way to the bottom."

"It could get real dirty," Karson said. He stood up and took his coffee cup to the sink. "I have to work out some ground rules."

"The confidential thing?"

"Exactly." Karson walked to the door. *"I'll* tell *you* a thing. If you weren't serving divorce papers, Emery would have snapped you in two at the cemetery."

"That so?"

"And here's another thing to think about. The minute you've completed your go-between role in the divorce, he'll come after you for Chris."

"Why does he hate you?"

Karson chose his words carefully. "Some people say I helped Jesse and Chris get out from under his thumb."

Harry spent the rest of the day cleaning up the mess. He called his insurance agent in St. Paul and explained about the car. He'd need a police report for the claim. He ate warmed-over spaghetti and watched the evening news. The phone rang in the middle of the weather report.

Don Karson's conscience, working out ground rules: "Karl Talme teaches English at the high school. He's the guy Chris pulled the gun on. Maybe you should talk to him. Use my name." Karson hung up.

It was a crooked road that wound through Maston County and a man needed a few crooks of his own so as not to lose his way. Harry methodically searched for something to drink, down on his knees going through the kitchen cupboards. Finally he stooped over the garbage can and extracted the Jack Daniel's bottle. An amber corner winked at him through a scum of damp coffee grounds.

The veins on his strong right arm popped out tight as he squeezed the sturdy glass and wrung the few drops onto his tongue.

32

Gunshots woke Harry at dawn. He rolled out of his covers, put his hand on the shotgun, and went to the window. Just hunters up on the ridge. The fog had cleared off and enough sun slipped through the clouds to breathe orchid into the steam drifting across Glacier Lake.

He put the coffee on and paced. His insides churned cold and his nerves were on their knees, whiskey beggars. Stay ahead of it. He glanced at the bearskin on the wall. Time to give Emery a tweak in his den.

At 8 A.M., he called the Maston County Sheriff's Department and asked to speak to Lawrence Emery.

"He ain't here. He's out hunting," said the deputy.

"Tell him it's Harry Griffin. I'm at the Maston lodge."

Harry spent two hours splitting and hauling wood to shake the cramps out of his muscles. The phone rang and he jogged inside.

Emery set the tone immediately. They would talk around Chris. "You know, Griffin, there's some people up here willing to give you the benefit of the doubt, but after that stunt you pulled Tuesday . . ." His voice was sly, weary sounding.

"Is it against the law to serve divorce papers, Sheriff?"

"No. But the timing sure as hell is bad judgment."

"Am I still part of an ongoing investigation?"

Emery sighed. "What's on your mind, Griffin?"

"I want my rifle back."

"What?"

"It's still deer season. I have a valid license and I want my rifle back to go hunting."

"You gotta be shittin' me."

"If there's no legal reason for you keeping my rifle, I want it back."

"The BCA has your rifle for running ballistic tests. It's routine in a gunshot death. Common sense should tell you that."

"So you're still investigating the shooting, huh?" Emery didn't answer. "Well, I can get another rifle. Any reason I can't go hunting then?"

"You got in mind deer or people?"

"The Klan came through on snowmobiles the night of the funeral—"

"Yeah, yeah. I heard. You wanna press charges, come down to the station."

"Don't want any drunk snowmobilers having a serious accident, is all."

"Put on some coffee. You an' me's going to have a little talk."

The coffee was ready when the Wrangler tires of Emery's Blazer slushed to a halt in the soot in front of the lodge. Jerry sat in the passenger seat.

Harry went out to meet them and decided to put Chris on Front Street, in perspective. He nodded to Jerry and faced Emery. "I know Chris was your kid and whatever else can be said about you and me in that regard, it leaves you with a hell of a conflict of interest."

With chilling nonchalance, Emery ignored the comment. He inspected the war zone in the drive and grunted, "Deadly fuckers, they killed the porch."

"I need a police report to file my insurance on the Honda," said Harry.

"Awright," said Emery. He needed some coffee. His face was poached with fatigue and part of his red-eyed stare could have come from peering into the miserable wet woods for a whitetail, but the scent of morning whiskey squeezed out from peppermint breath mints.

"You been getting enough sleep, Sheriff?"

"Fuck you, Griffin. Go home. Go huntin' someplace else."

"Nah. Think I'll stick around," said Harry.

They entered the lodge and Jerry assumed the quiet presence of a German shepherd, boots spread, thumbs hooked in his pistol belt.

Emery shrugged off his Mackinaw and looked around. He wore a Pendleton shirt, khaki trousers, and Sorel boots. The trousers were damp to the knee with snow. He stared at the BUD IS A FUCKER graffiti scrawled next to the fireplace. "Was going to get Becky out here to clean that up but you being here and what happened at the funeral, probably ain't a good idea."

"Karson was here. He said Becky's dropped out of sight."

"She runs off. Had to go to the Cities and get her once. She's around here somewhere."

"Girl off alone?"

"She'll turn up."

Harry pointed to the bearskin on the wall. "What do you want to do about that?"

"Leave it. Goes with the place." Emery's casual demeanor set Harry's teeth on edge. He decided that was the method Emery had adopted to use on him.

"You like to shoot bears?"

"Used to. They got be a nuisance, coming into town after the garbage. Messing with the fishing trade. Got so I didn't like them. Then after I bagged that guy on the wall I was camping out at the other end of the lake and this big storm came up. Damn if this bear didn't run right into my tent and chase me out on all fours. Bear run one way. I run the other. Big crack of lightning and this dead maple blew over and fell slam on my tent right where I was sleeping. I liked bears ever since."

"Uh-huh," said Harry. Emery's rustic charm concealed spread steel jaws.

Emery moved silently in that disturbing light way of his up the steps into the den and sat at the table. Jerry shifted his position, maintaining his two-step distance. Emery slapped down a sheaf of computer print-outs. "Know what I got here?"

"Uh-uh," Harry poured coffee and held up the pot toward Jerry, who did not move a muscle in response.

"Story of your life from a police point of view."

Harry lit a cigarette. Emery took out one of his toothpicks.

"Yeah, so?" asked Harry.

"So . . ." Emery twirled his toothpick in his blunt fingers. "I think you're one of them interesting guys that things happen to. Fact is, if I was on vacation and met you in a bar somewheres, I suspect we could trade a few stories. But you ain't the kind of person I appreciate setting up housekeeping in my county. So when your business here is done, I want you gone."

Harry offered him a cigarette. Emery shook his head. "Gave it up."

"Like Jesse gave you up for Bud Maston?"

Intimidating pathology toyed in Emery's smile and a mean street-wise sneer replaced molasses and cornbread in his voice. "How's a fuckup like you and a rich fatboy like Maston get to be friends any-way?"

"Met in Vietnam Veterans Against the War."

Emery snorted with contempt. "You serve together over there?"

"Nope. First time I saw Bud was in 1969. Protest rally at the U in Minneapolis. Then it was AA. You heard of Alcoholics Anonymous? For people with drinking problems?"

"You're the one needs crutches, man, not me," said Emery. He sipped his coffee and spread the printouts on the table like a poker hand.

"Dee-troit City. You got this habit of assaulting people. Six months in the House of Correction. What happened there, Griffin?"

"I used to smell like you in the morning. It got me in trouble."

"Uh-huh. Was you drinking when your wife filed this assault charge for hitting her?" Harry didn't respond. "How you go from wife beater to working for a newspaper?"

"Grew up."

"July sixty-seven. Conviction for aggravated armed assault during the Detroit riot. You got a suspended sentence. One of the parties involved in the incident was a black guy, lawyer, now a judge in Detroit. He bargained the suspension." Emery showed Harry a fax of a military DD214 discharge and grinned. "Got you a bunch of medals. Uncle Sam appreciated your knack for armed assault." Emery tapped the discharge. "Says here you were assigned to Advisers. Story in the newspaper said you were in Special Ops. You get off on that kind of stuff?"

"You've been busy," said Harry.

"Computers is wonderful things. Assaulting a National Guardsman with a knife during a riot and insurrection, it says here."

"It was a bayonet and it was two Guardsmen."

"Tell me about it."

"You wouldn't get it. You hadda be there." Harry came forward in his chair. "So you know where I've been. I'm curious where you were the morning your kid took a shot at Bud Maston."

"Scoff-law attitude, Griffin. I'd watch that. Don't tempt me to kick your ass and dump you over the county line. Fact is, I got ample cause not to like you much."

"It's mutual. I think you're a poor excuse for a sheriff."

Jerry moved a little closer and Emery grinned and ruffled the print-outs. "You only served six months of a twelve-month sentence in the House of Correction. Somebody sprung you. Copper I talked to in Detroit said it was a government deal. Took me a while to figure it out." Emery's lip curled. "Got into your military records. You was discharged from the army in May sixty-eight. You was wounded in Vietnam. You collected some disability for a couple of years. Seventy to seventy-two. Thing is, on the VA paperwork, there's a record of you being treated for gunshot wounds in an Air Force hospital in Udorn, Thailand, in January, sixty-nine. What happened? You get shit-faced in Dee-troit, take the wrong bus, and wake up in Thailand?"

"This is all crap . . ." said Harry. But he was impressed with Emery's persistence as a hunter. In the woods, in computer banks. Shit.

"That buddy of yours down in the Cities, Randall the hotshit writer. He was regular army, then he got mixed up with the CIA. I think you went back over there as a fucking mercenary. You're Maston's trained dog, ain'tcha? Kind of scumbag who does it for money."

"And what do you do it for, Emery? Love?"

Jerry stood at the table. "Okay, guys, take it easy."

Emery projected menace softly. "Lemme explain how it works, newspaper artist. Maston has projects. Some are good for the town. The hospital, the school, the Christmas tree farm. He wants to come off as a guilty fatboy making amends for when his family raped this whole end of the state."

Emery took a sip of coffee. "'Course it ain't gonna do any good. In ten years they'll be no town left, and birds will be building nests in the new hospital. Jobs ain't there. Last year we voted the town mayor's office out of existence. Closed the library. Half the stores and half the classrooms in the high school are empty. All 'cause do-good Bud Maston used his clout to get the mill closed so the fishies wouldn't die. Fish are fine. Town's dying. He's still a Maston, and he's still fucking people."

Emery scratched his ear lobe. "Now here's the problem. You're one of Maston's projects that has went and got itself lost."

"Nice how all you people are so worried about me. Karson and now you."

"Fuck Karson."

"He on your shit list too?"

"Let's just say he ain't the kind of guy I like to see teaching kids in Sunday school."

"Seems like a pretty intelligent guy."

"Yeah, right. Been to college and everything." Emery grinned. "Fact is, you and him got a lot in common. Reason he's up here in the bumfuck outback is he had some emotional problems down in Minneapolis when he was pastor at a big parish. Nervous breakdown and getting high with the kids in his church is what I heard. I can guess at the rest."

Emery stood up. Anger came silently in him, like his tread. He threw the police and medical records and Jerry moved between them.

"They paste you back together in the VA?" Emery snarled as Jerry covered him. "Drug dependency. Stress groups. Did ya tell 'em where it hurts? They ask you why you couldn't handle it on your own? Fuck!" Emery turned away.

Then he spun around and pointed his finger. "What I been trying to tell you is you don't do so good on your own. You're walking wounded, another loony like that goddamn Cox. Maston collects you guys. Should keep you in a kennel. You need structure. Man, you're out in the fuckin' woods alone."

He tugged Jerry's arm. "Tell him, Jerry, you wouldn't been watchin' his silly ass the other night, those ole boys from the VFW would have made him into bait."

"Speaking of which, I was you I'd run Cox's name through your computer."

"I'll make sure Jay walks the line. You take care you do the same."

"What about Jesse? Anybody ever get her to walk the line?"

"Jessica's got her faults. But she's the one who give these people up here hope. We wouldn't have the new gym or the hospital without her. She holds this community together. Don't forget that."

"You through? I'd like to hit the woods. I'm losing daylight," said Harry.

Jerry Hakala sighed with relief and walked Emery out to the Blazer.

After they left, Harry took the coffee cups to the sink. Something clinked in the one Emery had used. A button. A metal button with a distinctive bellied-out inner curve. The hair at the nape of his neck tingled. It was the missing button from the surplus wool British Army trousers he'd been wearing that morning.

Harry sat quiet as a stick on the ridge overlooking the swamp with the lever-action rifle across his knees as the damp afternoon freshened, bent back on itself, and crunched with cold.

Emery had a point. He did need structure. Now it was a footrace to see whether he could solve the mystery of Chris Deucette before the booze took him down. He grimaced at the rifle in his hands. He'd meant it, what he'd said to Karson. A Buddhist mosquito had bitten him over there. This tiny inoculation of . . .

Wife beater, Emery said.

Cathedral silence sifted through the tall pines and Harry remembered why he'd quit hunting. Reminded him of ambushes. Why go hunting when there are supermarkets? That's what Kate, his wife, had said.

Marrying that woman had been like going through Tet again. A fight in a cramped apartment ended it. She slung an electric frying pan of pork chops at him, he backhanded her getting out of the way. An hour later he was in a bar fight. Some asshole pulled a knife. He'd snapped off a pool cue, wound up putting it through the jerk's neck muscles. Busted. Coulda beat it, self-defense.

Then Kate filed charges, showed up in court with a black eye. Pregnant.

So his buddies intervened. So Fucking Laos.

When he heard, Randall thought it was folly, taking Hollywood's deal to get out of jail early, going back as a contract employee. A paid thug.

Six months under the Jolly Roger. Ammo flying in, opium flying out. Powered by amphetamines, he'd prowled the Ho Chi Minh Trail with Vang Pao's Hmong, calling in airstrikes, trying to close down a ten-mile stretch. When he started they were wheeling supplies down on bicycles. By the time he was nicked in the hip and called it quits, they were driving trucks.

A flock of crows rose silently over the trees and Harry remembered the searching look on the face of that one-legged dude on the street in St. Paul. Those black eyes knew him. Bugged out again.

Not this time. This time out he was going to win.

He shivered and walked back to the lodge. Keep busy. He looked up the name Karson had given him in the local phone book. Dialed Karl Talme's residence. A woman answered.

"Karl there?"

"Tonight's Karl's group night," said the woman.

"What, AA?"

"No, uh, he and Don Karson, they go to Duluth to this group for men."

"They run out of men around here?"

"Who is this?"

"Friend of Karson's. I'll call back."

Weird.

Then the call came that Harry had been avoiding. Bud. "I want you to leave. Lock up and leave," he said in a furry, thoroughly detoxified voice.

"Who told you?"

"Karson called me. He's a minister, right? So they got me out of group. He said you've been drinking. That you're up there looking for a fight. Let the sheriff watch the place. Get out."

"Emery's job is looking the other way. I leave, these bandits will rob you blind."

"I don't care. Just get out of there before somebody else gets hurt."

"Hey, Bud, grow some balls!" Harry didn't disguise the contempt in his voice.

"You're back walking on all fours, Harry. You're going to fuck up. Dammit! Don't make me come back up there." Both a threat and a plea.

"Just worry about getting an injunction against Jesse."

"Christ. You really did that? The funeral?"

"You wanted her served. She's served. And Becky's disappeared. I told Emery; he didn't seem too concerned."

"It's like a different culture up there. They have their own way of doing things. I can't worry about Becky. I have to let go of all that stuff."

"Don't worry, man. I'll hold down the fort," said Harry.

"It's not a fort . . ." Then Bud erupted. "Goddammit, I know what you're doing. You found some . . . adversity, and you can't let it go." His voice accelerated, "Karson told me about you and Jesse. The way—"

"I gotta go now," said Harry. He hung up the phone. Almost immediately it rang again. Busy night.

"Hi, remember me? Ginny from the Timber Cruiser?" said a breathy voice.

"Sure, the astrology lady." Harry grinned. He picked up the button Emery had left, tossed it in the air. Caught it.

"You got the whole town talking about you, pinning Jesse's ears back with those divorce papers. Shooting at those guys."

"That why you called, keep me up to speed on the local gossip?"

"Actually I was thinking of going out to the VFW for a drink, only thing is, this guy I used to go out with might bother me—"

"And you could use a little male companionship?" Harry grinned. It was just the oldest setup in the world, baited with pussy and whiskey. Well, why not, as long as he could squeeze in a few drinks before the killing started. He gave the telltale button a shove with his index finger and wondered what Ginny Hakala's game was.

"Fact is, the right kind of male companionship could get lucky tonight."

"You always this forward?"

"I don't know. Tell you what. You bring the apple and I'll bring a snake and a tree and we'll find out. Say eight-thirty . . ." Her voice dropped a register, somewhere between sophistication and guile. "And, Harry, leave the suit home. It's not that kind of place."

33

Outside, some comedian had pasted a smile face label over the cracked thermometer on the VFW door. Inside, Ginny Hakala sunned her stuff below the bent neon helix of a GRAIN BELT BEER sign. Her personals ad would be upbeat. *"Man wanted; must have muzzle loader that can keep up with my six-shooter. Thirty-year-old single white natural female. Smokes, drinks, never leaves a spec of chrome on the trailer hitch."*

Here we go. Eyes turned as Harry came down the bar. The men in dirty blaze orange who packed the stools and booths exuded a musk of beer, bar whiskey, the grease pit, cold winter alfalfa dust, deer guts, and heavy machinery. Their stumpy hands had trained for doing shot glass curls by twisting frozen hex nuts off rusted bolts. Most wore snowmobile boots and suits, unzipped, arms out, hanging down their backs like capes. Some of them probably had fresh memories of his buckshot whistling over their heads.

A game was in progress on the pool table. Alabama cursed Neil Young on the Wurlitzer. He did not see Jay Cox.

Ginny draped sideways in a booth next to the pool table, and made no concessions to the weather. Her thin, stiff, ox-blood leather car coat popped open to let her cleavage shine and the hem of her black clingy minidress crept high on her blazing thighs. She saw him and crossed her legs.

Harry grinned, big easy grin. Pretend it's 1968.

She'd swept her hair up, went easy on the eyeliner and makeup. As he slid into the booth she tugged at the cuff of his sheep-lined Levi's jacket. "You didn't wear your suit."

"Get yourself an outfit and be a cowboy too," said Harry.

"Dig it. Everybody is watching us."

"They don't look very excited. In fact, I expected it to be louder in here."

"Too many Finnlanders," she said. "We're into melancholy, big time. There's a saying. Whatever happens, we'll be on the losing side."

A waitress appeared. Ginny ordered a Black Russian. "Pabst and a doubleshot of bar whiskey," the words rolled naturally off his tongue.

"What I heard is you don't drink." She cocked her head.

Harry took off his coat, rolled up his sleeves. "Just chipping."

She traced the griffin tattoo on his left arm with a cool finger. "Like your identity there on your arm." She nodded. "Jay's got one, too . . . From the marines. His says 'Death Before Dishonor.'" She curled her upper lip. "Probably crawled off his arm out of pure shame."

Their eyes met and he saw more range in hers than he'd anticipated. She let her hand rest lightly on his forearm. With the other she lit a Winston 100 with a plastic lighter and blew a stream of smoke.

"I'm not *dumb*, Harry. You and Jay Cox got a thing." Her secretive smile broadened, revealing the slight overbite. Her fingers lingered, a clairvoyant sweep along his arm.

"You got any other tattoos? Or scars?" she asked.

Harry knit his brows in mock concern. "You one of these weird backwoods hippie chicks? Into disfigured men?"

"It's a problem," she said. "Exciting guys have scars and tattoos. Unfortunately they also have lots of unresolved baggage. Are you like that, Harry?"

"For sure."

Maybe it was all his pores cranked open to the barroom scent of tacit danger. She turned him on with a flick of her eyes. She would always turn men on and they would always worship her in private as long as they were horizontal. But they would always get up and leave her for women who were more respectable, conventionally better looking, and lousy in bed.

Their drinks came. "You know a lot of things," he said.

"For a waitress, huh? Who's almost pretty as long as she keeps her mouth shut." She mocked the unintended condescension that had crept into his voice. Joke was on him.

Jay Cox walked into the bar and conversation paused a beat. Half a dozen of the barflies gravitated to him.

"Here comes trouble," said Ginny gamely, sitting up and self-consciously fluffing her hair with both palms.

"What is this, a test?" Harry muttered.

"Just want to see what you're made of, Mr. Harry Griffin."

Cox pushed between two guys at the bar and ordered a drink. He watched them over his shoulder with sullen eyes. Harry could almost smell the gasoline on him.

Cox sipped from a shot glass and Harry felt the fight pack in the air, tight as an ice ball. People moved away. The murmur of the barroom picked up a raw, static zing.

Harry gulped his whiskey and it seared his throat and started a memory dance of physical blows and ignorance behind his eyes. Why is it I always pick the bars with tilted floors? Why is it, the one violent asshole in the joint always runs downhill to me?

Cox, egged on by his huddle of cronies, made his move. He swaggered to the pool table and took a cue stick from the wall rack. Slapping the cue in his palm, he strutted in front of the booth. The stick vibrated in his bone-prominent hands.

"Hiya, Cox," said Harry. His voice trembled. Scared. *Until he got hit.*

Cox panted a stubble ugly grin and Harry noticed a web of scar tissue on his throat that crawled with his Adam's apple. He was building menace and he had an audience. Christ, they were two middle-aged men. This was going to be real dumb.

Cox snarled, "Doing your number on him now, huh, Ginny? Thought better of you. Out with this guy. Fact is, I bet he don't even like women."

Ginny put a plastic swizzle stick between her teeth, bit it, drew it slowly out. When she was confident all eyes were on her, she delivered her cameo lines in the Stanley soap opera: "Jay has this problem. He can't let go of anything. He's insanely possessive." She smiled sweetly. "Right now he's got this real dilemma for a possessive man. He's out at his trailer shacked up with Jesse Deucette and she's the local nymphomaniac."

Cox's glower flamed into rage. Harry began to shake in anticipation, and Cox took encouragement. He wagged the cue in Harry's face. A tic-tac-toe streak of blue chalk crossed his scabs. Harry pushed the stick away and stood up. His muscles felt loose, ropes shaking out. Cox was too big, too powerful. The sense of déjà vu almost made him smile. He focused on the stick. Sure worked last time. Landed him in jail instead of the morgue.

Cox grinned. "We got us a sissy boy treehugger here. Lookit the fucker shake."

The cue stick lashed out and stung Harry's chest. Yeah. Now I remember. The muscles across his back flared out tight.

"Hey, you guys," yelled the bartender, "take it outside."

"Don't think he'll make it," said Cox. "I do believe he's going to piss all over the floor right here."

The cue rapped forward and stung Harry's chest again. Pain oriented him and the tightness scalded from his back and out his arms. Harry grinned, stepped back, and planted his right hip against the pool table.

The third time the cue flashed at his face, instinct took over and his breath ignited. He twisted, set, blocked the stick and slid up it with his left forearm and clamped his hand behind Cox's. With a sharp twist he broke Cox's grip, reversed the cue, and, holding it like a clubbed rifle, pounded the fat end at Cox's throat.

Cox drew in his chin and the handle hit muscle. He backed up, stunned, and started to tuck into a fighting crouch. Not quick enough. Harry twirled the cue and did his barroom trick. Stuck the tip in the end pocket of the pool table and snapped it off. Harry uncoiled, holding the shortened stick two-handed and laid the jagged, splintered tip against Cox's carotid artery.

Cox poised on the balls of his feet with the cue lodged secure at his throat just a shiver away from serious damage as rage did a somersault in his peppery eyes. With a mad grunt he pressed forward, thrusting his throat against the jagged wood. Blood streaked his neck.

Cox's mad eyes baited. "You ain't got the guts," he sneered and he looked like he'd push the sharp end through his own throat to get at Harry. Harry hesitated. Cox knocked the cue clattering against the table. His knobby fist cocked at his shoulder.

That's when Harry moved ahead of the punch, dropping slightly on flexed knees. His right hand snaked between Cox's legs, grabbed a handful of denim, zipper, and nuts and mashed and wrenched up and Cox was in dance class, levitating with a strangled howl. All he needed was a tutu and toe shoes. Harry released his grip. Cox staggered back against the pool table, gasping. Harry glanced down the bar. Everybody slunked over, looking down their noses into their glasses. Broke-dick silence.

"Okay, break it up. Fun's over," drawled an amused voice next to Harry's ear. Emery. Doing his silent approach. Harry turned. Emery smiled. He was alone, Jerry was nowhere in sight. He wore hunting duds and snow clung to the cuffs of his trousers. Just in from the woods.

Emery moved Harry aside and stepped up to Cox. "Wanna push somebody around? Come push me. One teeny little push. I wouldn't mind, Jay. Fact is, coming from you, I'd kinda appreciate it right now."

Cox was still game. Harry saw the bartender look around nervously. These two tuskers could wreck the place.

"Was between me and him, Larry," Cox said in a labored voice.

"Bullshit. Leave it alone. Tell Jessica I said for her to do the same."

Cox gnawed his lip and glared at Harry. "Got no quarrel with you, Larry."

"That's big of you, Jay, seeing's I'm the fucking sheriff!"

Cox appraised Harry. "Next time," he promised.

"Ain't gonna be no next time. Now get outta here," said Emery, who put his hands on his hips and narrowed his eyes at the crowd. When Cox had left through the front door he spoke softly. Nobody had trouble hearing. "Now listen up. No more fun and games on Maston's land, you hear?"

Then he slouched, hands deep in the Mackinaw pockets. He pulled out a rolled-up paper and closed his right fist around it. With deceptive speed, he dropped his shoulder, rotated, and slammed the fist into Harry's stomach—knocking the breath out of him and nearly lifting him onto the pool table.

"Police report for your car insurance. Been meaning to give it to you." Emery grinned. "Now pay for that cue stick and get the hell out of here."

Harry gasped for breath, peeled two twenties off the roll in his jeans, and threw them on the pool table. Ginny stepped up and handed Harry his coat. "C'mon, hon, let's blow this pop stand," she said briskly as she helped him toward the door. She rolled her eyes back at the silent crowd. "Now that's what I call foreplay," she chuckled, running her tongue over her teeth.

Emery tipped his hunting cap to Ginny and his face resumed its mournful repose. "Y'all have a good night, now."

Outside, Harry sucked in huge draughts of air. "What the hell happened to Cox in there? You see the way he threw himself at that stick?"

"Poor Jay," said Ginny with a sad shrug. "Off his meds since Jesse's been messing with his mind. Too bad. He's really this sweet guy."

"Huh?" Harry grumbled, one hand to his belly.

"Don't feel bad," said Ginny helpfully. "No shame in a run-in with Larry Emery."

34

Once Harry got past the blood bruise on his stomach, it was fun. Racing back to the lodge, Ginny riding his tail in her red Camaro. Laughing through the door, building the fire, and turning off the lights. Undressing.

He discovered her body and his own dog-happy arousal. Between the fight and getting naked he had acquired nineteen-year-old eyes. Glowing nineteen-year-old skin.

She held up a twinkling tinfoil square and Harry groaned.

"This is your basic casual encounter. And this is a rubber," she said.

Still fun with galoshes on.

Before the problems began, Linda Margoles used to accuse Harry of being addicted to mood-altering flesh. Not true. Addiction was a struggle to stay ahead of physical tolerance. Good sex doesn't go away after the first time and you never get used to it, and done right, it was still the only race where both people get to win.

"Man. I needed this." Harry rubbed his knuckles through his messed-up hair. His sweat smelled good. His skin tingled.

"It's a relief to be with a guy who doesn't have problems with sex," Ginny said as she ran her tongue across his bicep.

Harry grinned. Down the line, of course, lurked the jack-in-the-box nightmare.

"Don't laugh," Ginny said. "There's a lot who do."

"Like Jay?"

Her brows knitted. "You into comparisons?"

"Everybody's different, huh?"

"No." She crossed her eyes. "But truth and the male ego can wreak havoc on a bedroom real fast."

Sweat glistened on the milky slopes of her shoulders and hips and pooled in her navel. Down below, the cesarean scar made a crooked welt, deep scarlet in the firelight. His finger followed the slick furrow into her pubic hair.

"Kids?" he said.

"Little girl."

"Married?"

"Separated."

"He live in town?" Harry cast his eyes around warily.

"Heck no," she laughed. "He's an assistant sociology professor at Moorhead State."

"Good." Harry fell back into the covers, relieved. "My luck, he'd be another Paul Bunyan look-alike." He shook his head. "Hakala, Emery, Cox. Aren't there any normal-sized guys up here?"

"You," she said with a sly smile.

He lit two cigarettes and passed her one. They lay side by side and stared at the ceiling. She smoothed the scar on his hip with her fingers, as if to blend the dead tissue into the living skin. She relaxed. At ease with him and more poised with her clothes off.

"What's your husband like?"

"He wouldn't let me smoke in bed."

Harry turned, supporting himself on his elbows. "Then tell me what Cox is like?"

"Too fast," she said. "Slow down." She raised her head to be kissed. His kiss was mechanical. His mind, which had bucked off during their lovemaking, was back.

She patted him on the cheek and her expression set and tightened. "How quick it gets away," she said.

"You're not really a waitress, are you?"

"Can't we have this conversation over coffee, say in the morning?"

"Ginny, you took me to that bar knowing Cox would be there."

"We sure got his attention, didn't we? I confess, I'm not perfect."

"And you're not a waitress."

Ginny toyed with the mole on her cheek. "What gave me away? The Ph.D. in oral sex?" she smiled. "I teach elementary school. Did. I took a year's leave of absence from Moorhead public schools when my marriage went down the tubes. My dad's letting me run the diner till things straighten out."

"Which one's your dad?"

"The bank."

"Christ, your brother's Jerry the cop."

"Jerry's all right. I'm surprised he wasn't there tonight. He's sure taken an interest in you, making sure Larry doesn't catch you out in the dark some night. Just don't mention the Maple Leafs. He's sensitive. They cut him from the team his first season."

"Great." Harry shook his head. "Why in the hell did you go out with someone like Cox?"

Ginny sat up and pulled the sheets to her shoulders. "He's a sweet guy. He has these incredibly sensitive hands. Wish he could touch a body the way he touches a piece of wood. He can't help the way he looks."

"The sonofabitch is crazy, Ginny. Look in his eyes."

"What do you expect? He got mixed up with Jesse."

"You really don't like her."

"Actually, I feel sorry for her. She's got it all. Looks. Brains. In her own way, she has a lot of heart. But she's this beautiful plane that'll never take off sitting on the runway."

"So why didn't she get out of here?"

"She got as far as Duluth and Larry Emery brought her back," said Ginny. Goosebumps prickled over her smooth shoulders and she shivered and pulled the sheets tighter. "Larry loves Jesse. Except he loves the wild parts of her and his love winds up like a cage."

"So she married Bud."

"That doesn't mean she got away from Larry." She touched his forehead. "You know, you have these two lines between your eyebrows from scowling. They go away when you make love." Her hand was drawn back to his left hip. "What happened here?" she asked.

He closed his fingers over her hand. "I need a little help, Ginny. What do people really think about the shooting? Why did Chris try to kill Bud Maston?"

"Uncle Mike says Chris was stoned out of his gourd—"

"C'mon, Ginny. I fought King Kong to earn your favors."

She shrugged. "Chris was different. He was pulled in every which direction between Larry, his mother, and Reverend Karson. Like when Larry and Reverend Karson had their fight about Chris."

"What kind of fight?"

Ginny made a face. "Chris got in trouble at school—"

"Pulled a gun?"

"No, before that. End of the school year last summer. Don Karson became real . . . involved . . . you know, counseling him. Larry lost it what with Jesse leaving him and living with Maston. He dragged Chris out of the church. Karson insists Larry assaulted him. It was a real scene. Karson gave this sermon about the rights of children and abusive men who were too rough on them. Larry walked out and took a bunch of the congregation with him. Jay was the only one Chris would talk to."

"Doesn't explain why Chris pulled the trigger."

Ginny rolled her eyes. "Look. Larry and Jesse had—have this really strange relationship. Chris and Becky were both twisted from it. Uncle Mike says Chris was shrapnel that finally went off."

"Where's Cox fit?"

Ginny sat up and smoothed the sweaty tangles in her hair. "Jay is just this guy who's been seriously run over by the wheel of life. He showed up last May, drove into town in a rattletrap truck full of tools, and started remodeling this place."

"He's driving a new truck now. Where's he from?"

"He was in the service, then he had a contracting business up in the Pacific Northwest where it rains all the time. Seattle."

"You wouldn't know his birth date, would you?"

Slow revelation peeked in her eyes. "So that's why you got me in bed. Shame on you." Her eyes narrowed. "You're doing some kind of investigation. For the newspaper?"

"Help me out a little here, will you, Ginny?"

"What the hell. Sure, I did his chart. Aquarius. Jason Emmet Cox. January twenty-first, nineteen forty-one. You want me to write it down?"

Ginny got up and hunted through the room until she found a pen and stationery on the desk. She wrote briefly and came back to the mattress.

Harry was genuinely distracted, watching her come willowy through the firelight. He reached for her.

"Oh my. One of those city guys who likes to get his ears greasy," she sighed deep in her throat as Harry nuzzled, sliding down her stomach.

A clatter on the porch brought him up for air.

He lurched and caught a glimpse of a shadow by the window. He surged out the door, barefoot on the freezing mud porch. The kindling he'd stacked was toppled and footfalls pounded past the cabins. From the steps, he caught a flash of ponytail in the pole barn light.

"Who was it?" Ginny asked when he came back in.

"Becky Deucette, my guess. Playing Peeping Tom."

"Crazy damn kid," said Ginny, summoning him back beside her. Her hand floated back to its perch on his hip, exploring the scar.

"You know, I think you're all right," she said.

Later, Harry walked Ginny to her car and she lifted a chaste kiss from his face in the glare of the yard light. A haze of burned wood and tires drifted around them.

"Ginny, you think you could talk to your brother, quietlike? Find out if there's really a serious investigation about Chris's motives in the shooting?"

"You mean spy."

"I mean help me out."

Ginny cocked her head. "I might. If you tell me why you're really here poking around in things. Is it for the newspaper? Or are you working for Bud Maston?"

"Working? Ginny, I have to know what happened with Chris so I can sleep nights."

She drew a cool finger down his throat. "You know, I believe you mean that."

He watched her taillights disappear down the drive. Ginny Hakala did not make a convincing tramp. And Jay Cox wasn't the kind of guy to quit in a bar fight. The night had been choreographed. He'd underestimated these people. They were handling him.

35

Harry, in Bud's baggy terrycloth robe, hunched over the dining room table drawing with a felt-tip pen while a CD of Beethoven's Ninth rebuked the overcast morning.

He hummed along with "An die Freude" as the pen sketched spidery lines in the style of Heinrich Kley.

Jesse, in her moonlight mode, hair uncoiled in serpentine tangles; enough character in the eyebrows and dark eyes to be recognizable.

Siren torso, arms extended, hands open in offering but, where her belly curved down, instead of well-shaped legs, her hips became the twin slat uprights of a guillotine. The triangle where her thighs came together formed the weighted, suspended knife.

At the base of the sketch, a Yogi Bear with a sheriff's star dragged a tumbril containing a plump Porky Pig. A raven perched on Jesse's shoulder. Cox.

Harry Griffin's cartoon theory of criminal investigation. Go with instinct. Offstage a banquet table would be prepared. The Hakala clan, in horned helmets, napkins tucked at their throats, knives sharp, waited to carve the ham.

It made a great picture. The problem was, Chris wasn't in it.

And what about Ginny? He studied her penmanship. A distinctive, angular, printed hand. All lowercase letters. jason emmet cox.

Could he know Cox? Some collision from the past during a zombie blackout? Nah. Cox had loose marbles. Or did he? He'd looked the squared-away ex-jarhead at the funeral. Harry shook his head and crumpled the drawing and threw it at the fireplace.

He started another sheet of paper with names and a rough chronology. Bud drops out, comes to Stanley. Meets Jesse. They start the development Coop. Blue birds and happiness. Then last summer something happened and everything went kaput and Bud started drinking and getting fat. And Jesse decided to get her pound of flesh. Harry circled the words: *Last summer. Chris: trouble at school.*

If they *had* planned a hunting accident Emery would be in position to cover it up to protect Jesse and Chris. Could Emery get Chris to do that? The Chris he'd met looked far beyond any adult's control.

Then where did Cox figure in? And what about Emery's animosity toward Cox? A falling out? Harry shook his head. Too complicated. Too many people for a plan—he remembered the names on the monument in the graveyard—unless they were all in on it.

He wrote Karson's name and a question mark. Chris told something to Karson that made him suspect Emery. Below Karson he scribbled the name of the high school teacher, Talme. Check him out.

He came to Becky's name. Was she hiding something or hiding from someone? Harry wrote: Green Jeep Wrangler. He added Mitch Hakala to his list of names.

Becky was hiding, but she was snooping in windows, too?

Harry walked down the hall and stood before the closed door of Chris's room. The thing he avoided. He put his hand on the doorknob, but didn't turn it.

Start at the beginning. With Chris. The loop of film flickered in memory. The deafening shot. The kick of the rifle.

Doubt. Bud's weak-ass voice. "I was trying to talk to him."

They could just be tolerating him out of deference to Bud. All of it ... just ... shock radiating from his rifle shot that precipitating a messy divorce to a hasty doomed marriage. What if it *was* just Chris, stoned, on his own, flipping out?

What if I shot too fast?

And Bud was covering for him. Harry jerked his hand from the doorknob as if it were hot.

He dressed, pulled on an orange vest, the fancy lightweight boots Bud had bought for him, and loaded the heavy .45-70. Walk it off in the woods.

But the tiny corkscrew of doubt had grown to meat grinder proportions in his brain. Boring in. Whatever Ginny Hakala's agenda, her memory had been warm on his skin when he awoke. Gone now—

what they called mood swings in the sobriety business. He stood in the door for long minutes scanning the blackened debris in the driveway.

Serious shit, man. Shots fired.

The air shattered into a million snowflakes that pinwheeled down and blotted over the fire rings in the slush. Harry stepped into the driveway and tilted his head up and opened his mouth. Felt a snowflake touch on his tongue.

Used to do that when I was a kid.

How much of life had I tasted at sixteen? Adolescent confusion going to black. That's what I gave to Chris.

This moody shit was what he got for playing with the booze. Today is day one. One day sober.

The snowmobile trail stretched before him. He knelt and tried to pick out Becky's footprints. Fresh snow blurred the crusted impressions. He got up.

Annoying damn snow. Got at his eyes. He blinked away moisture. Heavy walking even in the light boots.

Exhausted before he'd even started. He found a stump and sat down. Snow. No sun. Black trees. Lonely out here.

He imagined the forest without humans in it. A world in which he did not exist.

And he could see how people went crazy. They suddenly just felt the full weight of life. Scales and a ruler. How much you weighed and how far you'd travel between the womb and the grave.

Christ. Maybe this is how Bud feels all the time. Fuck that.

Bring him up here to help some kid, Bud's nutty idea. Well, he'd helped all right.

Dammit! I saved his life. Kid was going to shoot him again.

What would a father do? Take a chance and yell, "Son. Put down the gun." Try to talk, like Bud. Take a bullet and still try to talk?

He imagined it. Yelling in his loud voice that could carry over gunfire. *Put it down, kid!*

Harry shook his head. There hadn't been time. He couldn't see it going down any different. He took off his gloves and touched his eyes. Not the snow. Tears.

Snap! Branch breaking in the crisp air, maybe 30 yards away . . .

Movement in the trickling snow. Oh boy! Off balance. Not ready for this. Something cutting through the brush. Deer? Not a deer. A person watching him? A running figure blurred in the trees.

"Hold it," yelled Harry, bringing up the rifle.

Becky Deucette froze in place, mired in knee-deep snow. She wore a black watch cap, a baggy army field jacket, and the damn dirty wind suit.

Harry lowered the rifle, shouted, "It's all right, kid. I won't hurt you."

She bolted and Harry ran after her.

She made it to the snowmobile trail and opened her stride. But she was clumsy in snow-pac boots. Still, no way he could match her encumbered with a rifle. She opened the distance.

He dropped the rifle and sprinted. Their gasping breath came closer together and she slipped and lost her balance in a skid. Harry tackled her.

They rolled over, grappling, and he felt her young body burn through her clothes as she arched up and her pelvis bucked, trying to throw him off.

"Knock it off," panted Harry.

He pinned her arms into the snow and surged down. She struggled, knees gripping, trying to get her feet under her.

She clenched her teeth and her dark eyes smoldered and hair twisted across her face in greasy unwashed ropes. Squirming, she almost threw him and her jacket rode up, and shoving her back down, Harry tore her bra. One of her breasts bobbed in the cold. The skin there was incredibly smooth and the brown aureole puckered and the nipple was rigid as a coffee bean.

She strained, laying the whole length of her body against his. She thrust one last time with her hips.

"You gettin' a hard-on?" she sneered. "You're stronger than me. You could make me do anything you want."

He released his hold and sat up, straddling her, holding her in place with his thighs. He panted, "You been watching me, haven't you? At the lodge last night."

"I saw you with that whore Ginny Hakala, you bastard!" She swung a short chop with her right hand. Harry caught it in his fist.

"What are you doing here?"

"I was out running. I run along the snowmobile trail."

"Not dressed for running."

"Dress any way I want."

He let her hand go and she struggled up on her elbows. "Get off me," she said. "I'm getting snow down my pants."

He pulled away and stood up. "Do yourself up," he said curtly.

Her eyes raked his face. "Get a good look?" she asked.

He pushed her back up the trail while she worked with her bra and pulled the coat around her. He picked up the rifle.

"You going to shoot me?" she asked in a petulant tone.

Harry rolled his eyes and slung the rifle over his shoulder.

"Where we going?" she asked.

He pushed her ahead of him. "Get you warmed up. Then I'm taking you back to your mom."

"She'll love that," she said contemptuously.

He pushed her. "Move."

She jammed her hands in her pockets and hunched her shoulders, with the collar of the jacket turned up, she looked like a smart-ass kid getting arrested for the first time.

When they got inside the lodge he asked. "Where is she?"

"Depends what time of the month it is. Mom's calendar's got men on it instead of numbers." Becky flopped down on the couch and folded her arms sullenly across her chest.

Harry found Cox's number in the slim directory next to the phone and took a chance. His fingers shook, dialing the number. On the third ring, Jesse answered.

"Jesse, this is Harry Griffin." Silence . . . "I've got your daughter out at the lodge."

"Hold on to her," Jesse said quickly. "Don't let her out of your sight. Tie her up if you have to."

"I thought she was following me. She spooked me," said Harry.

"But she's . . . okay?" Jesse asked slowly.

"Just a little shook up. You tell me where you are, I'll bring her home."

"No. I'll come pick her up. Don't come here. It wouldn't . . . I'll come get her."

Harry hung up the phone. "She's coming to get you."

"Yeah, sure she is," said Becky.

Harry walked past her to his duffel bag in the den, dug around, and held up a pair of sweatpants, a hooded sweatshirt, and heavy wool socks. "Put these on."

She took the clothes and began to undress right before him. He turned his back. She laughed. "Sure you don't want to watch? I don't have stretch marks like Mom."

Harry faced her and she grinned at his chagrin. She had stripped and was delicately balanced, putting one pointed foot into the gray sweats. She looked sideways at him through her greasy hair and held up her soiled underwear. "You ripped my bra."

He looked past her, at the words "Bud is a fucker" still scrawled in garish green on the wall by the fireplace, and felt irritated with both himself and her. With himself, because he should have removed it that day he returned to the lodge and encountered Cox in the driveway. With her, because he had a feeling she'd written it.

He went to the kitchen, threw open drawers and cupboards, and came back at her with a can of Comet, a bucket of water, and a copper scrub. He yanked the sweatshirt down around her outstretched arms and pushed her across the main room to the fireplace.

"Till your mom gets here, you take that writing off the wall."

"I'm not your fucking maid!"

"Just do it," muttered Harry.

Harry paced. Becky scrubbed. The minutes dragged by. She gave him a disgusted look when he splashed cold water on his face in the kitchen sink and ran a comb through his hair.

"How nice. You combed your hair for Mom," she said sarcastically. "She's probably doing *her* hair."

36

Fifteen minutes later, a blue Ford Escort—muffler rattling, rusting rocker panels—pulled up in front of the lodge and Jesse got out in wrinkled jeans and a heavy sweater with unraveled elbows.

She wore neither lipstick nor makeup and her hair hung slack, unbraided, frizzed with static electricity. Strain etched the corners of her eyes and mouth. She was the most desirable woman he had ever seen.

Charcoal crunched under her snowboots and she winced at the debris. When he opened the door, she saw the 12 gauge leaning against the wall and it had to be the grimmest moment of his life when he looked into her eyes.

Becky, back in her jacket, tried to shoulder by. Her face flushed as she passed through the wall of tension in the doorway. She grabbed Jesse's elbow. "Let's go."

"Wait. What happened?" said Jesse, hauling Becky back by the jacket.

"I was out hunting." Harry's words sounded bitten. Bruises on the cold air.

"He was crying," said Becky. "Sitting on this stump crying just like a baby. Then he must have heard me as I was trying to get out of there and he came after me with his gun."

Jesse scanned Harry's face as her daughter spoke. "Go wait in the car," she told her.

Becky shook her head. "Not leaving you alone with him."

"Git," said Jesse.

Becky drew herself up. "Jay said . . ." She pursed her lips. "Don't get alone with him . . ."

Jesse said starkly, "Jay's back with Ginny."

"But . . ." Becky ground her teeth together.

"Move. Right now!" ordered Jesse.

Becky's dirty face exploded with hot tears. "You're blind, all of you are blind. Why don't you just fuck him on Chris's grave!"

Jesse drew back her hand and slapped Becky, burning the palm across her face and Becky slumped and began to sob and walked down the wobbly steps. She stood staring at her shoelaces for a moment. Then she burst into a full run and disappeared around the pole barn, toward the snowmobile trail. Jesse started to follow and her shoulders sagged and she stopped.

They were alone in the driveway, facing in opposite directions. Motionless.

"She was out there that morning, on skis. She saw us in . . . the trees," said Harry.

"Perhaps," said Jesse.

"She's been spying on me," Harry said, his voice too loud. "Keep her away."

"How am I going to keep her away?" Jesse shot back. "I can't even find her. Did you see how she looks? Like she's been sleeping with cats and dogs. God knows where she gets herself off to."

When they turned to face each other, Harry wasn't sure if they were looking back or if they were looking forward to Sodom and Gomorrah.

She took a cigarette from her sweater pocket and tried to light it, but her fingers didn't have the strength to push the little wheel on her lighter. Harry brought out his Zippo. His own smokes. They lit up.

Jesse turned away again and put one hand to the soot-blackened porch for balance. Harry spread his fingers and brought them to within an inch from the back of her hair. A fuzz of energy tickled his fingertips.

When she spoke, he pulled his hand back.

"That took a lot of balls, what you did with those divorce papers. I thought Bud might try to come to the funeral. I never thought I'd see you again."

"Yes, you did," said Harry.

Jesse's shoulders rose and fell and she turned around and he could not name the expression she formed with her lips. He should say some-thing—some impossible word he didn't know that was made out of love and sorrow and distrust.

Her hand came up and he moved to block it. "Hush," she said with total authority as her fingers lightly brushed his hair. "You look like a high school boy after gym class with comb marks in his hair."

She bit her lip and looked away and then noticed the soot on her hand from the porch and realized she'd marked his forehead with it. She rubbed her fingers together, then dragged on the cigarette. "Leave Jay alone. He's in real rough shape."

Harry nodded. "Then tell him to stay away from me."

She took a deep breath. "This all has to stop. It's time to be . . . practical. We have to talk."

"We're talking right now."

She shook her head. "Someplace away from here."

"About what?"

"A divorce settlement."

"That's for lawyers," said Harry.

"We could meet for dinner . . . I know a place on sixty-one."

"I'll think about it," said Harry.

"You do that. Think real hard." She walked down the steps and got in her car. Completely exhausted by their conversation, Harry watched her drive away. His hand was up next to his temple where she'd touched him and came away faintly smudged with soot.

She called an hour later.

"The restaurant's called the Shore Wind, just north of Gooseberry Falls. I can meet you there at eight," she said.

"I'll be there."

"I'll be alone," she said.

"So will I."

He spent the afternoon watching the day turn cold as bone, so damn cold that only Eskimo and Indian curses had the grit to do it justice.

He made a pot of very strong, very black, coffee.

Bud called at 6 P.M. while Harry was cleaning the rifle. Radio Free Ojibway was back on the radio, dropping out of a hole in the sky.

"What's that in the background?" asked Bud.

"Drums."

Bud's voice sounded hollow over the long-distance connection. "I was hoping you wouldn't be there. You got me worried."

"Look, Bud. I was having some trouble. But I'm all right now."

"I said that very thing this morning in my group. They suggested that I stick around."

"I saw Jesse. She wants to talk. Tonight. About a divorce settlement."

"Be careful," Bud said quickly. "Whatever you do, don't get sucked in to trying to get her approval."

"Anything you want me to say? Know about?"

Harry listened to Bud's rapid breathing. "Talk to her," Bud said tightly. "Find out what she wants."

37

He arrived early and walked along the beach behind the restaurant and the cold gnawed down and Lake Superior clicked in the dark like a pane of glass.

Jesse arrived punctually. Her face was porcelain, bare of makeup, and she could have just emerged from an icy shower of grief. Or calculation. Wordless, he helped her off with her coat.

She wore a severe ivory silk blouse with a high buttoned neck and a long dark skirt and her hair plunged down in strict black lines against the tendons of her throat.

His suit wouldn't do, so he'd put on one of Bud's sweaters that he'd found in the bedroom closet. His dress shirt and tie. And his scabs. Her eyes sparked when she recognized the sweater.

The manager took her hand and expressed his condolences about Chris. They spoke intimately and Jesse noticed a few changes he'd made in the decor as he ushered them to a table by the windows overlooking the shore.

"They know you here," said Harry.

"I did some work for them once."

A small bar situated along one wall. "Tending bar?" he asked.

"I worked on their books."

"So you're not a bartender?"

"I'm good with numbers. Taxes, things like that."

"Bud leaves things out."

"Definitely." Her eyes hardened. "Bud likes me in jeans and a lumberjack shirt. When I was a kid my dad taught me to flip flapjacks in a frying pan. Bud saw me do it once and decided that's who I was."

"Was he right?"

"I took tap-dancing lessons when I was a kid, too. Doesn't make me a chorus girl." She ordered a vodka martini. He had black coffee.

"So how do we begin, you and I?" she asked frankly, holding the martini glass in both hands.

"We already . . . began," said Harry. She raised her eyebrows. "I think you tried to kill my friend for money. That you used your own kid to do it."

"Prove it," she said straight back.

"Never happen in Maston County." Harry inhaled and said the rest of it. "I'm also obviously attracted to you."

"Prove that, too," she said.

Harry spread his hands on the linen tablecloth in what he meant to be a slow stable gesture. His fingers blundered into a water glass and nearly tipped it over.

She studied him. "Don't get hung up on appearances. You have this knack for walking into the middle of things. You should try to catch some beginnings." Her voice chiseled, matching her eyes. "One thing Bud knows about is appearances. He creates people and assigns them roles. He made you into the best buddy. First he gave you a lot in common, then he got you to owe him . . ."

She lit a Marlboro and leaned forward.

"He gets things on people to hold over them. Then he tosses in a curve and enjoys watching you scramble. And you can't shake him. He—" she searched for a word—"adapts. It scares me what he could do if he got into politics."

Harry had not expected this kind of conversation. He couldn't tell if she was testing him for weaknesses or for strengths.

"He knew," she said.

"Knew what?"

"That we couldn't keep our hands off each other. What we had wasn't even ours. We're stuck. Like two butterflies on a pin." She blew a nervous stream of smoke. "The biggest mistake I ever made in my life was marrying him."

Harry raised an eyebrow and she jerked her lips in a nonsmile. "And your biggest mistake was coming up here. But I did and you did and . . ." Her voice trailed off.

Harry took the button from his pocket and placed it on the table.

"What's that?" she asked.

"Came off my pants, that morning in the woods. Larry Emery found it."

"He would." She pursed her lips and turned her head and her breasts rose and fell under the silk. When she looked back, the precise finish vanished from her eyes. They clouded, rapture in one, everlasting damnation in the other.

"You're trying to turn me around . . . just like that morning," Harry said, guarded.

She cocked her head and the movement rippled her straight hair. "He took you off the street, fixed your teeth, got you your job. You're his hard guy Frankenstein. Wasn't for him, you'd be exercising those fifty-caliber shoulders on a loading dock somewhere, going to seedy AA meetings every night, and having tense dreams about glasses of draft beer."

Harry gave her a tight smile and sorrow bunched the corners of her lips. He couldn't decipher what impulse sucked the tears back from her eyes. One second it was vulnerable, the next it shriveled into the bitterest of smiles.

"You can fuck me, but you can't see me, and I'm sitting right here in front of you," she said.

"Jesse . . . we have to talk about Chris."

Her eyes slapped him. "Nobody's innocent. All clear?"

Maybe all they had were random moments. This one was gone. Her words came in tight wire bundles. "Listen carefully, wise ass. Tell your master I want the lodge, the lake, the land . . . and a million dollars."

"That's pretty steep blood money for a murdering kid."

A spark of hellfire flew in her eyes. "Combined business and divorce settlement. He can cash out. Simple round figures."

"Why don't you tell him?" he asked.

"He slapped an injunction on me. We're not supposed to talk."

"So get a lawyer."

"Why? When you're here. The invaluable friend." She laughed bitterly. "The best man, the best shot . . . the best fuck."

They became aware of the waiter poised nervously to take their order.

"I lost my appetite. How about you?" she said briskly. The waiter retreated.

She pulled some bills from the pocket of her purse and dropped them on the table, getting ready to leave.

"You don't have much of a life, do you?" she asked as she stood up. "You're not interested in money, or power. Just some myths about who you are and a few moments when they seem to come true. Chris was one of those moments, wasn't he?"

"Why's Becky hiding?" he countered as they walked toward the coat rack.

"Keep it simple, stupid. The lake, the lodge, the land, and the money."

He took her arm and pulled her around to face him. "You don't fit up here, with Emery and Cox."

Her face flashed. "We don't all get to wind up where we fit. Sometimes we wind up where we get stuck." She pried off his hand and put on her coat.

In the parking lot they hunched in their coats, leaving, but not finished. Harry dropped all pretense of control. "Why's Cox look at me that way?" he demanded.

"You mean like he's seen a ghost?" Abruptly she turned and walked down the path among the boulders to the shore. Harry followed her. She turned up her collar and huddled close to him.

"Why are we here?" he asked.

"Open your eyes."

He peered into her face. She took his chin in her hand and pointed it out over the lake. The horizon flamed pale green and vermilion where the Aurora Borealis made a million-car pileup at the edge of the world.

"Pretty," he said, looking into her face.

"It's fucking beautiful, Harry. The most beautiful thing you'll ever see."

Another situation, another woman; it would be the time for a kiss and the kiss was spectral between them in the warm, white vapor of their breath mingling and gone in the night.

He opened his mouth to speak. Her finger pressed her lips and gently moved to his, sealing them. She was so good it looked like a real tear bent in the corner of her eye when she said, "The worst part of all this is it had to be you."

She turned and walked up the path. Halfway up, she spun and made an electric figure against the flickering sky.

"What the hell do you want?" he yelled at her.

"I want you to take a chance on me."

Then she disappeared into the darkness. He caught up to her in the parking lot.

"Anything else you want to tell Bud?" he asked in a hoarse voice.

"Sure, tell him life is unfair." Composed now, she got into her car and rolled down the window. "I'm a damsel in distress. Since you served those papers at the funeral, the local cavemen think I'm up for grabs. Larry has it in his mind that the guy who gets the biggest deer gets me. Men, huh?" she said as she drove away.

Her presence lingered and the caress of evil came as softly and innocently as a breeze stirs a flag. Shoot a deer. Fuck a dragon. Betray Bud. Out on the black arena of Superior, ice cracked like a starter pistol.

38

Take a chance.

The old infantry gamble. Stay low in the weeds with nineteen. Or stand up and walk toward it and tempt the bitch.

Hit me.

It wasn't her sensuality that stayed with him. It was the credible way she plunked down her demands.

She meant a million bucks. Harry thought about it. A dollar sign, a one, and six zeros. And Bud, pickled in guilt about Chris, would probably roll over for it. So what kind of a risk did she have in mind?

Bud's Jeep found its way to the front door of the Stanley Municipal Liquor Store and Harry was going two out of three falls with a powerful urge when the counterman flipped the closed sign on the door. He took the hint. Tie match for tonight. He drove up Highway 7.

The large manila envelope was tacked to the lodge door with a push pin. No writing on it, brand new, unsealed.

Harry placed it on the dining room table, went back out on the porch, and listened. Only the cold biting down and the cooling tick of the Jeep engine.

The envelope contained a yellowing page from the *Duluth Times.* He glanced at the date on the folio as he smoothed out the folds in the faded newsprint. Six years old.

Damn.

A circle of red Magic Marker swirled around a photograph on the page. Jesse's hair was shorter and she was more trim and tanned-looking and she wore a white party dress and held a bouquet of flowers. A tall rugged man in a tux stood next to her and their hands were joined around a champagne glass. They stood in the cockpit of a sailboat and the boat's name danced in stylized white script across the transom.

Tyche.

Harry blinked and read the headline over the picture: KIDWELL TIES THE KNOT BEFORE HE SAILS.

Tip Kidwell. He read the cutline: "Tip Kidwell toasts his solo round-the-world voyage with his new bride, the former Marie Bursac. The couple were married on Kidwell's 36-foot-sloop just before he sailed."

Bursac? Her maiden name?

Kidwell had been a story. Harry'd made a map of the voyage for the paper and updated it as Kidwell navigated the globe. He'd sailed back into the Duluth harbor a hometown hero. The big news twist came the next day. Kidwell had been killed in a confused shootout with Duluth police who had a warrant to search his boat for a load of cocaine. Their timing had been bad. A shipment of drugs was found in Duluth, but not on Kidwell's boat, and a huge legal stink resulted in a lawsuit against the police department. Harry couldn't remember.

Suddenly very sober in his thinking, he grabbed the phone and called Randall's number in St. Paul.

"I wake you up?" Harry asked when Dorothy answered.

"No, I was reading. What's happening?"

"Randall there?"

"Put him on a plane this morning. He's gone to a conference in D.C. Harry? He's been scratchy on the subject of you. Did you guys have words?"

"Ah, he was riding my ass about coming up here, I barked at him. Forget that, listen. Remember Tip Kidwell?"

"Sure, I interviewed the pompous bastard."

"You remember anything about his wife?"

"No. I didn't work that end of the story."

"I just came home here and there's this envelope with a page from the Duluth paper six years old tacked to the door. Picture of Kidwell just before he sailed. Staged a wedding on the boat. Dorothy, he married the same lady Bud did. I'm sure of it. Name's different, face is the same."

Dorothy's voice sat up, alert. "Really."

"Whoever left it for me circled her face in red."

Her voice perked up. "This is creepy, in an interesting way."

"Somebody up here wants to tell me something."

"You talk to Bud about it?"

"Not yet. Dorothy, are you still on speaking terms with that Minneapolis homicide cop with the blow-dry hair and the black Porsche?"

Aghast, Dorothy protested. "Harry, that was *years* ago."

"But he'd trip all over his big gun to do you a favor, wouldn't he?"

Her voice squirmed. "I don't know. Randall did sort of scare him half to death."

"Get something to write with." Harry scrambled through the sheets of paper on the table, found Ginny's note with Cox's birth date.

"Do I have to?" Dorothy asked reluctantly.

"You have to. Pulling in my chits."

"Okay. Ready," said Dorothy.

"Have your cop run Jason Emmet Cox, born January twenty-first, nineteen forty-one, through the computer. But mainly see if he can find somebody in the Duluth coppers who'll give him the dirt on Kidwell, the bust, the shooting, all the stuff that didn't get in the press."

"What are you looking for?"

"Maybe the reason they didn't have a grand jury . . . Dorothy, find the name of the cop who shot Kidwell. And what the widow wound up with."

"Now there's an ugly thought. I'll get back to you." Low-key newshound excitement made a tin rattle in her voice. She hung up.

"Tyche," Harry said aloud. Tyche Fortuna—the bitch goddess of gamblers and mercenaries–was a realpolitik deity the ancient Greeks turned to after they lost their civilization. That dumb country-club prick Kidwell had the wit to name his sloop after Jesse.

Bud said what? She married a guy in Duluth and he died. Right, in a hail of police bullets.

Okay, so who left the clipping?

Karson. Had to be. Doing his backwoods Deep Throat routine.

A car horn blared in the drive. Harry jumped up and ran out the door and saw the now-familiar shadow dart past the pole barn.

He hadn't locked the Jeep. Becky had turned on the lights. When he went to turn them off he saw the note pinned under the windshield wiper.

"Meet me up on Nanabozho Point in the morning. Early."

39

Harry dressed in the predawn dark, made coffee, filled a Thermos, and packed it, along with two sandwiches, in his knapsack. He tossed in Bud's fancy Zeiss binoculars, loaded the rifle, and tested the bindings on a pair of Bearpaw snowshoes.

Then he studied a Superior Hiking Trail map on the back of a Snowshoe Lodge brochure. Trails trickled through a long rectangle marked "privately owned" that started at the highway and stretched back over the top of the ridge. Bud's property.

He wanted the dotted line that branched off from the lakeshore and meandered up the ridge to the overlook at the peak: Nanabozho Point.

Quiet as a shadow, Harry slipped into the greater shadow of the forest.

The muscle below his left shoulder blade twinged hot—the vulnerable place on his body he couldn't touch. For years he'd superstitiously believed that a bullet orbited Detroit, waiting to land on that spot, and he could feel them out there, sniper eyes plucking at his clothing.

He followed the snowmobile trail and it was smooth going on the snow cushion over the hard pack the sleds had left. No need for the Bearpaws slung over his shoulder.

The moon sailed in Persian lamb clouds and spun spidery shadows. The shadows reminded him of Jesse.

Keep it simple. Stay alert.

He followed the snowmobile trail to the cross trail and squinted to make out the sign. An arrow pointed up to the point. Junction. Always an apt place for an ambush. He slipped off the trail and found a spot in the pines. He cut a pile of boughs to make a nest 20 yards down a long moraine from the crossing.

He sat motionless and his hearing unplugged by stages until it seemed that he could hear the sun roll up the ridge to the east and disrobe the moon.

Up ahead somewhere, a deer started, then bounded through the undergrowth. Dry branches snapped. Then silence. Harry poised and cupped his hands to his ears.

The footfalls were soft at first. Too steady a rhythm for a deer. They came from the north, along the snowmobile trail, and he picked up movement in the faint light.

Becky in jeans, his sweatshirt, Emery's field jacket, a black watch cap, and running shoes. She loped gracefully along the trail, resting her forearms in a cradle formed by a pair of snow-pac boots tied by the laces and slung around her neck. She slowed to a walk at the trail junction. He could make out her hair in a ponytail and see the white puffs of her breath.

Dawn poked through the trees and a lattice of shadow crept across the snow and Becky raised a mittened hand. Her body arched alert. Listening. Satisfied she was alone, she turned to face the sun and set her shoulders in resignation and plunged up the trail to the point.

Strange way to hide. Running the trail. Follow her? Better wait. See if anybody was after her.

Two does wandered down the far side of the moraine, fat and idle as cartoon mice. Harry let them pass, then left his perch and followed Becky's fresh footprints up the ridge.

From the corner of his eye he caught a smudge of red up the slope. Hunter? He reached the spot where he'd seen the movement and found snowshoe tracks. Becky wasn't carrying snowshoes. Her tracks were knee-deep in the snow and their shape was different. She'd changed to the boots. He strapped on his Bearpaws and started up the incline.

It was a steep goddamn trail and the sign of wandering hunters fell away as he climbed. Only animal tracks. Rabbit. Deer mostly. Piles of their black braided shit. Through breaks in the pine and birch he saw the lodge illuminated by the fading yard lights. Headlights on Highway 7 made semaphore flashes between the trees.

The granite shoulders of the ridge increasingly jutted from the snow cover and a cloud of mist rolled in from the lake. Trees floated, twisting from the crannies with tangled roots swept bare by the wind. Troll country.

His snowshoes slid on rock and he took them off and tied them to the backpack. The tracks disappeared on a windswept escarpment.

Climbing now, rifle slung across his back, he needed both hands to pull himself up the massive bluff of fissured granite that rose above him in a hood of mist.

A weathered sign tilted on a tree and pointed up the rock face: CAUTION. HAZARDOUS AREA. CHILDREN SHOULD BE KEPT IN HAND.

He cocked his head to a crisp arrhythmic rattle from above. Not rock or wood or metal. The click of bone on bone.

Alert, he scrambled up the rock and sweat ran in his eyes and the snowshoes and rifle lurched on his back. The face broadened out and a dome of furrowed granite spread before him with a foot trail sketched into the rock that led to the promontory. He scaled the last fold of rock and passed through a pygmy pine jungle with a soft moss floor. The layered mist parted. Good. He could see.

The rattle was louder now. He unslung his rifle and approached cautiously and the trees ended and the Big Water did its endless float to the horizon. Far below, Stanley was a pastel watercolor that turned off its night lights one by one.

A tortured birch grew from a tangle of roots in a rock cranny on the apex of the point and the rattle came from a pair of deer antlers tied together and hung over a branch.

Spokes of sunlight thrust through the clouds and raced over the granite-barnacled backbone of the ridge as daylight soaked up the slumbering mist and Harry's eyes followed the racing edge of dawn. A visual slap—the evergreen spine of the ridge collapsed into a immense concave shadow.

The Stanley open pit. Hidden, except from up here.

His calves trembling from the climb, Harry took off his pack, set his rifle and snowshoes aside, and opened his Thermos. With a cup of coffee, he found a seat on the gnarled roots.

He lit a cigarette and watched the magic slowly seep out of the dawn. Then he took out the binoculars and scanned the terrain below.

Something.

He dropped the binoculars and reached for his rifle.

His hand grabbed empty air.

Sheriff Emery stood three feet away holding the rifle, inspecting it. Harry lurched up suddenly and spilled hot coffee on his wrist.

No sound of his approach. Only the sigh of the wind in the pines below and the rattle of the antlers. No Jerry for a chaperone today.

Emery was bareheaded and his dark hair was longer when it wasn't combed back. He wore the red Mackinaw with the black band striping the sleeves and the hem and his jeans were tucked into the top of worn, greasy leather boots with thick, upturned moccasin toes. A scoped .30-06 hung from his shoulder with a pair of slender snowshoes that gleamed wet yellow.

Emery took a step forward and Harry backed up defensively, then, realizing he had a sheer drop of thin air a foot to his rear, he stood his ground.

Emery's hand came forward, returning the weapon. "That's an old gun you got there, Harry Griffin," he said, friendly enough, as if he'd left the words they'd exchanged at the lodge down below with the load of his life.

Harry squinted around the rock bluff. "Where . . . ?"

"Heard you coming up the trail. Thought you might be a deer. You, ah, got another smoke?"

Harry held out his pack. Emery selected a cigarette and tore off the filter and lit it from Harry's lighter. His hands, cupped around the flame, were ruddy olive brown, powerful and thickly veined in the thin sunlight. He nodded at the antlers. "Leave these horns up here. When the wind's right, can sound like two bucks going at it. Once in a while it draws in a big guy." His face was tight and clear-eyed as he scanned the surrounding country.

"I saw Becky on the snowmobile trail," said Harry.

"Uh-huh."

"She's been following me. Peeking in windows at the lodge."

Emery nodded. "She can be like that. Sneaky."

Harry refilled the Thermos cup and offered it to Emery. "'Fraid it's just coffee," he said.

Emery didn't comment. He sipped the cup. "Good," he said. They smoked in silence for a moment.

Harry gestured toward the gigantic open pit that broke the back of the ridge. "Sure wrecks the nature walk."

"Yeah," said Emery, "My dad said he took a coupla battleships out of that hole in the ground." He flicked the coal from his cigarette and field stripped the paper. Then he kneaded the remains between his fingers, raised his hand, sniffed it, and let the wind carry the brown strings off his fingers. He was different up here, his energy straighter.

"You were a cop in Duluth, weren't you?" said Harry.

Emery's tobacco eyes passed slowly over Harry's face. "Let me ask the questions." He handed the cup back. "Fact is, not a good idea to ask too many questions of people you meet up here in these woods. You might not like the answers you get." said Emery.

He left like smoke, without a sound.

Harry sat back down with his rifle firmly across his knees and drank another cup of coffee and smoked another cigarette. The only sound was the click click click of the antlers swaying over his head.

"He gone?" Becky called out.

"Got me," said Harry. All he saw was trees and sky.

"He has this way of just showing up that can give you the creeps." Her voice came from over the lip of the drop. By holding on to the tree roots, he could lean out and see her six feet below, sitting on a concave shelf of rock. She stood up and dusted off the seat of her jeans. "Got any food?" she asked.

"Sandwich."

"What is it?" she asked.

"Ham and cheese."

She climbed up, took his hand, and swung up beside him. She stood with her hands thrust deep into the baggy pockets of the field jacket. Her running shoes were tied together and thrown around her neck. When she pulled off her sweaty wool cap, he smelled an outdoors broth of body odor and unwashed clothing.

She squatted on the thick tree root and devoured the sandwich and washed it down with coffee.

"Shouldn't you be in school?" he asked.

"I've learned all I'm going to learn in that school. I'd rather watch all the grown-ups. That's real school."

"So, you learn anything lately?"

"Uh-huh. You were out with Mom," she accused with food in her mouth.

"There's food on your upper lip," said Harry.

She wiped at her face with her sleeve. "You fuck her again?" she asked.

"Watch your mouth."

She grinned at him. "Bet you did, fuck her. If I was home I could tell cause she gets this dreamy full-like glaze on her eyes. Sorta like a python I saw on *National Geographic* after it slowly squeezed a baby pig to death and swallowed it. Women are supposed to glow, aren't they? Not Mom. She just swells up a little. Men are Mom's food of choice."

Harry ignored her. After an interval, he asked, "Emery follow you up here?"

"Yeah. He's never far away."

"He watching us now?"

"Probably." She hugged herself. "Maybe he wants to see if you'll throw me off this cliff."

Her nimble eyes tingled with secrets and budding beauty under a layer of dirt and Harry cautioned himself, mindful her IQ was way ahead of her teenage emotions.

"Somebody left something pinned to my door last night," he said.

"Uh-huh. I read it."

"See who left it?"

"Dumbass Don Karson. Who else."

"So, tell me about Tip Kidwell."

She yawned with cosmic teenage boredom. "Kidwell was a jerk. Mom always marries jerks."

Again, the sensation of eyes plucking at him. Somebody *was* watching them. Harry could feel the crosshairs of a high-powered scope crawl on his neck.

"Why's Emery trying to catch you?"

"Figures I know something."

"Do you know something?"

"Yup," she grinned nervously. "He could figure it out if he wasn't drinking." She hugged herself and shivered. "It's all so *obvious*."

"So just go tell him, or tell me."

"Can't. Not yet. I'll let him catch me when the time's right, like I let you catch me by the lodge," she announced. Boldness flared in her eyes. Too much. She didn't know how to adjust the flame. For the first time, she resembled her mother.

"Let me catch you," said Harry.

"Uh-huh. It was a test, to see what you'd do. You could have murdered me and stuck my body in the bottom of the lake."

"Like I 'murdered' your brother?"

She looked away. "You didn't kill Chris on purpose."

"Then why'd you do this to my face?"

"At the time I didn't know. But I've thought it all through and now I know."

"You saw us that morning. You swept the tracks so your dad wouldn't . . ."

"Uh-huh. Mom's got enough trouble without that."

Harry seized her jacket and pulled her forward. "For Chrissake, Becky, quit screwing around—"

"Watch it. Dad could be out there, but Mitch is there for sure watching you through a rifle scope," she cautioned as her eyes roved confidently toward the treeline. Harry sat back and opened his hands to show they were empty. She smiled. "Sorry, I have to do this my way and I have to trust you more."

"How do you propose to do that?"

She shrugged. "Tell me about yourself."

"Like what?"

"What was your mom like?"

"She taught me to read and to draw. She died when I was young."

"What about your dad?"

Harry took a breath and it just came out; because he was sitting on a mountaintop talking to a kid, he figured it was all right. "He was an officer in the army—he was in Europe and Korea and Vietnam. Now he's a writer."

"Poor Harry," said Becky as she stood up and dusted damp bark from the seat of her trousers. "Just then, you reminded me of Chris—afraid to face the truth." She chastised him with an intelligent frown. "You lied. Bud told us all about you. Your father was in the army all right, but they were going to send him to jail for being a coward and he died drunk in a bar. Bud said that's why you never quit once you start."

Harry sat perfectly still, not even reacting when he saw Mitch Hakala step from the trees 50 yards away wearing illegal gray tree bark camo and carrying a scoped rifle.

"You're a pretty smart kid," said Harry.

"I'm pretty smart, period," said Becky. "And I need to know exactly why you're here, but it looks like you still haven't figured it out for yourself."

"Why'd you get me up here?"

"To tell you to go see Miss Loretta. Take her a present when you go. A carton of Pall Malls." She turned and walked toward Mitch and the trees.

"What? Who's Loretta?" he shouted after her. But she and the boy were gone. Harry sat alone on the gnarled roots of the twisted tree and watched the sunlight play checkers on the vast plain of Superior.

You're eight years old and you creep to the edge of the stairs in a rural Michigan farmhouse and listen to your uncles drink their beer and tell their war stories and you hear a few words and suddenly you're more alone in the world.

You learn how your dad really died in the war, how your dad could savage other men in the ring and beat your mother when he was drunk, but when it came to the German army . . .

Learn how your uncles and your dad went to fight Hitler as brand-new paratroopers in the same company of the 82nd and when the time came, how your dad chickened out in the door and refused to jump into Sicily.

So they brought him over to the invasion beach on a boat and sent him to the line, to the Biazza Ridge, where his company was dug in and he took one look at the panzers of the Hermann Göring Division and he deserted his buddies and ran away.

Back in England, waiting on a court-martial for cowardice, he got himself stabbed to death in a drunken bar fight over a whore and you weren't even born yet.

Harry threw pebbles over the drop, one after another. His sense of physical fear had always been acute by a factor of imagination squared, but he'd also had his dad's reflexes, so he went into Golden Gloves and the factories and streets of Detroit and then the jungles of Vietnam to put his blood through the hairiest strainer he could find to cleanse the coward gene and he never ran away.

He dropped his chin on his chest. Except from his wife and kid. Except from Linda Margoles and his whole goddamn life.

He didn't plan it, but he wound up coming down through the low ridges and the swamp where the shooting happened.

When the deer snorted in the thicket, he didn't even break stride. Damn deer was laughing at him from deep inside the rhubarb-colored briar patch.

He walked an arc around the brush and the deer started its stamping and blowing. Arrogant fucker. Serve him right if I put one up his nostril.

Harry trudged back to the lodge. Karson. The schoolteacher, Talme. Now Miss Loretta? The list was getting longer.

Not even halfway through the morning and he was beat. Should have bought that bottle.

40

Stanley High School was near the hospital in the hilly streets above the town. The spacious tented halls echoed with departed iron wealth.

In the principal's office Harry asked the secretary, "Where would I find Karl Talme this hour?"

She gave him an officious once-over. "Are you a parent?" she asked.

"Yes," said Harry. Which was true, but not accurate under the circumstances. "It concerns a student."

"You must be new?"

"Yup. Just moved in."

"People are moving out, not moving in," she said dryly. Talme taught Senior English the next two hours. He had a break between classes in twenty minutes. She gave him the room number and craned her neck over her desk as he walked back into the hall.

On his way out to the parking lot, he passed beneath Bud's photograph enshrined above a brass plaque commemorating the new gym. The old Bud, Huck Finn playing Citizen Kane, his face radiating civic virtue and noblesse oblige.

Steam came from the grille of the green Jeep Wrangler parked next to Bud's Jeep. Mitch. His car hadn't been there when Harry pulled into the lot. He smoked a cigarette, watched two firemen flood a skating rink on a snowy athletic field, and kept an eye out for Mitch Hakala. Back inside, he quick-stepped at the bell to get to Talme's room before classes changed, found the room number, and glanced through the glass-paned door. Talme sat at his desk. Students filed past him picking up assignments.

Not that many students. Even during class change, the halls were half empty. Harry let the sparse herd jostle him. When the room was empty, he went in.

Talme had the build of a fireplug that liked to eat a lot. Comfortably powerful. He rearranged his thick glasses to focus on Harry.

"Mr. Talme, could I have a few minutes of your time? My name is . . ."

"I know who you are. You disrupted the funeral, you called my house the other night. My wife said you were rude on the phone." His tone was matter-of-fact. Competent, grounded guy.

"You were Chris Deucette's homeroom teacher . . ."

Talme cut him off. "Don Karson told me he was talking to you. He runs his mouth too damn much."

"Yeah, he does. How about I buy you a cup of coffee and we talk about it."

Talme's sigh conveyed an appreciation of the absurdity of life. "Sure. What the hell. You know where the Timber Cruiser Cafe is?" Harry nodded. "Meet me there at noon." Talme dropped his heavy eyes back to his study plan.

The students moving through the halls parted around an immovable object ahead of him. Mitch Hakala wore a varsity jacket with a shoulder patch. Hockey. The word *Captain* was stitched across it. His hunting boots dripped melted snow.

"Hiya," he said.

"Hello, Mitch."

"You want to know about Chris Deucette?" Mitch asked.

Harry nodded. Mitch's eyes were serious as ball bearings and Harry absolutely believed they had been tracking him through a rifle scope up on the ridge.

"Talme won't tell you all of it." The incorruptible temper of hard youth was in his face and it reminded Harry of a whole generation of other young faces. GIs.

"So?" said Harry.

"C'mon," said Mitch, "I gotta take a leak." Harry followed him down the hall and into a tiled lavatory that smelled nostalgically of stale cigarette smoke. Mitch pointed to the toilets. "In there. Middle stall."

Harry entered the stall, lowered himself to the seat, and closed the door. The interior had been freshly painted. A crude drawing of a vagina was laboriously sketched with pencil over the toilet paper dispenser. The walls were scarred with eroded graffiti beneath the paint.

One of them had been scratched deeply into the metal of the door with a sharp object. He angled around to use the light to see the scratches in relief.

CHRIS DUCETTE SUCKS DICK.

Mitch waited in the hall. He inclined his head, "You wanna talk?"

"I'm staying out at Maston's," Harry nodded.

"I'll let you know when I'm coming," said Mitch.

Karl Talme canted his shoulders sideways to fit through the door to the cafe, came to the booth where Harry sat, and tossed down a high school yearbook. Last year's. A paper marker stuck from the pages. "Go on. Open it," said Talme. A slender waitress brought coffee. Ginny Hakala was nowhere in sight.

The marked page showed small pictures of the sophomore class. Harry scanned the young faces. "He's not here," said Harry.

"Sure he is, his name's there."

Harry found the name and backtracked through the block of pictures. His eyes raised to Talme. The picture, even in small scale, was not the Chris he'd met. The boy had shorter, tidier hair and a wry, devilish smile on his face.

"Here's the class picture he handed out," said Talme, putting the picture on the yearbook page. The resemblance to his sister was pronounced in the bone structure and the wide intelligent eyes. No raccoon circles. No morbid druggy smirk.

Talme lit a pipe and puffed while Harry flipped the picture over and read. "To Mr. Talme. Huzzah! For showing me the difference between commas and semicolons. Next year on to the ablative." It was signed Chris "Hemingway" Deucette.

"Next year, on to the ablative . . ." Harry's lungs caved in with a long sigh. "Not the kid I met," he said.

"You killed," said Talme. His smile was phlegmatic. "I'm not judging you, Griffin. The law does that, and they found you—what?—a victim of tragic circumstances."

"When was this picture taken?"

"Over a year ago. He was my best sophomore English student. I have some things he wrote at home, if you're interested. He had talent."

"Where was he living then? I mean, who was his mother with?"

"Jesse." Talme said heavily. A sound to conjure with. He sucked on his pipe.

"Who?"

"Larry Emery." Talme struck a match and relit his pipe.

"Were they ever going to get married?" asked Harry.

"That's one of the big local mysteries. They did go to Don's church together."

"Church?" Harry raised his eyebrows.

Talme studied the bowl of his pipe over his glasses. "I know what you mean," he said. "She has a quality of animal magnetism. Or you could say she's a cunt."

"They broke up," said Harry.

"On a regular basis. She started tending bar at the VFW. To spite Larry."

"You know Jay Cox?"

"Drifter . . . good carpenter."

"Jesse take up with Cox?"

"They were never an item. Cronies maybe. Chris was close to Cox. They did things together."

"Did Emery try to get her back?"

"Larry's our local paradox. He's solid as a wall. But he lets Jesse walk all over him." Talme shrugged his sloping shoulders. "When Chris was living with Emery he was an *A* student. Then Jesse moved out and he grew his hair and started wracking up *C*s and *D*s. Played rebel."

"Bud Maston arrived," said Harry.

"Exactly," said Talme. "Our own hundred-proof millionaire. He had the biggest house in the county and a lake to boot. Jesse saw him coming a long way off."

"That simple?"

"No, in fairness, she blossomed at first with Maston. They were going to change the world, those two."

"Karson told me about their plans for the mill."

"Then Maston quit on her. Just went to hell."

"And the kids?"

"After Jesse moved to the lake, Chris really went off the deep end. Truancy. Drugs. Maston couldn't enforce discipline, you ask me."

"What about Becky?"

"Genius-range. Four-point-oh grade point average. Maxed the SATs. She's talking to Carleton College about a scholarship. Becky will land on her feet."

Harry leaned forward. "Will she? She's gone missing."

"Maybe," said Talme. "Or maybe she's just grabbing for attention." He busied his stumpy fingers, digging at his pipe bowl with a shiny tool. "Oh, she's comfortable with being bright. It's puberty she runs from."

Harry cocked his head.

Talme shrugged. "Just my admittedly chauvinist opinion. Now that she's developed tits and an ass, maybe she's nervous that her mother will hatch out in her hormones."

"And Chris?"

"The opposite. Becky has her negative role model to measure herself against. Chris had confusion."

Harry waited for a full minute. Talme fixated on his tool, folding it and twisting it.

"Something turned in Chris. He developed a . . . hatred for everybody who tried to help him," said Talme softly. "It was a horrible thing to see in a boy."

"He pulled a gun on you?"

Talme raised his shoulders. "Ah, yeah. About a month ago. He came to school stoned in the middle of the afternoon. I grabbed him and pushed him into the teacher's lounge. He stuck the gun in my face and said if I ever touched him again, he'd kill me."

"What'd you do?"

"I took it away from him."

Harry raised an eyebrow.

"I teach Judo," Talme said simply.

"You had many kids pull weapons on you?"

"Once a boy took out a knife. But he was showing off and I talked him into putting it down."

"So Chris wasn't showing off?"

"No. Chris had a reason for carrying that gun."

"What reason?"

"Why do you carry a gun, Griffin?"

Harry was silent for a moment. "For protection," he said. "The other kids? They pick on him?"

Talme exhaled. "This is really more Don Karson's province."

"Why Karson?"

"School retains him to counsel students in certain situations. He's got a master's in psychology—"

"Talme, how far out in the woods are we? Do people up here say gay or do they say faggot?"

Talme took off his glasses, pulled out a handkerchief, and slowly cleaned them one lens at a time. "I guess they'd prefer not to talk about it at all. Which is the problem."

"What happened?"

Talme cleared his throat. "There was an incident involving Chris and another student. The student handled it quite well, but it was overheard by other kids and—"

"Give me a date," said Harry.

"Last June, end of the school year. Chris propositioned another boy. Here at school." Talme grimaced. "The boy came to me for advice. We didn't deal with it well. We thought we did at the time, but now, thinking back, we didn't—"

"Run it down," said Harry.

Talme spread his hands. "We didn't bring in the parents."

"When you say 'we,' who are you talking about?"

"I called Don in and we kept it between us. I would have gone to Emery but Don convinced me to let him deal with it. He has this notion that kids are entitled to their privacy same as adults." Talme shook his head. "Nothing's private in this town. Emery knew and he and Don had quite a scene. Now, after the shooting, Don's real nervous. You know, what if there's a grand jury and Emery uses it against him somehow."

"There's not going to be a grand jury. So why's Karson antsy? Minister? Pillar of the community?"

Talme exhaled. "Don used to have a big church in a fat suburb down in the Cities. There was a scandal. He's up here doing penance. We're his hair shirt."

"A scandal with boys in it?"

"A perception of impropriety among tight-assed members of his congregation. He smoked a joint—the kind you set on fire, not the kind you pee through—with some kids on a retreat. Emery dug it up and accused him right in church in front of God and everybody, as it were."

"So Karson looked for something on Emery?"

Talme's gaze deflected, explored the middle distance. "It goes back and forth. Don likes to play politics. There's this . . . animosity between him and Emery. This clash of styles. Almost as if Don was gleeful that Chris was experimenting with sexual adventure. Like it was a repudiation of Emery's moral standing. He won't admit it. Hell, he's not even aware of it. But I think, when he counseled Chris, he was trying to turn him against Emery. Whether they meant to or not, those two turned that boy into a battleground."

"This have something to do with those groups you go to in Duluth?"

"Hell," Talme rumbled. "I'm just curious. I even tried Tai Chi once. Wasn't built for it. But Don gets pretty deep into that men's group stuff."

"So he sees Emery as the old-fashioned, two-fisted macho man?"

"Wish it was that simple, Griffin." Talme peered into his coffee cup. "It's about a certain kind of credentials that gives someone authority. Don's an intellectual. He gets furious when I talk like this. But kids sense it in people."

"And?"

Talme shrugged. "Kids like Emery more than they like Don. I mean, Don's good to talk to—"

"But Emery's the one who takes you deer hunting."

"Yeah. Karson is Wonder Bread shipped from Minneapolis. Emery's the real thing in this county."

"Except now the real thing is drinking a lot."

"Yup. And everybody's walking soft, scared shitless of what he might do. First Jesse marries another man. Then Chris."

"What about Bud Maston?"

Talme laughed. "He's sort of like the Goodyear blimp. He flies over us little people on his million-dollar skyhook. We wave."

Harry put a five on the table to cover the coffee. Out on the street, they shook hands.

"He was a real sensitive kid, Griffin. Wrote, drew, played trumpet. I can see him stealing those guns, but I don't buy the part about him selling dope. At least, not in the winter. Dope shows up with the summer crowd. Everybody's hooked on the legal stuff up here. Liquid variety." He shook his head.

"Why'd he do it, Talme? Your best guess."

"Don's got this harebrained theory, you know—that Larry Emery's behind it, pulling the strings. He likes that conspiracy stuff. But I think Oswald and Chris acted alone. Chris was stoned. You read about it more and more. A parent tries to discipline a kid, the kid comes back with deadly force. Guess fresh air and pine trees are no insurance. Some shitty world, huh?"

"Yeah, well, thanks for the time." They shook hands.

Talme held Harry's hand in a vice of tendon and bone and as Harry narrowed his eyes, he added, "Jesse might fuck around and maybe she's up to a gold-digger game with your rich friend. But Emery's the one who really loves her."

Harry nodded. Talme lowered his voice although no one was remotely within hearing distance. "Don't provoke him about Jesse. Not when he's drinking."

Talme left. Damn. He meant to ask him who Miss Loretta was. He went into the drugstore and bought a carton of Pall Malls. When he emerged, snowflakes littered down on the clean white slum of Stanley, Minnesota. Across the street, a chubby man in a blaze-orange parka, wool trousers, and hunting boots twisted a chain of yule boughs around an ornate light pole in front of the bank.

Then the man hurried down the street and joined a crowd of hunters forming in front of the sheriff's office. Jerry Hakala stood in the bed of a pickup, his breath striking frosty commas in the air. Harry walked close enough to hear snatches of conversation. Search party. For Becky.

Harry had just got the Jeep in gear when he saw Jay Cox's blue truck drive by with Ginny Hakala sitting in the passenger seat. The truck made a right turn at the north end of town and drove out the jetty toward the Lutheran church. Harry followed it.

Cox went by the church and stopped in front of the Historical Society. He and Ginny each took a bag of groceries from the cab and carried them up the steps. The lady with the ramrod posture, the one Harry'd seen raise the flag the morning of the funeral, met them. She opened the door and Cox and Ginny carried the groceries inside. Then they came back out on the porch and Cox bent his head, listening, while the woman talked to them. Cox bobbed his head. She reached up and patted his scarred cheek. Ginny saw Harry first. She tugged on Cox's sleeve.

Harry tensed behind the wheel.

Jay Cox did the strangest thing. He smiled at Harry. A simple straight smile. Then he raised his right hand and split the fingers into a peace sign.

Stunned and wary, Harry coiled in his seat as Cox ambled over to the Jeep.

"Owe you an apology, man," said Cox, offering his knobby hand.

"I don't get it, Cox," said Harry, accepting the handshake.

"You ain't supposed to, troop. Life is strange."

41

Karson's station wagon was parked in the Trinity Lutheran Church lot.

It was a time for caution. Too many jack-in-the-boxes were popping out of the woodwork in Stanley, Minnesota. Not a time to rush in.

Harry took the steps two at a time, shoved open the church doors, and entered a Germanic thicket of oak pews, pulpit, beams, and a choir loft. Stairs in the small lobby led to a basement common room.

Karson sat, head bent, pen busy at a desk in a glass-partitioned office thinly ruled with Levelor blinds. A secretary guarded his office door from behind a typewriter and telephone. Harry pointed at Karson.

"Do you have an appointment?" she inquired with enough blood rushing to her face that Harry figured she was hip to who he was.

"It's all right," said Harry, opening the door without knocking.

Karson's eyes snapped up and he dropped his pen.

Harry tossed the manila envelope onto the desk. Karson saw his secretary talking urgently on the phone. Reassured, he opened the folder, looked at the page, folded it, and put it back. His eyes practically cracked the lenses on his horn-rims with the strain of keeping his face expressionless.

"Somebody nailed that to Maston's door last night like Martin Luther nailed his edict to the cathedral," said Harry.

"Not here, not now," said Karson in a calm voice.

Harry plopped down into a deep cushioned chair in front of the desk. Comfy chair, comfy office. He had to look real hard among the piled bookcases, past the Native American pottery and Inuit stone carving to find a solitary picture of Jesus.

Karson rose from his chair and closed the blinds. He returned, lit a Winston, and flipped on a Norelco clean-air machine next to his desk. "You have a very invasive style, Harry," he said.

"You can't have it both ways, Don. Either you keep confidences and let it all lay or you point fingers."

"It's not that simple."

"Talked to your buddy Talme. Only straight guy I've met up here." He emphasized the word "straight." Harry tapped the envelope. "Why me? I might jump to some conclusions. That what you want? Me going off the deep end because Emery and you have this feud?"

"I'll deny having this conversation," said Karson.

"And here I thought you and me had a dialogue going." Harry shook his head. "So the squeeze is on, huh?" Harry's eyes perused the book-cases behind the desk and stopped at a framed photograph on the book-case behind Karson's chair. He stood up, went behind the desk, and scrutinized the picture. "Well, no shit." Karson and Talme stood arm in arm with Tad Clark, the men's guru. Bud's place in the background draped in summer maples.

Karson kept his eyes fixed on the wall clock. Harry removed the pic-ture from the bookcase and dropped it on Karson's desk. "The men's movement?"

"You wouldn't understand."

"Sure I would. I was in a big men's group, cut my hair short, wore green all the time, slept in the woods . . ."

Voices out by the receptionist's desk. The door opened. Karson's face relaxed.

The creak of cold leather announced Jerry Hakala. "Everything all right, Don?"

"I was just asking Griffin to leave," said Karson.

"I'm a little worried about Don here, Jerry. I think somebody cut out his tongue," said Harry amiably.

"He, uh, bothering you?" Jerry asked Karson.

"I just want him to leave."

Jerry tapped Harry on the shoulder. "Why don't you and me step outside?" Harry picked up the envelope, winked at Karson, and fol-lowed Jerry out of the church into the parking lot. "Leave him be, Grif-fin, he don't need encouragement spreading poison about Larry." The young cop grinned and sunshine traced a faint webbing of scar tissue around his chin and eyebrows where he'd been massaged with pro hockey sticks.

Harry looked around. "Where'd you put Emery? In day care?" Jerry smiled patiently and Harry pushed it. "I met your sister. She was just next door with Cox. Looks like they're back together. When exactly did they break up?"

Jerry shifted his stance and cocked his head.

"If I'm such a pain in the ass, how come you guys let me hang around?" Harry asked.

"Just keep your nose clean and drive the speed limit, Griffin. Try not to annoy people."

"Saw you in front of the police station giving a speech," Harry persisted.

Jerry smiled, showing expensive bridgework. More hockey sticks. "Becky Deucette hasn't come home. Sheriff's not too worried, but Uncle Mike thought it was time to organize a search."

"Squared-away cop like you, doesn't it bother you working for a sheriff who's out hunting all the time, who smells like a bar towel? You ever think of running for sheriff, Jerry? You have the name recognition."

"Have a good day, Mr. Griffin."

"Hey Jerry," Harry called to him as he was getting into his Blazer. "Who's Miss Loretta?"

"That'd be Loretta Emery." Jerry pointed to the Historical Society next to the church. "She's in there. If you're planning on bothering her, you're on your own, brother."

"Like in Sheriff Emery?"

"Everybody's got a mother, Griffin."

Jerry stood by his Blazer and watched Harry go to the Jeep, remove the carton of cigarettes, and wander out along the jetty, scuffing his boots against the snow-packed red shingle.

He kicked at some gravel a plow had dredged up in frozen clumps like fat liver pills. He stooped, poked, looking for flat ones. When he found one he skipped it into the restless harbor. Looked over his shoulder at the Historical Society. *Christ. She was Chris's grandmother.*

A hollow knock sounded behind him. Turning, he saw a shadowy figure hover in the bay windows of the old building, tap again on the glass, wave, and then draw an arm in a summoning gesture.

Harry mounted the granite stairs and crossed the porch. The striking woman who met him at the door was in her sixties and had deep Native-dark eyes and a remarkable trim figure in snug jeans. A black leotard top pressed her still-full breasts flat against her chest and delineated the firm line of her rib cage. Her vigor brought the notion of yoga to mind.

Her face was smooth and doeskin soft, except for little gathers at the corners of her eyes, and where the curve of her jaw anchored to her ears. A hefty silver and turquoise barrette fastened the knot of her ponytail. She held a Phillips head screwdriver in her hand.

"Hello there," she said. Her smile revealed even, slightly nicotine-stained teeth and drew faint stress lines, fine as thread across her cheeks.

Harry was at a loss what to say.

Swiftly, she rescued him. "I saw you throwing rocks. I've been watching boys throw rocks into the lake for . . . well, all my life. Would you give me a hand for a minute?"

Nervously, he handed her the cigarettes. She took them without comment. "Are you the . . . custodian?" He balked.

"Live-in caretaker. And you're Bud Maston's . . . houseguest. You're the one who shot Chris."

Harry lowered his eyes.

"Don't look at the ground. Chris was trying to be strong. You were stronger and now you should know why. Come in. I've been expecting you." She smiled warmly.

Nuts.

Reluctant now, Harry went in. The rooms were heaped with antique junk like a circa 1900 garage sale. Storyboard pictures papered the wall. Men driving horses, pulling timber. Miners. Rafts of pulpwood behind tugboats. Stacks of musty newspapers, books, and magazines blocked a spiral staircase to the second story. A veil of dust covered everything. Motes sailed in the air. Harry spotted four cats in the first ten seconds.

A tall stepladder sat among the clutter. Above it, a new light fixture hung at a sprung angle at the terminus of exposed wires.

She set the carton of smokes aside on a table and asked, "Could you steady this ladder for a minute . . ." Harry gripped the ladder and she nimbly went up the steps. A spray of plaster dust sprinkled down as she attached the fixture with her screwdriver. "Ladder's a little tippy," she muttered from the corner of her mouth. "There. Go over and hit that light switch by the door."

Harry flipped the switch and the light came on. Miss Loretta descended the ladder, brushed dust off her hands, and looked around. "I used to keep it clean, but I just gave up," she said. "Would you sign the ledger?" A book was open on a table next to a rolltop desk. A hand of solitaire was laid out on the desk. Harry took the pen and signed. The last entry was a month before.

She studied his handwriting. "Slopes. An introvert," she said. "Griffin," she mulled the phonetic rish, but you don't look Irish." She placed her fingers on hi drew back. "Easy," she said softly, exploring his face. She her hand. "Hard to read the aura, could be classic Slav or . ould even be one of us." She rubbed her fingertips together. "Suffering. Burns a little."

She pointed to a table next to the bay windows. A carafe sat with two coffee cups, an ashtray, and a pack of Pall Mall straights. Harry sat down. She poured two cups of coffee. Then she held up the cigarettes.

Harry declined. "Too strong for me."

She smiled merrily. "We invented tobacco to give you cancer."

"You're Indian?"

"Enough so I don't try to pass for white, like some people I know."

"What tribe?"

"Hard to pick one." She blew a stream of blue smoke. "My family got around a lot."

Harry took a sip of strong chicory coffee. "Miss Loretta. This morning I was up on Nanabozho Point with your son—"

She made a distasteful grunt in her throat. "That boy and I haven't been talking. I give up on him five years ago when he came back from Duluth with his dirty money and built the house for Jesse."

"Becky Deucette was up there."

"Ah, Becky," she brightened. "Is she well?"

"Hardly. Your son—" She glowered at him. He rephrased. "The sheriff is trying to find her and question her. She's off running through the woods like a—"

"Buck-ass wild Indian," Miss Loretta said happily. "Good. I told her to stay clear of it. Silly damn business that's been going on forever." She leaned back and closed her eyes. "Ever since eighteen-forty when the first Hakalas and Mastons shot it out over a trapline. All in there on the wall, you care to read it. They've been fighting back and forth more than a hundred years. When the Mastons found the iron, the Hakalas brought up the Reds to organize the union to strike the mine. My late husband arrived from Tennessee in the latter stages of that invasion. Latest round is Bud Maston closing the mill. Doesn't surprise me one bit Chris tried to shoot him."

"Becky said I should talk to you," Harry said uncertainly.

Loretta Emery smiled. "Yes, she wants me to take a look." She pressed her finger to Harry's chest. "To see what's in there."

Harry was trapped humoring a crazy old lady. "Becky knows something I need to know," he began.

She smiled at his discomfort. "She knows that greed built Maston County. Now greed is going to tear it down."

"I was looking to get a more specific description of things."

Miss Loretta laughed. "Okay. I'll tell you exactly. You say you were up on the point this morning. When you look around up there, what do you see?"

Harry shrugged. "Lake Superior."

"What else?"

"The ridge."

She nodded. "You're getting warm. And . . . ?"

"The open pit."

"Yes. The pit." Her dark eyes kindled. She raised her finger. "You understand that if you ask for something, you might really get it?"

Harry sat politely. A shaggy gray tomcat arched its back against his leg. Out the window he saw Jerry Hakala lounging against his police car, arms folded. "Sure," he said.

"Sure," she chuckled and her eyes danced. An exotic granny Beatnik hanging out in musty piles of junk.

She put her hands behind her head and undid her barrette. With a toss of her trim neck, she shook out her hair, stroked her fingers through the thick graying strands, and pulled it down along her throat. She offered the Pall Malls again with ceremonial graciousness. This time, politely, Harry took one. A cloud of smoke rose over the table.

"I will tell you a story about Nanabozho," she said very circumspectly.

"Pardon?"

"Indian fella you meet wandering up in those woods on the point. Got to be careful with him. He's the trickster. He was very strong around here at one time."

"Uh-huh," said Harry cautiously. Ojibway culture hero. Some local color mentioned in the Superior Hiking Trail brochure. Christ, coffee and smokes with Miss Loretta came with an obligatory oral history recital.

"Well," she said, getting comfortable, "way back, he was out walking through the woods and he met the first white man. He'd never seen one before, so he was curious. They sat down and had a talk. The white man showed him a little piece of yellow metal. Gold, of course. The white man was looking for it.

"Nanabozho pointed out all the other things in the forest, the herbs, the trees, the animals. But the white man only had eyes for the yellow lump."

Miss Loretta paused and her eyes held him with the power of deep forest. Empty, to casual inspection. Teeming, to the greater senses. "Go on," he said cautiously.

She nodded and continued. "Well, Nanabozho was puzzled. So that night when the white man was asleep, he pulled his chest apart, and removed his heart to inspect it. The answer was clear. A very big spider of a kind he'd never seen before had all eight legs tightly wrapped around the white man's heart."

She lowered her voice. " 'Gold,' whispered the spider."

Harry sipped the bitter chicory. "I see," he said.

"Good," said Miss Loretta. "The spider was a European import and Nanabozho saw he had a problem. Now that the spider was out of the white man's chest, it could get loose and raise hell in the forest. So Nanabozho put the heart back in the chest and tied the arms and legs in a tight knot to keep the spider from getting out. Then he carried the body deep into a cave, way down to where there was a little shiny vein of gold. He piled tons and tons of rocks on that body so the spider would never get loose in the world."

Miss Loretta sighed. "Then, unfortunately, Nanabozho went off on one of his long trips."

Harry nodded and stood up. "Well, thanks for the coffee."

"Sit down, young man. I'm not done yet," she commanded.

"Yes ma'am," Harry sat.

"You see, Nanabozho screwed up. He thought the white man was a freak. A one-of-a-kind creature. Trouble was there were millions of other white men. And one of them was Bud Maston's grandfather. When old Stanley Maston dug that pit to get the iron, damn if he didn't let that spider out. That spider was hungry. Only thing he had to eat was the white man's heart, and he developed a taste for it. Other thing, that spider was pissed at Indians."

This time Harry got up and started walking toward the door. "Well, I got to go. Been nice talking to you."

She followed him out onto the steps. "When I told that story to Jay Cox, he understood it. Chris understood it. Becky understands it . . ."

Harry kept moving, avoiding her eyes and her words.

"To understand the story you have to go up there," she tilted her head at the ridge. "Go without a compass into the woods until you are lost. Then when the sun goes down, listen to the winter voices in your heart—"

"Be seeing you," said Harry.

"Harry Griffin," she pronounced. "Do you really want to find what you're looking for?"

Jerry Hakala wiggled his eyebrows as Harry walked past. "She get you all straightened out?" he asked.

Harry grunted and climbed in the Jeep. He drove slowly down a side street and pulled to the snowbank in front of the liquor store. Bubbleb-bubble, toil and trouble, the three Indian winos, stood shifting from foot to foot in the cold.

He glanced up at Nanabozho Ridge. Take these tourist woods any day over the Laotian highlands. He summoned one of the Indians.

"How about you go in there and get me a fifth of Jack Daniel's?"

"Whatsa matter chief, you ain't twenty-one?" asked the guy. His face was a burst sweet potato and his tapioca eyes perused the bill in Harry's hand. "That's Mr. Franklin."

"Just be a pal."

The dude returned with a bottle in a brown paper bag and a handful of currency. Harry took the bottle and told him to keep the change. The wino raised his eyebrows.

"Back rent," said Harry as he drove away.

The switchboard at St. Helen's Hospital defeated him. Harry hit the disconnect and tried Dorothy. Phone machine. He called Linda Margoles at her law office.

"Talk to Bud lately?" he asked.

"It's easier to ring up a federal prisoner than penetrate that damn hospital."

"I talked to his lovely wife. She wants a million dollars."

Linda Margoles whistled. "How are you doing?"

"Fine," said Harry as he jammed shells into the Remington pump. He set the shotgun across the dining room table and took a slug of whiskey. "Just signed up for a wilderness experience field trip."

"What?"

"Check you later, Linda."

Harry found a seat among the granite polyps overlooking the lake and sipped from the bottle. The shotgun made a comfortable brace for his elbows across his knees.

Whiskey was funny. Sometimes it slammed you hot and sweaty as Saturday night wrestling. Or, like now, it walked you slow and mercilessly through every mundane act of cowardice that living straight and drawing a paycheck from an American corporation required.

The sun flamed out against the black sticks of the forest and briefly he pictured Jesse and Emery padding through the trees, silent as wolves. He did not hear Miss Loretta's voices. He thought, instead, about a book that had been his sophomore bible. *Man's Fate* by André Malraux. The scene where the baron, on a mission to warn the hero that the bad guys are coming to snatch him, tarries at a casino, drinks, and watches the roulette ball tumble round and round in fascination as his friend's life runs out.

That was close to what Jesse meant, he supposed, when she asked him to take a chance on her.

42

Working on One Day Sober Twice. The Sequel. Harry was thinking he had to figure out a way to shave the hot bristles growing on his eyeballs when the phone rang.

"Maybe you're not so dumb after all," said Dorothy Houston.

"What you got?" Harry took the call stretched on a chair, pointing his bare feet toward a roaring fire.

"My cop friend made a few calls."

"What'd he turn up on Cox?"

"Cox schmox. Small potatoes. A couple of drunk and disorderlies in Seattle years ago—"

"But Emery is a different story," said Harry.

"You nailed it. My friend found a detective on the Duluth force who used to work with him."

"Lemme guess."

"Detective Lawrence Emery shot Kidwell. Fact. But then it gets tangled depending on who you believe. The cops said Kidwell was resisting arrest. Kidwell's family—brother and sister who co-owned his custom sailboat operation—insisted he was defending his business against intruders. There was a question about whether the cops properly identified themselves going in. The family sued. They settled it out of court for an undisclosed amount."

"What about Emery?"

"The coppers all stuck together, said Emery did it by the book, was fired on, returned fire. They found traces of cocaine big-time in the sailboat, but no weight. Emery was cleared on the shooting, but the word was, if he'd stuck around, he'd have been walking a beat in the Boundary Waters."

"The money? Did the wife get any of it?"

"Nope. She got the life insurance."

"How? He was shot allegedly in the commission of a crime."

"The insurance company investigated. They came up inconclusive on Kidwell's involvement in a felony. No evidence. Where's the crime? It was—"

Harry took a breath and let it out. "An accident."

"Double indemnity for accidental death, Harry."

"How much did she get?"

"A half a million bucks. He had tons of insurance. Even had one of those Lloyds of London specials for the trip. She couldn't collect on the policies he took out when they got married. There's this two-year contestability thing. She was on the policy he'd had for ten years."

"And Emery and the grieving widow disappear into the sunset, to friendly Maston County," said Harry. "Fuckin' Bud. He hadda know this. He wanted Jesse to be this earth mother in a lumberjack shirt, so that's what she was."

"You think this Emery and the Deucette woman were running the same kind of game on Bud?"

"Damn straight. Except this time they were after a hunk of the Maston estate. Why didn't someone in the Duluth media pick up on this?"

"She went by her mother's name in Duluth. Her picture wasn't in the paper and she was never interviewed on TV. No one put it together."

"Hakala handled the media like a pro. That's why he put it to bed so fast. Get Bud in treatment, politics, and Bill Tully. Sure. Right. Who investigates a county prosecutor?"

"State Attorney General or the Justice Department. You have to make a case for probable cause that there was a conspiracy to violate Bud's civil rights."

Silence on the connection while his mind raced.

Dorothy said, "The thing is, you have to connect that kid you shot. Without that, you just have a vivid imagination and a compelling coincidence. You're right on the cusp of a conspiracy theory. Without proof you wind up sounding like a nut. Go slow. A lot of this is police department gossip."

"You run any of this by Randall?"

Dorothy exhaled. "Mentioned it on the phone. I gave him Cox's birthday and he said he'd get Hollywood to snoop around in the Justice Department computers. He called back and said he might have found something."

"What?"

"Didn't say." A tired concern wove through her voice.

"Everything all right?"

"The last time he hooked up with Hollywood he tried to party himself young. You know how they get going." Dorothy paused. "And he told me to get you to come home. It's not your scene up there."

"C'mon, Dorothy. You too?"

Dorothy's voice changed, a bit of the childless matron in it. "We all love you, Harry . . . but you're an amateur."

"Right. Thanks, Dorothy. Talk to you later."

Connect the dots. No wonder Emery looked so bummed that morning. He taught Chris how to shoot.

Harry called Linda Margoles at her office. She was on another line. He left a message. When the phone rang, he leaped at it.

"Harry?" Linda's voice was cautious, concerned.

"What's probable cause?"

"What?"

"The legal definition of probable cause. C'mon—"

"Harry, listen a minute. We got other stuff. I told Bud about the settlement. He said okay, if we can counteroffer the money minus the amount she cleaned out of his account. She forfeits the property."

"I figured he'd go for it."

"Harry. I *talked* to him. In my office. He's out. He left the hospital."

"Aw shit."

"He wants me to get on the calendar in Maston County court. Finalize the terms of the separation. I have a call in to them right now—"

"Don't let him come up here."

"Harry, I'm an attorney; he's my client. He wants to settle the money part of this fast. As a private person, I share Bud's concern that you're playing unguided missile—"

"The guy should be committed. He's not responsible—"

"He says *you're* the one who should be committed. It's a wash. If I didn't know you both I wouldn't go near it. Screw the fee and travel time."

253

"Travel time?"

"I have to go to court with him."

"Linda. I gotta go."

Harry was exhilarated and wary, climbing a scaffold of toothpicks he was building as he went. But dammit, there *was* something here!

So they left Duluth with a pile of loot. Dirty money, Miss Loretta called it. Wonder where they put it? He dug through the local phone directory and found the listing for Lawrence Emery. Then he placed the address as best he could on the township map in the front of the phone book. He tore the page out, threw on his coat, and jumped in the Jeep.

To get to the county road Emery lived on, Harry had to drive around Bud's property. The road was a boundary between two different countries. On one side, the timber was thick and towering. On the other, the land was bog and spindly jack pine. Hunters dotted the sparse swamps. Probably all the deer headed for the thick cover of the Maston acres.

His stomach growled. Nothing in it but black coffee over massacred digestive juices. He lit another cigarette and ran his fingers across the sweaty stubble on his chin.

Emery lived on quite a piece of land. The acres of rolling, fenced pasture were divided by a fishing stream, the house was cedar, modern Tudor. But desolate. A hay feeder sat barren in the pasture. The barn looked empty. No horses in sight. No tracks in the windswept snow.

He could see Jesse's lethal ass poised in an English saddle, putting a thoroughbred through its paces in a paddock. Looking over the spread.

Nice. But no lake. And just a sheriff's salary.

A house like that, new, might go for around 250,000 bucks. With the barn, the land, and the horses, it would eat up Jesse's insurance settlement from Duluth.

His eyes traveled the landscaped drive and stopped at the three-car garage. There was a basketball hoop, the net stiff with ice. He couldn't picture Chris shooting baskets. Becky, maybe.

What does a sheriff in a depressed county make a year?

Harry drew stares as he marched down the hall toward Mike Hakala's office. He yanked off his wool cap and swatches of hair stuck at wild angles. The scabs on his face didn't help.

One of Hakala's brothers and a woman sat in the easy chairs in front of Hakala's desk. They viewed Harry with mild alarm when he appeared in the doorway. The woman stood up in a businesslike skirt and sweater. Her long legs didn't flash so much, muted by nylons. She clutched a yellow legal pad in her hands and her face turned crimson in contrast to her long blond hair.

Harry grinned. "The Hakala politburo I presume. Ginny. Didn't recognize you with your clothes on."

The Hakala brother rolled his eyes toward the sheriff's office down the hall, *Should I get someone?*

Hakala pursed his lips and discreetly shook his head. *No.*

"Harry," said Hakala, rising from his desk. "What can I do for you?"

"Like to talk, you and me," said Harry.

"Sure. Uh," he turned to Ginny and the brother. "Take a break. Say fifteen minutes."

Ginny's heels clicked past him. She did not meet his eyes.

"Close the door, Harry. Sit down. Coffee?" said Hakala.

Harry looked down the hall at Ginny. "She cleans up well, your niece."

"Ginny picks up a few hours a week with the county, when she isn't managing the diner."

"Right," said Harry, sitting down.

Hakala passed him a cup of coffee, leaning over his desk far enough to make a production of recoiling from Harry's breath and his appearance. "Any more trouble at Maston's? We've been keeping an eye out. We checked out the serial number on that snowmobile that got . . . left behind when those hooligans came through. Guy it's registered to said it was stolen that night."

"Uh-huh. Who hired Larry Emery to fill out the old sheriff's term?"

"Why, the County Board, on my recommendation," said Hakala.

"What's a county sheriff make a year?"

Hakala shrugged. "Low forties. Somewhere in there."

"How much you figure that house he's got is worth? Looks pretty pricy for a sheriff's salary."

Hakala smiled. "You, uh, recall a conversation we had in this office? About how civilians shouldn't try to do the system's work?"

"Absolutely. Which part of the system checked out Emery's resume?" Harry tossed the newspaper page on Hakala's desk. "You recognize the lady circled in red?"

Hakala studied it for a moment and rolled his eyes. "Don Karson's already been through here with that. What else is new." He sighed.

"He's dropping big hints that Emery had something to do with Chris. Then, to be fair, Emery is making sounds like Karson is the local pederast. Yeah, I went round the bases. I been to the high school and seen the writing on the wall."

Hakala's desk phone buzzed. "Hold my calls," he said brusquely, then paused, "What? When?" He tightened his eyes shut, listening. "Well, give them a good talking to. No. I'm staying out of it." He slammed down the receiver and sighed. "Fight at the high school, my kid just beat the dog shit out of one of the guys on the hockey team. I swear, this whole damn town is going batty. Where were we—okay," said Hakala, rearranging his thoughts like notes. "Larry had some bad luck in Duluth. If he'd caught Kidwell with the dope it could have been the biggest drug bust in state history."

"Too bad, so he settled for Kidwell's wife. Imagine my surprise when I discovered that Jesse was the wife. She collected quite a piece of change. Like half a million bucks in insurance. Doesn't it tweak your curiosity, the way Jesse Deucette's husbands are prone to death by gunshot wound?"

Hakala's robust face clouded. "The bullet that passed through Bud Maston's body came from Chris Deucette's rifle. I have the forensic report right here."

"Let's see it."

"Listen, fella," Hakala cautioned. "I been going out of my way to be civil with you." He rose out of his chair and walked back and forth behind his desk. "I realize you've been through a lot. I thought we had a working agreement. Get Bud some help and let it lie. Word of advice. After what you did at the funeral, Emery would like to nail your balls to a stump and push you over backwards. Don't crowd him, Griffin."

"Why is Becky Deucette a missing person? Could it be she knows something about her dead brother and her dad? Something you overlooked? I didn't tell you when it happened, but I think I saw her out there that day."

Hakala picked up some papers and threw them down on his desk. "You're paranoid, fella. You're starting to look like a loose cannon."

Harry stood up. "Your loose cannon is wearing a badge. And that's not all. Bud's checked himself out of the hospital and is headed this way with a pillowcase full of money to cash out Jesse."

"Not good," Hakala breathed.

Harry pointed an accusing finger. "There were flags on Chris start-ing back last summer. And last month you let him slide on a stolen gun offense. That kid needed help or he should have been put away and you let Emery put a rifle in his hand. You let him be turned into a weapon."

"Wait a goddamn minute. You can piss in the wind. I have to operate within the constraints of the law."

"Oh yeah? So what happens if Bud cruises into town to file his sepa-ration papers and some overeager deer hunter shoots him between the eyes, say, in front of the police station? One of those accidental deaths like what happened to Kidwell in Duluth?"

Hakala watched him closely. "So what's your point?"

"What happens to his estate?"

"Arggh," Hakala growled dubiously. "Bud has no children. As far as I know he's the last of the Maston line. And a decree of separation, which does not terminate a husband and a wife's legal connection, is not a final judgment of divorce—"

"In other words?"

"The surviving spouse could go after the whole thing," Hakala said. "Not only that, but the estate would be disposed in the domicile of the deceased. And since Bud has resided here for a year, has voted in a local election, banks here, has attended Don Karson's church, and since he has assets here, the land, the lodge . . ." Hakala clicked his teeth. "They'd carve it up right here in the probate division of the Maston County court system. My Uncle Toyvo presiding."

"No grand jury. That was a slick move, Hakala. Fuck!"

"Hey," Hakala opened his hands reasonably. "I was trying to help the guy out, for Chrissake."

"Let me help *you* out," said Harry. He held up his hands and framed a rectangle of air. "Lightning strikes twice in Maston County. Helpless widow inherits millions. Then it comes out. Helpless widow has fucked sheriff. Fucked sheriff sired her bastard kids and has a habit of shooting widow's husbands."

Harry turned his back on Hakala and was going through the door when the district attorney went into a conniption:

"You've been drinking and picking fights! Now you're hallucinating spurious allegations! You're way out of line, Griffin!"

Harry passed Mitch Hakala standing at the dispatcher's desk in the company of a deputy with black sideburns. Morris, the tobacco-chewer, from the morning of the shooting. Mitch leaked blood from his gauze-bandaged right hand and his face was a mask of permafrost. He stepped in Harry's path. "Need to talk to you," he said.

Harry pushed by. "Later, you're busy."

Mitch pulled Harry aside with surprising trained strength in his hands. "Be at the lodge. A couple hours from now. Four-thirty."

"Take it easy, Mitch," said the deputy.

Ginny Hakala was on the sidewalk in front of the sheriff's office. Warily she watched Harry approach. "Okay, I'm busted," she said. "I combined a little business with pleasure. Actually, it was *Jerry* who wanted *me* to get next to *you* and I saw a way to make Jay jealous." She shrugged sadly. "And it worked. We're back together."

"You don't look very happy about it."

Ginny grimaced. "Larry's pushing for a grand jury. He wants to sub-peona everybody, including me."

"Why you?"

"Because he's after Jay." Ginny Hakala had tears in her eyes as she turned and went back into the county offices.

Jay my ass.

Harry let it all float, words and faces. He stood on a lip of granite overlooking Glacier Lake as the sun dipped into the tree line. But tonight he was drinking reheated black coffee from a stout stoneware cup.

Almost time for Mitch to show up. Flashlights swung in the woods at the far end of the lake. Emery's search party.

The cry slid on sheets of crystalline air, eerie, echoing along the shore.

Wolf.

Out there hunting.

He had to find Becky before Emery did.

43

Mitch Hakala steered his scrupulously waxed, olive-green Jeep Wrangler through the wreckage of the Battle of the Snowmobiles and parked, out of sight, behind the pole barn. Harry met him at the door. Mitch's steely blue eyes bored straight ahead and beneath his blank, manfully contained adolescent fury, he looked like a very shook-up young man.

"So Ginny's your cousin?" Harry started slowly.

Mitch nodded stiffly. "Look at the phone book. There's forty of us." Inside, Mitch inspected the plume of soot over the mantel, the empty socket in the woodwork, and the scrawl of paint on the wall. "They really did a number on this place," he said.

They sat in front of the fire. Mitch slid a Lucky Strike from a steel cigarette case and lit it with tight-banded reflexes. Harry nodded at the orange stain of Iodine and the bandage on Mitch's swollen right hand.

"What happened?"

"Nothing. How'd it go with my dad?"

"He's hiding something."

"Older people get, the more they got to hide." Mitch raised his eyes and fixed them on a spot on the balcony overlooking the main room. His eyes stayed pinned there with intense concentration for long seconds.

"Mitch, why'd you steer me into the boy's john?"

"People lie about who they really are."

"Was Chris like that?"

"No. Chris tried to be up-front, but they all fucked him over. He had guts, but it wasn't the kind of guts the people in this town could understand."

"You're the guy he came on to in school, aren't you?"

Mitch gingerly flexed his battered knuckles. "Yeah, but it wasn't like people say. I mean, he didn't grab my zipper or anything . . ." His eyes tightened. "We just talked."

"So what did you talk about?"

Mitch shrugged. "Life. Our parents. Fantasies. He was, you know, real open . . . maybe too open."

Pain corroded Mitch's face. Harry went to the fire, put on another log, stabbed a few times with the poker. When he turned, Mitch was watching him intensely.

"Guess trust is hard to come by in this town," said Harry.

Mitch rubbed the heel of his battered right hand across his cheek, smashing a tear. "Trust is a bitch, ain't it," he said.

"Whatever you got broken off in you, you might as well pull it out."

"Yeah, well . . . Chris said that your fantasies are the key to your sex," Mitch dragged on his smoke, exhaled. "He said when he jacked off he always wound up thinking of me. Then he wanted to know who I thought of . . ."

Mitch bit his lip. "It was like a real serious talk we were having, so I had to tell him the truth. So I told him I thought about his . . . sister, Becky."

Harry smiled. Mistake. Mitch looked like he might break into tears. Soberly, Harry asked, "How'd he take that?"

"Well, at first he looked hurt but then he laughed, too." Mitch stood up and began to pace. "I felt like his older brother. I'd look out for him at school. He had a way of pissing off the other guys. Quick with words. But it kind of worried me, too."

Mitch paused in front of the fireplace.

"Chris made me promise not to tell anybody about . . ." Mitch shook his head. "But I decided he needed someone to talk to. Someone older he could trust. What the hell did I know? I was a junior, he was a sophomore. I mean, he was not real strong and able to take care of himself. And he was freaked, having Sheriff Emery for his dad and being fifteen and wondering if he was, you know, a homosexual."

"Did Emery know any of this?"

"Hadda hear the gossip." Mitch allowed a tight smile. "Before they moved out, I'd be over there and Sheriff Emery would come home for dinner and Chris'd tease him about Jesse. You know, if he was so damn tough why didn't he marry her. Sometimes Emery would look like he was about to explode inside."

"Did Emery ever rough him up?"

"No. He never laid a hand on any of them, not Chris, or Becky or Jesse." Mitch shook his head. "That's what pissed Chris off so much. That his mom could just walk all over Emery."

"So who did you trust with Chris's problem?"

"Reverend Karson and Mr. Talme." Mitch said sarcastically. "And I told Chris I thought he should talk to Karson." He dropped his eyes. "Chris felt I snitched him out."

"But Chris talked to Karson?"

"Oh yeah. Hardly talked to anybody else but. And Mr. Maston, who's into a lot of the same silly shit Karson is."

"What kind of shit?"

"You know, love the trees. Clean up the lake, close the mill, put everybody out of work. Brought those weirdo city guys up here with the drums. That's when he started doing the cyberpunk bit, the hair and the drugs. Was almost like Chris was daring Sheriff Emery to step in and straighten him out."

Harry thought out loud: "Sonofabitch. Would Chris try to kill Maston to get his mother and father back together?"

"I don't know." Mitch clenched his fists and winced. "There was a fight. Right in this room. Just before Maston and Jesse got married. My cousin Jerry got a call to come out here. There was Jesse and Jay Cox and Maston and they were trying to calm down Chris and Becky. I guess Chris was really nuts. Jerry said he had to drag Chris outside and sit him in the police car. He was yelling all this crazy shit like, how he'd tell his dad and he'd kill Maston if he married his mother."

"Did your dad know this?"

"Course he knew, everybody knew."

Mitch lowered his eyes. "Jerry told me I'd better try and talk to Chris and Becky." He grimaced. "Becky and I were going steady for two years and she dropped me cold. And Chris turned to stone. Next thing I know, Chris and Maston are getting along and Chris suddenly gets hot to go deer hunting and he's off in the woods with the sheriff learning how to shoot."

Mitch rotated his eyes around the lodge. "Becky wouldn't talk to me for a month, then the day of the shooting, I go to the hospital when I hear what happened and she comes running out and says to get her outta there."

"She's talking to you now."

"Not really. She leaves me notes in different mailboxes. Where to meet her on the road with food. I don't know where she's hiding. She wanted me along with a rifle when she met you on the ridge and before that, on the trail out by the lake." He exhaled. "She wanted to see if you'd try to hurt her. She's acting screwy. You killed Chris and she says you're the only one she can trust. It's driving me nuts."

Mitch walked to the window and pointed down the lake. "Lookit those dumb fuckers out in the dark," he said.

Lights, coming up the east shore of the lake.

Mitch laughed. "They'll never catch her. Not in these woods. She's too damn smart for her own good, Mr. Griffin."

"How's that?"

"She saw it that morning. The whole thing between Mr. Maston and Chris. That's why she's hiding."

"What did she see?"

Mitch's muscular interior lines bunched with anger. "Didn't tell me. There's a lot she didn't tell me. Just that she was there. She says no one can see it because it's right in front of their noses."

"That's why Emery's looking for her."

Mitch heaved his shoulders. "Ask her. She's waiting out past the cabins on the snowmobile trail. Give me five minutes with her first."

Harry waited on the porch, dressed for the woods, impatiently smoking a cigarette, watching the darkening space between two of the cabins where Mitch had disappeared. Mitch came jogging back, his eyes tracking, wary.

"It ain't good," he said, biting his lip. "They posted some guys down on this end. The rest are making a drive along the lake. She says some of those idiots have guns, and the light's going. She says it's too tricky to come in right now."

"So let's get her outta there."

"Don't you think I tried," said Mitch between clenched teeth, and the yardlight punched up the glaze of tears in his eyes. He glanced back toward the trees and shook his head. "She . . . likes it. Having everybody worry about her."

Without further comment, Mitch jumped into his truck and drove away with his lights off.

Trying to flush her like a deer. "Bullshit," said Harry. He ran into the lodge, grabbed the Remington pump, and jammed the .45 automatic in his waistband. With luck, she'd find a way to let him find her.

44

The bewitching hour, when the last light ink-stains into shadow and the deer start to move. It had gotten noticeably colder since Harry had begun searching.

"Becky! I know you're out here, goddammit." His harsh whisper echoed with the crunch of snow under his boots. "I won't let them get you—"

"You dummy, you got it upside down. You the one getting got." Her voice thrilled in the twilight.

Out there, pacing him silently in the snow. Where was she? He stopped and his breath came in bleached, shivering clouds.

"Can I trust you, Harry?"

"You wouldn't send Mitch if you couldn't."

"I'm not sure. I've seen pictures of you—"

Pictures of me? Harry moved toward her voice. "Dammit girl, come on in. It's freezing."

"Scary, too. We're not alone out here." She stepped onto the trail, a lithe, wraith-haired shadow with one hip thrust out and the whites of her eyes hyper-alert in the failing light. She smelled dank with sweat and kerosene fumes and she trembled violently.

Harry removed his glove and touched her sooty face. Bits of leaves and a burr snagged in her stringy hair under a dirty wool cap. "You been out here too long. You're suffering from exposure."

"No shit," she giggled. "I been exposed to a lot." Then she arched, her whole body acute. "Shhh. Hear that? One of them's right up there."

"Who," he whispered. "Emery? Cox?"

She stifled a nervous giggle and for the first time she looked like a frightened trapped animal. "Mitch tell you?" she asked hesitantly.

"He said you were out there the morning of the shooting."

She nodded her head vigorously and her teeth chattered. "What else did he tell you?" A branch snapped above them on the ridge. She shuddered and started moving, ready to run. Harry followed.

"Look, I don't have much time before I have to split," she said. "Tell Mom not to take the money. It's not too late if she stops the divorce." She was scared stiff, freezing, talking crazy.

"Becky, let me take you to St. Paul, we'll talk to some real cops."

"No. We have to do it my way or it won't work."

"Fuck," whispered Harry. "You think this is fun."

Her teeth flashed in her grimy match-girl face. They both cocked their ears as footsteps punched through the frozen snow up the slope. Lights bobbed in the trees up ahead. Deepening shadows closed in. The trail cut a hazy gray arc.

He seized her arm. "You're coming with me. I can protect you."

"No one can protect me the way it is now."

"'Nuff of this shit." Harry tightened his grip, balanced the shotgun in his right hand, thumb off the safety.

"No way. Ow!" she protested. No longer whispering. Their voices rang in the dark. "They'll catch us. They'll ask me . . . questions. My dad would kill me if—"

The steps above them stopped. A blubbery whistling sound.

"What the hell . . ." When he looked up, she slipped from his grasp and sprinted down the trail.

The blowing came louder.

"Goddammit, Becky . . ." Harry ran after her.

Crack-beoww!!! A rifle shot cracked. High.

"Search party my ass!" he bellowed, ducking, turning to the ridge.

Crack! Crack! The third shot clipped a piece of branch. Splinters rattled on his parka. But he fixed on the muzzle flash. *See you, motherfucker.* Extreme range for the shotgun, up the slope. Harry aimed high. Scare 'em off. The 12 gauge boomed. A load of buckshot wapped through the upper branches where the aftershadow of the muzzle flash sparkled out. He crashed into the underbrush, wracking the pump action. *Boom. Boom. Boom.* Marching fire. Still keeping it high. In the intervals between the shots he heard the buckshot thunk into trees, slap through the brush.

A scream echoed down to him. Fear. Not of pain. Harry dropped the shotgun, yanked out the pistol, and charged up the slope, smashing through brush, chasing the tripping footfalls ahead of him. "Get you, you fucker!" Could see him now, a dumpy shadow waddling against a wall of snow. Pistol upraised, Harry ran down the wheezing man.

"Oh God, oh God, please," yelled the guy.

Harry pushed him face first into the snow. "Fuck the ground, asshole," snarled Harry.

"What?" came the bewildered response.

Harry knelt and frisked him. He'd dropped his rifle. Wasn't carrying another weapon. "Stand up," he ordered. "Who the hell are you?"

"Na-Na-Norm Patton. I wa-wa-work in the Ba-ba-bank."

"What are you doing out here?"

"Sa-sa-searching."

Harry seized him by the collar and pulled him to his feet. "Down the hill. I'm right behind you."

Pushing Norm Patton ahead, he retraced their footprints, retrieved Patton's deer rifle, then his shotgun. Snowmobiles scurried loudly up the trail next to the lake. Other lights, headlights, it looked like, flashed between the cabins by the lodge. A crumpled cellophane squawk, police radio.

Backlit by the headlights, two figures jogged toward him and his hyperventilating prisoner. Harry slid the .45 back into his belt, out of sight.

"*Griffin!*" shouted Larry Emery. "*Now what, you sonofabitch!*" Jerry Hakala's only slightly less furious face bobbed next to the sheriff's.

"Calm down, Larry," yelled an indignant voice from the snowmobiles convened on the trail. Don Karson.

"I seen her, Sheriff," said Norm Patton. "Sh-sh-she was right down here on the trail with him."

"This asshole shot at me," yelled Harry, throwing Patton's rifle into the snow.

"Did not," stuttered Patton. "I tried to blow my whistle like you said, but it had slobber in it and was froze. So I fired three times in the air—"

"Air my ass, shot right over my head!" Harry shouted.

"Did not! Then this nut started shooting the woods apart."

"Norm," growled Emery, struggling to keep his voice under control,

"How come you had you a rifle up there? I said no guns. *No guns!* We're looking for a screwed-up teenage girl. All she needs is to think people are shooting at her!"

"Hell, Sheriff, was still light when I got into position, thought I might see that big bastard deer's 'posed to be in Maston's swamp."

Emery snarled deep in his throat. "Griffin! What the hell were you doing out here with a shotgun?"

"He's got a pistol too, pulled it on me up there."

"Shut the fuck up, Norm."

"Sheriff Emery, sir," Harry said with excessive respect. "I heard somebody moving round back of the cabins, went to take a look. Last time somebody came through there they set me on fire."

Don Karson stepped up. "Still solving problems with guns, Harry?" he asked. Then he turned to Patton. "Norm, you all right? You're not injured—shot or anything?"

Norm laughed nervously. "I crapped my pants."

A ripple of laughter chorused through the crowd of deputies and citizens.

"This isn't funny," Karson was indignant. "Not one damn bit funny. This isn't a search. It's a damned circus. What's needed here is some adult leadership."

Emery's derisive chuckle turned murderous. "Too bad the paper went out of business. You could write a letter to the editor."

Karson drew himself up and faced Emery. "People are getting real tired of smelling your whiskey breath."

"Get your big mouth out from behind the hem of Jesus' garment and say that, Don," Emery said between clenched teeth.

"All right, you guys . . ." Jerry Hakala stepped between them. "It's been a long day."

Emery turned toward the Blazer. His shoulder sideswiped Harry, pushing him off balance.

"Stand by, fucker!" Harry warned.

Emery spun, his face hideous in the headlights. Jerry shepherded him with a broad shoulder. "Larry . . ."

"Just what we all need. A little more violence," Karson said in a jerky voice.

Harry watched the blaze-orange posse troop down Bud's driveway. In the lodge, frustrated, he threw the shotgun on the dining room table.

He was inside something where you don't get to think anymore. Like everybody, he was reacting.

Tell Mom to stop the divorce?

Numb, with circles of pain ringing in his ears from the gunfire, he looked up Cox's number and dialed it.

She answered on the second ring. "Hello?" The first hello was bright and husky. Hope.

"Hello? Becky? Is that you? Honey?" Desperate hope, then cancel the hope.

"Who is this?" A tin quiver of fear.

Harry couldn't do it. He hung up. It was torture, just like she said. Two butterflies stuck on a length of pain. Unable to move toward each other.

Do the responsible thing. Call Bud. No idea where he was. Harry called Linda's office. Closed down, the machine on. He tried her home. Another machine.

"This is Harry. Find Bud and tell him I talked to Becky. She saw the whole thing that morning Chris tried to shoot him. We have a witness. Emery is mounting a search for her. I'm worried she might meet with an accident. Call me ASAP."

45

Harry cleaned the shotgun in front of the fireplace. There was no convenient ramrod to swab the folly of shooting up the hill at Norm Patton. Dumb.

Then shivers. That was killing hate he'd seen in Emery's face. The bottle of J.D. flickered in the firelight. Just a reach away.

Pictures, Becky said.

Okay. His eyes roved the lodge. What happened here in October? Abruptly he got up, picked up a flashlight on his way through the kitchen, and pushed through the plastic sheeting that walled off the new construction and entered the addition.

The light meandered over a carpenter's belt discarded on the deck, bulging with tools, and shined on Cox's rusted Skilsaw, abandoned on the sawhorses. If they were cleaning out the place, why would Cox leave his tools behind? He thumbed the rime of rust on the saw blade and evaluated the dust on the blueprints spread on the sawhorses.

Whatever was going on here stopped a month ago. When Chris made his threats, when Bud and Jesse decided to marry. Harry squatted on the plywood decking and played the light across the Sheetrock. The light stopped on the diagonal shadow of a ladder behind another sheet of plastic.

The ladder was placed into a stairwell and led to the second floor. Harry swung the light ahead as he climbed the ladder. Cages of naked two-by-fours defined the rooms. Nothing but scraps of lumber. Nails and dust.

A bit of color snagged the light, out on the balcony. Harry stooped to a swatch of red and blue ribbons. High school track awards. Girl's events. 440. Half mile. High hurdles. They were fouled with something and stuck together and coated with dust.

And next to them lay a curl of tan-gray plastic. Little sprocket tracks on one side. He'd been around enough news photographers to recognize 35-mm film. Sometimes they tore off the end leader to mark the roll. He stood up and felt along the thick sheeting that walled the balcony off from the main room. The seam was parted. The staples had been removed and placed in an orderly line on the balcony railing. He pushed the plastic apart and looked down on the couches and chairs and his makeshift bed in front of the fireplace.

Pictures.

He left the ribbons and the clip of film exactly where he'd found them and went back down the ladder. Now is when you make your mind empty, Randall had taught him that. Just melt open your senses so everything makes an impression. Don't think. Just see.

He flipped on the TV and watched the weather report out of Duluth. Another cold front was shuffling in, arrows from the northwest. A stack of video tapes were piled next to the VCR. One stood out from the commercial movie names. A tape with a white label handwritten in felt-tip pen: *PBS, Clark Group.*

Pictures.

He poured a cup of coffee and ran the tape. Clark in his buckskin shirt. Another twenty sensitive guys in a semicircle on the floor of the lodge main room.

Clark moved ponderously across the screen, a fleecy cloud trying to turn into a thunderhead. His sermon was the shadow that dwelled in men. The primal force of their manhood. Harry killed the audio and watched the camera pan the seated men. Uh-huh. Don Karson sat next to Karl Talme. Karson's face was focused, really into this shit. Talme looked politely bored and uncomfortable sitting on the floor. The camera tracked. Bud's wide back with red suspenders making an X in the middle of his spine. He turned, his face wreathed in the pride of authorship.

In a corner of the shot, Karson raised his hand and summoned off camera. He slid over to make room. Chris, his hair shorter in length, scrambled across the floor and hunkered next to Karson. Karson smiled and put his arm around Chris's slender shoulders, pulling him close in a hug. Leaned close to the boy, whispered in his ear. Chris's face shone in the camera lights, his expressive eyes sparkled.

Beautiful kid.

The angry emotional assumption proceeded at the speed of light. Same conclusion Emery must have made. He stopped the tape, ran it back, watched Karson summon Chris, froze the tape there, and studied the skewed image of Chris's smiling face until the pause function blipped off into static.

Chris's death chose this moment to claw its way out of Harry's chest. *When the ghost of the person you kill chops a hole in your heart, he makes it roomy. Big enough to house his unlived life, an addition for the kids . . .*

And suddenly more damn black clamoring night rushed behind his eyes than in the whole North Woods. No hope of sunrise for it. A mighty urge for a drink sliced the darkness like a fin. Dipped down.

Call some folks.

Harry picked up the phone and dialed the house on River Road in St. Paul. He needed to talk to the man who he wished had been his father.

No good. Randall was still in the big city. "How you doing?" he asked Dorothy.

Her voice caused Harry to wince. Warmly ironic, a little high, she pondered, "My bed is a lonely raft in a rising tide of menopause. How's by you?"

Harry rubbed his eyes. "My probable-cause theory is falling apart. Now I think the local Lutheran minister who's been feeding me a line on the sheriff is into boys. Coulda been screwing the kid I shot."

"Proof?"

"Just my intuition."

"Harry, your intuition has a magical three-second attention span. After that you need a seeing-eye dog."

"You could be right."

Dorothy sighed. "My man done stood me up, stayed on in D.C. with the boys. I had a bubble bath and three glasses of wine. Now I'm reading Anne Sexton."

"Hope you have the razor blades locked up."

She laughed. "I'm in my comfy bed. You're up in the chiller-diller woods. Why don't you give it up, Harry, walk away."

"Can't. There's rules, Dorothy."

"Are there? Sometimes I think there's just lines painted on the road. All we do is hope everybody stays in their own lane."

That struck him as very funny, very apt. He thanked Dorothy and hung up. What you get for messing in other people's lives. For trying to figure them out. You cause accidents.

Peering into the embers in the fireplace, he recalled the painting that had hung over Chris's bed. Saturn devouring his son. Emery, Cox, Bud. Chris wanted a father and his mother went on "The Dating Game." What was scarier than looking too deep into a human family?

He was seeing through the hole that killing Chris had torn in his life. Young civilizations looked through that window and saw God. Older ones just saw the void.

Harry saw a bottle.

He got a tumbler from the kitchen, sat it down on the cluttered table in the den, and poured it half full of whiskey.

Looked harmless. The golden eye of your favorite dog. Faithful, obedient. Forget the last time it bared his teeth.

The glass leaked a water ring on the pages of his detective musings, the names crossed out and rewritten, the arrows going in circles.

All the dots that refused to connect.

The .45 made a steel angle next to the glass. Scraps of cardboard from ammunition boxes, shotgun shells, and rounds for the .45-70 thick as brass fingers littered the table. Stumpy bullets for the .45 nestled, spring loaded in a spare magazine. He'd cleaned out his pockets. Change among the bullets. Keys. A wadded roll of $100 bills.

Another bad night in America getting ready to happen.

Harry reached for the glass. It was evil out and he didn't want to be alone. There was company in the alcohol. Ghosts mostly. He could almost hear the runaway train of the first half of his life.

He arm wrestled with the glass. One last grab for something to brace on, 'cause this time he wasn't playing with edges. This time he was going in, down, to the bottom.

He moved the glass back and forth across the table, pushing aside a stray .45 round, two quarters, a dime. The goddamn button Emery had found in the snow . . . Gouged in the wood grain, painstakingly carved with a knife, the blocky vandal letters shouted:

Huzzah!

The archaic cheer brought a sad smile as he hoisted the glass. Kind of prank he might have carved as a kid—always off in a corner reading books, dreaming of battles and chivalry . . .

Well no shit! Back in the game, he rose and hurled the tumbler across the lodge. Glass shards exploded off the fireplace.

The class picture Talme showed him. The writing on the back.

"Next year on to the ablative," he said aloud.

The kid wrote.

Maybe journals or a diary, just like Harry had kept at that age, and Chris would hide what he wrote—hide it so good that Jesse, cleaning out the place, would never find it.

Harry dumped the liquor down the sink. This time he rinsed the bottle out with water. No diving for corners in the garbage pit. Deep breath, let it out. He walked down the hall and turned the knob on the door to Chris's room.

46

The heat vent was shut off and the cold room was stripped clean except for the Iron Cross that hung from the light bulb. Harry closed his hand around the German doodad and squeezed for some lingering presence of Chris Deucette.

The closet doors were pulled open on their tracks, the shelves empty. The wire hangers tangled like bad nerves. The mattress was bare. The desk barren. Nothing in the drawers. Strips of tape stuck to the walls where posters had been torn down.

He felt around the mattress and box springs for any sign they had been altered to create a hiding place. He checked behind the desk, the edges of the carpet. Place was clean. This is crazy, he thought, sitting on the floor, smoking a cigarette, trying to make his mind fifteen years old—sixteen. Trying to reconstruct the glitter in Chris's eyes, talking about guns in front of the fireplace. The fascination.

He tore the room apart.

Methodically, he ripped up the carpet and yanked the shelves from the closet. Then he did the same to Becky's room. In Bud's room, he took all the clothes out of the closet, out of the drawers. He was looking for a notebook, a diary. Frustrated, he kicked at the scattered clothing and went back down the hall.

Nervous sweat coiled in his armpits as he rifled the desk in the den. Lifted the computer to look underneath . . .

Harry stared at the IBM.

Dummy.

Chris probably never owned a pen. He had a *computer*. All the drawers in the desk came out. All the floppies. He flipped on the PC and began opening files, going through the disks, one by one.

Business correspondence. Budgets, proposed expenses, and spreadsheets that costed out the creation of Snowshoe Lodge. Hours in front of the screen pushing the keys. The computer sat like a squat plastic cyclops and defied him.

Harry sagged in the chair and ran his eyes over the long shelves of books that lined the den floor to ceiling. *Smart kid might hide it in plain view, where he could smile to himself when people walked right by it.*

He made a pot of coffee and turned on the tuner. Radio Free Ojibway tiptoed in the static. Russell Means cut in and out, giving a speech. Harry started on the top shelf, opened every book. Thumbed through the pages of books that had gathered Brahman dust in an Ivy League dorm.

He ruffled the pages of *The Iliad*; paper swollen and gray from mildew, the cover chewed by jungle. *Cam Lo, 1969*, written on the flyleaf. Tossed it aside. Conrad, Camus, Bellow, Malraux littered the floor. The books of his own youth.

The drums got the range at 3 A.M. and came hoofing out of the ionosphere—loud—wailing. They carried him out onto the porch. Giddy with black coffee, he sucked down a recharge of fresh air and listened to Glacier Lake sigh, waiting for the ice.

He found it just before dawn, in a much-handled copy of *Neuromancer* by William Gibson.

I've seen pictures . . .

The diskette was taped to a postcard and a photograph. The card was a close-up of Michelangelo's *David*, the head, torso, and hips. With red felt tip, two cherries and a sprig were drawn on the statue's left hip. The Polaroid was something else . . .

"Jesus," Harry's breath rattled. Chris posed like the David in bad light, against a rock background. Looking off camera, one arm raised to his shoulder. Slender, ribs showing, penis tumescent. Tattoo on his left hip. Two cherries and a green sprig.

He inserted the disk in the PC and opened the solitary file, which was titled: "Martin." With the Ojibway drums pounding in his ears, he read:

The Life and Death of Martin

Men lie. Especially they lie about war. They lie about how they get their kicks, too. Some men will be sneaky about getting you to suck their dick, then they'll lie about it later.

When someone you love lies, that's worst of all. Martin had these thoughts as he walked through the red dust toward the hill.

Martin was a soldier. All the other men in his platoon talked real tough about what they'd do when they met the enemy. Martin figured they'd all run away.

The enemy was strong. He controlled the land. It was the land of Martin's ancestors. Everybody said they wanted to fight, to take back the land for the people. But Martin knew beneath their talk they were chicken. When it came right down to it, Martin would have to do the hard work.

The Sarge walked next to Martin. He was old and instead of guts in his belly he had whiskey. He had been in the war too long. The Sarge hated Martin. He hated him because Martin was beautiful.

And he hated Martin because he didn't approve of Lt. Mitchum being in love with Martin. Lt. Mitchum was popular. He was the platoon leader. He was tall and handsome with blond hair and a wonderful smile. He wasn't like the other men. Martin could talk to him. It didn't bother Lt. Mitchum that Martin was different.

Brambles of nicotine lacerated Harry's breath and a powerful sense of trespass came over him, reading this dead boy's innermost thoughts. He sipped lukewarm coffee and forced his eyes back to the orange letters glowing on the screen.

They started to climb the hill. The old Sarge carried a heavy pack and he fell down. Martin picked him up. Sarge pushed him away. "Don't touch me, you faggot," said the Sarge.

Martin forgave the Sarge, who was old and afraid of everything.

But it was true. Martin loved men. You couldn't tell by looking at him. He had the body of a Greek athlete. But he didn't always look that way. He had been born without all the muscles in one of his legs. As a boy he limped and other boys teased him. But he had an operation because of a new technology that could grow synthetic muscles. The new muscles were stronger than ordinary muscles. Now Martin was the strongest man in the platoon.

Martin didn't lie about who he was. He was up-front and now all the men knew the two things that he liked above all else. He liked to fight and he liked to suck dicks. But he'd only go out with someone he was in love with.

Martin was in love with Lt. Mitchum. Martin had showed Mitchum how not to be afraid of who he was. They ran naked together through the jungle.

Martin saw Lt. Mitchum come up the hill. It excited him to watch him. Martin loved the way he walked and the way the sunlight outlined his handsome face. He loved the way the sweat ran down over his muscles. Martin pretended his fingers were the sweat, touching Mitchum all over.

Mitchum came up to Martin and squeezed his shoulder. "We're in for a rough night," he said. "The enemy is very strong here and we have to defend the most dangerous part of the hill."

They smiled at each other. They would die for each other. There was no greater love.

That night, Martin could feel how afraid they all were. Even Lt. Mitchum. They could hear the enemy moving around in the dark. Getting closer. It was the blackest night there ever was.

Then the enemy came. They fought and fought but there were too many of them and the other men were so scared they couldn't speak. Finally, even Lt. Mitchum was too scared to even fight. They ran away, even Lt. Mitchum. Martin wouldn't run. Even though the other men despised him, even though his heart was broken that Lt. Mitchum had left him. Somebody had to stay and keep the enemy from getting to the top of the hill.

Martin was hurt. He was shot in many places. The bullets had torn his new muscles all to shreds and he was a cripple again. But he wouldn't leave. Even though they'd all betrayed him.

He had to go on. He had to finish what he'd started.

He cried out in his pain. In hatred for Lt. Mitchum who'd let him down, who had betrayed him.

Only one man was so ashamed that he came back. The old Sarge.

Together they held the hill and saved the company. But Martin was dying of his wounds. He was dying in Sarge's arms. There was no love left in Martin. He'd used it all up fighting. All he had left was hate and pain for Lt. Mitchum. The old Sarge kissed him as he died and swallowed all of Martin's hate.

Harry read Chris's warrior fantasy three times and with each reading he descended another rung into a private hell and the rifle kicked and Chris spun in his awkward snowshoe jig. Eyes wide open, crucified upon the thorns.

Trying to be strong, Miss Loretta said.

The Polaroid suggested a partner. Could this be some kind of allegory? A love letter? The reference to Mitch Hakala was transparent. Unrequited? Maybe from Chris's end. Couldn't see Mitch . . .

No. The answer was in the slime somewhere between Karson and Emery . . .

Something else. Something Chris said that night in front of the fireplace. Harry shook his head as his brain cranked. Metal thoughts grinding, out of oil. Too many cigarettes. Too much coffee.

He took the last of the coffee and sat on the porch steps. Out there, people were stirring in their peaceful beds with nothing more complicated in their heads than picking up their toothbrushes and making coffee. Soon they'd be watching morning television. Linda Margoles would take a shower and would draw a sponge along her smooth skin. Dorothy would sit in her roomy kitchen, butter toast, and listen to public radio.

Usually when Harry looked inside himself, he saw locked doors. Do not enter signs.

He knew Chris better now. Knew what it was like to be different, to move off to the side in the shower stall when they got to snapping towels. To be frightened by the escalating chorus of giggles that formed up the pack. Be an artist. Mom's wishbone hope.

Calling me chicken, Ma. Fairy. Gotta fight 'em. At the bus stop. In the parking lot. Gotta stand up when everybody is ass in the grass. Hurt people out there. Americans. The more they scream the stronger I get . . .

Harry stood up, poisoned with fatigue. He turned and started back into the lodge. The muscles below his left shoulder blade lit up. *Danger.*

Harry spun. Larry Emery stood 100 yards away in his red Mackinaw, unmistakable among the snow-draped pines. He lowered the scoped rifle. The red blanket quivered. Like a goddamned ghost, Emery disappeared.

All right, Emery—you and me!

47

Harry grabbed his hunting knife, found a white sheet in the hall closet and slashed a hole for his head. At the fireplace he scrawled a quick winter-camo pattern with a chunk of charcoal, threw it over his parka, and pulled on his boots.

Not the only one who can play snoop and poop in the woods, Emery.

Pack? No time. Going out the door, he barely remembered his hat and gloves. He hefted the heavy lever-action rifle and sprinted into the woods on sheer adrenaline.

You been hunting that kid, you fucker. Why don't you try hunting me?

He picked up Emery's tracks and slowly started up the ridge. Walk three steps, stop, listen, scan 360 degrees. Boonie Walk, an Australian conceit of fieldcraft he'd learned.

He wiggled on his belly through a stand of dwarf pines and saw Larry Emery's red square back dip over a hill 200 yards away.

Emery took a trail that skirted the ridge and twisted through the ravines. Harry came to a sign disfigured by a rusted stipple of buck-shot. Snowmobile logo in a circle behind a diagonal slash. Hiking trail.

Emery traveled at a smooth trot, working a pattern through the trail network. Harry kept the 200-yard interval, his lungs banging against his ribs. Snake breath. Formaldehyde sweat gushed in his eyes. Keep going. The old tie breaker. He can do it. You can do it.

Emery left the trails and climbed the ridge and the silent chase ate up the morning. No watch. No compass. Hour and direction lost in the swirl of exhaustion. Emery skirted the ridgeline and went down the other side. Oatmeal for sky. No sun. No shadows. Just follow.

Back on the trails, the red target stopped. Harry squatted, caught his breath, and relaced his boots. Within a minute, Emery moved again. He'd paused at a county road. An unfiltered cigarette butt smashed the snow. Across the road, an empty pint of Old Grand-Dad lay in his tracks with amber beads of liquor still wet on the bottleneck.

A couple hundred yards down the road Harry saw a country mailbox, set on an overhang to let the snowplow through.

More switchback hills. Swampy, thick second growth. Jack pine. Off Bud's land. Emery removed his Mackinaw and tucked it under a bough. His slate-gray shirt blended into the snow and Harry closed the distance, afraid he would lose him in the hills. Once he thought Emery might have heard him. He fell back. The track of a plow blade wound through the trees. Road? No, a driveway. Power line running in. Emery went back for high ground. The tang of wood smoke stained the air.

The big trailer had a screened-in porch on one side and an addition on the other with a stovepipe off the addition putting out the smoke. Jay Cox's truck. Jesse's Escort. A Quonset garage had been converted to a workshop and looked full of power tools, lumber.

Emery lay motionless, scouting the trailer.

An hour passed. The sun made a platinum smudge in the clouds and disappeared. The wind came up. When the plume of smoke came directly at Emery and Harry, Harry took advantage of being downwind to calm himself with a cigarette.

The trailer door opened, the sound out of sync with the distance, and Jay Cox stepped out, clad in blaze orange. He shouldered his rifle and walked to his shed where he pushed out a fat-tired three-wheel scooter. He mounted it and putted down the driveway.

Harry kept his eyes on Emery. What would he do? Go after Cox? Go down to see if Jesse was in there alone? A meeting?

Emery moved almost immediately, scrambling to where he'd left his coat. He put it on and began to walk in the direction Cox had taken.

Harry waited another thirty minutes to see if Emery would double back. His eyes snapped back on the trailer.

She was in there alone.

He circled, staying in the cover of the trees, and came at the trailer from the end where there was only one window, the curtain drawn.

He hoped that Cox didn't keep a dog. A dog inside the trailer would be barking already. No dog, decided Harry. From the edge of the trailer he could see through the framed eight-foot-high thermal windows, twelve of them, four to a side, that formed the addition.

A nude copper shadow rippled through the tinted glass as Jesse moved into the addition drying her hair with the end of a towel.

Harry pulled back behind the end of the trailer and gripped the rifle with both hands and willed his heartbeat to slow down. Then he rounded the trailer and gained the screened porch in long strides. Through the porch. The door opened to his grasp. He was in.

"Hello," she called out over the whine of the hair dryer. "Jay?"

A couch and chair. TV. Coffee table. Shelves held more books than Harry was prepared to think that Cox was inclined to read.

Flat cardboard boxes adorned with the script of a Duluth women's apparel shop were strewn on the couch amid tatters of beige wrapping tissue that gave off a new expensive scent. The table was littered with brightly colored travel brochures, scattered among plastic pill containers. "Mexico" in warm terra-cotta type. Harry picked up one the bottles. Elavil. From the Twin Ports VA Clinic in Superior, Wisconsin. Cox's name typed along with a lengthy description of doses and contraindications.

Travelers checks. Thick booklets of hundreds. Two airline tickets. Northwest. Duluth to Ixtapa, Mexico. Somebody was headed to the beach to beat the winter blues.

The electric whine shut off. "Oh my," said Jesse.

She merely stepped into the doorway, but she danced in his vision, his own backroads Shiva, with her hair down and her bare shoulders more rounded than he pictured them and her skin as pale as blooming peonies and the clustered triangle between her legs as black as ants.

Her face had mellowed, no longer drawn in sharp lines, and a burnished quality had replaced guile and grief in her dark eyes. The look evoked a memory of his mother's eyes. Against all odds. Hope.

"Marie Bursac," said Harry.

Jesse smiled. "Smart, aren't you? It's Jessica Marie. And Bursac was my mother's name." She shook her head. "I knew you'd come eventually, but I really thought you'd dress better."

"Sit down. Put something on."

"Which should I do first?" Stretch marks drew faint ironed-on purple bruises down the curve of flesh below her navel and delicately webbed above the nipples of her breasts. "Bud send you or are you on your own errand this time?" she asked.

Too hot in the trailer and her naked optimism smelled faintly perfumed and as flimsy as the wrapping paper on the couch. He began to sweat. "Is Becky in danger?"

"Becky's onstage."

"She says you should stop the divorce. Don't take the money."

"My God." Painted thoughts rolled on her eyes like fruited symbols on a slot machine. She stopped them on the jackpot. "The money's all I've got. They're just kids, they can't understand that."

Unnerved by her lapse of tenses, Harry shifted the rifle, keeping the muzzle angled away from her. She put her hands on her hips. "If you're going to shoot off your gun, go ahead. If not, get out of the way. I have to get dressed. I have an appointment with a lawyer."

"Did you know that Chris thought he was a homosexual?"

She walked past him, moving the rifle away with her index finger. "C'mon, Harry. You mean that silly business with Mitch Hakala? That was just boys playing. That's old thinking from the Kinsey days. Calling a boy queer just because he has an experience to orgasm with another boy."

"Did Karson seduce Chris?"

Jesse sniffed. "My God! Are you serious? Don Karson is a . . . prude."

"There was a fight last month at the lodge. You called the cops because Chris was threatening Bud. And you let them go *hunting* together?"

"That wasn't me. Larry and Bud worked that out."

"Whose idea was it to go hunting?"

"You're thinking city. It was supposed to be a way to make up. And it gave Larry an excuse to spend some time with Chris."

"Goddammit! Emery's out there hunting your daughter like she's some animal."

"Yup. She's got his full attention, just like she always wanted. Good old reliable Larry," she said sarcastically. "Reliable *now* for Becky. For Bud. For Chris . . . sure wasn't there for me, that's for sure." She shot a venomous look out the windows. "Made me drive that goddamn Ford all these years. Every woman in town's got something better. Giving orders all the time. All because I wouldn't marry him." She caught herself. "The man is a drag."

"Tell me about Tip Kidwell."

The painted drum rolled in her eyes. "I'm like you, Harry. I never look back."

He shook his head. "You're some kind of goddamn monster."

"Oh yeah?" She glided past and trailed a hand across his jeans. "Who's that for? Godzilla?"

Damn. Put them in the same room and the flute started.

He leaned the rifle against the wall and lowered himself to the rocking chair in front of the wood stove. Jesse moved off the porch, into the trailer, and hangers rattled in a closet. He yanked off the silly camouflage and unzipped his parka. Snow melted off his boots and ran in giddy rivulets along the shiny oak grain.

Jesse reappeared in panties light as foam on her shadowed tummy. She pulled on clean ironed jeans and tucked in a crisp beige blouse and stroked her hair with a brush. She tossed her head. No braids. No bra. Free.

Snowflakes began to crash silently against the tinted windows.

"You make a lousy go-between, Harry. You've been out of touch, Bud and I agreed on a figure," she said brightly. "One zero zero zero zero zero zero. How do you like those measurements?"

"Bullshit."

"Hey, I talked to his lawyer. Bud said you used to go out with her. She sounded like a real nice girl."

Her smile mocked and her husky voice did that bourbon trickle in her throat. "Is she? A real . . . nice . . . girl?"

Now there were Christmas lights in her eyes as she laughed at the expression on his face. "Bud's coming up. We'll settle it all then."

"Not if I can help it," he said.

"You can't stop it. It's ticking along like a Swiss clock. I'm finally getting out of here. Away from Larry Emery."

She pulled on a pair of snow boots with tufted liners, put on a bright red parka, and slung a purse over her shoulder. New clothes, new purse. Harry inhaled expensive leather and the mysterious interior scent of cosmetics. Her soap and body lotion. Her crazy smile like burning wires.

She withdrew a tube of lipstick. "Come with me," she said impulsively.

"Huh?"

"To Mexico. You have a passport?"

"At home. In St. Paul."

"Go get it."

"So I won't be around when you guys kill Bud?"

"You're *so* melodramatic. You're just like Jay. Your head's all jammed up. Didn't you ever just want to be . . . happy?"

Harry squinted at her. "What's with Cox? First he gets in a fight with me at the bar, then he acts . . . real friendly?"

"Decided you were just stuck in the middle." She knelt before him and put her hands on his thighs. Looking into her sparkling eyes, it occurred to him how wrong he could be. Nothing shrewd. No cares. All she could think of was her ticket out.

Blaming her. Emery. Could that be *his* ticket out. From the simple truth? He saw in the alluring mask of her face a mother who couldn't accept that her son had been cut down.

It hadn't really hit her yet. She'd taken her tragedy to the mall and went shopping. Doubt eclipsed him as he felt all the lives toppled over by the bullet that killed Chris.

He lurched forward, seized her shoulders, and shook her.

"He's dead. Chris is gone," said Harry. Nothing showed in her eyes but the bright images of his own face. He started to sit up, to push her away.

"Hush," she ordered, "just hush."

Deftly, with a metal hiss, she drew down his zipper, and freed him from the tangle of his underwear. Her fingernails teased.

Harry slapped her face. She slapped him back. A carnal greeting.

"We know each other, you and I," she said gaily.. "I'm your missing rib."

She twirled the bottom of her lipstick tube and daubed it on the glans of his penis. Her dark head tipped forward, took him in her mouth, and rolled in a figure eight.

Just a quick visit that inflamed him. When she looked up, she was smiling, and she had her lipstick on. She stood up briskly, shouldered her purse, and walked from the room. "I'll come see you tonight and we'll work on the rest. Turn out the lights when you leave," she said.

He walked toward the wooded hills in back of the trailer and put one foot in front of the other, aimlessly, in the blowing snow. Where he'd sought enemies, he'd found afflicted people. This whole week, not even people. Dogs running loose, a foam of pain dripping from their jaws.

All he had to show for the day was lipstick on his dick.

The weird orange light of the north stirred embers of storm-charge in the snow and he kept walking, deep into the woods.

Not sure anymore. Were they going to kill Bud? Arrange another accident? This time, coincidence would have a better aim. Jesse would walk away and lay on a beach and sip snappy rum drinks. Harry tried to imagine Jay Cox in a Hawaiian shirt and sunglasses. Cha cha cha. Becky the witness would disappear, be found in the spring when it thawed. Patient Larry Emery would do the paperwork and wait for Jesse to return to him. Then they'd all sharpen their knives and go after the will . . .

Ice cracked and his feet went out from under him. *Yikes!* Waist deep in frigid black water. He scrambled for solid ground. Soaker. Great. He'd blundered into a fucking tamarack swamp.

Walk *around*, dummy. In minutes, his leg muscles were cramped from jumping from one clump of roots to another. His gloves were drenched and his hands cut raw from grabbing at saplings. Solid sheets of ice clung to his jeans. Boots cased in it.

The wind burned the sweat running in his eyes and sleety snow slashed his face and dreadlocks of frozen sweat clicked in his hair. *Forget Jesse and Emery. You're lost, man.*

Harry began to shiver in a cloud of steam and he wished it was from fear. His body was losing heat faster than it could replace it. Okay. You're wet, wind's rising, the temperature's plunging. You have daylight. But how much?

Calmly, he smoked a cigarette and stared into the bleak maze of trees and marsh. You have a lighter. No matches. He smiled at the irony. Raised in the woodland shadows of the Great Lakes, he'd made all the obvious mistakes. Not just being disoriented without a map or compass. Soaked to the bone. Been up all night, hadn't eaten. Plus all that coffee. Dehydrated for sure.

Build a fire and dry out? Or walk out while he had light. Walk out. He'd have to backtrack. No calm way to get out of the swamp. He lurched on stiffening feet. Patient black water pooled under patches of thin ice. Trick was not to . . . Don't think the word. He'd already thought lost.

He broke the ice off his pants and began the long march back. Hadda be that goddamn fat sticky snow that fluffed up. Mistake to be going this fast, but he had to go on tracks while he still had them. He fell into a jerky trot doubling back on the boot prints that swelled with new snow. The ground was pulling zippers shut. Fainter, fainter. Gone.

No more walking tracks, just his fresh lost tracks.

He stood perfectly still and strained his ears. Hoped to hear a truck, a chainsaw, some reference.

Mistake. The wind spooked him with a low groaning among the trees and panic creaked ajar in the switchback moraines and the jack pine wagged their skinny boughs. Thumbs down. The snow blew almost horizontal in the limbo light.

Shaking uncontrollably now, an ominous solidity bonded his feet and boots together and a painful sting tightened in his fingers. Harry began to jog to get his circulation going. Blindly, just to move. The synergy of wind and snow torqued him and loosed a trampling surge in his chest.

He'd held on to the rifle. Useless damn thing, fringed with ice. He pressed it to his chest to rein in his runaway heartbeat. The wind scythed him and hacked off a corner of the light. And he came down with bone-deep shivers and it was hostile everywhere he looked and the idea of night entered his mind.

Nanabozho time.

A carnival of jack-in-the-boxes went booga booga in the wind. Control slipped a notch and Harry had a peek at full-blown panic. It occurred to him that Tad Clark should have his group out here on the bone lip of hypothermia. Talk about the Shadow. The primitive power of wilderness.

The only heat came from the pulsing tick under his left shoulder blade. Not alone out here. Harry tried to wrack the lever on his rifle. Frozen solid. He yanked his knife from its scabbard. It fell from his numb fingers. He lurched after it, digging frantically in the snow. Couldn't find it. Lost.

The wind soared, the branches rattled like a gallows tattoo, and the cold sliced right through him. He felt the blood turning gray in his veins and the whiteout was erasing him like a small mistake and when it passed, the forest reached for him.

Join us, beckoned the line-dancing trees and the wind chanted, midwife to the Windigo. *You winter soul of men. You spirit of starvation, of cannibals, of incest, of murder . . .*

He took a deep breath and stared it in the face. Don't fight it, you'll just mess it up. Be calm. He tried being calm. Maybe he could be calm if he was a Tibetan. But he wasn't.

Well, fuck this shit! Harry staggered to his feet, pulled off his gloves, and with spasming fingers, dug out his Zippo and cigarettes. He held fire in his trembling cupped hands and blew smoke at the goblins.

Had his own bullshit savage voices from Knox and Benning.

All right if you die, you pussy, just don't quit on me . . .

Harry drew a rectangle in the snow. As best he could, he transposed the map from the Snowshoe Lodge brochure. He'd followed Emery east from the lodge. Wandered east from the trailer. Cox's driveway opened on a county road that ran north and south. He hoped. The last weather picture on the TV news showed a cold front moving from the northwest. So. Face the goddamn wind and guide left.

Harry counted cadence and kept the stinging wind on his right cheek. Thousands of numbers later he saw the sweep of lights through the trees. Trolling headlights in the dusky snow, two, three sets of them. Other lights, swinging, moving, closer in.

His stiff feet picked up the step. A road had never looked so good.

The road was just as barren, cold, and windshot as everything else. He turned left toward the nearest lights. He'd gone only a hundred yards when he halted in mid-stride, staggering. His nostrils distended.

Whiskey on the wind, sour as coal oil in the turbulent, charged air. Out of place . . . Harry turned.

Silent and furred with snow, Larry Emery loomed in a surge of fury. A gloved fist. No time. Stars. Or the ice cracking on his eyebrows.

The trees spun.

48

Broke his fucking nose!

Emery's eyes bulged with tears as he stooped and seized Harry's dropped rifle. Two-handed, he smashed it against the trunk of the nearest pine. Harry gauged Emery's madness by the force that splintered the weapon. Emery tossed it aside.

He gave Harry two seconds to come out of a stagger and concentrate the spinning stars into a bee storm.

"Leave her alone, damn you. Can't you see she ain't well?" Emery muttered as his brawny hands opened and closed, struggling for control.

Harry cleared a loose wad of phlegm and blood from his throat and spit it into the snow at Emery's feet and choked out red-finned words, "Not your business she can't keep her pants on!"

With a tormented sob, Larry Emery, six-two, 220 pounds, charged and his right hand jarred Harry's left shoulder to the bone. A haymaker left uppercut went wild and missed his nose.

Harry drove his right fist with all his might into Emery's middle. Mistake. Lumped muscle. Gut was a sack of potatoes. Emery's hand came down, grabbed a handful of Harry's frozen hair, and flung him to the ground.

"Get up, you meddling piece of shit," rasped Emery.

Thing about pain. It sure warmed you up real fast. "This how you did in Tip Kidwell? Bounce him around and then shoot him?" Harry baited as he rolled to his feet.

"You don't know . . . nothing!"

"How'd you do it, Emery? How'd you get Chris to shoot Maston?"

The sheriff's face swelled with drunken fury and his roundhouse right looped wild. Ha! Harry timed him, stepped in and jackhammered a stiff left jab that went in sharp under the right eye. Followed immediately by a right cross. Another mistake. Boxing in a streetfight. Emery didn't even back up. With a spasm of sheer animal strength, he smothered Harry with his arms and pistoned a sharp knee into his groin.

Too old for this shit. Harry cringed into a fetal ball. Nausea gushed up from his pelvis.

Emery glared down. "Stay away from her, you sonofabitch, or next time I'll really . . ."

Suddenly it was a threesome. Jason Emmet Cox burst down the road in his truck and screeched to a halt ten yards away. He hit the ground running, deer rifle held high in both hands.

Horizontal butt stroke. Manual perfect. Cox buried the rifle butt into Emery's left kidney.

"Lay off 'im, Larry!" shouted Cox.

Lights in the snow, coming down the road. The whine of an engine.

Emery and Cox struggled over the rifle, went down, rolling. "Your fault!" Emery screamed. "Belong in a mental ward. Crazy sonofabitch! Leave her alone. She ain't well."

"I never laid a hand on her, goddammit," Cox protested. Now Emery was on top, elbows locked, forcing the rifle down on Cox's throat.

"Griffin," gagged Cox. "A little help would be appreciated."

Harry got his feet under him and flung himself at Emery. The three of them toppled over in a flurry of fists, knees, and elbows. Grunts and spit. Emery's drunken nightmare breath scalded them.

Harry threw his arms around Emery's neck and wrapped his legs around his waist in a child's desperate wrestling hold. Cox smashed his fist at Emery's hands, trying to break his grip on the rifle.

Deputy Jerry did his famous four-wheel skid.

The Blazer was still rolling when Jerry Hakala came out the door at a dead run brandishing a billy club.

"*Knock it off!*" He dove between them. The club flailed indiscriminately.

"Cuffs," gasped Cox. "Cuff the fucker . . . can't hold him . . ."

Harry had one of Emery's hands, Cox had the other. Jerry pried the rifle from his grasp. Emery surged, kicking with his feet, his jacket and shirt torn open. Bloody streaks from fingernails gashed his barrel chest.

"Shut your eyes!" Jerry yelled. Harry saw the canister in Jerry's hand, clamped his eyes shut, and strained his face away. Astride Emery's hips, Jerry squirted the Mace into Emery's face. Emery roared and clawed at his eyes. The knot of men broke apart. Coughing and gasping. Emery crawled in a mad circle on all fours. Through teared eyes, Harry watched oblivious snowflakes sail down and stick to Emery's swollen face.

They were all half blind, staggering from the chemical. A jingle of metal. Jerry had a pair of handcuffs. Emery struggled up. His arms flailed. Jerry stepped in, grabbed the sheriff's wrist efficiently in a twist, and snapped a short vicious body check into his armpit. Then he swept Emery's rubber legs out from under him. Using the rigid locked arm as a lever, he forced Emery face down in the snow. Cox trapped the other arm. Like two men hog-tying a steer, grunting, tears streaming down their red faces, they grappled the arms together. Jerry clamped the shackle. They jumped back, their breath coming in long torn clouds.

"What's . . . going . . . on?" Jerry demanded.

"Police brutality," gasped Cox with a predatory grin, his pepper-fog eyes watering. "Like I said on the phone. Emery was following him. Jumped out from behind a tree and sucker punched him. Saw it all coming down the road." Cox cleared his throat, snuffled, and spit out a wad of bloody mucus. "Then he kicked him in the balls. When he was down. It was very unsheriff-like."

"Kill you motherfuckers." Emery gasped in a strangled growl. On his knees, struggling for breath, eyes black and wild. His body made a crazy jig, raging against the cuffs.

"Jesus, Larry." Jerry winced and looked away. He exhaled and cursed: "Jesse."

Emery lowered his eyes.

"Yeah," said Jerry, shaking his head, "Jesse."

Harry had trouble seeing. His head was cased in a tight Norman helmet with a thick flange of swelling pain welded for a nose. A cold ring radiated inside his neck where pain thawed into fiery spasms. He visualized vertebrae fused in a nerve-grinding mangle. With satisfaction, he determined that between them, he and Cox had blacked both of Emery's eyes and given him a hell of lumpy mouse on his right cheek.

"You all right, Griffin?" asked Jerry.

"Fuck you *and* your sister," spat Harry.

"This weather, you were lucky Cox called. Said you were turned around in the swamp and that Larry might be after you. We had some guys out looking for Becky." Jerry paused to catch his breath. "Shifted the search this way."

"You gotta do something with him before he hurts somebody," said Cox.

"I know, I know," muttered Jerry. "Jesus, what a fuckin' week. Okay. Larry? You hear me? We're gonna put you in the car."

Emery nodded sullenly. Head bent, his eyes fixed on the trampled blood-sprinkled snow.

"C'mon, help me get him in, before the rest of the guys get here," said Jerry.

Emery stood up, shook off Jerry's hand, and stumbled to the Blazer. Jerry opened the passenger door. Emery got in. Jerry pulled the seat belt over his cuffed hands, securing him. "We'll go like this till I get you home. Then I'll get you cleaned up," Jerry's voice strove for calm.

"Wait a minute. Aren't you gonna lock him up?" Harry said.

"Don't tell me how to do my job. Way I see it, you gave this man a lot of provocation. Both of you!" Jerry said in a level voice.

Cox rummaged at the side of the road. Found Emery's deer rifle, wracked the bolt, unloading it, cleared it, and handed it to Jerry. "Let it go, Griffin," cautioned Cox.

"You kidding? With Maston coming up here to see her? You want that crazy sonofabitch walking around?"

"We'll deal with it, okay?" said Jerry. He picked up his radio handset and briskly explained that they'd found the lost guy. He didn't mention anything about the scene with Emery and signed off. "Now, you guys need a ride?"

"Fuck that," said Harry. Cox shook his head.

"Okay, that's it." Jerry closed the door. Emery hunched in the seat, staring straight ahead. Jerry got behind the wheel, put the Blazer in gear, and drove away.

Harry trembled and watched the taillights recede. "He's gonna let the sucker go. Jesus."

Cox gave a hollow laugh, stooped, retrieved Harry's rifle, and squinted along the shattered stock. "This puppy's fucked unless you got crooked bullets. Maston might have a few of those, but I don't think you do." He tossed the rifle into the brush.

"How'd you happen to be here?" asked Harry.

Cox shrugged. "Found you guys' tracks by the trailer, doubled back, Emery had done the same, was watching you in there with Jesse. He followed you when you came out. Lost your tracks in the swamp when the storm whipped up. I called Jerry."

So something *was* out there. Not the Windigo. Men were still the scariest thing in the forest.

Cox shook his head. "Emery's right, you know. She's off her fuckin' rocker since Chris—"

"Do we know each other, Cox?"

Spooky laugh. "You might say we're connected."

"You and Ginny . . . I thought you were on the outs, but I was wrong, wasn't I? You've been keeping tabs on me together."

Cox grinned. "She got a nice way of checking a fella out, don't she?"

Harry shivered and cautiously dabbed at the elbow that was growing between his eyes. "Fuckin' Emery likes to hit."

Cox nodded. "Kind of guy who'll never quit. Hate people like that." Then he grinned. "I'm like that."

"He's a violent sonofabitch."

"We all are," Cox said. "That's why we're here. The lives we lived brought us together." He bent down and grabbed a handful of snow, packed it, and pressed it against Harry's swollen nose. "You best hold that there for a while for the swelling. Get to the hospital. At least slap some tape on it." While Harry adjusted the icepack, Cox shook two cigarettes from a pack and handed one to Harry. He popped a lighter and his gaunt face flared in the flame, warted, and scarred.

Harry pressed. "What went down at the lodge last month, when Jesse called the cops? C'mon, man. You were there."

Cox cast his eyes at the snow-blurred woods. "I was there all right." He chuckled and slapped Harry on the shoulder. "Never get greedy, troop, it'll fuck up your life."

"You're not a whole lot of help, Cox."

"*Sin loy.* Sorry 'bout that." Cox grinned enigmatically. "Kinda like being out at night with the gooks, ain't it? Don't know who's really next to you till it's too late."

He picked up his rifle and nodded toward his truck. "Run you home?"

"I suppose so," said Harry resignedly. His nose was beginning to throb. He threw down his cigarette and headed for the passenger side.

As the vehicle careened down the snow-clogged road, Harry tried to keep the conversation going. "I saw a lot of pill bottles back in your trailer, Cox."

"That's right. I'm crazy. Lock-ward certified. That's my excuse. What's yours?"

"Why'd Chris do it?"

"Semper fi, Griffin, semper fi," Cox cackled to the wind.

It wasn't that far to the lodge. Cox dropped him at the driveway.

"What about Jesse?" Harry asked.

"She's a lot of woman. 'Fraid this has her all mixed up. She ain't like a normal person. Throw her up in the air, she's not liable to come down. But it'll be over soon," Cox said.

"What do you mean by that?" Harry said, as Cox shifted into gear. The truck began to pull away. "Goddammit, Cox—"

Cox's reply was nearly drowned in the engine noise. "*Go armed! The Maston family got its start setting traps in these woods!*"

Harry couldn't stop shivering, even after a hot shower. He inspected the road-killed pumpkin of his face in the bathroom mirror and groaned.

Got my nose.

One of the few things he'd been proud of was that his straight nose had come through the first half of his life undamaged. He plastered a thick strip of adhesive over the swelling and smoothed the ends under his puffy black eyes.

Be honest. You're scared. Everybody you ran into today frightened you. Jesse hatching out of her vamp cocoon into a basket case. Cox— saving your ass—that was really creepy. *Christ, the two of us couldn't handle Emery.* If Jerry hadn't showed up . . . Okay, so you're on a snipe hunt with Franz Kafka. You been there before.

Talk to Mike Hakala. Showdown, nothing wild. Find out what happened in October and why in the hell he let Chris slide by making threats and hauling a gun to school. Get him to . . . what? Lock up the sheriff?

Not thinking clearly. The way to shake the fear was to do something. Anything. Just go into town. Get directions. Find out where Hakala lives and have it out.

He dressed quickly, snatched up the .45, and fishtailed out of the drive.

Highway 7 greeted him with raving cadenzas of snow that streamed down like the quadrillion of all his fears. Snug inside Bud's Jeep, though. The heater whirred reliably. The radio popped on at the touch of a finger and the Ojibway Tabernacle Choir beat their goddamn drums.

The shape war danced out of the dark, up out of the swirling white ground. Harry stabbed the brakes and the deer froze in the headlights.

Big goddamn buck. Long left tine.

Chris's deer, mocking him like everything he didn't know, standing there, a statue in the headlights. With a yell, he stamped on the gas. The deer scrambled, hoofs slipping on the icy asphalt. Harry drove off the shoulder and struck the animal a glancing blow with the left fender. The buck rolled over stunned and lay in knee-deep snow.

Groped for the .45 next to him. Fumbled, knocked it down between the seats. Reached into the back. Box with jumper cables. Tools. His hand closed on the wooden handle of the army surplus entrenching shovel. He sprang out the door and slid in the snow. The deer had his hindquarters up and planted his antlers as a fulcrum to push his body upright.

Harry skipped around the struggling animal and the ditch blazed in a jukebox frenzy of high beams, dome, and dash lights and the snow came on like fever in the galloping drums and the shadows of man and deer jumped huge against the snow-truncated trees.

Savagely, he stepped in and swung two-handed and hit the antlers with a stinging clang of steel on bone. Damn deer was up! Seriously up on all four feet.

Face-to-face. Harry felt the hot breath snort from the buck's nostrils and saw its neck swollen, thick, lowering, aligning the horns.

Harry stared into the wild eyes of the thing he didn't understand, that he was trying to kill, and saw its beauty and its fury.

Thirteen tines of cruel bone sliced the air and ripped the shovel from his hands. With a hysterical laugh, he dashed back behind the car door. The buck pranced once, turned sideways, and disappeared into the night.

Time out. Call it a day, man. What was he doing in a world where he wound up going hand-to-hand with jealous sheriffs and wild fucking animals?

Harry turned off the radio and as his breath returned to normal he watched the snow quietly smooth out the wrinkles of the bizarre encounter in the ditch. He found the shovel, dug out the mired wheels, put the Jeep in four-wheel low, backed out of the ditch, and returned to the lodge.

49

The blue Escort was parked next to the burned hulk of his Honda and Jesse sat on the steps, smoking a cigarette. He climbed out of the Jeep, still shaking from the damn deer.

A scarf hid her hair but her face shone in the yard light with a bags-packed, leaving-on-a-jet-plane smile.

Harry opened the door. Jesse removed her coat. She wore a pleated blue dress, low snowboots. She pulled the scarf from her head. She'd been to Duluth, he'd bet. Her hair bounced, waved with the pampered coif of a beauty salon. Had her nails done, too.

Her lacquered fingers were cool as dice on his chin. "Jay told me," she winced appreciatively at his swollen nose and eyes. "One of these days Larry's drinking is going to lose him his job," She reached in her purse. Took out a present wrapped like a party favor, twisted on the ends.

"What's that?" he asked.

"For you. Open it."

Sunglasses. Expensive RayBans.

"Put 'em on," she coaxed. "Do wonders for your eyes."

He placed the glasses on the table by the door. She reached back in her purse. "They go with this." She handed him an airline ticket.

"Thought this was for Cox."

"Jay?" She blushed. "Nah, Jay's got other plans. That ticket was for Becky, but she's still playing lost. What about it? A month on the beach. We could heal up. Forget about . . . winter."

She kicked off her boots and walked into the den area, unconcerned with the wreckage of the bookcases strewn on the carpet. Distracted, she walked past the orange glow of her son's story on the computer screen and punched the CD player. Harry trailed her and slipped the .45 under the scattered paper on the table.

She twirled back into the main room, improvising a few dance steps to the piano and guitar riff of "Riders on the Storm."

"How much are you going to get?" Harry asked.

"The basic deal. I'm out of here. On my own for a change so I won't owe anybody . . ."

Harry furrowed his brow, which hurt. "What's Jay get?"

She ignored him and glanced at the faint leftover scrawl on the wall: IS A FUCKER. She walked around the mattress spread in front of the fireplace. "Is this where you sleep? On the floor?" she asked.

"So when does it happen?"

"Tomorrow. He gives me a check, I sign some papers. I don't even have to come to court when it's final. One-stop shopping." She stretched her arms and fell backwards onto the couch. Whee! Like a kid.

"What about Becky?"

"Larry'll watch her."

"She's out in the woods, freezing!"

Jesse tidied her new hair. Minded a Cretan spit curl that curtsied over her forehead. Blew it aside. "Becky," she said, "is out there having a ball. Being the main topic of conversation. She's fine. Larry taught her. He used to run the winter survival course in the army, up in Alaska before he went to Vietnam. Probably what fucked up his head, the abrupt temperature change—"

"Jesse. Emery's out of control."

She shrugged. Brightened again. "So what do you say? Day after tomorrow, high noon, be standing in front of the Timber Cruiser Cafe. I'll pick you up and we'll drive that old rusty Escort to Duluth and leave it to rot in the airport parking lot."

"Why the hell would I do that?"

She curled her legs under her on the couch. The firelight licked the curve of her calves. She wound the springy, errant coil of hair around her finger.

"Chemistry. In case you haven't noticed, we have something . . ." She shifted her haunches. The pleats flowed across her thighs and carved knees. "And not just sex, Harry. This only happens to people once."

The phone rang. At the third ring Jesse inquired, "You going to answer it?"

"Uh-uh." Harry stared directly into her eyes. "If I did, we both might disappear."

She softened when he said that, shucked off an entire layer. "It's Bud." She pursed her lips and cocked her head. "You don't owe him anything."

"You here. Be hard to explain—"

"Do me a favor?" she asked. "Don't say his name for the rest of the night, okay?"

"Okay."

The fire crackled and a tongue of flame shot up. Jesse shivered and hugged herself.

"You all right?" he asked.

"Feel like that piece of wood. Like you're going to burn me up. Felt that way the first time I saw you."

He took a small taste of the optimism that radiated from her eyes. She was so good, so believable. Tip Kidwell believed. Bud believed. Somewhere out there Emery was loading a gun.

"We'd be great," she said.

"You don't say," said Harry.

"Just knew this was going to happen the minute you walked up the steps," she said.

"This," said Harry dryly.

"Yes." She slipped off the couch and approached him. Their hips touched. She inclined her head, her large dark eyes tilted up, and the Barbara Stanwyck hairdo tumbled across her face. "So you going to burn me up or what?"

His hands melted into the warm firmness of her shoulders. She felt so good . . .

"Undress me," she said.

Harry thought about it.

Her, lying there naked in the firelight. Once he got that far, he wouldn't be able to imagine her anywhere but in a bed close to him. This was the art of her changeling energy, to have this effect on a man.

Her face in the firelight was upturned, open, and guileless. Just like that first morning in the woods under the horned moon. Isn't it supposed to be like this, her wide eyes prompted. Like magic?

Their bodies would consume each other, as hot and graceful as the flames, and drop by drop the fire would dry their sweat.

But most magic is just tricks. She was recruiting him for the Flying Scrotums, her high-wire sex act. A pyramid of men with her at the center designed so that at the last second they would all collapse and she would be left standing. Don't buy into those dewy eyes. Those are Aztec eyes.

She drew her finger down his chest, indolently circling his heart. "What're you thinking about, Harry?"

"Evil. It's just like love. You need two people to make it work."

"That's the truth."

"You fucked them all, didn't you?"

"I *know* you all. And none of you know me because as soon as your pricks get soft you go blind."

"We never talked about precautions."

"Don't worry. I'm not fertile. The pill made me swell up. And I never trusted those IUD things. Diaphragms always struck me as something you see hanging on a rack in an auto parts store." She took a deep breath. "And getting a guy to wear a rubber is like getting a kid to eat broccoli. So I had my tubes tied. Now when my period comes, it's like empty cars going by."

He moved back, wary of the power of her sincerity.

She locked on to his reaction, stepped forward, closing the distance. Touched his cheek. "Tell me what you want, Harry . . ."

Her fingers plucked at his belt, undoing it. She popped the buttons of his jeans. "Okay then, I'll tell you. You want what you all want. To be forgiven," she said. "For all your crimes, all your sins, and your dirty little thoughts."

She knelt, easing his jeans down over his hips, tethering him at the knees.

Her hair grazed the skin below his navel. "Why is it," she mused, "that when men want to be forgiven I'm the one winds up on my knees?"

Something about the way her fingers moved, fluttering across the scar on his left hip.

Like she'd done in the dark bathroom that first night.

Like Ginny Hakala. Checking him out.

Rough, his hand seized her hair and pulled her head up. "What is it?" He growled. The wet smile on her lips froze into shock.

"What?" She wavered.

Harry wrenched her to her feet, hauled up his pants, and dragged her tripping across the main room, up the steps into the den. With his free hand, he scattered the piles of paper on the dining room table. She saw the Colt lying there and pulled away.

"Jesus, Harry, now wait a minute . . ."

He found what he was looking for. The *David* postcard and under it the snapshot of Chris with a hard-on, displaying the cherries tattooed on his hip. He thrust it in her face.

"What is it?" he demanded.

"My God," she muttered, wincing, averting her face from the drugged smile, the aroused nakedness of her son. She shut her eyes. Her throat muscles gagged. Harry shook her.

"Tell me, goddammit!"

"I don't know. Where'd you get . . . *that?*"

She could fake anything. Palpable horror. The tears coming to her eyes. Anything.

"You people," he hissed. "What did you do to that kid?"

She shook her head. "Stop it, Harry, you're . . . scaring me."

He pulled her to him, bearing down on her wrists. There'd be bruises.

"That hurts!" she cried. Defiance crowded the pain from her eyes. She surged, fighting him. Her fists hammered his chest. He raised his hands to defend, but somehow his arms wound up around her and they embraced and it was like he'd never kissed a woman before and she was crying, kisses full of salt all over his face.

"Hold me," she cried.

"No." The muscles in his arms and shoulders cracked and burned with the strain of pushing her away.

"We only got this one chance. We gotta take it . . ."

He shoved her away and she fell to the carpet. She sobbed and pounded the floor. "I only want what's due me, goddammit. I worked my ass off and I'm still driving that goddamn Ford with a loose muffler.

Bud and I had an *agreement*! He lied. You all lie to get what you want!"

"I don't believe you." He kicked the picture at her. It skittered off her knee.

She began to cry again. "It all went to hell when you showed up! I *don't know* what happened to Chris. Now everybody's acting crazy. Jay. Larry. I don't know where Becky is or what she's doing. I'm scared, Harry . . . I know I did some things wrong. I'll make it up." She reached for him.

This is how she lives with Emery. She expects to be taken back. "Stay away from me," he yelled at her.

"Please," she pleaded. "Let's get a motel room. Away from all of them. Just stay with me till it's over."

He couldn't deal with it. If she stayed around, he'd melt down. He went to the main room, grabbed her coat, boots, the airline ticket. The ridiculous sunglasses. Stuffed them in her purse. Opened the door, threw them past the porch into the snow.

Then he pulled her up. She clung to him. "Harry, look at me! *Please see me*," she pleaded.

"*No!*" He manhandled her to the door and pushed her out. She stumbled back and forth barefoot on the tilted porch with her hands tangled in her new hair. Then she began pounding on the door. He shut his eyes and turned his back, wincing each time her fist slammed the wood. Finally, exhausted, she grabbed her things and went to her car. For a few more agonizing minutes she idled in front of the steps, face slick with tears in the yard lights. Snow poured silently.

"Get out!" He shouted. Sheer will. Go out there, kiss away the tears. Don't trust it. He wanted to believe her.

The Escort lurched down the drive. He dashed outside. "Wait," he yelled after her lights as they turned onto the road. His heart caved in when he saw her boots crumpled where he'd thrown them. He picked them up and ran after her, down the driveway out onto the road. Her taillights disappeared around a bend.

Lifted him right out of his life. Right, wrong, up, down. Didn't cut shit with her.

"You crazy, vulgar beautiful bitch!" he shouted hopelessly to the blowing snow and with the words, fear scooped his chest. Shit! Desiring her was an incantation that would summon Emery out of the storm like that goddamn buck.

He ran for the lodge and snatched up the Colt. A few minutes later, the phone started ringing. He ignored it and switched off the lights. Embers glowed in the fireplace. Deep wood's eyes. Emery's eyes.

He hugged the pistol to his chest and waited.

Got a problem? Call a cop. Harry laughed dryly.

Damn. He wished Randall were here.

50

Must have nodded off when the phone jarred him upright and, fumbling for the pistol, he cracked open crusted eyes and very clearly, he recalled standing face-to-face with the deer.

Damn deer kicked his ass. Just like Emery.

Then Jesse . . .

Ring-ring-ring.

"Stay in your own goddamn lane," he yelled. Finally the ringing stopped.

He tried to bring up spit but he came up bone dry with an 800-pound mongrel thirst gnawing on him with sloppy salivating gums, yellow teeth, and a huge wet tongue.

The pain radiating from his nose had been fluid and hot and now it set in his neck and shoulders like cold cement. He lurched to a sitting position and discovered that his whole body had the muscle flu and he had cardboard for skin.

The phone again. Fuck it. Jesse's voice could cast a spell. Wasn't going near it. He'd get his head straight. Then go find Hakala. He made coffee. Had to rebuild himself block by block.

Came to believe that we were powerless over alcohol . . .

Christ, back to square one. *I pray the Lord my soul to take . . .*

Screw that. Too late for that. He slapped a Doors CD on the sound system and turned up the volume. Harry put himself back together with Jim Morrison, coffee, and cigarettes.

The phone rang intermittently and he ignored it and he was on his second pot of coffee, and the third time through "Moonlight Drive," sitting at the computer in the den, worrying his teeth with his toothbrush, staring at the orange type of Chris's strange story, trying to make it all fit, when he heard tires in the drive and saw the flash of lights.

Automatically, he reached for the Colt.

Jerry Hakala climbed out of the police Blazer and, with a noticeable sag to his usually athletic gait, his boots crunched through the broken glass and creaked up the porch boards. His square fist banged urgently on the door. Harry yanked it open.

"Now what?"

"Hold it there. Harry . . ." The cop had never called him by his first name and it conveyed a peculiar vibration of alarm. "You didn't answer the phone." Jerry wasn't good at looking contrite. His eyes swept back and forth at knee level. "Just wanted to check on you."

It hurt when Harry tried to grin.

Jerry chewed his lip. "Yeah, well, we got a problem. Larry's loose." The words had the laconic brevity of correctly gauging the approach of a typhoon. Harry nodded. Their eyes agreed. They'd just as soon be somewhere else.

"We sent a deputy out to Cox's trailer. Put another out on the road in front of here. Just a precaution."

Harry grimaced. "You should put a sign at the edge of town. Caution: Sheriff Dangerous When Drunk."

"Think it could be a little more serious than that." Jerry toed the porch boards with a polished boot.

"What happened?" Harry asked and realized he'd been standing there with a cocked pistol hanging in his right hand and Jerry hadn't mentioned it. His eyes scanned the black treeline.

Jerry inhaled, held the breath. "Took him home, cleaned him up. Looked like he was coming out of it. Then he went to the bathroom. He was butt-naked in a towel . . . and . . ." Jerry clicked his expensive bridgework. "Bathroom had two doors. Breezeway goes to the garage. Musta had a pack with hunting gear stowed out there. From the garage was boot prints. So, ah, he's on foot. Near as I can tell he's up Nanabozho—"

"Armed?"

"Be my guess."

"Great."

"Harry. Me and Uncle Mike need you to look at something."

"What? Now?"

"I need your help, man. Get your coat on," said Jerry firmly, hooking his thumbs in the thick leather belt that supported his 9-mm Glock, cuffs, spare ammo, and can of Mace. "Just been crazier'n hell with the funeral and Jesse and Maston getting divorced like they are . . . now this."

Harry queried Jerry's intelligent, uncomplicated, powder-blue eyes, and saw duty there, durable as a coat of paint on a wooden soldier. Neat silver badge. Thin blue line. All that good shit.

The wooden soldier dropped his eyes.

"What is it, Jerry?"

"You know how to use that piece?"

Harry nodded. Jerry cleared his throat. "Well, better bring it along. He shows up—if he's like he was last night—and for some reason he gets past us . . . don't take any chances."

"Jesus? Where we going?"

"Back to his house. Shake it up."

Now the snow comes down as quiet as a separate peace and inside the speeding Blazer the dash lights leak gloomy lime bubbles across Jerry's face.

"Mitch was in a fight. What about?" asked Harry.

"Ah, that was high school stuff. Kid made an off-color remark about Becky. Mitch lunched him." Jerry drove in silence for a few minutes, then he said, "Uncle Mike ain't exactly been candid."

"No shit."

"He's been covering for Larry. Not calling the grand jury wasn't for Maston. That was to go light on Larry for babying Chris." Jerry ground his teeth. "Weird thing is Larry wanted the grand jury. Wanted to grill Jay Cox and Karson. And you. That threw us."

"Mitch told me about the scene in October. Chris threatening Bud."

"You gotta know the history, Harry. He loved those kids and suddenly everybody's taking them away from him. Now this is just between you and me, but around Labor Day it looked like Jesse had given up on Maston and was putting out feelers to go back to Larry. He got antsy about Cox, said something wrong was going on out at that lodge and he had to get Jesse and the kids out of it."

Jerry grimaced, the Blazer skidded through a turn too fast. "Then she does a one-eighty and decides to *marry* Maston. That's what the big fight was about. The kids thought they were going back with their dad. After the wedding, Chris started acting up and took a gun to school. Larry stepped in and made Uncle Mike back off. Had this idea he could work with Chris, go hunting together, get close to him again after everything that'd happened. But then Chris turned it around, after Larry taught him to handle a rifle, he decided to go out with Maston."

"Or Emery talked him into it, for obvious reasons."

"Hell, we knew it stank to high heaven and then you came back to remind us and Don Karson was running around playing Johnny One Note about the Duluth stuff. And word getting around about Jesse's big divorce settlement. But goddammit, there was nothing solid."

"Where was he that morning?"

"Exactly. He was in the police station, getting ready to go out hunting, standing next to the dispatcher when the call came in about Maston."

"Doesn't mean he didn't talk Chris into it."

"Yesterday I'd a given you an argument." Jerry shook his head. "Figured it was too sloppy and obvious for Larry, putting Chris, fucked up like he was, in the middle. Hell, he'd of found a way to have Maston eaten by a bear or break his neck climbing a tree. Now, I don't know. Could be Don Karson is right." Jerry exhaled. "Normally Larry doesn't spend all day in the woods and all night in a bottle."

"He's in the woods after Becky. She knows what happened. If he'd use his son to commit murder, he might make his daughter disappear. It's about Jesse and the money. And if Bud Maston dies before the divorce is final, we're talking a lot of money."

"I don't want to believe he'd do that to his kids," said Jerry.

They pulled into Emery's driveway. Two more Blazers and a red Bronco were parked in front of the garage. A deputy waved them in. "Mike's in the basement," he said.

The first thing Harry saw in the hallway was a picture of Becky and Chris, younger, smiling. The place where Jesse should be was cut out. Night of the funeral, after the Battle of the Snowmobiles, digging in the basement—that picture . . .

"This way," said Jerry. Months of dust cloaked the living room furniture and gave off a musty lived-in smell that turned piquant as they entered the kitchen.

"Phew." Harry wrinkled his nose. Bags of garbage heaped against the stove. Spores of mold festered on fruit rinds. Opened cans. Pots gluey with leftovers on crusted burners. Jerry grinned tightly. "My dad always said you have the heart-to-hearts sitting at the kitchen table."

A family album had been ripped apart, cellophane page minders scattered and torn. Scraps of cardboard. Photos littered the grubby table and the woman's face had been cut from all of them.

"I count four empty whiskey bottles," said Jerry. He jerked his head ominously to the basement stairs. "It's down here. When he split on me, I thought maybe he got into the basement, so I went down to take a look."

The basement was divided into two areas. An unfinished utility area with the furnace, laundry sinks, washer and dryer, storage closets. The other half was a paneled den.

Mike Hakala hadn't taken the time to get all the way dressed. He stood barefoot next to his kicked-off Sorels, in pajamas under his parka. Staring.

A couch and chair faced a fireplace and a small bar was built into the wall. Next to it, a broad workbench held a mounted apparatus Harry vaguely recognized as a reloading press. There were shelves with tools and firearm paraphernalia and two rifles lay on the bench. A large abstract painting, six feet by three and a half, four feet, was propped on the top shelf over the bench.

A third rifle was secured by rubber bungees to a snow tire on a table at one end of the room. Sandbags wedged the table legs.

"Don't touch anything," said Mike.

Harry nodded and followed the direction of the rifle muzzle. At the other end of the room, a plywood frame held a backstop of thick phone books. Bud's face, thinner, a poster from his stillborn political campaign, was taped to the phone books. A grid had been drawn with precision over his features with a red felt-tip pen. It exactly matched the grid on a sheet of paper taped next to it. Harry had seen the sheet of paper before. A target grid from an army instruction manual they used on the rifle range to zero M14s. Something about the trajectory being the same at 20 feet as at 200 yards.

"What the fuck?" Harry poked a finger at a tight group of six bullet holes a foot off the poster two o'clock high on the right.

"Don't touch, just look," said Jerry.

They went back to the bench. A plastic baggy containing a lump of smashed lead lay next to a bottle of Old Grand-Dad. Three unfired cartridges, all tagged. The tags labeled: Chris, Maston, Griffin.

Harry pointed to the old Remington on the counter. "That's my rifle. I thought—"

"Yeah, so did I. All three guns went down to the BCA in St. Paul for analysis. Larry got 'em back. What the fuck was he up to?" Mike winced and looked away.

Harry gave his full attention to what leaned against the wall over the bench and his battered sinuses cleared and the hallucinatory after scent of whiskey and cordite that lingered in the basement became a witch's brew of obsession.

"Holy shit," he breathed.

"Right," said Jerry tersely. "You're an artist. Give me an artistic opinion about *that*."

Harry's skin rippled as he sensed the brooding presence of Larry Emery all around him. A man who watched everything and missed nothing.

"It's a photo montage," said Harry quietly as his eyes roved and his knees got weak. He dropped to a stool and groped for a cigarette. Jerry backhanded him on the arm, held out his hand.

"Huh?"

"Gimme one."

They lit up and viewed the intricate wall hanging. Bud. Hundreds of pictures of Bud Maston. Meticulously cut out and fitted together with headlines and blocks of type. A public record of his shining life. Bud in his baby shoes. Bud walking with his father on the Stanley waterfront. At the funeral after his family died in the sailing accident. On the football team at St. Thomas Academy in St. Paul. The debate team at Harvard. Grainy photos from the Pacific edition of *Stars and Stripes*. Sleek black-tie snapshots from society pages. Banquets. Dedications. Dates. The most recent pictures were from his political campaign. Gleaned painstakingly from dozens of publications over more than forty years.

Richard Nixon hanging the Congressional Medal of Honor around his neck at the White House.

Mike Hakala's voice was quiet, glum. "How hard is it to make something like this?"

"Not the technique, Mike. It's the time . . . assembling all the pieces."

"Whaddya suppose that means?" Jerry pointed at a color picture of a muscled torso, male genitals. A portion torn from a larger picture. No face.

Harry strained air through clenched teeth. A sprig of cherries, drawn on, like a tattoo on the muscle of the left hip.

"These cherries all around?" Jerry pondered, indicating several large groups of cherries cut from glossy ads sprinkled over the montage along with Marine Corps insignias plastered next to a bold headline. LOCAL MAN WINS HIGHEST HONOR.

Harry shook his head. The thing dripped with cold patient pathological hatred. "I don't know, man . . ."

Their eyes met. Jerry gritted his teeth and whistled. "So Larry coulda kept like a scrapbook all these years and then . . . after Jesse left him . . . been down here drinking and putting this together." He clicked his teeth. "And Chris . . . somehow in on it?"

Mike Hakala's voice rasped. "Not common knowledge but I saw it on the coroner's report. Chris had cherries tattooed on his hip."

"Jesus H. Christ," muttered Jerry.

Harry turned to Mike Hakala. "So, Prosecutor, what do you think?"

Mike Hakala shook his head. "Fuck me dead! This goddamn thing won't go away, will it?" He exhaled. "This . . . gun setup, that could be tampering with a state agency."

Jerry hitched up his gunbelt. "Uncle Mike, I think we better have us a manhunt. Fast."

Harry watched Mike Hakala pace while Jerry stood with his arms crossed; the more Mike speculated the more determined the expression on his nephew's face became.

"You say he threatened Cox and Griffin last night?"

"We had to cuff him, Mike. Took all three of us."

"And you let him go?"

"Jesus, I thought it was just a drunken piss-off, that he'd sleep it off."

Mike pointed to the montage. "That ain't no drunken piss-off. That's psycho shit. That's . . . weird. And those pictures in the kitchen. Jesse's face cut out?"

"We gotta pick him up," said Jerry flatly.

"Well, sure. What's the charge?" Mike wrung his hands.

"How about he's an armed, dangerous sonofabitch who's out to kill every man who ever screwed Jesse Deucette? And I think Bud Maston is way up on top of the list," said Jerry.

"How do I put *that* in a warrant?" Hakala laughed nervously. "I don't know what this crazy shit means. Is there intent here? Does it prove anything?"

Jerry pointed down the room at the red grid traced over Bud's smiling face. "Do I have to draw you a fucking picture? Don Karson's out there just dying to give his theory of things to a reporter. Hell, he spoon-fed it to Harry. And what if he's right? History could be repeating itself here. Like Kidwell in Duluth. Or have you forgotten about that?"

"Christ, Larry and I are . . . friends. We were on the goddamn hockey team, went down to the state tournament together. We dated the same girls . . . you know how he keeps everything inside. I thought he'd get through it. I thought he was working on something—"

"Make a decision, Uncle Mike. It's what we pay you the big bucks for." Jerry put his hands on his pistol belt. "I sure as fuck ain't going up against Larry Emery with nothing but good intentions backing me up!"

"He did that to your nose?" Mike asked Harry.

Harry nodded. "Cox saw it."

"Unprovoked attack?" Mike asked Jerry.

"Well, he did mumble something about losing it when he looked in through Cox's windows and saw Jesse coping Griffin's joint."

"Christ," Mike Hakala put his face in his hands. Then he looked up at Harry. "Maston's been trying to get ahold of you. He left a message at my office. He's in Duluth. Said you weren't answering the phone. He's coming up here tomorrow—" Hakala glanced at his watch "—today, to go to court on a separation agreement with Jesse."

"Could be a setup. We better get Jesse in to talk to." Jerry shook his head. "You should have gone to a grand jury on Chris, Uncle Mike."

"I know, I know." Hakala took a breath. "This time if we err, it'll be on the side of caution. First we get Larry."

"The number. Where Bud's staying?" asked Harry.

"Uh, left it at the office. Look. Jerry, you secure this place. Who's dispatcher tonight?

"Billy Munger."

"I'll get Billy to wake everybody up. Get another guy out here to take pictures. Nobody disturbs this—"

"Two more guys here, and two out at Cox's and four at the lodge. Be straight with them. Tell them Larry's wrong on this. And warn Maston off till we lock him down," said Jerry.

"Okay. Griffin, we're going to town. I'll find that fucking message. What else?"

"Becky Deucette," said Harry.

"She's all right, she's with my crazy kid. They got some damn hideout up on the ridge."

"Better find her, Uncle Mike, before Larry does," said Jerry.

"Okay. Okay. Collect Becky. Arrest Larry." Mike Hakala made dizzy swimming motions with his hands. "Jesus, we need more guys."

"You gotta put it over the radio in plain goddamn view," said Jerry. "Highway Patrol. Lake and Cook Counties. Hell, if we have to take *him* on in the woods—"

"Yeah, yeah," muttered Mike Hakala, "I might have to call Rudy and ask for the National Guard."

They went out the door and Jerry grabbed a radio handset and put out an all points on Larry Emery. One of the other deputies walked off a few steps and aimed a kick at a snow tire. "Yeah, *our* Larry Emery," Jerry yelled back at a query from the static. Mike Hakala pointed to the Colt stuck in Harry's waistband. "That thing loaded?" he asked. Harry nodded. "Keep it handy," he said, stomping into the snowy night, pajama top flapping.

51

Hakala bobsledded his Ford Bronco down Highway 7. "Live situation. Important to keep it simple. No time to figure it all out. First, warn Bud off till we find Larry. Second—Christ," he giggled nervously. "Every shadow in the goddamned headlights . . ."

Harry eased the Colt from his belt and held it in his lap.

"Keep your eyes peeled, I saw that sonofabitch drop a deer at 400 yards with open sights once," said Hakala.

Streetlights sieved the steady snow falling on Stanley's barren streets and nothing moved except a cloud of exhaust that surrounded a Blazer running in front of the police station. Hakala opened the door to the police car and turned off the engine. Then he stormed through the door, yelling.

"Everybody out. We got trouble. Larry Emery's off his fucking nut!"

Deputy Morris stood in the hall, parka open, sandwich to his mouth. Another tired-looking deputy behind the radio desk gave Hakala a deadpan once-over. "We heard. Jesse," he said, shaking his head.

Hakala threw a set of keys at Morris. "Don't leave your unit running with the door open, Morris."

"Huh?"

"Do I look like I'm kidding *at three A.M. in my fucking pajamas!* Extend all shifts. Go down the list. Wake 'em up and tell 'em to get in here. Shoot two men to Emery's house to back up Jerry. Get two more out to Jay Cox's trailer—you know where that is?"

The dispatcher nodded. "Where Jesse's at."

"Right."

"I volunteer *not* to be in that party," said Morris.

313

"Anybody cruising up north call them down, work County Road X, Y, and Highway 7. Tell them to arrest Larry Emery on sight."

"What's the charge?" The dispatcher was disbelieving.

"Aggravated assault on this guy," Hakala pointed to Harry.

"Jesus, Mike, a bar fight?"

"Listen, dummy. Jerry had to cuff Emery last night!"

The dispatcher's mouth dropped open. "You ain't kidding."

"Billy, I'm telling you, he's finally flipped. Could be bad craziness. He's on foot, last we heard. Probably armed for bear. Jerry thinks he's moving around the base of Nanabozho. If anybody reports a missing vehicle, jump on it. And call the fucking Highway Patrol. Call Lake and Cook. Do it, Billy. Armed and dangerous. All that good shit. Do it *now*!"

Billy bent his microphone. With his other hand he picked up the phone, referred to a list of numbers taped to the desk, and started punching numbers as he spoke into the mike. "Net Call! Listen up out there . . ."

Harry followed Hakala to his office. Hakala scattered paper on his desk. "Goddamn. Goddamn. Knew I should have done something about the drinking. Ah, here it is. In Duluth, at the Radisson." He handed Harry the message slip.

Harry put it in his pocket. "How bad a spot you figure you're in?"

Hakala grinned. "Oh, I just ignored a police report that a kid was threatening the life of his future stepfather and didn't bust him when he was caught carrying a concealed weapon. Instead I let his real father take him out and teach him to shoot a rifle. Accessory is the term that comes to mind." Hakala waved his arms. "Hey. We're doing it. We'll find him. Don't get carried away."

"Then why all the extra cops?"

"It's Larry. It could get out of hand. Shit, I don't like it. Coming off that basement stuff is like taking a leap of faith except it's not faith, it's dread. I'm bringing in an army. What *if* it's just him drunk and hitting you in the nose? I'll get laughed out of the county."

"You weren't talking like that twenty minutes ago."

Hakala shuddered. "That's it. I gotta go with my gut." He reached in his desk drawer, took out a bottle of Pepto-Bismol, toasted Harry, and swigged. "To the public safety."

Then he grabbed the phone, punched in a number, and raked his knuckles across the stubble on his jowls. "It's me," he said, "wake up our number-one son." He put his hand over the receiver. "I don't think Emery will go after Maston. Sounds like he isn't thinking that far in advance. I think he'll head for you out at the lodge. How are you at playing tethered goat?"

Hakala turned his attention back to the phone. "Mitchell, this is the guy who pays the mortgage. Rouse your young ass and go find Becky. Yeah, yeah, I know you don't know where she is. *Find her* and get her to the police station. Tell you later. I know what time it is. Just do it."

On the way to the front door two deputies looked up from a map and the one talking on the phone yelled, "You want a SWAT team?"

"Why not?" groaned Mike Hakala.

52

Tethered goat implies lion.

If he didn't keep his mind flexed just right, he got this image of Larry Emery sitting at that kitchen table with his elbows in a puddle of Campbell's soup, cutting Jesse's face out of pictures, and a chill began to curl at the back of his neck.

Like something you read in seedy news shorts buried in the Met section—estranged boyfriend comes after woman and her new lover. Later, he bounces off the blood-spattered walls blubbering "I'm sorry" to the coppers.

Fear worked up through the floor and puckered his asshole and cotton-mouthed him dry of spit. His blood congealed into a billion floaty bubbles of pressure-sensitive mercury and with Mount Palomar eyes he saw Larry Emery ready to pounce in every snow-dancing shadow.

The deputies Mike Hakala put around him did little to diminish his anxiety. They'd pulled their trucks off the road and now three of them squatted outside the lodge in the trees. Morris sat in the corner of the main room with firelight glimmering on the barrel of his 12 gauge and, on the ride up from town, communication with the deputy had consisted of one laconic question: "Larry do that to your face?" And Harry nodded and Morris sucked on his teeth.

Morris was a wiry man and his black sideburns trimmed crafty pointed features and he wore his shiny dark hair swept up and back with Brylcreem. Thirty years ago in high school he would have worn his shirt collar up and his jeans down to the crack of his ass. Now, as Harry sat in a bull's-eye of light at the dining room table, Morris was stricken by speech.

"If there's like a shot you get on the floor real quick," said Morris. He added a nervous "Hee hee."

"You have a problem with arresting Emery?"

"The *idea* don't bother me at all. It's the practical doing it that could be tricky. You ever notice how quiet that man can be. How you just look up and he's there."

"Well, to get here he'd have to travel through the woods at night. What are the chances of catching him out there?"

Morris snorted. "He's a fucking Indian."

"His mother's got Indian blood, but he looks like he lives pretty white."

"You take your normal soul brother like you got down in the city. Man's bound to have some white blood in him but nobody'd call him part white now would they. Uh-uh. Larry's a fucking Indian and for all I know he can turn into a fucking owl and fly through the woods at night." Morris grinned philosophically. "Don't discount anything out of hand I always say."

"Okay, he's Indian."

"Indians are difficult people. You know, extreme. Like that Red Feather Veteran's bunch Larry was in for a while. Need *three* of them Purple Hearts to join. Man, that's extreme. Yeah, he was over there in Vietnam. Showed me this picture once from *Life* magazine. All these empty boots lined up after this battle. Said he was in that picture, in the back, but you couldn't see him. That's Larry, hee hee."

"Morris, shut the fuck up please."

Dawn dripped down the windows the color of sweat and Morris's radio crackled and he spoke to the guys outside. Then he leaned over and spit tobacco juice into a copper antique wastebasket that was embossed with a Maston Mining logo. "It's quiet," he said. "Three more of the boys showed up. State Patrol's out at Cox's trailer. Bunch of guys from Lake County are at Larry's house. And cops on the roads thick as fleas. Be a big search come daylight."

Harry made coffee for the cops who now sat warming themselves in their trucks in the drive. Then he called the hotel in Duluth. At first the clerk wouldn't ring Bud's room because of the early hour.

"This is a police emergency," Harry said in his best storm trooper voice.

"Huh? What?" Bud's groggy voice.

Finally. "Hey, fucker, Wake up! Where you been?"

"Harry?"

"Man, you won't believe all the shit—"

"Where've *you* been?" Bud demanded.

"Tip Kidwell. Duluth. Larry Emery hiding in the woods. That's where I been."

"What?"

"Emery's flipped out. He tried to take my head off. We got a game of tag. Cops with riot guns. The sheriff is fucking it."

"You're not making sense."

"They got an all points for him. Armed and dangerous, just like in the movies. Bud, he's got Chris's rifle down in his basement and this target of you on the wall and all these pictures—"

"Pictures?"

"Yeah, this collage. You and Nixon. A million fucking pictures. There's other stuff. I found this story Chris wrote. That's *really* weird. It ties in with what Emery's got in his basement but damned if I can figure how . . ."

"Story?"

"Karson has had Emery pegged from day one, man."

"Harry, slow down. It's all skewed."

"Yeah, tell me about it. Just stay away, far away, until we drop a net over this guy."

"Bullshit. I'm getting dressed. Give me an hour and a half. I'm getting you out of there. You at my place?"

"Christ—don't come near here."

"Goddammit!" Bud shouted. "I live there! I'm going to settle this damn thing with Jesse once and for all."

"I doubt the court is doing any normal business today. Mike Hakala has a gang of coppers watching Jesse out at Cox's place. And he's bringing Becky in. With Emery flipped out there's bound to be a grand jury into Chris now. My bet is Jesse'll come down in price. Call Hakala at the police station. Get an escort. Stay on the main roads. This guy's got it in for you. He's doing the Kidwell thing all over again."

"Call you back." Bud hung up.

Harry paced, peering out the windows. The phone rang ten minutes later.

"Jesus Christ. What's happening up there?" said Bud soberly. "Hakala said he was using you as bait."

"Now you believe me?"

"It's six-thirty. I'll meet you at the Timber Cruiser at ten. Calm down. Hakala said not to overreact. It's all over cops. Some cooperative thing with other jurisdictions. Emery's not downtown, for Chrissake. And what did you mean a story?"

"I'll print out a copy. It's something else."

"Whatever."

53

Ten-fifteen. Bud was late. Harry lit another cigarette and motioned to the waitress for a refill on coffee. The Cruiser was jammed with hunters and cops from all over coffeeing up before they hit the woods. Faithful Morris had followed him back down the hill and sat at the counter contemplating a mountain of blueberry pancakes. Four husky guys in black fatigues and snappy little black SWAT caps occupied one table with the air of trophy hunters out for exotic game. The lady reporter from Duluth, Sherry what'shername, sat with them.

Ginny Hakala walked through the crowd in a mountain parka, wool pants, and beaded mukluks. She sat down. "Lookit all these guys raffling wolf tickets. What a fucking mess."

"Where's Jerry?"

"Uncle Mike's got him tailing Mitch, looking for Becky."

She lit one of Harry's cigarettes. "Between you and me, this isn't like Larry Emery. Uh-uh. Not one bit. I don't care what he's got in his basement." She blew a plume of smoke. "You all right?"

Harry, going on sixty hours without sleep, laughed.

"I'm worried about Jay," she said frankly.

"The guy can take care of himself. He convinced me. And there's a million cops."

"That's exactly what worries me. Doesn't all this prove that nobody can take care of themselves?"

A deputy stood up at the counter and motioned for her. She rose to her feet. "I gotta go guide in a search party."

Two cigarettes and a cup of coffee later, Bud slowly hoisted himself out of a gray rental Isuzu Trooper. A green Honda Prelude pulled in next to him—Linda Margoles.

Deferential silence accompanied the blast of icy air as Bud pushed through the door. Cold-eyed sober and bullet-headed in a gray three-piece pinstripe suit, he filled the cafe—ponderous as an icon of power visiting from another era. An expensive silk tie was knotted at his throat and he'd already sweated a ring through the collar of his shirt. His top sheet of fat had melted off.

"What the hell's she doing here?" Harry demanded when Bud and Linda came through the crowded restaurant.

"I'm working," said Linda, who was crisp in a tailored charcoal suit with razor creases and a fluffy silk bodice layered between her lapels. Behind a pragmatic lawyer's smile, her face was compact with resolve.

"She's like my lawyer. We'd hoped to file papers in court," said Bud. He squeezed Harry's arm in a steel grip. "Now what happened to your face?"

"Sheriff Emery and I went half a round."

They sat down and Harry smelled him. Gray-faced, rank with nervous sweat. Linda, right next to him, pretended not to notice. His eyes were flat as two blue buttons. Linda's smile was so tight it threatened to crack her face.

Bud lit a Camel straight and pushed the pack across the table. His hands were clean but the fingernails were untrimmed, grimy ribbons.

Another dose of ice water air announced Mike Hakala. He had a picture ID clipped to his parka and carried a growling police radio. "No court today, Bud," he said.

"What's your situation, Mike?"

"You can see we're knee-deep in cops. We have teams assigned to Jesse and Cox and Don Karson, and we'll have people on you and Harry. And I'm working on getting Becky into protective custody."

"How dirty is he?"

"Technically, all I got on him is jumping Harry. But I think I have probable cause to hold him as an accessory in the attempt on your life. Once we nail him, we'll have a showdown investigation like this county's never seen and the chips are going to fall where they fucking fall."

"Do you think Jesse was involved with him?" Bud asked.

"We're sure as hell going to ask her some questions."

"Mike, I think I should get Harry out of here, he's starting to look frayed around the edges."

Hakala shrugged. "Fine, but as long as you're in my county, you'll travel under police escort until this emergency is over. Now, I've got to get these people moving." He nodded and went to the SWAT team table.

Bud turned to Harry. "Now what's this stuff you've got?"

Harry took the page from the Duluth paper and Chris's story from the manila envelope and spread them on the table. He unfolded the page and thumbed his finger on the red-circled photograph.

"For starters, you left some stuff out," Harry said, reaching for a Camel. The .45 in his waistband clunked against the table.

Alert to the sound, Bud came across the table and pushed Harry's parka back from his belt. "Detroit Harry's got a gun," Bud announced in a weary voice.

"Oh, Harry," said Linda.

Harry glanced from Bud's face to Linda's and back again. He tried to find a way into Bud's fixed eyes.

"You don't get it, do you?" Harry insisted, stabbing his finger at the page. "They tried it again. Except this time it's a bigger target."

Bud smiled tightly. "It's over. She gets a check. It all goes away. Unless she's implicated."

Incensed, Harry banged his fist on the table. "You're not going to pay her a *million bucks!*"

Heads turned. Hakala paused going out the door with the SWAT guys, shook his head, moved on. Bud grimaced and drew his chin into his shoulders and Linda leaned forward, warning Harry with her eyes. "He can pay her anything he wants. Calm down. You're making a scene."

Conversation ceased. A waitress hovered uncomfortably. Her eyes were riveted on the butt of the .45 sticking out of Harry's belt.

"Coffee," said Bud in a hollow voice. The waitress retreated.

"Where'd you get this?" Bud brandished the newsprint.

"Don Karson stuck it on the door of the lodge. He's seen *All the President's Men* one too many times."

"Then I'll go talk to him," said Bud. His hand ruffled the printed sheets. "And this?"

"Something Chris wrote."

Bud picked it up and began to read. "Jesus, this is sick," he said and set it aside.

"Becky's been hiding in the woods because she knows the whole deal. Once they get her to talk . . ."

Bud pondered it with dreamy eyes, going back in time. He patted Harry's arm. "You always just have to go at things, don't you?" Nervously, the waitress leaned across the table, putting down the coffee cups. Seeing that the menus were stacked unopened, she said diplomatically, "I'll be back in a little while."

Bud's face tightened and he pursed his lips. "See how he is?" he said to Linda. "He's obsessed and he's armed." Turning to Harry, Bud gathered himself and said forcefully, "You have to stop all this, right now!"

His voice was loud enough to cause the restaurant patter to miss a beat and faces turned again. Bud's rich baritone erupted from the ashes of his life, commanding: "You get in trouble when you're excited like this, Harry. You want to break things and kill things like a dangerous little boy."

"What is this?"

"He told me why you left Detroit," said Linda gravely.

Harry clicked his teeth and fatigue took his last reserves away in a slow, sad brass strut like a New Orleans funeral.

It was funny how your past was never far away. It crouched just out of eyesight, ready to bite you in the heels. Sitting there, the years rolled away, calling forth images of that night: Cherry's—a bar where he'd hung out after the afternoon shift at Eldon Axle. Different after so many years away. The town had changed. Everybody pulled a gun. Harry had one too. Confused shots and then . . . one very dead black who'd picked the wrong night to be macho. He'd hopped a Greyhound for St. Paul the next day. Thanksgiving. The Lions were playing the Minnesota Vikings, an away game in a foot of snow.

"You fucker," said Harry. "What are you trying to pull?" His eyes jumped to Linda's face. The intricate codas and grapples of the legal system revolved in her cool brown eyes. "You told . . . *her*?"

Bud's voice deepened, absolutely steady. "She has a copy in her briefcase of the *Detroit Free Press* from the morning you left Detroit."

Linda pulled her briefcase up on the table. The latches clicked under her thumbs.

Harry put out his hand. "I believe you."

"That was your Fifth Step. Admitting to God and one other person the exact nature of your wrongs—"

"So you must be God, huh? 'Cause she's the other person now." Harry said in a steady voice.

"Nobody's saying you did this," Linda said quickly, tapping the briefcase. We just don't want it to . . . happen again."

"Give me the gun," said Bud, extending his hand. "Go back to St. Paul with Linda. I'll bring your stuff."

Harry shook his head. "I'm staying till Emery's in a cage."

"You can't use a mess in my life as an excuse to go out of control again, *I won't have it.*"

"You just going to roll over for those fuckers? Try and buy your way out? You don't owe them shit. They set you up, man. Jesse unzipped my fly to keep me from going into the woods that morning!"

Bud recoiled and sparks ignited in his eyes.

"Yeah, you married the town pump, buddy. Wake up."

Bud's eyes crackled and his voice shook. "I always tried to help you . . . and this is how—"

"I saved your ass," retorted Harry. "I blew that kid all over the fucking county."

"And you enjoyed it. You should have seen your face."

"Guys," said Linda in a tense voice, aware of all the forks suspended in midair around them.

"No," snarled Bud. "I have to tell him this. I been there, too. I went over there and it was twisted, but it was service. You, you sonofabitch, you went back, to Laos, and you went back as a mercenary. You did it for money and for kicks. Christ, those CIA creeps even sprung you out of jail in Detroit—"

"Jail?" said Linda.

Harry shook his head. "Not jail. The workhouse."

"Because he beat up his wife."

"You're outta line, Bud. You can't handle this stuff anymore," said Harry.

"I can," said Bud. "I'll show you, you big-dick sonofabitch!" Bud lurched across the table and tried to grab the gun in Harry's belt. Harry blocked him, shoved Bud back. Breakfast stopped. A fork clattered to a plate.

A Maston County deputy came over. "Is everything all right, Mr. Maston?" he asked.

"Fine. It's a personal matter that we should not have aired in public," said Bud, busying his hands with his lapels. The deputy moved away. Bud stood up, folded the Duluth paper, and put it in his suit pocket, then he picked up Chris's story and mashed it into a ball in his fist. Before Harry could stop him, he went to the Fisher stove, opened the door, and chucked the ball of paper into the fire. Harry started out of his chair to follow. Linda held him back with a cautioning hand. "Let him be alone for a while."

Harry shook his head. "He's going to fuck up."

"You really cut him," said Linda.

"Aw, shit," Harry stood up. He caught a flash of Bud's determined eyeballs through the windshield of the Trooper as he pulled away from the diner with two police cars in tow.

Linda plucked his sleeve. "Did you really beat up your wife?" she asked in a serious voice.

"Huh?" Harry put his hand in front of his eyes. Where was she from? Venus? Didn't she know what was going on?

"Well, did you?"

"Christ no, Linda . . . it was . . ." He reached for a handle in the thin air to steady himself. Nothing. Bud hadn't left any ground under him. And the look on Linda's face. "You wouldn't understand . . . Why the hell did you have to come?" he asked.

"We thought we could talk to you . . ."

He stared at her hard.

She drew herself up. "Because I love you, you dumb sonofabitch. So does he. He's reaching out to you and you slapped him down. He's not well, he's depressed . . . that was crude, what you said about that grasping bitch he married. You screwed her, didn't you?"

"I don't know what I did."

Linda tucked her briefcase under her arm. "Well I have to get a new court date so I can smile at her and arrange to hand over a check like I get paid for. Then I'm outta here. Last chance for a ride home."

"Linda, you don't get it. See all these cops? There's a guy out there who's this one-man army and all he wants to do is kill your client. There's a manhunt."

She looked at him, perplexed.

"I mean a person hunt. Fuck it."

She gave him a frosty look and gripped her briefcase. "Where's the court house?"

"One block down across the street, in the back room of the liquor store," said Harry. "Jesus, wait. I'll walk you."

54

Harry watched Linda drive out of town and the dreary damn overcast promised more snow and hung thistles of fatigue in the iron light and Nanabozho Point brooded down from the top of the ridge and he shouldn't have said that to Bud about Jesse. That hurt him.

Cops came and went down Main Street. Harry sat in the Jeep and smoked a cigarette. Morris came over and knocked on the window.

The deputy grinned. "All the people with college educations are to meet at the lodge. You, Maston, and Karson. Just got a call from Maston's escort. Follow me up."

Halfway up Highway 7 Morris's flasher erupted into a blue meteor and two cop cars topped the rise ahead of them. Hogging both lanes, the cops bore down and forced them off the road. Morris's tires showered Harry with snow and gravel as he whipped a 180 and joined the pack.

Great. There went his guards.

He found the front door of the lodge wide open. Okay. Light-headed and fatalistic with exhaustion, he swung the Colt and step-by-step cautiously checked out the rooms, then the basement. He entered the addition, climbed the ladder, and searched the unfinished rooms and the balcony. Back in the den, he saw that the computer port was open and the disk was gone.

So was the picture of Chris and the Italian postcard.

The visitor had left an unsubtle calling card. A fifth of Jack Daniel's sat amid the clutter on the dining room table.

My brand. Nice touch. Emery's idea of a joke? He hurled the bottle across the main room into the fireplace. Another shattered whiskey

327

flower bloomed from the soot and creosote and smelled like Larry Emery's breath.

Emery could be here. Right outside. No, the cops were piling on to something. They must have spotted him. Not thinking too clearly right now.

The phone rang and he grabbed it.

"Now what?"

"Najoong, motherfucker," said an energetic voice from the crypt.

Harry sagged to a chair. Hallucination wasn't out of the question.

"Hollywood?" Harry's lips slowly formed the question.

"Long time, buddy."

Harry visualized a mountain airstrip in the Laotian highlands, gray helicopters in the creeping mist, and the thick compost scent of jungle . . .

The voice went on. "Me and Randall's sitting here killing a bottle of tequila talking about you, so we decided to call you up."

Harry rubbed his eyes. "What?"

"Me and Randall . . . hey, you all right?"

"Yeah sure. Great." Harry's head swam. Hollywood. Another Randall prodigy who'd stayed on and on. Turned out the lights in the embassy in Phnom Penh and then Saigon. Fuckin' Hollywood.

"Hear you had some bad luck hunting—"

"Uh-huh," said Harry tonelessly.

"Still a hero, still flawed, eh? So apart from still being able to shoot, how'd you turn out? You ever get to be an artist?"

"Hack artist at a newspaper." Unbelievable.

"I can dig it. Turned into a hack Republican lawyer myself."

"I figured you'd be dead. Or swabbing cankers from the foreskin of some fascist chimpanzee in El Salvador."

"Same old Harry. Say listen, Randall's here and wants to talk to you."

Randall came on the line. "How's it going?" He slurred his s's. Wonderful. They were loaded.

"Weird. Dorothy tell you—?"

"Yeah, you're living in a game of Clue. Old newspapers pinned to your door. Wild girl in the woods. Listen, forget that, me and trusty ole Hollywood were hunting in the computers just for the hell of it and we've turned up something on this Cox guy. We're on our way to check it out. Just so happens it fits in with Hollywood's current line of work so we're traveling on Uncle."

Traveling? "Where the hell are you?" asked Harry.

"Arizona. You should come on down. Catch some rays—"

"Forget it," said Harry, rubbing his eyes. "The other guy, the sheriff, went bonkers. Looks like he was in it with his kid to kill Bud. All these cops are chasing him all over the back forty. He's got these cutouts of Bud . . . Aw, fuck it. Tell you later. And Bud's up here with Linda Margoles getting set to hand over a million bucks to get free of a three-week marriage. Can you believe that? Soon's they catch the sheriff I'm going home, man. I been too long at the fair."

"Question: Why's Bud have Linda handling his divorce? Linda's one smart lady, but the Maston family has used Deal and Noble in St. Paul as legal council for over a hundred years."

Harry shook his head. "This isn't a game of three-dimensional chess like you used to play with the Vietnamese. Just a bunch of backwoods thugs pulling off a get-rich-quick scheme. And it's my fault. Bud's stuck paying blood money because I killed that kid."

"You sound pretty rough."

"Randall. I been in a fight with a deer."

"A deer?"

"I'll explain later . . ."

Cars in the driveway. Harry bolted upright. "Have fun in Arizona. Tell a few war stories for me." He slammed down the phone. Agitated voices, hurried footfalls up the porch. Harry rolled out of the chair, snatched up the Colt, and had his arm extended when the door opened.

Don Karson took one look at Harry's menacing face squinting over the sights of the pistol and gasped.

Bud pushed the minister through the door and planted his hands on his hips. "For Chrissake, Harry. Put that thing *down!*"

55

"Look out," Harry admonished. "There are pieces of glass on the floor."

"What happened?" asked Bud.

"Somebody was here. They left a bottle of booze for me. Thoughtful, huh?"

Bud's eyes swung, watchfully. "You think it's another setup?"

Harry shrugged. "The cops that were here split."

"Ours too, took off with the ones hauling ass down the hill. Could be they found him already . . ." Bud's voiced trailed off and he licked at an open sore where stitches had been on his lower lip. "Or maybe he's right outside." He picked up the 12 gauge off the table and wracked it open. A shell popped out. He put it back in, slammed the slide back, chambered it, thumbed the safe.

The shotgun's steel clash brought Karson to attention. His eyes darted out the windows. "Emery?"

"Who knows," Bud said absently. Circulation had returned to the haggard face and his pupils wrenched down tight to pinholes.

"You didn't have to say that in front of Linda," Harry said.

Bud looked him straight in the eye. "I had to get your attention. Didn't I?"

Harry nodded tightly. "While you were getting my attention, they ripped the place off. Chris's floppy was in the computer when I left."

Karson seemed visibly shaken, but Bud waved his hand in disinterest. "Do you really think a boy's fantasies are proof of anything?" he said. He raked a polished wing tip through the books that littered the den carpet, then snapped the plastic latch on the disk drive of the IBM and clicked it open.

"They took other stuff," Harry went on. "This picture of Chris posing naked. Did you know he had cherries tattooed on his left hip?"

"Cherries?"

"Yeah. And the collage in Emery's basement . . ."

Bud nodded. "Hakala told me."

"It had a picture like that, some stud with a cherry tattoo. Left hip. They took those flicks for a reason," said Harry.

"They?" said Bud, scrutinizing Harry. He went out on the porch and stared at the wreckage in the drive. "Same 'they' who tried to burn me out?"

His eyes met Harry's. It was cold on the porch but both men sweated profusely and reeked of nerves. "This is a fucked-up place. Why did I ever come here?" said Bud softly. His eyes wandered up. "Good, it's starting to snow." They went back in.

"Karson," Bud called out. "It's time for show and tell." He grinned and his lips curled back too far, revealing receding gums and slivers of root above his shiny dental work. "What if Emery *is* out there?" he asked Harry. "Jesse made half a million cool ones when Emery put a bullet in Tip Kidwell in Duluth."

"Should have paid more attention to *that*," said Harry.

"As you pointed out, I wasn't tracking at the time. Christ. I think *I'm* the one who needs a drink." They laughed. Bad dream kind of laugh.

Karson joined them in the den and winced when Bud swept the clutter off the dining room table with a brisk arm. Scraps of ammunition boxes and bullets scattered among the books on the floor.

"Sit down, Reverend." Bud balanced the shotgun stock on his hip.

Karson sat. Bud stood behind him. Harry slid a hip on the table so he was above Karson. Bud leaned forward and spread the newspaper page out in front of the minister. Harry put the pistol on it.

"So?" said Karson.

"Real simple, Don," said Bud. "Why didn't you go directly to Hakala? Why feed it roundabout to Harry?"

Karson squared his shoulders. "I went to Mike. He dismissed it as a cheap shot because of the animosity between Emery and me. And people thought you sent Harry up here to investigate what really happened."

"But you think Larry Emery and Jesse are implicated in what Chris . . . did?"

"Larry, yes. Jesse . . . I don't know."

"This computer disk and the photo of Chris that Harry says is missing—you know anything about that?"

Karson shook his head.

"Chris ever show you a story he wrote about . . ." Bud raised his eyes to Harry. "What was it about, anyway?"

"A homosexual fantasy."

"No. Never," said Karson.

Harry took over. "Jesse and Chris told you certain things in confidence as their minister. And Emery accused you of making sexual overtures to Chris and turning Jesse against him under the guise of counseling."

"Any of that true, Don?" asked Bud.

"It's not that crude and simple. Yes, I talked to Jesse and Chris when they moved out on Emery and in with you, Bud." Karson took a deep breath and let it out. "Chris told me in the fiercest way that he'd do anything to get his family back together. He wanted Jesse to marry his dad."

"God," said Bud. "No wonder the boy flipped out the night we told him we were getting married."

Karson sighed. "But *Jesse* said she'd do anything to escape Larry Emery's control. That makes it hard to place all three of them in a conspiracy."

"So?" Bud glowered.

"So, after the marriage, I think Emery planted the idea that Chris could redeem himself and force his mother and father back together by killing you."

"What about you, Don?" said Harry. "What did you plant in your private little discussions with Chris about his sexual . . . preference?"

"Jesus, Harry," Bud said, grimacing. He eased Harry aside and pulled a chair up next to Karson. "Look, Don, we know each other, right?"

Karson nodded.

"You never told me that Chris was obsessed with getting his parents back together."

Karson pursed his lips. "When people talk to me in confidence, I'm supposed to keep it that way." He sighed. "Now I've violated that trust."

"Okay, okay. What about the other stuff—the sex thing. Could Emery have used it to manipulate Chris?"

Karson sat straighter in the chair and smoothed his thumb and index finger across his mustache. "Possibly. Chris escaped his home life in fantasies and later in drugs. And he had . . . anxieties about his sexual identity. Emery was a very violent man and his mother was—"

"A tramp," said Bud.

"He was old enough to remember that." Karson tapped the newspaper page. "Emery killed his stepfather. Then took his place. And Jesse kept fooling around. I think both those kids lived in fear that Emery was going to do it again. He was trying to escape the man. But in the end, he tried to please him."

"You really think so?" Pallid wrinkles creased Bud's forehead. "I thought he was just . . . rebelling."

"No. He was contemptuous." Karson erupted with sincerity. "Remember when we had Clark up here and he talked about the importance of fathers? How fathers and sons have to row together, cross over together. I think Chris desperately wanted a father figure he could trust. He wanted to love Emery but he couldn't tell him he was . . . gay. Maybe he thought Emery would respect him if . . ."

Bud gingerly touched his side, glanced at Harry, and winced. "So he shot me to get his father's approval? Jesus."

"They did it for the money. This is bullshit," Harry grunted.

Karson smiled. "That's the same thing Larry said when he found out that I was talking to Chris. It didn't fit into his sick macho worldview."

"Worldview," said Harry, shaking his head. "Now he's giving us the big picture." Harry walked to windows, stared out.

"You're another savage, Harry. You're just like Emery," Karson said.

Harry turned around. "This is a small-town sideshow, Bud. He despises everything Emery stands for, but his refined sensibilities won't let him admit it. He even used Chris as a pawn in that game."

"That's unthinkable," Karson protested.

"Not saying it was conscious, Don," said Harry, turning to Karson. "Emery has more clout in town than you do. And Emery got in your face in public and humiliated you. This is your way of getting even. You want to see Emery take a fall. And that's sick macho bullshit of a different order."

Karson was on his feet, angry. "You never felt a drip of remorse about Chris. It was just another kill. You glory in your violence. All of you. Your never-ending crucifixion. Because you were in Vietnam, you bully people who weren't."

Bud and Harry exchanged fast glances. Harry shook his head. "So that's why you hate him. And us. *You're* carrying some weird baggage, Karson."

Karson spun and glared at Bud. "You really shocked me after the shooting. All you worried about was this psychotic, how it might screw up his head, killing one more person. You should have seen him at the funeral. He was like some . . . Nazi."

"How much of that story did you read?" Harry asked Bud.

"Just the first few sentences."

"It was a war story."

"That doesn't surprise me," said Karson. "Chris was fascinated with the honors that Bud and Emery won in the war, that he could never hope for because he was crippled." Karson exhaled and lowered himself back to his chair. "I tried to bring him out of that, tried to show him . . ." Karson balled his hand into a fist. "There's other masculine feelings just as deep . . ."

Bud had put his head in his hands, elbows leaning on the table. One eye peeked between his fingers and Harry saw a yelp of dark humor in it.

Weary of it, Harry shook Karson by the shoulder. "So just how deep into his masculine feeling did you get?"

Karson pulled away. "I refuse to dignify that with an answer." He relished Harry's frustration. "There's a dark side in all of us. We talked about that. The wild men in our dreams . . . there is always temptation."

"You laid this shit on a confused sixteen-year-old? I should whip you through hell with barbed wire," Harry said coldly.

"I tried to help him," stated Karson.

"You don't get it, do you? Chris wasn't like you. You want the war paint without the war. He picked up a gun," Harry said.

Bud came between them and pushed Harry away. "Everybody calm down," he ordered. Bud and Harry towered over Karson, their eyes drilling into him.

Karson cleared his throat. "Obviously I lost him to Emery when he decided to go hunting."

Sadness gathered in the room, mushrooming, shutting off light. Harry looked out the windows. Just the snow coming thicker.

Karson's chin sagged to his chest. "Tell me the story he wrote. Maybe I can interpret it for you."

"Fuck," said Harry.

Bud fingered his strong chin and inspected his ragged fingernails. "Tell him. I'm curious."

"I've heard enough," said Harry. He strode to the table, snatched the pistol, and shoved it in his waistband. "Bud, let's get out of here."

"C'mon, Harry," Bud jerked his head, beckoning, "Tell it."

Harry exhaled. "I don't know. There's this queer GI—"

"Gay," corrected Karson.

"He has a crush on his officer. They get in this fight on a hill and everybody bugs out. Basically the guy stands his ground and dies saving everybody who ran away. There's this drunk sergeant who comes back at the end and fights next to him. The description of the officer sounds a lot like Mitch Hakala."

Karson's fine features held a brittle edge of compassion. "Chris struggled with the warrior inside. There's some things you should see right off. Bud, you were decorated in a hill fight. So was Emery. Isn't that true?"

"I don't know about Emery."

"I do," Karson said with distaste. "Chris told me. And Emery was a sergeant."

Harry watched the snow come faster against the windows. He was getting tired of Don Karson. Real tired, when he launched into pop psychology.

"Besides unrequited love, the other theme of the story is betrayal. Both of Chris's heroes betrayed him. Emery couldn't control Jesse and make the family whole. Bud, you threatened to turn him in for selling drugs. And the fact is"—Karson lowered his eyes—"you couldn't control *her*, either. Chris took a desperate gamble to reunite his family with heroic death as the alternative."

Bud looked to Harry and raised his eyebrows.

Harry shrugged. "Going down in the act of taking a shot at the last Maston confers martyr status in this fucked-up county. Least that's what Emery's mother, the local witch, suggested."

Karson shook his head. "He committed suicide out there that day."

Bud disagreed. "Too romantic, Don. You leave out the fact that he had a head full of PCP."

"That too," said Karson sadly.

"You're forgetting Becky," said Harry. "She knows something."

"Did she tell you that?" asked Bud.

Harry shook his head. "Not details."

"Becky's the smart one," said Karson. "Maybe she's hiding something or maybe it's more obvious, maybe she's just disassociating herself from the whole mess. She's damaged, too. The human family can be a machine of torture."

"Give me a fucking break," Bud said scowling. "I'm tired of this hindsight soap opera about a bunch of wacko people jumbled up in trauma. We ought to put an end to this . . . suffering, don't you think?"

Two shots cracked down the lake and Karson turned toward the sound. "Hunters," he said hopefully.

"Only thing they're hunting today is Larry Emery. I'll call the sheriff's office," said Bud. He sighed, hefted the shotgun, went to the phone, dialed, and hunched over in conversation. Suddenly he spun around and shook with hysterical laughter. "They got him. Get this. They found him sleeping off a hangover in the Historical Society. His mother came to the police to explain why he was late for work."

Bud's hilarity was infectious and created a giddy aura of amnesty between the three of them. "Poor Mike," said Karson, grinning. "All those cops. Who's going to pay all that overtime?"

Harry shook his head. "Emery's still got a lot of explaining to do. This isn't over yet."

Karson stood up. "I'd better get down there. He might need someone to talk to."

Harry raised his eyebrows. Karson smiled sadly. "It's my job." He paused at the door. "You're right, about the baggage. I shouldn't have prejudged the man. And Harry, you can put that away now." He pointed at the pistol.

Bud stood at the windows and watched Don Karson's station wagon accelerate down the driveway and pondered. "They'll probably put Emery in drug-dependency treatment." He giggled. "Nothing will be resolved. You're right, you know. If I were found on this floor tomorrow morning with a bullet between my eyes, the legal system of Maston County would rule accidental death. Stray hunter's bullet." Bud mused softly, "And that bullet would have been fired at my grandfather before I was even born. Fuck 'em all. I guess we can't really change people. I can't change you. And I can't change me. Maybe we should just be who the fuck we are, huh?"

"I have one last thing to do, file assault charges against that bastard Emery," said Harry. "Then let's get out of here."

"Might as well. Too bad they canceled the court appointment. That's going to be something. When Jesse meets Linda." He giggled again. "The daughter of Scarlett O'Hara meets the daughter of Gloria Stein-hem."

"You're not giving her all that bread? After what's happened?"

Bud grinned. "She's probably sitting out in that trailer with Cox making lists of things she wants to buy. Her mad minute at Kmart."

"Don't sell Hakala short. She might downsize her figure once the grand jury cranks up," said Harry.

Bud regarded him through lidded eyes. "Good point. She took advantage of her kid's death. And what did being a soft touch ever get me? Dead, almost." He patted Harry on the shoulder and stared into the falling snow. "You fuck up a few times and they never leave you alone." He whistled softly.

Bud slipped out of his suit coat and vest, loosened his tie, and rolled up his sleeves. In his pinstripe oxford-cloth shirt strapped with black suspenders, he looked solid, purposeful. He glanced at his fingernails. "I should clean up. I haven't been taking care of myself." Then a know-ing smile played across his scabbed lower lip and his lidded eyes. "You fuck her?"

Harry couldn't help grinning. He saw his old friend in that smile. A touch of the unaffected grim elegance he'd always envied in the younger, thinner Bud. Getting stronger. Fought his way back through that wall of black plate glass, came up here and faced it.

"Well? Did you, you devious, airborne crud?"

"C'mon. Knock it off. I guarded Castle Frankenstein here against the serfs when they came with their torches to burn it down."

"You did, didn't you?" He held up his hand to stay Harry's pained expression. "No sweat. I wouldn't have married her sober. But you were sober when you fucked her. It was . . . predictable. Like you com-ing back up here was predictable." He smiled. "Even you shooting Chris was predictable."

"Bud—"

"Let me be a bit irreverent, Harry. It's healthy."

"So you're coming out of your funk?"

"Yeeeaah," said Bud. "There's a downside, though. Considering that things couldn't get more fucked up than they are." Bud's freckles did that rivet-pop on his pale skin and Huck Finn mischief twinkled in his eyes and the old charismatic smile was back. "Why in the hell are we sober?"

Absurdity tumbled in their eyes and they laughed at the same time.

56

"How about it? One drink to celebrate catching Emery," said Bud with convivial glee as he opened the cabinet next to the fireplace. He moved the gun rack aside and withdrew a long shimmer of old glass. No label.

"Hundred-and-fifty-year-old sherry." Bud winked. "Before we turned inland to trap, we were pirates. Story is, my great grandfather got it from a shipwreck off the coast of Maine. Family heirloom. This we have to drink out of glasses. Be right back." Bud started for the kitchen.

Harry held up his hand. "Make mine ginger ale, there's some in the fridge. One of us has to stay straight. To drive."

"You being predictable again?" Bud yelled back. He laughed and reappeared with two water glasses. "We're short on crystal . . . these'll have to do." He handed the one fizzing with soda to Harry and then he struggled with a corkscrew. The ancient cork crumbled. "Fuck it." He broke the neck of the bottle on the fireplace.

The impulsive gesture galvanized them with laughter. Bud slopped the amber liquid into his glass and the wine glistened on his hand.

"I'm the designated driver," said Harry, studying his glass.

"All you have to do is make it to Duluth. We'll spend the night. Big steak at the Pickwick." Bud raised his glass. "Down Eros, up Mars," he toasted.

"Whatever," said Harry, tasting the pop. His face screwed up. It had a chalky, chemical bite. "Shit's gone sour."

"Down the hatch, buddy," said Bud. They drained their glasses.

Bud gestured with his empty glass, one arm on the mantel. "You flatter these people, Harry. They couldn't put together a *plan*. That would involve thinking past the next paycheck."

Harry grimaced. Something was seriously wrong. A flush and a tingling wave of euphoric nausea radiated from his stomach and into his veins. He lowered himself to the couch. Bud leaned against the mantel, drinking now from the broken lip of the bottle. Soot made a broad slick on his shirt under his arm and down his side. "Hey, you don't look so hot, partner," he said.

Harry grinned weakly, lit a cigarette, and adjusted the .45 in his waistband so the barrel didn't jam his nuts. "Need some sleep."

"When we get to Duluth, let's really tie one on. Then we could *both* go through treatment. Be roommates again."

Bud tipped the bottle and the antique wine ran down his chin onto his suspenders. Harry sprawled, very involved in the intricate curl of smoke seeping from the cigarette.

"Pictures," he mused. "I think somebody was up on the balcony, behind the sheeting, taking pictures . . ." his voice trailed off, disappearing in the air like the swirls of smoke.

Bud arched his eyebrows. "Really? Ah, fuck 'em all," said Bud. "Especially Jesse." He swung the bottle, taking in the overturned den. "To fucking women, may they all rot in hell."

Harry's vision was getting furry and Bud smiled at him. Bud looked . . . happy.

"Just keep squeezing tighter and tighter," said Bud. "Crush all the life out of a guy. Eat their fucking young . . ." Bud loomed in Harry's vision and his smile jerked into a distorted grin and Harry had seen that rictus of a smile before, on a picture hanging on the wall in Chris's room, and things were becoming very fucked-up.

"Don't know if I'd go that far," said Harry.

"Cows," said Bud. "Milk machines. Hook 'em up in a barn in stanchions, one long production line pumping out milk, babies, and pies of shit."

Harry winced at the image. But he smiled too as the edges on objects in the room acquired a hazy nimbus. He was sinking through the cushions and ever so slowly his fingers touched the handle of the pistol in his belt. The idea—*danger*—formed in his mind. "Jesus," he muttered.

"What's the matter? You get some bad Schweppes?"

"Man, I don't know. Something . . ."

Bud's devouring grin yawned. "Could be the qualudes. You just swallowed enough to stop an elephant dead in his tracks."

Harry struggled to get up and fell back onto the couch. Bud lifted his head, put a pillow under it, and patted him on the cheek. "Sorry, Harry, but you're going to sit this one out. Like Karson said, no more sick macho bullshit." He lifted the pistol from Harry's jeans and tossed it aside.

Then Bud stalked back and forth in front of the sooty maw of the fireplace and he'd cut his lip on the wine bottle and a dribble of blood made a crimson thread down his wet chin. "The thing I loved about Nam, man. No fucking women. Well, except for the gooks, but they were more like monkeys chattering. But a rifle company. It's this perfect thing. There were times when I felt like Leonard fucking Bernstein with the New York Philharmonic. Just raise my baton. Andante. Allegro . . ." Bud sketched grace notes in the air with his hand. "It was beautiful."

"Sounds like officer talk to me," Harry mumbled.

Bud grinned at him and put his arm over Harry's shoulder. "That's because you were always a lone wolf. Special Operations. Out there playing Lord Jim with Tim Randall. You never had to submit."

"P-p-paid my dues. Sat still for a lot of shit—"

"No, you never *really* accepted discipline. You'd be so good if only you could. But there's something in you that resists it."

Harry tried to focus his strength. Words blew out his lips like soap bubbles. "Called being an American, you asshole."

Bud shook his head. "You'll always be a member of the mob. You never were a soldier. You were just a thug from Dee-troit City. I had some men like you in my company, they wouldn't accept discipline . . . they were flawed. Like your crooked teeth were a flaw, Harry. You had this dynamite body and then those teeth. I'm so glad you had them fixed."

Harry started to pour sweat and Bud was going in and out of focus. "Slipped me a mickey, you devious fuck—"

"You're so hard on people, Harry. You make people hide because you hide from yourself. I could show you who you really are if you'd let me." Bud sighed. With a flourish, he drained the bottle and the wine squeezed through his thick knuckles.

"You called me . . . that night. Phone booth . . . needed me," said Harry.

"It was a dream, Harry. Like this is a dream," Bud towered, thick,

341

powerful, smiling. "Did you really think that I was . . . weak?"

Bud stooped, grimacing slightly with pain, one hand going to his wounded side. Harry didn't want his lips to be smiling. Didn't want his reflexes spread around him in a soft, silken puddle. Bud's fingers were in his mouth, placing something against the back of his tongue.

Harry started to gag. Bud gently massaged his throat. "You're having a dream, Harry. One of those double-scream backcrawlers. Flashback City, my man."

"Wha . . .?" Harry's tongue was lolled. His eyes rolled.

"Sorry, buddy. This time you're not running interference. So I'm giving you a little cocktail. Some Thorazine, to go with the ludes and a little filthy yellow Mexican heroin I found lying around. All packaged in neat gelatin time-released capsules."

Gently Bud massaged Harry's throat until he swallowed. He sputtered, gagged, coughed. But far away. It was all happening far away.

"Just take a little nap."

Bud's face filled his vision as florid as a marbled cut of meat. But getting thinner. Soon he would be handsome again. Sleek. Up at a podium surrounded by microphones in the spotlight. He caressed Harry's face. "Do you know your Shakespeare, Harry?" he crooned. "*Henry the Fifth?* No, of course not. Thugs don't read the classics. Well, there's this part the night before the battle of Agincourt . . . when fear is all around . . ."

Bud's voice rolled, rich, warm, baritone:

"His liberal eye doth give to every one,
thawing cold fear; that mean and gentle all
behold, as may unworthiness define,
a little touch of Harry in the night.
And so our scene must to the battle fly."

It seemed that Bud laughed. It seemed that he bent down and kissed Harry on the lips.

57

It smelled like a dog had been rolling in guts and deep in his burning insides a little red fire engine of adrenaline managed to leave the station.

Slumped forward against the Jeep's steering wheel. All sticky. Vomit caked his throat and chest. Throwing up must have woke him up. Snow whirled against his face. *Get up. Get up.* He lurched and looked around. Car door was open, groaning in the wind. Snow blew all over the leather seat.

Eyes weren't turned all the way on yet. Banging sound. Bang. Bang.

Blood—felt like slick snot ropes of it on his jeans and something hard. The .45 made a steel cramp across his belly. He shuddered. Sounded like a scream. Definitely a scream and the sound jellied his muscles and all the slipknots were sliding and Harry pissed his pants. He gritted his teeth and willed his sphincter into a tight fist.

Light out. Or was it? Tin-pan sun as pale as the moon in the snow, streaming past a grove of birch with long twisty trunks jointed like knuckle bones . . .

Sparks crashed inside his head. Eyes hooking up. Okay. The banging sound was the door of Jay Cox's trailer swinging in the wind. The scream came from . . . his own mouth.

He saw. Becky. She ran out the trailer door and fell to all fours. What the hell was she doing? Stuffing her mouth with snow. Her nose. Trying to smother herself?

He was back in the fucking blood swamp with the jack-in-the-box and fear savaged him into focus and he fumbled the .45. Sniffed the breech. Inhaled the baked metal crisp of cordite. He took out the magazine, pushed his grisly finger against the spring-loaded bullets. Three or four missing. Think? It had been full. Reloaded, pulled the charging handle. Used up all his dexterity.

Where was Bud? Harry took a deep breath and it popped open for him and he finally got the big joke.

He staggered from the Jeep. Cox's truck was there. Jesse's Escort. Snow filling in other tire tracks. At least one other vehicle had pulled in, backed up, and turned around.

Stilts not feet. Sleepwalking past Becky . . .

She trembled violently. Couldn't be helped. Her eyes plunged at the snowy woods, then at the trailer. Her lips made a silent O. *No.*

Harry turned his back on her. Saw Cox's black cap and a bloody drag-trail in the snow that led to the trailer door. The pistol fell from his numb hand. He followed it, dropping comically on his rump. He had a good smell of himself.

Retrieving the Colt with cardboard fingers . . . it felt like he was wearing gloves. Brushed away the snow. No gloves. Just more blood stiffening in the cold. He stared at the swinging trailer door. Thought Hakala had cops guarding her.

It was going to be real bad.

Go see. Unsteadily, he approached the trailer. In the door, swung the pistol in a clumsy uncoordinated arc. Radio on. Polka music. Idiot sing-song accordion.

She had fought hard. The living room was in shambles. Table overturned. Cox's pills were strewn on the carpet. On the hallway wall, leading to the bedroom, the stigmata of her bloody handprint. The light was on.

His curse had always been to be at his best in the presence of horror. A battlefield stench scattered his drugged fog.

He bolted from the room and smashed the gun's butt into the radio. Then he closed the door on its creaking hinges. Silence. Slowly, solemnly, he went back. SEE MEXICO. A gaudy confetti of travel brochures was glued wetly over the posed naked bodies.

Harry did not decipher rage on the smeared walls. Not even sickness. Something evil had *played* here and dumped her forward from the headboard in a final contraction over her own evisceration; legs spraddled, knees bent, her heels had been tucked into the stirrups of Cox's collarbone.

Harry took a deep clarifying breath and saw the shovel on the floor. Bastard had used the entrenching tool on her. But the bloody finger-prints on the handle would belong to Detroit Harry. *Don't think about the handle.*

Cox had been killed with two shots to the back of the head. Jesse . . .

The splintered haft protruded between her legs. In his frenzy, the fucker'd snapped it off after he had hacked . . .

Harry touched the graying clay of Cox's bicep, moved a strand of Jesse's matted hair from the tattoo there. Bayonet piercing a heart: Death Before Dishonor.

He drew a sheet over their obscene posture and covered the hairy tongue of severed testicles that spilled from between Cox's teeth.

North Vietnamese trick. Seen that one before.

Harry withdrew carefully, closed and latched the door. As he went out, the survival armor girdled him. *Can't feel it now, worry about the living. Becky.*

Snowflakes pelted through the Jeep's headlights. He stooped and picked up Cox's hat with the Snoopy emblem as the cold pure air hit him like a whack of Zen.

Blind spots, Randall had cautioned.

Remember patterns.

He adapts, Jesse'd said. One seamless puppet show from the minute his phone rang early that morning. Bud propositioning Murphy for the story. *You're so predictable. Knew I'd shoot.* Bringing in Linda, getting her up here so she could see him strung out. With this damn gun. And Karson at the lodge. And he'd had plenty of time to drop in at his home, no problem with cops, and lift the computer disk and pictures.

Harry swung the .45 in a two-handed grip, scanning the snow-span-gled trees. Not Emery. Wrong about Jesse too. Pushed her out the door straight into . . .

Raining shit and blood in a blacked-out Hell. They'd say he was drunk again and this time they'd say he murdered two people. He'd been here before to this terribly lonely place. But Randall had been there that time. Need Randall.

"Becky?" Dammit. Where was she? The Jeep beckoned, lights on, running in neutral. This was no place to be. He was a survivor. Time to boogie.

Not this time.

Couldn't survive leaving her in there like that. More than dead. Negated. Harry didn't consider himself a Christian. But maybe she was. Sung in the choir . . .

First he washed his hands and took off his spattered shirt. Then he found a bucket under the sink and filled it with hot water. From the bathroom, he took clean towels, a washcloth, and a bar of her scented soap. He reentered the ghoulish room and threw back the sheet. Eased Cox from the bed and gently laid him on the floor. Put a blanket over him.

She'd always said he didn't see her. He saw her now as he plucked scarabs of filth from her face and dealt with the shovel handle. He straightened her legs and did his best to tidy the wreckage of her stomach. Working with the patience that tenderness required, he washed her limbs, taking care to get between her fingers and her toes. When he was finished, he tucked a sheet to cover the worst and went back for a fresh cloth to cleanse her throat and face. Then he unknotted the ugliness from her hair and drew a brush through it. When it was done, he bent to close her eyes and some trapped water spilled from the open clouded iris and trickled down the stiffening cheek.

Harry turned out the light.

Too late, he realized there was another vehicle in the drive. A blue-and-white sheriff's Blazer.

"Drop it! Don't move! Swear to God I'll blow your fuckin' head off!" Jerry Hakala's voice shook, about a foot behind Harry's back. Thing about snow. Made it easy for people to sneak up on you. Was like friendship . . .

Harry pulled the pistol from his belt. He didn't drop it. "I saw through the window, you creepy fuck!" Jerry yelled. "Looks like a kill floor in there."

"Where's Emery, Jerry?"

"Spit my name out of your mouth, you fuck."

"I mean you pulled the cops outta here when you spotted Emery," Harry said.

"Blood here's not even cold. He didn't do this, asshole. You did."

"Jerry. I don't want you to get any more excited. I'm not moving too good right now."

"*Drop the damn piece!*"

Harry didn't move. "Becky's here somewhere," he said.

"You sonofabitch," Hakala hissed. Lynch law was in that voice. Harry was betting Jerry wouldn't shoot him in the back.

"I mean . . . alive. She was right out front here—"

"Put it down. I mean it." Jerry's voice wrapped tighter.

"Who tipped you, Jerry?"

"Maston came downtown looking for you. Said you were drinking, on the prod. Last chance, fucker."

Jerry's finger was probably down to the hot end of the trigger pull and Harry's .45 was pointed at the ground. No way to even it. Jerry was going to shoot him. Shoot him the way he did everything; properly, by the book, three warnings followed by three rounds, center spine. Never find Bud this way. Reluctantly, Harry dropped the gun.

The blunt barrel of the Glock jammed in Harry's right ear—hard. "Okay, now lower yourself real slow. Down on your knees. Now lean forward. Put your head against the trailer. Arms behind your back. Lock the elbows. Lace your fingers. Now grab your hands together."

Harry did as he was told. Awkwardly balanced forward, he heard the jingle of the cuffs coming off Jerry's belt.

"Okay, fucker, I'm arresting you on suspicion of murder. You have the right—" Jerry stopped in midsentence.

"Yo, Jer!" A hard young voice. Tilting his head to the side, Harry saw a fluffy snowball splatter playfully on Jerry Hakala's chest. Mitch Hakala, in his varsity jacket, stepped from behind the end of the trailer.

"Mitch? What the fuck?" Jerry blurted.

Mitch bent, scooped up snow, and packed another snowball.

"Get back," ordered Jerry. "This is a fuckin' crime scene."

"No shit," said Mitch, advancing, casually slinging the snowball. Jerry ducked to the side.

"What're you, nuts?" Jerry shouted.

"Pretty close," Mitch said with a tight grin. He packed another snowball.

Confusion gobbled Jerry's face. His eyes turned toward his car. The radio. The Glock wavered uncertainly away from Harry, toward Mitch, who was now only an arm's length away.

"What're you gonna do, Jer? Shoot me for throwing a snowball? Shit, man. I'm your cousin."

"You're interfering in an arrest. Now get back!"

Becky's voice. "Whatever you guys are gonna do, you better make it quick!" she yelled.

Then the radio in the Blazer squawked: "Jerry, this is Billy. Where the hell are you, over."

"He hasn't called it in," said Harry.

"Yeah," said Mitch.

"Nobody fuckin' move," shouted Jerry. He was losing control of the situation. Mitch tossed the snowball up in front of Jerry's face. The instant Jerry's eyes flinched, Mitch struck the gun out of line and swept Jerry's legs from under him. Swift martial arts choreography locked the gun hand. Jerry dropped the weapon. Harry watched, amazed.

"Goddammit," Jerry yelled, going facedown. "Don't fuck around! You can go to jail, you dumb . . ."

Mitch wheezed, tightening his grip. "'Member you laughing at me about Mr. Talme's judo class the last three years, cuz . . ."

Becky raced out of the darkness. She seized the Glock and held it to Jerry's head just as he was lifting Mitch bodily off the ground. She didn't have her finger on the trigger, but Jerry didn't know that.

"Get his handcuffs," yelled Mitch. Jerry pounded at the ground with his left hand, trying to get leverage. Mitch and the pistol held him pinned. Harry lurched on his knees, grabbed the cuffs from Becky, and slapped one bracelet on Jerry's left hand.

"You'll be sorry," shouted Jerry.

Harry put his knee in Jerry's back and wrenched the cuffed hand over toward the hand Mitch had in a wrist lock. Jerry was cuffed. Mitch let him go. The infuriated deputy rolled over and sat up.

"Fuckin' felony you're looking at, Mitch!" he roared.

"Way I see it, Jer, there's the law, there's family, and there's Becky. Becky comes first."

Harry glanced at Mitch. "This is some deep shit you're getting into," he cautioned.

"You got no idea," said Mitch. His stony eyes did not waver. "Now help me get him to his car."

With Jerry's keys, Mitch opened the hatchback, shoved Jerry inside, and bound his feet with a rubber bungee. "You're all headed right down the tubes," Jerry yelled. Mitch slammed the rear hatch. Becky and Mitch embraced.

"You sure you're not mad at me?" she said.

"Shush. Call when it's safe. You know where," Mitch instructed. She nodded. Mitch turned to Harry. "Me and Jerry's gonna take a ride in the woods. Way back. I suspect we'll get stuck for big ass. Might not find our way out till tomorrow. You get her as far as you can and lay low. You have money?"

Harry felt the wad of hundreds in his pocket, the shape of his wallet. Visa card. He nodded. Looked toward the trailer. Dropped his eyes to Becky. "Bud is a fucker," he said.

Becky bit her lip to stop the tears.

"Chris didn't attack Bud," said Harry. He swallowed. Couldn't get the words out of his mouth.

Becky helped him. Bitterly. "You all had it backwards. He was defending himself when you . . ."

Hell wasn't even other people. It fit neatly inside his own skin. Harry took a deep breath of sulfur. He put his hand on Mitch's shoulder. "Did you see what happened here?"

Mitch shook his head. "We got here after. Then Jerry pulled in, I hid my truck behind the trailer . . . Look, there's no time. If she don't get far away, Maston will kill her. When Jer gets over being pissed, he'll listen to me." Mitch climbed into the Blazer, ripped the radio handset away from the dash, and tossed it out the window. "Run for it," he said.

They watched Mitch drive away. Becky began to tremble. "He's smarter than everybody."

Harry put his hands on her shoulders and shook her. "Listen. We have to *function*, you understand?"

She shuddered against him, "He's got everything figured out. He plans things years in advance."

"Nobody has everything figured out."

"Take me somewhere it's safe. It's gotta be real safe or I won't say anything."

"I don't know where that is."

"Find it," said Becky. "Find it fast. It's everything I can do to keep from screaming and if I start, I don't think I'll ever be able to stop."

Randall.

They couldn't travel the way they were. They had to clean up.

Harry had to physically carry her over the threshold into the bathroom and stand by the door until she took a shower. He handed her a

349

wind suit and low soft leather boots Jesse had laid out for the trip. When she finished, he ducked under the water, soaped, shampooed.

Becky waited outside, insisting he keep the trailer door open so she could see him when he used the phone. Jesse's purse lay on the counter leaking a maddeningly normal cosmetic blush that drifted sweet on the stink of death. Harry picked the RayBans from the purse. Put them on. His fingers ruffled the airline tickets that slanted in the side pouch.

He made two calls. Wrote quickly on a notepad. Then he opened the hall closet, some drawers, until he found a pair of Cox's jeans, jean jacket, and a shirt. A pair of cowboy boots. He rolled the pistol in his bloody clothes and stuck them, with Becky's wind suit, long underwear, and shoes, into an AWOL bag he found in the closet. He dressed in Cox's clothing. Loose fit. Stylish these days. A leather travel bag lay on its side in the clutter. Harry snatched it up.

"We'll freeze in this stuff," Becky shivered.

"It's warm where we're going."

The bloody palm print on the wall gave him a red push. "Let's go."

Becky pulled a knapsack from next to the trailer steps and grabbed Jesse's travel bag, looked up, and nodded. He pulled Jay Cox's black cap with the Snoopy emblem down over his eyes, pushed the RayBans up on his swollen nose, squeezed Jesse's car keys, and walked toward the blue Escort with the rusted-out rocker panels.

Pulling out onto the county road, Becky turned to him. "You could have got away. Thank you. That was ... decent, what you did for Mom."

Harry shook his head. "The way we are now, it was disturbing evidence."

"No, it was decent."

58

Going south down 61 an adrenaline backfire contained the chemical inferno in his blood until his last reserves snuffed out at Two Harbors and he forged a finely wrought hate and drove on that and the snow tapered to flurries and they spotted the high bridges of Duluth. Becky worried him; huddled, staring straight ahead, hugging herself in her mother's jacket, she had not spoken one word since they left Stanley.

Harry pulled into a shopping mall. Hit the grocery and a Nutrition World. He bought a bottle of Tabasco sauce, Niacin 500 mm tablets, chewable Vitamin C, and spring water. Back in the car, he poured an ounce of Tabasco into a Styrofoam cup and knocked it back with six of the Niacin.

Becky watched curiously as he grimaced and tears came to his eyes and he muttered, "Detroit hangover cure." He swigged from the half-gallon of water to hydrate himself.

Slapped alert by the pepper sauce, Harry consulted a map and found the turnoff for the Duluth airport. They left Jesse's car in the lot, went into the terminal, rented a locker, and stowed Cox's AWOL bag. Hat pulled down, sunglasses low on his battered nose, he went to the ticket counter and bought passage on the Northwest flight he'd reserved when he called from the trailer. They had a short hop to the Cities, then connect to Denver and on to Phoenix. It left in 45 minutes.

Becky shouldered her mother's travel bag and said she was going to the john. Harry sat in a smoking area making a circle of butts on the floor as the Niacin came on and blasted his capillaries and sandpapered his skin. The crimson rush subsided and, hopefully, it rooted some of the gunk from his veins. He chewed a dozen 1,000 mm Vitamin Cs and washed them down with the water. Checked the time.

When he'd called Dorothy from the trailer, she didn't even pause when he told her about the killings and the time Mitch had bought them. She'd said: "Move fast, Harry. You were right from the start. It's a blackmail situation that got out of hand. Hop the first thing smoking to Phoenix. Randall will explain. I know it's dicey, but Hollywood thinks there could be a federal angle and maybe he'll be able to help. Bring the girl. Call me when you get to the airport."

Harry dropped quarters into the pay phone and dialed the number in St. Paul. As the phone rang, he watched Becky stroll across the lobby. She'd changed into a light pair of pedal pushers and a quiet silk blouse Jesse must have packed. She lowered a pair of sunglasses over her eyes. Absolutely poised, she lit a Marlboro, folded her arms, and watched an airport security man walk across the terminal.

Dorothy answered crisply and he asked, "How many laws am I breaking right now?"

"Give me the flight number and arrival time in Phoenix." Harry did. "Somebody will meet you," she said.

"Dorothy, the sonofabitch has been setting me up—"

"Longer than you think," said Dorothy cryptically. "Don't miss the plane." She hung up.

At the boarding gate, Becky turned to him. "You try to pretend something didn't happen. But it really did." Her voice had aged ten years.

"We all pretend about a lot of things," said Harry.

"This guy where we're going, you trust him?"

"He's like . . . my father."

"Has he ever killed anybody?"

"He quit counting people when he started counting governments."

Minnesota, with its corpses and its snow, receded below them and Harry crashed to the whisper of jet engines. They landed in a Denver snowstorm and were delayed. Waiting on their connection, Harry grabbed a few more hours sleep on a terminal bench. They ate breakfast and caught their plane and, from 10,000 feet, Harry watched Denver erect a drowsy brown tent of pollution against the Rockies. He slept all the way to Phoenix and jerked awake when the wheels lowered for landing. Becky was holding his hand.

A burly man—mid-forties, twelve-inch wrists—waited in aviator sunglasses, khaki desert pants, a Banlon body shirt, and a thin, blue nylon windbreaker with uppercase letters—DEA—stenciled on his left breast. His golden mane of curls framed classic North American features that grappled in a ceaseless tension between beast and boy.

His given name was Dwayne Milan and he traced his family tree back to the Alamo. He had flawless Texas manners, the kind that would smile patiently at an insult right up until he reached for an excessively calibered handgun.

Hollywood's quick handshake radiated military urgency. "You got your teeth fixed. What the fuck happened to your face?"

"Zigged when I should have zagged. What's Randall up to?"

"Don't sweat the small stuff. You're safely back in Uncle's bosom." Hollywood flashed a tight smile.

"What? Are you still with the fucking CIA? I thought—"

"Justice Department. There's a war on, don'tcha know? Drugs," Hollywood whispered.

They looked at each other, burst into crazed laughter, and both blurted at the same time. "You haven't changed . . ."

"Becky meet Hollywood," said Harry.

The woman of mystery behind her dark glasses, Becky extended a slender hand.

"You have any baggage to claim?" asked Hollywood.

"Just what we're carrying."

"Wait here a second." Hollywood walked off a few paces and whipped out a cellular phone. Becky leaned against Harry's shoulder and said, "He's got a gun on under that jacket." The first words she had spoken since they boarded in Duluth.

Hollywood rejoined them, gallantly took Becky's shoulder bag, and walked them through a door, down a stairway, and through a basement corridor. They came out onto the tarmac and the dry, bright heat stunned them. Mountains floated in a wreath of smog.

"Where are we going?" asked Harry.

"To jail if we get caught. I'm cutting some corners on this one."

They stopped in front of a hangar and Hollywood jogged into a small office. Two Bell UH1 helicopters sat with drooping rotors on the sun-cooked cement. And a Cessna.

Hollywood came back out and pointed to the Cessna. "That's our chariot." Becky and Harry climbed in while Hollywood made his pre-flight checks.

"You ever flown in a small plane?" Harry asked her.

She ran her hands over the interior of the craft and lowered her sunglasses, looking at him with large eyes. "Harry, I've never flown in anything before today. This is like . . . a video."

Color and curiosity were returning to her face. He squeezed her hand. "Good girl. Hang in there."

Hollywood piled into the cockpit and cranked the motor. As they taxied to the runway, Hollywood talked to the tower. Becky came forward, leaning between them, fascinated at the radio traffic, all the dials and gauges. She clamped her eyes shut when they took off.

Harry watched the compass spin as they banked through a turn, gained altitude and leveled off. South.

"Mind if I smoke?" he said.

"Go ahead. Your funeral. Hardest part of the Nam to give up. The goddamn cigarettes."

"So what are you, a narc?"

Hollywood laughed. "Justice Department. Special Task Force. I'm down here narking the narcs. Too damn much money in the drug industry, Harry. Too few men who can't be bought. Assholes in Washington gotta realize it's time to bring back the firing squad." He grinned. "Need to breed another generation of fanatics like we were. A little fucking American fundamentalism."

"You like your work, huh?"

"Most of the time I feel like a cockroach on the *Titanic*."

Harry tried to absorb the vast desert sky and the mountain ranges. He shook his head. "Yesterday I was in the woods in northern Minnesota. It was snowing. Now I don't have a clue—"

Hollywood smiled. "Just like old times."

"What's Randall up to?"

"He's operating in midair. Something popped up on a computer screen in my office and considering that you're our old asshole buddy . . . we put all this together in one day flat."

"Put what together?"

Hollywood had yet to show his eyes behind the sleek black glasses. He chewed his lip, "Another little Valentine from the heart of fucking darkness."

*   *   *

Harry dozed to the warm chug of the propeller. When he awoke, he heard Becky quizzing Hollywood about the mountains. They flew over desert and mesa, parallel to a highway. A mountain range loomed ahead of them, speckled in sunlight.

"Those are the Chiricahua Mountains. Down there, that wide place off the road that looks like a junkyard? That's Chato, Arizona. We have a couple rooms in the one motel," said Hollywood. He dropped low and skimmed over the mesquite and cactus, flying toward the foothills of the mountains.

Harry turned soberly to Hollywood. "This is all great eye-fucking, the scenery and all, but you guys could wind up accessories to murder."

Hollywood grinned. "Story of our lives, huh?" He pointed out the window at an abandoned airstrip with a decrepit hangar, the sides caved in. The figure of a man stood next to a station wagon, staked to a long shadow. A wind sock fluttered from the vehicle's antenna.

The shadow of the Cessna swooped over the car. Hollywood waggled the wings, put the left one practically into the mesquite, and veered back to the runway.

"Where'd you learn to fly?" Harry gripped his seat.

"Air America. Laos. After you split. Strictly an amateur. Sure miss those short landings and takeoffs."

"Hold on, Becky," said Harry.

Hollywood cut power and wallowed down onto the cracked, weed-choked tarmac. They came to a jarring halt. Becky's hair was in her eyes.

They got out. Becky looked around at the mesquite, Spanish bayonet, and prickly pear. The space and light. "Weird," she said.

Hollywood smiled. "When the going gets weird, the weird turn pro."

The guy on the ground was hardcore DEA cowboy; short, cropped hair, weightlifter muscles, black baseball cap, and a face unavailable behind sunglasses. He removed a solid-state radio, a small cooler, and a Tom Clancy paperback from the station wagon and walked to the shade of the plane.

Hollywood drove toward the highway. In seconds they were painted with red dust.

"Where's Randall?" asked Harry.

"With the guy you're going to talk to. Owns a gas station in town."

Life had passed Chato by when the new highway detoured around it. They turned onto the old highway and entered a museum of boarded-up storefronts and streets that ended in the sand. The gas station was left over from *The Grapes of Wrath*. A closed sign hung on the door.

"C'mon, he lives around the back." said Hollywood. Jay Cox's cowboy boots kicked up a horned toad among the bull thorns as they went around the building. The back room of the station had been converted to living quarters. A concrete patio was being reclaimed by the desert. Rusty abandoned cars clustered in the mesquite.

Tim Randall sat at a wrought-iron table in the shade of an umbrella. He wore the same clothes he'd been wearing the day Harry'd met him on the street in Hue City: a frayed pin-striped shirt, tennis shoes, a leather vest, jeans, and a Chicago Cubs baseball cap. He was smoking a taboo Pall Mall.

Even dignified with age, he was still the last guy in the joint you'd ever want to meet.

The man who sat across from Randall was a sinewy, dark Latino in jeans, a tank top, and slick black hair gathered in a ponytail. His sturdy mechanic's fingers drummed on the table and jailhouse tattooes twined on his arms like plump coral snakes. He stood up and watched Harry, Hollywood, and Becky approach.

Hollywood spoke offhand. "His name is Hector Jefferson Cruz. An L.A. street entrepreneur who didn't quite make the grade as middle management with a multinational out of Bogata. With a little plea-bargain evangelism, we made Hector see the light. He's our Lobo now. Watches the border," said Hollywood. He nodded at the guy. "Hiya Hector."

Hector's glassy obsidian eyes fixed on Harry.

Hollywood clucked his tongue. "Hector's been down some pretty hairy ratholes for us. But he never mentioned Witness Protection until we showed him a picture of you and this Maston guy."

They stood at the table, Harry face-to-face with Hector Cruz. Randall had not moved from his chair. Impassive, he ignored Hector and seemed more interested in Becky. Hollywood said, "Tell Hector what happened last night to Jason Emmet Cox."

Harry engaged the nervous shine in Hector's eyes. "Bud Maston killed him."

"Does he kill like a man or like a devil?" asked Hector.

"He mutilates."

Hector nodded. "Remove the shades."

Harry took off the RayBans. Hector raised his right hand and made the sign of the cross. His fingers stayed on his muscled bronze chest, clasping a crucifix on a gold chain, and his eyes jockeyed, eerie, in trance. His voice made a hoarse whisper in the dry air. "*Hombre*, this ain't right. I seen you dead." He held up his powerful hands. "Martin, I put you in a body bag with these hands."

59

Becky was drawn to Randall and they sat at the table and began a quietly intense conversation in the shade of the umbrella. Hollywood, Harry, and Hector drifted to the edge of the patio and, as they began to talk, they squatted peasant-fashion on their haunches. Harry drew nonsense designs in the sand with a stick. Every time he looked up, Hector was staring at him.

Hollywood ran it down.

"Sheer damn luck. Drinking in the basement at Justice after hours. For the hell of it, we ran Cox through the computers. At first he turned out innocent enough. Retread, lots of mileage. Jarhead lifer. Three tours in Nam. Wounded. Ninety percent disability. Great Lakes, then mucho VA hospital time out in Washington State. Defaulted small business loans and a few hassles with the IRS. He had a small construction business in Seattle."

Hollywood looked at Randall. "Colonel says dig deeper. So I ran a spot search through the files of current DEA operations. Cox's name pops up in a surveillance log they were running with Hector. Year ago, September. Time frame ring any bells?"

Harry squinted. "Just before Bud Maston dropped out of the primary for Congress."

Hollywood nodded. "Uh-huh. Cox visited Hector here in Chato. DEA ran his stats. No drug connection. Just like Hector reported. So we ran a parallel check on both their backgrounds to see if they were associated any time in the past."

Becky left the table and joined them and sat cross-legged with Jesse's saddlebag purse between her knees. Slowly she poured sand back and forth between her hands. Randall stared at the mountains, stroking his chin in the cleft of his palm.

Hollywood went on. "Both jarheads, in the same platoon at the same time in Vietnam in 1969. Guess who their commanding officer was?"

Harry chewed his lip. "Bud Maston."

"Right. So we decided to fly out here and have a talk with Hector." Hollywood stood up, he put his hand on Hector's shoulder like the snitch was his pet Caliban. Hector shook the hand off. Hollywood smiled and removed his sunglasses. His lynx-eyes were the color of cold honey. "Had Dorothy fax some pictures of Bud she had around the house from a party. The idea was to show him Bud's picture."

Hector broke in, "One look and I freaked. Not about Maston, but you in the picture."

"The same way Cox reacted the first time he saw me," said Harry.

"Randall told me that. I ran your military records against Hector's and Cox's. No way you two were in any of the same places at the same time, either in Nam or stateside." Hollywood nudged Hector, who pulled a picture from his back jeans pocket.

Hector shrugged. "I had it in my stuff."

A young Bud Maston, his shirt off, warrior-lean in a bush hat, arm in arm with a young man who bore a striking resemblance to Harry Griffin. In the background, a mamasan in baggy pantaloons bent under the weight of a carrying pole. Rice paddies. Mountains. The photo was sepia-toned but Harry could see the heavy saffron air, the red dirt, and feel the sweat on the young bodies.

"Jesus."

"Creepy, ain't it?" said Hector.

Becky held up her hand. She rummaged in her bag and pulled out a battered mask cut from a photograph. It was an enlargement of the expression on the man's face who stood next to Bud.

"I've got a twin," said Harry.

"Not quite," said Hollywood. "Look at the teeth. His are straight. Back then, you looked like a werewolf." He turned the mask in Becky's fingers. "So what the hell is this?"

Becky looked away. "Bud made Chris wear this when they . . . had sex."

"Christ," muttered Hollywood.

Hector stood up and walked like a matador into his house. He returned with a can of Coke and bottles of Mexican beer. He gave the Coke to Becky, then he twisted the caps off the beers with his callused hands and handed them around. Harry did not decline.

Hector gazed through the shimmering heat at the far mountains. Watching him, it struck Harry that Hector was probably the future. The golden mud of his skin had been spit in by African slaves, Mexican Indians, Chinese coolies, and white trash.

"Okay," said Hector softly. "This is for Gunny Cox." The reflexive sneer went out of his handsome, ravaged face.

"Who is he?" Harry pointed to the Adonis marine with his arm around Bud Maston.

"Martin Kessler," said Hector with a wistful smile. "We called him Fearless Faggot." Hector waffled his hand, loose at the wrist. "A homo." Hector paused and a pocket of memory deepened his eyes. "Didn't put it on Front Street but didn't deny it, either. He had this tattoo on his thigh, two little cherries. Three months in the bush and he added some words. KILL MORE GOOKS." Hector gave a dry laugh. "He was a crazy fucker, you know, from loving and hating the war. But he carried the platoon radio. He took care of us all."

"And Jay Cox?" asked Harry.

"Gunny," said Hector. "Platoon sergeant. On his third tour when I met him. His nerves were shot after we hit the shit at Cam Lo. Other two platoons in the company got really torn up. The skipper and all three lieutenants got wasted. Martin and Gunny pulled us through. Didn't lose a single guy from our platoon except the lieutenant. We got so we were superstitious about Martin. And then, we drew Maston as our new lieutenant . . ." Hector stopped.

"What's wrong?" asked Harry.

"The chica. Maybe you should send her away," said Hector.

"Talk," said Becky.

Hector took another sip of beer. "Lieutenant Maston. You could just see it the minute he showed up. He had that look. That Kennedy light on him. He was going to do everything at least once. The war was his dime store and we was his toy soldiers."

A desert hawk drifted over them and Harry watched its shadow sail across the sand and a cloud covered the sun and the hawk's shadow metastasized and covered everything.

Hector lit a cigarette. "This is a war story. You know about war stories. That's where everybody lies." He smiled tightly at Becky. "Just as soon not talk in front of her."

"Fuck you," said Becky.

Hector appraised her. "You're tough, huh? Okay, so Maston. At first we thought, cool. He's a good head. Like he went out of his way to take care of us. He remembered everybody's name and where they were from. But then stuff started to happen."

"What kind of stuff?" asked Harry.

"Creepy things. Even for over there. We captured this sniper. Some of the guys were gonna shoot him, I mean, he was wounded and all. And he was a fucking sniper. But Maston had this idea—he wanted to hang him." Hector shrugged and hugged himself like he had bumped into a sudden chill in the 90-degree heat. "He said he'd never seen any-body hanged before. Like curious, you know. Woulda too, if Gunny Cox hadn't talked him out of it."

"What else?" Harry felt the goose bumps start at the base of his spine, radiate out his shoulders, and pop down his arms.

"There was this ville the zoomies blew to shit, and we made a sweep through it. Some civilians were killed, and ah, some cows and pigs . . ." Hector licked his lips and drank greedily from his beer. "And Maston, he carved this hunk out of this dead lady's leg and was roasting it on his K-Bar over these embers. He just took one bite though—you know, curious again."

They watched Hector drink half his beer. Then Hollywood asked, "What about Martin and Lieutenant Maston?"

"Well, it was like the other stuff. Maybe he was curious. Maybe he wanted to try Martin too. Just one bite." Hector shook his head. "But Martin never fucked around in the field and anyway, I think he was like, only into niggers. We kidded Martin about it, you know. How Maston was gonna stick him on his K-Bar like a weenie and put the fire to him and eat his ass up.

"But it wasn't funny. We were all getting strung out." Hector bared his teeth. "They left us out there too fucking long, man. We needed a break. Gunny Cox was losing his shit. And the way it got to Maston is . . . I guess he like, fell in love with Martin. Which was really flaky because Martin was the one holding us all together."

The cloud passed and white-hot sunlight transformed Hector Jefferson Cruz's face into a twitching Mayan sculpture.

"We were sick. Guys had fevers of a hundred and one, a hundred and two. Guys had dysentery and malaria. Afraid to take their boots off because how bad their feet looked. Maston tried to get us a stand-down. Instead they gave us another brilliant fucking operation. Everybody was just too . . . fucking . . . strung out.

"This goddamned hill. Company night position up by the Rockpile. Everybody was spooked because there were these rumors that the NVA had tanks. My squad got stuck on an exposed finger. The flank. Hanging in the goddamned air. Martin and Maston set up with us."

Hector's voice took them into the time machine. "Gets so damn dark like night is older there. Then the crickets stop and you hear the bamboo clicking, those little rice-propelled fuckers signaling. Then the whistles. Tough bastards, they came right through their own mortars. In five minutes we had 50 percent KIA, everybody wounded. But we held. Maston said we had to pull back. Martin said we had to hold that ridge 'cause if the NVA got a machine gun up there, they could enfilade the whole company, it'd be all over."

Hector stood up, gesturing with his hands. "Then they came again and it was just too hairy. We grabbed our wounded and booked. Maston ran. I ran. We all ran.

"Martin stayed. On that ridge with the radio and the machine gun. The crazy fucker held them off. Cox come by checking the line and found us. He was furious that we left Martin up there. He was screaming and kicking Maston, but nobody was going. So he went back up there alone to help Martin, and Maston kept saying, 'Don't worry, it'll be all right if we all stick together.'

"Whole place was lit up with flares and Martin was running the fire from his radio, bringing it in real close. All of a sudden this creepy quiet and we heard Martin scream, 'All of you but one' . . . Over and over. The whole company heard him, they thought he was screaming about the gooks.

"Then Maston went back up there. We heard some shots and then everything was quiet. So we crept back up and got in our holes. Cox was real fucked up, shot to shit. When we put him on the medevac the guys in the chopper got out a body bag. Martin was dead. And Maston was wounded, shot bad in the leg."

Hector sighed. "Well, shit, the colonel come out and the general come out and everybody come out and Maston didn't say shit. Just sat there, refusing to be medevaced, in that hole with all them dead gooks Martin and Gunny wasted piled up around it. And everybody thought it was him out there running the radio, manning that gun that saved the company. So we all rode with it. It was, you know, officer shit. Maston got us safe gigs in the rear. He said he'd take care of us. We heard Gunny Cox died of wounds on the way to Japan. And Maston got nominated for the Congressional Medal of Honor."

Hector flipped his cigarette away. "We didn't think much of it. Officers were always doing stuff like that, writing themselves up for medals. Nobody talked about it. Nobody wanted to hear Martin screaming up there." He looked at Harry with a jerky smile and asked, "You think there's a Hell?"

"I think we're already there."

Hector gnawed his lip. "Cox thought there was a Hell. He was legally dead for three minutes, he said. Went down to Hell. Said they sent him back for Maston. That fucker wouldn't die. He showed up, a year ago. Tracked me through my address of record from the marines and got my Mom, in L.A., to give him this place. Man, he was *intense*. Been traveling the country tracking down survivors of the squad. He said him and me were it. All that's left. The only witnesses.

"He showed me this *Newsweek* magazine story about Maston. How he was going to run for the U.S. Congress in Minnesota. Cox was like—driven. Had this picture thing in his old truck. He'd spent years putting it together. All these flicks of Maston, wrote all over to get them, he said."

The silence became so dry and hot that the friction of two rough words could ignite the air.

"Then Cox tells me what really happened up on that ridge. How he was hit and feeding the ammo and Martin was staying on that gun bleeding to death and how Martin started screaming. And his screams got weaker and weaker and Maston came back and got down in the hole with Martin, stroking his face and not doing anything to stop the bleeding. But he did other things . . . and the guy was dying and that fucker was—"

"Steady," said Hollywood, taking Hector's arm in an iron grip.

"Fuck you, man," Hector warned Hollywood, cautioning him with an extended middle finger. Hollywood put his arm protectively around Becky's shoulder. "Riiight," said Hector, "protect peaches and cream so she don't know what it's really like out there."

It was quiet on the desert as they waited for Hector to find his voice again.

"Cox said that then Maston starts firing the gun. Maston starts calling in the artillery, blowing everything to shit. But all the gooks were gone. How he picks up an AK from one of the dead gooks and shoots himself in the leg—"

"Shit," muttered Harry. He turned and looked at Becky. She regarded him with wide, solemn eyes and nodded her head.

Hector shook his head. "Goddamn Cox. Wanted me to go to Minnesota with him. Said we had to expose Maston and keep him out of politics. Make him confess what he did. How we had to go to the president and get Martin his medal, get it away from Maston.

"Fuck that. Who's going to believe *him*? Or me. He's got to check into a VA hospital every winter so they can change his Thorazine antifreeze. For the last five years he's been mostly getting his mail in a lock ward. But damn if he didn't go."

Harry stood up and turned away.

"Hey," called out Hector. "Did Maston ever run for the politics?"

"No," said Harry. "Cox stopped him."

"No shit. Gunny Cox did that, huh? Well I'll be damned," Hector shook his head. "He said he should kill the sonofabitch, but he didn't think he had it in him anymore."

"He got some help. It was the wrong kind of help and it didn't work out," Harry said.

Hector perused Harry's face. "You probably *amused* him. You musta looked real good to that sicko bastard. Like death warmed over."

Harry walked off a few paces and squatted. He put a hand out to steady himself. Texas harvester ants scurried between his fingers. They were sturdy and fierce-looking and as heavily armored as bronze warriors. The word *marines* formed in his mind as he picked one up between his thumb and forefinger. He hardly felt the sting.

Chris had tried to be the hero of his story after all.

Out of reflex, he reached for a cigarette. He understood the habit of smoking. As long as you had a cigarette you were never alone. There were times when being alone with your thoughts could kill you.

Randall was next to him, his face braided in the heat. Harry stood up and Randall embraced him with iron strength in his withered arms. Then Randall stepped back. Dry-eyed, implacable. Randall's generation didn't show their feelings much. They'd lived them.

He remembered what Randall had tried to teach him. Words spoken long ago in the tropical heat, in the shadow of another mountain range.

Just because you discover that everything you know and believe is wrong doesn't give you an excuse to quit living.

"This won't change anything, Randall. He's got me boxed. I'm going down for two murders."

A transit of admiration flickered in Randall's spooky eyes. "Maybe not." He turned and studied Becky.

60

Chato, Arizona, had two gas stations, one convenience store, three taverns, and the motel. The motel room's back door opened on a sand-choked patio and the sand led to the town's former business district, where siding hung from the original adobe walls. Farther into the desert, the skeleton of a coal chute stood guard over abandoned railroad tracks.

A scrawny chicken pecked its way across the patio. Twenty yards away two Mexican kids with starchy bellies hung over dirty undershorts played in a rusted-out 1957 Chevrolet.

Down the highway, under a Fellini-twilight tiara of pink and blue neon, a fat man in bib overalls played an ancient upright piano on an open court behind a cantina.

The air conditioner didn't work and they all dripped sweat. Hollywood questioned Harry and Becky about the sequence of events at the trailer. He particularly didn't like the part about Jerry Hakala seeing Harry with the gun, or the overpowering and kidnap of the policeman.

Patiently, he tried to walk Becky through it from the beginning. "Did your brother go into the woods that morning planning to kill Bud Maston?"

"To fight him. To make him leave Mom alone," said Becky.

"Becky, you're going to have to tell us exactly what happened. It will all come out in court," Hollywood explained.

"I don't want to go to court," she said through clenched teeth.

Randall signaled with his eyes to ease up. "Okay," said Hollywood, "so what did you see in the woods?"

"They got into an argument."

"Could you hear what it was about?"

She shook her head. "Bud hit him and Chris tried to fight back and Bud grabbed his gun and it shot in the air. Then Bud pulled the barrel into his side and held it there. They were struggling, but Bud had his hand on Chris's on the trigger. It went off again. He pulled open the bolt and stuffed it with snow. Then he pushed Chris down."

Her voice quickened. "Chris was trying to load another bullet but his gun wouldn't work because it had snow stuck in it. By then, Bud was screaming, laying in the snow, but now he had his own rifle pointed at Chris. Just when Harry came over the ridge, he threw his rifle away. Chris got unjammed and aimed at Bud and you know the rest."

Harry saw it. Bud, the unlikely high-wire artist, methodically growing his love handles to cushion the bullet and meticulously planning the timing, lining up all the trapeze bars for his circus of the real and thrilling to the split-second risk.

"Why didn't you go to Sheriff Emery?" asked Hollywood.

"I was scared. I thought Bud brought Harry to kill us all." Becky buried her hands in her hair and when she looked up, her eyes were two sores. "Don't you see? I did something too . . . and he took pictures of me . . . and now part of . . . of what happened has even gotten back to my boyfriend." She shut her eyes and shook her head violently and ran next door to her room.

"Give her a few minutes, Harry," said Randall. "Then go in and just listen to her. She's about to talk."

Harry drifted with it while Hollywood and Randall haggled about the law. He didn't hear the words, only the intensity of their voices and, the way they held their bodies, it could have been twenty years ago, they could have been weighing the best way to approach a hostile village.

They decided to call Mike Hakala in Maston County and let it all hang out. Hollywood picked up the phone. Harry went to the adjoining room.

Becky was in the shower and a cloud of moisture preceded her when she came out of the bathroom saronged in a towel. The towel swished against her thighs and a peek of pubic hair caught a thread of fire off the lowering sun.

"Put some clothes on," he said.

"I want to dry off," she said. Her face was baby-butt moist and shiny. "You'd feel better if you cleaned up," she said.

Harry didn't want to feel better.

Becky tilted her head. "It won't help. What that guy said. He's just a junkie. A nobody. There's only one way for us now."

She leaned her damp body against him in a chaste embrace, went up on tiptoe, and kissed him with affection on the forehead. Then she sat in a chair next to the air conditioner and toyed with the off-on toggle switch.

"Out of order," said Harry.

"Figures." She sighed, fanning her face with her hand. The chair jerked back under her weight and disturbed the folds of the cheap polyester curtains behind it. The chintzy abstract curtain design shivered a foot above her head and a large pale-green praying mantis flexed its lethal mandibles and settled back into anonymity.

He stared at her.

"We have to finish what Chris started," she said frankly.

"I wish it was that simple." He shook his head. "There are rules, Becky."

"Oh, right! After listening to what that Hector said, there's no rules and there's no God."

Becky pursed her lips and looked out at the desert. "I know I'm going to cry about it, but not yet. I get into the trailer and down the hall and when I try to open the door to the bedroom the door's locked. I can't get it open."

Harry sat down on the bed and waited. For a full minute the only sound was the hot swish of tires passing on the highway and the faraway tinkle of the piano.

Becky sagged in the chair and fingered one of her mother's cigarettes from the crush-proof box on the desk next to her chair. She lit it and French inhaled. The smoke trailed up over her head and the mantis moved an inch.

"She wouldn't marry Dad. She always married the wrong goddamn guys," she said irritably. And then, meeting his hard, measured gaze, she raised her voice. "Don't give me that. If I'd talked, there could be a trial and I'd have to be in court and a lawyer would ask me . . . questions. By the time he got through nobody would believe anything I said. He's got us, Harry. I thought it all through." She took a deep breath and said, "The only way to stop him is to kill him."

Harry watched shadows walk out from the mesquite. "How do you propose to do that?"

She lowered her eyes and sulked. Randall and Hollywood stood on the patio, listening through the screen door. Quietly, they entered the room. Hollywood asked, "Why wouldn't anyone believe you?"

Becky hugged the towel, walked to the bathroom door, and turned. "Because I saw more than just Bud and Chris fight. I saw it all from the beginning. If I knew about it and didn't tell, that makes me part of it. Bud planned it that way."

They waited while she changed into a pair of jeans and a blouse and fastened a bone necklace around her throat and methodically braided her black hair.

"Mom had one of her fights with Dad and she moved Chris and me to Grandma Loretta's and she rented an apartment in town and started tending bar at the VFW because that would really piss Dad off.

"One night she took us out to dinner and there's this guy with her who turns out to be Bud Maston. Chris and I were impressed. We'd seen him on TV and his picture's in the hall at school."

"When was this?" asked Harry.

"A year ago almost exactly. He was thin then, and really funny in a sad way. Mom wasn't tense around him like she was with Dad.

"He took us places—skiing, we even went on a dogsled into the Boundary Waters. But always out-of-the-way places, because Bud was sensitive about publicity after the political thing. But he kept his hand in. Pretty soon he and Mom were making all these plans about the town.

"We moved into the lodge and at first Chris was really against it. He wanted to go back home. But it was like one big party. Chris and I could do whatever we wanted. Like no curfew. I could stay out all night with Mitch if I wanted. Bud let Chris smoke and even drink with him. And that's when Mom made her first mistake. She was always downtown at that office they opened up, driving Bud's new Jeep, being important, going to meetings with Don Karson. Chris didn't have to answer to anybody."

"And what was your dad doing?" asked Randall.

"Getting furious. Bud wasn't afraid of him like the other men in town. He owned the town. So he got the prettiest girl in town."

She walked to the screen door and traced with her finger on the mesh. "Then Jay Cox drove up one day in an old truck full of tools and it all changed."

"Last summer," said Harry.

"May," she sighed. "Bud and Jay went to the bank and Jay bought a new truck and a trailer and some land."

"Apparently Cox decided that keeping Bud out of politics wasn't enough," said Randall dryly.

Becky nodded. "Jay figured Bud owed him a life-time job to keep his mouth shut. But we didn't know that then. Next thing, Jay had these plans drawn up and he starts in on the lodge. Mom started getting nervous about Jay's hold over Bud. But she thought the lodge was a good business idea, so Bud let her take over the finances." She shivered violently. "Bud would sit up all night and drink and stare at the fireplace. Sometimes he'd build a fire and it was June.

"Bud left dope around and Chris started getting high a lot and trying to shock people. Then dumbass Don Karson came to Bud about the mess at school, the silly gossip about Chris being gay. And I was feeling like a real fool because the kids were saying that my brother had the hots for my boyfriend."

Becky shook her head from side to side. "Karson should have talked to Mom and Dad. Chris was real vulnerable and Bud started getting him off alone. Mom was in this panic, Bud was falling apart on her. She didn't see . . . or she pretended not to.

"He said he wanted to show Chris something, this secret place up on the ridge he found when he was a kid. When they got there, he said he needed to talk and he swore Chris to secrecy never to tell Mom. He said Jay was blackmailing him and that Jay was . . . sick, that's why he took those pills all the time . . ."

A tear worked its way down her cheek.

"He confessed to Chris and told him how he had to leave the city and politics because Jay threatened to tell about him having a secret boyfriend. That's when he showed Chris the pictures of Martin from the war. And that's when the weird stuff started with the drugs. And Chris got that tattoo.

"Then Jay caught Chris and Bud together up there. It was ugly. Chris was passed out stoned and . . . Jay . . . stopped . . . Bud and was going to tell Mom, but Bud had already started to turn it around. He pointed out that Jay had taken money and so he was a blackmailer.

"Chris told me how Bud got him high and . . . did things to him and it got very weird at the lodge. All of us, except Mom, were knee-deep in secrets and it stayed that way all summer. Jay was building the addition and the cabins and Mom was getting more and more nervous watching Bud sit there and drink and get fat.

"Except now Jay protected Chris from Bud and told him what really happened with that Martin guy and the medal. It was starting to stink. Mom'd see Chris and I whispering and Chris talking to Jay. And I think that's when Bud Maston decided to get rid of all of us.

"So Chris and I tried to talk Mom into going back to Dad. And she did . . . a little. She always did when she got scared. And that's when Bud laid his trap. It was his idea. The million dollars."

Seeing the expression on Harry's face, she laughed bitterly through her tears. "God, why are you so surprised? What do you think people are? You and Chris. You want to believe in knights in shining armor." She rolled her eyes. "They agreed on the divorce settlement *before* they got married."

"You just watched it, didn't you?" Harry said quietly.

She touched his cheek. "Hush," she said in a voice that chilled him. "Let me tell it all."

Harry glanced at Randall and Hollywood, who observed Becky with quiet fascination.

"God, you're so dumb," said Becky. "They were *all* guilty! They made a *deal*. Mom, Jay, and Bud. Right at the dining room table. Bud told Mom a cleaner version of what Hector said. How Jay could ruin his reputation. And how she could help him satisfy Jay and get what she really wanted, which was enough money to get away from Stanley. Think! Why the hell would Bud Maston, one of the richest guys in the state, marry my mom? He needed a way to pay off Cox so they couldn't trace the money, you know, later when he got back in politics."

"You were there?" Randall asked.

"Sure," said Becky. "That way Chris and I were involved. Bud was real sorry and said he wanted to make amends and settle it once and for all. But the main thing he said was a million dollars. Mom and him would get married, then split up in this big fight, which wouldn't surprise anybody. Bud would agree to a big divorce settlement. The lodge, the lake, and his land. The money."

Down the highway, the piano player banged insistently on one key.

"All she ever wanted was to be on her own. She couldn't resist it." Becky began to cry silently. "We were *so* pissed at her. Chris blew up and hit Bud and Mom called the cops and it was a real scene. Everybody left. I drove into town in Mom's car and ran into these two guys at the Cruiser, they're on the hockey team, friends of Mitch's, and I was feeling kind of crazy and mad at Mom and I said, well, nobody's home and Chris has this weed and there's lots to drink and we . . ."

She buried her hands in her hair and gagged on her words. "Do I have to say this to three guys?"

Randall shifted in his chair. Hollywood tugged on his earlobe.

"We went back home and I got really loaded and I just didn't give a shit . . . I hear this awful laughter and I look up and there's Bud on the balcony with a camera. Those guys deserted me, grabbed their clothes, and ran like hell. And Bud said if I didn't keep my mouth shut he'd show the pictures to Mitch and my dad."

Becky began to sob. "Except one of those guys made a crack to Mitch, and Mitch beat him up for it. And now when the whole truth comes out he probably won't have anything to do with me."

Randall exhaled, cleared his throat. "Keep going."

Becky wiped away the tears and took a deep breath. "We wouldn't go to the phony wedding. Chris said we couldn't trust anybody except each other and we couldn't tell Dad after what we'd done. He decided it was up to him to get Mom away from Bud before she took any money. So he broke into Dad's place and stole that gun. Then he got caught with it at school and Dad jumped in and got him off."

"Did Emery know any of this?" asked Harry.

"He was suspicious. Mom had started to make up, then suddenly she marries Bud. How could anybody know. I wouldn't even talk to Mitch."

"Dad tried like hell to get Chris to tell him what was going on out at the lodge, but Chris just wanted to learn to shoot. Then he dared Bud to take him hunting. Like a challenge."

"So he *did* go out there planning to nail Bud Maston," said Hollywood.

"I don't know, he wanted to face him with a gun. He said he'd been down into the spider heart and he had to get clean."

Randall and Hollywood exchanged quizzical glances, but Harry understood it perfectly. When he wrote his story he was romanticizing Martin, but when he went into the woods, he was his father's son.

Becky smoothed a hand down her braided hair and turned her profile to the setting sun. "The last part of the deal was bringing Harry up so he would think Mom was taking advantage of Bud. Bud said Harry would 'rescue' him." She turned to face Harry. "And you did, didn't you?"

Long shadows twisted across the room and snatches of raucous laughter drifted from the cantina and mingled with the steam of sagebrush in the boiling air.

Becky held up her hands and let them drop. "Then . . . everybody became Bud's puppets while he played poor, drunk Bud and just . . . amused himself. Jay and Chris freaked because you looked like Martin." She exhaled and stared out over the desert. "But Mom liked you. She thought she could trust you . . ."

She cocked her head and a queer reverence crept into her voice. "Bud's an . . . artist and Jay said he can turn on a dime. He makes a picture in his head, then he fits the right people at the right time to make it come true."

Hollywood stepped forward. "You have to go on the record with this, Becky. Back in Minnesota."

Becky squinted at him. "You're like a cop, aren't you? Am I arrested or anything?"

"I'm like a cop," said Hollywood. "And I just talked to Mike Hakala in Maston County—"

"Yeah?" Becky gritted her teeth.

"No formal charges have been brought in the deaths of your mother and Cox. In fact, they haven't even made it public yet. The sheriff's deputy you guys had the run-in with? Hakala said that was just a family misunderstanding. He said that the best thing for you and your family would be for the both of you to go back there."

Becky shut her eyes and took a deep breath. "Okay," she said.

"Good," said Hollywood. "Hakala wants me to formally depose Mr. Hector Cruz, get it on tape this time, and send it back with you."

"What's going on?" asked Harry.

"Local jurisdiction. Time is standing still in Maston County, Minnesota. They have Maston sealed off at his house, no phone, no wheels, and no official explanation," said Hollywood as he moved to the door.

"Where are you going?" asked Harry.

"Out of earshot of the rest of this conversation."

"Mom talked to Bud in the hospital right after he got shot and he accused her and Cox of trying to kill him. But they were stuck with it, he said, and nothing had changed, the deal was still on. She should get mad and wreck up the lodge and take money out of the bank and communicate through you, Harry. He knew that you couldn't let it lay, that you'd come back."

"Do you think this is some damn game where if you figure out the pieces you win, Becky? Are you really that smart?" said Harry.

"Indeed she is," said Randall.

"You mean, for a kid?" Her smile was elemental, catlike. "It goes deeper than that. Miss Loretta says, you shouldn't try to build a road through the forest. You should look for the path that's already there."

"Quit fucking around, Becky, this is serious shit were in," said Harry.

"The problem is, if I talk to Mitch's father, there's enough to arrest him on suspicion," said Becky very deliberately. "But I'm not a good witness, am I? Bud would make it all sound like it was part of the blackmail thing. And he has pictures of me with my clothes off. And he'd show those pictures to people in court too. Well, wouldn't he?"

"Very likely," said Randall.

"So if it gets to court, a jury wouldn't believe me. Never in a million years. And who will they believe now that Jay's dead? That guy Hector or poor rich Bud?"

She turned to Harry. "Juries believe facts. Jerry Hakala will have to put his hand on a Bible and say who he saw come out of the trailer with the gun in his hand. Not what he might believe but what he saw. They'll ask Mitch and me what *we saw* when we drove up. Harry again, all bloody, spaced out in the Jeep with the gun." Becky raised her chin as Randall and Harry weighed the full weight of her words.

"The law—" Harry insisted.

"Law's for right and wrong. He's *evil*," she charged, standing up straight.

And Randall, with his pale eyes that loved secrets and his wisdom

that could be as ruthlessly practical as locks and keys—and as cold—
smiled his bland, accommodating smile. "Bud missed the obvious thing
that can literally kill him, isn't that so, Becky?"

Desert sunset laved the darkened room and Becky raised her face
from shadow and stole a Moment of proud beauty from the red rock
light. In simple sentences, she showed Harry the way out.

61

It was last day of hunting season. A stream of vehicles with deer carcasses lashed to their roofs or trundling behind on flatbed trailers traveled south. Harry drove north on Highway 61 in the rattling Ford. The .45 was back in his waistband, making a steel angle in his lap. He wore soft buckskin gloves.

In his rearview mirror Harry could see Mike Hakala hunched in the front seat of his Bronco, talking to Randall.

Becky rode with Mitch Hakala behind the Bronco. Jerry Hakala, who'd apparently patched up his differences with Mitch, brought up the rear.

No one in Maston County law enforcement had slept much the night before.

Harry had declined to clean up and his hair stuck at odd angles and his face was a grease of sweat, lumped nose, livid scars, and dark stubble. His eyes were bloodshot behind Jesse's sunglasses.

The caravan turned up Highway 7. About a mile from the lodge, Hakala flashed his headlights. Harry pulled over. Hakala parked on the shoulder in back of him. Mitch raced on up the slope with Becky. Jerry followed them. Mike Hakala walked up and Harry rolled down the window.

"Give Becky about an hour to get in place. You go in in thirty minutes."

Harry nodded.

Hakala scanned the chilly pine crowns. "You, ah, want to wait back with us?"

Harry shook his head. He wanted to be alone.

Thirty minutes later, Randall leaned out his window and sliced his hand forward. "Go!" Harry took a last drag off his Camel and hotboxed it until his throat was raw as a scream. His gloved fingers shook as he flicked the butt out the window. He hadn't slept on the flight back from Phoenix. Past fatigue. They all were. In the grip of that extreme moral dimension where . . .

Fuck it.

He put the car in gear and drove the last mile to the lodge. Two County Blazers blocked the turnoff, their windshields faceless oblong mirrors full of clouds. They pulled back to let him pass. Bud's rental Trooper was stranded, all four tires flat, in the driveway,

Bud sat in a rocking chair, in front of the lodge. He hadn't changed his clothes except for trading his wing tips for Sorel boots and his overcoat for a heavy down parka. He held the 12 gauge across his thighs.

Harry got out of the car and removed the sunglasses in case Bud thought there might be mercy in his eyes.

The chair creaked, rocking back and forth. "I been thinking," Bud mused. "This is what Teddy Kennedy must have felt like after Chappaquiddick. How incredibly fucked up things get."

"Don't flatter yourself."

"I'm not." He exuded the confident sadism of a general reviewing the regrettable collateral damage. He sighed and stood up. "Nothing works the way it should anymore. Like, why aren't you in jail?" He nodded at the Trooper. "See what they did to my car? And the phone went dead." Bud swung the shotgun in an idle arc. "Couple dozen of the fuckers out there round the clock. Just watching me. Jerry Hakala dropped in this morning. Guess Emery's going to be suspended . . ." Bud smiled.

"Unless he goes through drug-dependency treatment. They got him in the hospital," said Harry with his own bleak smile.

"Where would we be without the self-help movement, eh, Harry?" Bud said.

The butchery in the trailer screamed unanswered in the silence between them. Perhaps he thought their conversation was being recorded.

Bud grinned, reading Harry's thoughts. "Apparently I'm being held in protective custody." His brilliant blue eyes sliced the air. "When I get done in court, this county will look like Carthage after the Romans were through with it."

He arched his back, working the kinks out of his neck. "They've even got some kind of drum. Last night they were beating on it. Subhumans."

He tossed the Remington on his shoulder, walked to the Escort, and kicked a patch of rust on the fender. "She always wanted a new car. Bitch. Bitch. Bitch." He turned to Harry. "So fill me in. Nobody's talking to me."

"We're supposed to bring Becky in."

"Where is she?"

"In the woods. They think you know where to find her."

"Did you fuck her, Harry?" Bud smiled.

The muscle in Harry's left cheek twitched.

"Not even just a little bit?" Bud grinned broadly. "Well, they're right. We have to collect her. Loose end. She's the smartest of the whole bunch, you know."

"I know," said Harry.

"Harry, I can understand you being pissed off, but you'll see, it's the only way for it to work out."

"She told me all about it."

"About what?"

"The divorce deal. You and Cox. The Ballad of Martin Kessler. Randall did a little digging around. Introduced me to a guy. Lance Corporal Hector Cruz. Remember him? He remembers you." Harry uncoiled and knocked the shotgun from Bud's shoulder, kicked it away with a swipe of Jay Cox's boots. He unbuttoned his jacket so Bud could see the .45 in his belt.

Bud smiled. Totally relaxed. Maybe he was adapting. "What a bunch of losers, huh?" He removed a glove. His fingernails were clipped and buffed, meticulously clean. He picked briefly at the scab on his lip, put the glove back on.

Harry rested his hand on the pistol butt. "Let's take a stroll in the woods."

"Psycho-drama, Harry? Returning to the scene of past and future crimes?"

"Move!"

"It was so perfect," said Bud. "God, the look in Cox's eyes when he saw you for the first time." Bud chuckled as they trudged down the snowmobile trail along the lakeshore. He threw out his arms and danced ahead.

"The first time *I* saw you standing outside Coffman Union in 1969, it was magic. You were so like him. You even moved like him. Except for the teeth, but we fixed that, didn't we? I just kept you in my pocket all these years. Every once in a while I'd take you out and look at you."

Harry smelled wood smoke and that's when the crazy tin-pan drum started up.

"Jesus, can you believe this shit," said Bud, shaking his head. Above them, on an outcrop of granite, the winos from the liquor store had a camp. They had a fire going and were bent over an upturned, rusted washtub. Sweet-potato face was there. He raised his wine bottle in a salute and did a slow drop-skip frug and a chilling, shaky cry warbled from his throat.

Bud sighed. "Okay, so I lied a little and the great crime of my life was that I fell in love with another man. Now that'll come out." Bud pursed his lips. "That's not all bad these days, you know. Especially in this state."

"You're not gay, Bud. Not straight, either. When they figure out what you are, they'll name it after you."

Bud winked. "Not who you're with, it's how far you go."

"Move, lard ass," said Harry. He yanked out the pistol.

"Do you want me to put up my hands? Maybe you want to tie me up?"

The hollow metal beat of the drum paced them to the turnoff to Nanabozho Point and they began to climb and, as they toiled upward, the wind freshened and it was an absolutely beautiful November late afternoon. By the time they reached the high ground, sundown groomed the snow-struck pines.

Sweating with exertion, Bud shoved his way into a thick stand of pines that filled a cleft in the granite face. Faintly, above them on the point, in pauses of the muted drum, Harry heard the rattle of antlers.

They came across a large drag-trail, streaked with blood.

Bud laughed and pointed to the big, field-dressed deer carcass strung up in a pine tree. The deer from the road with the long curved left tine. "Is this your idea of psy war?" Bud joked.

The sun dived and the woods rattled with distant gunfire in homage to the end of hunting season.

Bud grinned. "Don't shoot. I'm going to reach in this cranny for a flashlight." He felt around in the crevassed rock and pulled out a light and switched it on. They squirmed through the cranny and started down. "I planted those trees when I was a boy, to hide the entrance. This is my find. I suppose when this is over I'll have the Historical Society out here. Maybe I'll donate the land for a park."

The way led down through twisting galleries of lichen-covered rock and the air was claustrophobic and clammy with spores of mold and powdery sediment crumbled underfoot. The passage opened into a chamber and, veiled in spiderwebs, a hobo jungle took shape in the flashlight beam. A sleeping bag lay on a ragged futon, plywood plat-form underneath. Mats. A kerosene heater. There was a propane stove and a cache of canned and freeze-dried food. Two five-gallon drums of water.

Hundreds of candles dripped wax stalactites down the crannied rock. Bud removed his gloves and opened a box of Blue Tip matches. Harry stooped, grabbed Bud's gloves, and stuck them in his pocket. Bud began lighting candles and set the cave in motion. Frantic insect activity retreated from the light and cast crawly shadows and slowly the walls undulated into shape.

A neolithic Sistine of deer and bison arched above their heads. Stick hunters with bows and spears.

Becky's backpack lay on the dirty tatami mats. Bud shouted and his voice echoed in the cavern. "Come out, come out, wherever you are . . ." he turned to Harry. "So where's the cops, rocket scientist? That's the idea, isn't it?"

Becky's voice came from deep in the inky recesses. "How do I know you won't kill me with an ax thing like you did Mom?"

"What are you talking about?" asked Bud. "Come out where I can see you."

Harry poked him with the pistol and nodded at the pack. "Open it," he ordered. Bud unfastened the flap, picked out the mask of Martin's face, and held it in front of his own. "Pot's light, Becky," he sang into the shadows. Bud slipped his hand into his pocket. "Time to put in your ante."

"Watch it," warned Harry.

"Just some pictures, Harry." Bud sprinkled the prints on the mats. Laminated color ran wetly in the candlelight. "I have more, all X-rated. Back in St. Paul, in the offices of Noble and Deal."

Bud looked at them fondly and lined them up.

Variations of Chris. He lay on his stomach on the mattress, bathed in the glow of candles, looking over his skinny shoulder, a drugged smile smeared on his face. His narrow buttocks shining. The mask worn backward. Bud grinned, reached in his pocket and tossed another picture.

Becky—a sweaty two-six-pack-fantasy—thrust luridly naked on the spit of two adolescent penises.

Bud smiled and a tapestry of shadow creeped over his face. "Airtight Rebecca. The apple never falls far from the tree, does it? You never really know people. Look at the expressions. That's pure delight, beyond the limits. Chris gave me acid. Then we played spin the bottle. It started innocently with talk. Then you go to the right place. Create the right conditions and give your fantasies permission to come out. It could happen to anyone." Bud bent his manicured middle finger against his thumb and flicked it forward. Chris's picture skittered across the cave.

"Doing it with that murderous little creep was like putting a worm on a hook."

Harry leveled the pistol between Bud's eyebrows. *Steady.*

Bud raised his voice and leavened it with contrition. "Mike? Jerry? Drunkenness is no excuse. I freely admit what happened here. And I'm deeply ashamed."

Becky yelled again from the shadows. "Harry? What should I do?"

"What can we do, Becky?" shouted Bud. "Except tell the truth. Let the courts decide." He turned to Harry and whispered. "It's the only way. You just have to submit." Then he continued his confession in the loud voice. "He seduced me, Harry. Can you believe that? My wife's kid seduced me."

The pistol shook.

"You can't do it, Harry. Not when you're sober. Not without provocation. Go on, try to pull the trigger."

Harry explored the cushion of sweat against his index finger and felt the tiny grid on the trigger.

"You're weak," said Bud. "Like Martin was weak. Like Cox was weak. You have all these messy beliefs that make you a tar baby and get you stuck in the world. You'd all bumble over the cliff if people like me didn't organize you."

Harry swung the pistol and opened a gash in Bud's cheek. "C'mon, you sonofabitch," he rasped.

Bud staggered and held out his hands, smiling through a stain of blood. "I don't want to fight you, Harry. I love you. I've always loved you. You proved *your* love when you saved my life. And you'll learn to love me. I imagine it will be an awful trial. I'll be your best and worst character witness."

Bud paced, his voice by turns practical and dismissive. "I'll take some hits for being easily manipulated. By Jesse. By Cox, by these feral children. Have to deal with ugly rumors about my military record. But that won't be so bad in light of recent events, not like it would have been a year ago. Anyway, nobody really cares about Vietnam."

Harry shoved Bud hard, knocking him back against the rock. Bud kept smiling. "I think a classic post-traumatic stress defense will work best for you. I'll get anybody you want to defend you. I mean anybody. I'll visit faithfully when you're in prison. I've already provided for you. A generous amount has been put aside for you in lieu of the salary and retirement benefits you will lose. Even if something happens to me, you'll be taken care of. More money than you could ever earn.

"And in prison you will learn obedience. That's what prisons are for. To teach men like you obedience to other, stronger men."

The pistol burned in Harry's hand. Bud's vivid eyes twinkled in the candlelight over the front sight.

"Poor Harry. All you had was one grubby little penny. Your pathetic honor and all the tough-guy illusions that go with it. Where are they, now? After Chris? That was your cherry, baby, and I got it."

With a hollow click, the safety on the .45 snapped to firing position.

Bud wasn't impressed. "You have to make up your mind. Either you kill me or obey me."

"Fight, you bastard," said Harry in a calm voice.

Bud laughed. "Mother Goose. You still believe in all those American nursery rhymes. Even Chris, that crippled little fuck, thought he was on a mission from John Wayne." Bud clucked and shook his head and even now he could not resist giving a speech. "All of you kiddies, all the evidence to the contrary, you keep perpetuating the myths, keep paying your taxes and returning the politicians to office. You keep fighting the wars. Wise up. This country is just one big shopping mall run by murderers. *Those people were blackmailing me!*"

"You're going to jail," said Harry.

Bud laughed. "I *built* the goddamn jail to hold people like you. People who lose control. Who get confused and lash out. I can protect you, even inside. After the first time a bunch of those grunting animals hold you down and spread your cheeks, you won't refuse my calls or my intervention through third parties. By the time you get out, you'll be trained. You might even get a job sweeping up if you learn how to say 'Sir.'"

"Why'd you have to do that to Jesse and Cox?"

"Go on, say 'sir.'"

"Why them, like that?"

"But I didn't. You did it to protect me from a larcenous woman who'd use her son to attempt murder for profit. You figured it out, but in the process you went over the edge." Bud yelled into the shadows. "Olle olle oxen free."

Something started in the dark. Like a pebble being thrown.

Deliberately, Bud yelled into the shadows. "Somebody has to stop you, Harry, before you kill again!" Harry jerked his head. Bud lunged, one hand shoving the slide on the barrel housing of the .45 back, effectively disarming the firing mechanism. His other hand flashed up from the cuff of his boot and black steel guttered in the candlelight.

Harry blocked the marine K-Bar—Bud's cannibal knife—and took two inches of the tip in the muscle below his left elbow before it jarred into bone. The pain came in a clean bath and he grinned as his left hand clamped on Bud's right wrist. Bud warded off the pistol and, as they grappled, he puckered his lips in a mocking kiss. "C'mon, tough guy, wrestle me down." His voice was a wild giggle. Boys roughhousing. "Harder, Harry, faster—take it right to the edge. I always do. Are those steel bands of yours getting flaccid?" Bud thrilled.

Bud crowded him against the granite wall. Candles scattered. Hot wax dotted their faces. Theatrically, Bud yelled, "Run for it, Becky! I'll hold him as long as I can."

Becky darted from the shadows.

"Run, run, run!" shouted Bud. His bulk swept Harry in a jerky polka embrace across the gallery. Becky danced on the balls of her feet, maneuvering.

Enough games. Harry broke free and slapped him up with the pistol and his left fist. Bud recoiled, chastised, as if he'd blundered into the moving parts of a machine. He crumbled to his knees.

"Drop it, Griffin!" The mournful voice and the cold circle of steel against the back of his neck came moccasin-silent out of the shadows. Emery had got his deer after all.

Harry took a Moment to enjoy the confusion on Bud's bleeding face. Then he dropped the pistol.

"You said he was in the hospital," Bud gasped.

"I lied."

Bud struggled up, grinning. "Larry, Jesus Christ!"

"Surprise," said Emery.

Bud missed the irony in Emery's voice and blurted in relief. "Am I glad to see you. This crazy sonofabitch coulda killed somebody."

"Yeah," said Emery. "Looked that way to me, too. Pick up that gun, Maston."

Despite his blacked eyes, Emery cut an impressive figure turned out in the sheriff's uniform that was tailored fawn and gray with mother of pearl snap buttons neat on the pockets and a hand-tooled pistol belt low on his hip. A gold five-pointed star pinned his chest and the heavy revolver in his hand appeared very serious, Rock of Ages steady, and very straight indeed.

Harry stepped back to give Bud room to scramble for the pistol. "He said Becky might be here. I didn't know what he'd try but I thought maybe . . ." Bud's best civic-minded voice.

Becky spoke calmly, too calmly. "What do I do?" And Bud missed that too.

"You just go on outside, Becky," said Emery, moving swiftly to put his body between Bud and the girl.

"I want to stay," she said distinctly. Averting her eyes, she stooped to grab at the picture.

"No, leave it be," said Emery. "That's evidence, honey. You gotta learn to live with the truth. Go on now. Git."

Becky started through the narrow entrance. She turned.

"Go," said Emery. "Don't look back."

When she'd disappeared, Harry moved to cover the exit. Blood curled down into his palm and he blotted it against the granite, leaving a damp ochre handprint in the candlelight.

Bud sensed a little of it. A sip from Harry's hemlock eyes. "What?" he asked. Perplexed, he watched as Harry and Emery exchanged the barest of smiles. He extended the pistol like a pointer. "Larry. It's him. He's on drugs. Give him a blood test."

"No shit," said Emery. "How you doin', Harry? How's the nose?"

"How's yourself?"

"Mike says you'll drop the assault charge if I to go to AA. Looks like you got me after all."

"Larry," Bud shouted, "Becky! You shouldn't let her out there alone, she'll run off—"

"Nah," said Emery. "She'll be fine. Her grandma's out there. Everybody is."

"Who! What?"

Time accelerated for Bud and his electric eyes bulged with the meteor that was compressing him down to seconds. It all slowed for Harry and he thought, what a fine thing a cave is and his gaze wandered, slowly diagramming the movements some man or woman had made hundreds of years before, creating a buffalo by torchlight.

"So . . . what do we do now, guys?" Bud stuttered, shifting uneasily. "Just what is it you're up for?"

"Bud Maston, I'm arresting you for the murders of Jessica Deucette and Jason Cox," Emery said.

"Larry, hey, it's me, for Chrissake! I admit I did some awful things, but I was stoned, fucked-up . . . you can understand that." Bud fingered the pistol nervously.

"We took two slugs outta Jay. My guess is they came from that Colt there in your hand, that now conveniently has your fingerprints on it," said Emery.

"But Harry had the gun. Harry had it," shouted Bud.

"Looks like you got it now, bigshot."

"Larry, how's this going to look in court? Think about what you're saying," said Bud.

"You know what it was? The third shot Chris fired. Went over your head. That should have hit you. I taught that boy to shoot. He was a natural. You had the scope all out of square. That gun shot a foot off at twenty feet. And another thing. You gave Chris steel jackets, not soft-nosed hunting loads. So it'd make a neat, clean hole."

"Okay, Larry, that's the way you want it. Give me my rights."

"That picture board Cox had in his workshop threw me, so I brought it home to study it," said Emery.

"I want to talk to my lawyer," Bud demanded in a strangled voice. He hugged the pistol with both hands against his chest.

Harry noticed that Emery had his hair pulled back in a braid. Little blue ribbon tied to a dream catcher back there.

"Couldn't just shoot Jessica, could you? . . . had to . . ." Emery faltered, regained his voice. "She wouldn't marry me when I come back," he said in his mournful voice. "I didn't believe her when she said she was pregnant. I was on my way overseas. She never forgave me for that. Leaving her alone. Spent my whole life making up for that."

"Harry did it. Harry did it," Bud pleaded.

Larry Emery, the father of Jessica Deucette's children and the legal executioner of her husbands, continued to speak. "At first, when I came back, she wouldn't even let me see Chris and Becky. Years and years I took care of her, got her out of jams, but I was never good enough. Wouldn't let me tell them the truth. And finally when they knew, she wouldn't let them have my name." Emery's voice banged the granite walls. "Tell me again how you got my baby high on drugs and played games with him, Maston."

"You gotta help me here, Harry. Look at him, he's—"

"So long hero," said Harry.

"*You* can't do this to *me!*" Bud raised the Colt and fired. Rock chips drew blood from Harry's cheek and neck and the noise was a white-hot wire in his ears.

"Never hit anything shaking like that." The last thing Harry saw in Bud Maston's eyes was disbelief.

He turned his back and started through the narrow passage. It was personal what was going on back there. It required privacy. He never looked back, not even when the shots reverberated through the tight space almost rupturing his eardrums.

He walked into the cold night air toward the flashlights and the balloons of chilly breath. Randall. Ginny Hakala was there, crying softly. Becky, shivering in a blanket, leaned against Mitch. Miss Loretta held her chin high, as befits the Ojibway version of a Spartan mother. Mike Hakala and several deputies stepped forward. Jerry Hakala handed Harry a cup of coffee. Morris pressed a wad of gauze to his bleeding arm.

Far below, he could see the flicker of a fire on the lake and hear the happy drum.

Emery came out. Jerry held up the medical bag and raised his eyebrows and nodded toward the cave. "We need this?"

"Not fucking likely," mused Morris.

Emery shook his head and Becky sobbed and Emery put his arm around her and held her for a second. Don Karson stepped from the darkness. Emery reached out and squeezed the minister's elbow. "Stay with her. She might need to talk," he said. Karson nodded to Mitch and Miss Loretta and they walked Becky back down the trail.

Emery held out his hand. The big .44 magnum lay in his palm with tiny wisps of steam or smoke still leaking from the barrel and the chamber. Mike Hakala put his hand on the pistol, then Jerry. Harry covered the other men's hands with his own.

Emery holstered the pistol, unbuckled his gunbelt, fingered his badge off his chest, and handed it all over to Mike Hakala. Mike declined and handed them back. "There'll be a board. Turn it in when we get back to town. He resisted arrest, Larry. You were just doing your job."

Larry Emery nodded and cinched the gunbelt around his waist. His voice rang in the darkness. "Awright, people. Do it right. Process it. Don't touch nothing, take pictures. Get the medical examiner up here. And when it's all done, make sure you get all the pieces of him outta there. Be another four hundred years of bad luck if the spiders eat his fat ass."

62

Harry made the drive in Linda's car but was unable to bring himself to set foot back in that graveyard, so he watched the ceremony from a distance as they buried Jesse next to Chris in the cemetery beyond the old company housing on a quiet, chilly November day.

And the wind whispered down through the pines and scattered a lacy veil of snowflakes across the brooding ridge and the name we hear whispered at a graveside is always our own.

After the service, he drove directly back to St. Paul and attended his first AA meeting in years. Later he learned that, when no one claimed Cox's body, Sheriff Emery purchased a plot for him, next to the ring of granite stones.

It was too early to tell whether he would carry permanent nerve damage in his left hand from Bud's knife thrust. The lasting wound was more subtle and had to do with who he was now. Increasingly he caught himself facing north with the intuition that the healing was to be found in conversation with Miss Loretta's voices in the deep woods up on Nanabozho Ridge.

The casket containing Bud Maston's remains made the trip from the county morgue in Stanley, Minnesota, to the Fort Snelling Veterans' Cemetery in the open bed of Jay Cox's truck. Mitch Hakala received $200 for making the drive from the prestigious St. Paul law firm of Noble and Deal, which was none too happy about disposing of the Maston estate. Their client had been page-one news for two weeks, ever since he'd died resisting arrest for two counts of premeditated murder.

And ever since the detailed diary of Jason Cox—a document that read like the obsessed odyssey of a modern Ahab—had mysteriously showed up in Franky Murphy's mailbox. Palming off the diary was a modest touch of black propaganda in which Harry detected the hand of Tim Randall, and now Franky had a hell of a story going and Harry, inevitably, would be part of it.

Lots was going on. Harry had no trouble getting an indefinite leave of absence from his work. A strident national ad hoc gay and lesbian coalition demanded that Bud's Medal of Honor be reissued posthumously to its rightful owner.

He didn't relish testifying at the grand jury coming up in Maston County.

There was a sticky question concerning the disposition of the Maston fortune where Becky's rights as the surviving daughter of the deceased spouse were concerned. A flock of lawyers hovered over Maston County to puzzle that one out.

Becky had, as Dale Talme predicted, landed on her feet. She sent Harry a simple thank-you card. The enclosed photograph portrayed a seriously beautiful high school senior. Eyes uplifted, chin raised slightly to the future. After her name, she had written simply: "Valedictorian."

A preliminary reading of Bud Maston's will revealed that he had left Harry an amount of money that, after taxes, would exceed a half a million dollars—ostensibly a gratuity for saving his life, more likely the iron prison parachute he had mentioned. Dorothy's father advised Harry to stay clear of the will until after the grand jury.

Bud had included a thoughtful line in the will, something about hoping that Harry would openly enjoy the money, since he and Harry had been unable to openly enjoy the love they bore for each other.

Harry shifted from foot to foot in his icy dress shoes next to another open grave and heard a demented cackle that could have been Bud laughing in Hell. But it was just a raven with a broken wing that had been left behind, hopping among the gravestones in the tired snow on this endless white day.

Mitch wheeled up to the hole in the ground. He'd slapped a hell of a wax job on Cox's truck and the marine dress blue crackled smartly among the tidy white markers. Mitch nodded at Harry. He did not get out of the warm cab. A disgruntled federal employee, who was not real happy about working on the third Thursday in November, engaged him in conversation.

Harry watched an argument commence between Mitch and the groundskeeper about how they were going to move the casket from the truck onto the drop apparatus set up over the grave. There was no funeral party. No pallbearers. No flag. Just three TV vans and reporters and photogs from the two local papers and Sherry Rawlins from Duluth. She walked over and flipped open her notebook.

The expression on his face stayed her questions and she drifted back to the pack as the clouds stacked up like black cannonballs in the cold pewter sky at 1 P.M. on this gloomy Thanksgiving day.

Harry lit a cigarette and watched. He wore his new suit. He was not wearing an overcoat. He had not shined his shoes. He was freezing his ass. He wasn't carrying no coffin.

Necessity and the cold weather dictated that the only available able-bodied souls—the press—would carry the coffin the last few dozen feet.

Being carted to the worms by TV and print reporters was probably the loneliest fate that could befall a body and Harry thought it a just epitaph for Bud, who had so loved the limelight. After they lowered the box, they scrambled out of the way and the shooters snapped their shot of Harry standing there without a coat looking like a bandleader in a black suit—or maybe the Angel of Death—against the rows of white dragon teeth.

No thoughts came as he dragged on his cigarette. There were beginnings, middles, and ends. This ending would stay with him forever. His mouth and tongue felt like he'd spent his life licking the bottom of an ashtray.

He glanced at the green Prelude parked on the service road. Maybe it was time to quit. Make Linda happy. Harry walked past the grave, paused, and threw his cigarettes into the hole ahead of the backhoe poised to fill it in. "Day is done, motherfucker," he said under his breath.

Linda drove back to his apartment and they went up and he tossed off his suit on his new king-sized bed and put on his old corduroy sports jacket, a pair of jeans, and some comfortable shoes. Randall and Dorothy were expecting them.

He eyed the phone. He'd made a vow on the plane trip back from Arizona, along the lines of: if I get out of this alive and not in jail—I swear I'll do this thing . . .

He got out his phone directory and called the number in Michigan. A man answered.

"Is Kate there?" Harry asked.

"Who shall I say is calling?"

"Her husband," said Harry.

"I believe I'm her husband," said the man.

Polite fucker. Harry sighed and felt his belly tighten. "Her ex-husband."

Seconds passed. Very long seconds. "Harry?" And her voice was the wild bullet of his youth going right through his heart.

"Kate," he said.

"Harry?" she said.

He cleared his throat. "Ah, lookit. I came into some money and I thought—well, I should talk to the boy, you know, about . . . school. He must be close to graduation—"

"Next year," she said quickly. Then more slowly, "Uh, I don't know, Harry. That's . . . real thoughtful but, uh, maybe you should give me some time . . . to prepare . . ."

"Let me talk to him, okay? Please?"

Long sigh on the other end. "Uh, okay. Just a minute."

Harry waited. He began to sweat.

"Look, I don't want to talk to you," said a hard young voice. "I sure as hell don't want to talk to you on Thanksgiving."

Harry put both hands to the receiver, as if the voice were Braille and he could touch it.

"I . . . thought it's time we should talk," he said.

"Why? We never have before. Far as I'm concerned you're just noise in a piece of plastic—"

"Wait," said Harry. "Goddammit, I'm your father!"

But the line was dead. A little shaky, Harry managed a hollow laugh as Linda gently placed her hands on his shoulders.

"What's his name?" she asked.

"Randy. Sounds like a good kid. Tough, doesn't take any shit."

"It's a start," she said, then she took him by the hand. "C'mon, we'll be late for dinner."

"Right. Thanksgiving's the only uncorrupted feast day we have left." He smiled.

"What?" she asked.

He answered with his eyes. He was glad that he had someplace to go for dinner and that he had someone like her to accompany him.

Out on the street he reached for a cigarette. Then he remembered. He'd thrown them away.